THE DEAD SAINT

THE DEAD SAINT

BLOOD AND RUBIES

BOOK ONE

KATHRYN TRATTNER

for everyone who wants to kiss the villain

I found her on a night of fire and noise
Wild bells rang in a wild sky
I knew from that moment on
I'd love her until the day that I died

— Nick Cave

Each man kills the thing he loves.

— Oscar Wilde

WINTER PALACE
SUMMER PALACE
PAINTER'S TOWER
GREEN TEMPLE
THE
WORLD
OF
BLOOD
AND
RUBIES
GOLDEN CITADEL
MARE TESTA
ANDROPHAGOI
RED TOWER

Contents

Prologue   1
Chapter 1   5
Chapter 2   12
Chapter 3   18
Chapter 4   23
Chapter 5   31
Chapter 6   35
Chapter 7   44
Chapter 8   49
Chapter 9   58
Chapter 10   69
Chapter 11   72
Chapter 12   104
Chapter 13   128
Chapter 14   136
Chapter 15   144
Chapter 16   157
Chapter 17   165
Chapter 18   180
Chapter 19   188
Chapter 20   199
Chapter 21   220
Chapter 22   229
Chapter 23   233
Chapter 24   242
Chapter 25   251
Chapter 26   268
Chapter 27   271
Chapter 28   276

The Living Saint 295
Steel and Starlight 297
Sacrament and Smoke 299
Acknowledgments 301
About the Author 303
Also by Kathryn Trattner 305

PROLOGUE

The knife in her hand was cold and sharp, the blade reflecting the fire in the braziers nearby. Thick incense filled the air, overpowering the stink of humanity and the fires burning in the lower levels of the Golden Citadel. Soon, those fires would reach them. If the Horde didn't take the city first.

The constant sound of a battering ram beating at the gates grated on Sorcha's nerves. It had gone on for three days now, through the morning and night. It was incessant and methodical. The invading army had not paused once for rest, launching volley after volley of flaming arrows, vicious fire spreading as each one found a flammable target. Beyond the high walls, siege engines were rolling toward them, bridges half lowered, grappling hooks poised for flight.

Ines and Sorcha had stood on the temple roof and watched them being built. It had taken no time at all, the structures growing out of the earth as easily as wheat and just as prolific.

She had accepted what was coming, knowing there was no escape. But the ghost of hope, that faint trace she'd hidden and fostered, was now gone. In its place, a terrible numbness grew, expanding and consuming all other emotions.

The blade in her hand had chased the last vestiges of it away.

"I trust you," Ines said, gripping Sorcha tightly, staring into her eyes. "You will bring him back. You will bring us all back."

Sorcha shook her head, refusing to let the tears in her eyes fall.

Below them, deep within the city, the gates groaned—a long, drawn-out sound that vibrated through the air. Then a splintering crash reached her—an explosion of wood and iron, followed by triumphant shouts.

They'd done it then. The gates had been breached.

Now, it was only a matter of time.

Her hands shook, adrenaline flowing through her.

"I can't do this for you," Sorcha said, fighting the tremble in her voice.

"You don't have to," Ines said, taking the dagger with a tight smile. It was not an expression of happiness or joy, but one of acceptance for a task that would be unpleasant.

"Please, Ines." Sorcha reached for her friend, taking her by the shoulders. "Come with me. This isn't a choice you have to make right now."

Ines shook her head. "It will be easier for one person to escape the city rather than two. The Saint will protect you, Sorcha. You have nothing to fear."

"It's time," Rohan called out. "The Golden Citadel has fallen."

The others in the sanctuary turned to embrace each other with his words. Kisses were exchanged, their eyes wide with terror and conviction. A murmur traveled through the group of men and women, high and low priests and priestesses of the Saint. True believers each and every one. But a few familiar faces were missing. Kahina Kira—the most senior oracle and her mentor—was not here and had not been seen for several days.

Sorcha covered her mouth, waiting for the unstoppable horror.

"Sorcha, Oracle and Priestess of the Saint," Rohan, the high priest, called out to her from his place on the dais across the room, commanding everyone's attention. Their eyes met and Sorcha shivered. "You are his vessel. You are his chosen. Our faith now lies with you. Go south, over the Eversor mountains, to Androphagoi."

The high priest held a dagger to his neck, his gaze locked on her.

The others echoed his words, repeating them until it was a jumble of voices, nothing but noise.

"Do not fail us."

"You will bring us all back."

"Find him."

"Resurrect him."

Rohan sat and performed his death ritual. Others followed, until the room was full of terrible quiet and concentration.

Sorcha turned to Ines, shaking her head, her hand out to stop what was coming.

Ines cut herself, eyes going wide as the blade parted flesh, a bubbling gurgle escaping. A flash, blood pouring, and the woman sagged to her knees.

Sorcha dropped beside her, placing trembling hands over the wound in her friend's throat. But it was too late. The damage was irreparable, the spark of humor and determination that Sorcha loved so much about Ines gone in a few breaths. Sorcha swallowed a choked sob, leaning back on her heels and taking in the devastation.

With effort she stood, every muscle aching and bones weighing her down. Her lungs were full of incense and smoke, her nose full of the coppery scent of blood. She looked down at her gore covered hands—slick with death—and began to shake.

Do not fail us.

Sorcha took a step back, away from the sanctuary—away from the ruin of her life.

CHAPTER ONE

The city screamed as fire ate it alive.

Overhead, a gray sky swirled, large flakes of snow liquefying and then evaporating before the moisture could reach the burning buildings. Flames crackled and danced, sending joyous greedy tendrils over stone and wood—hungry and murmuring, expanding as it ate. Places once so familiar—the villas and temples Sorcha saw every day— were destroyed.

A thousand tiny fires converged to consume and transform, revealing the bones of a fallen civilization. Ash drifted around Sorcha, dancing on updrafts and settling between cobblestones and on window ledges, a flurrying storm of destruction and despair. The high castle at the center of Golden Citadel was a column of fierce fire, the huge stones at the base buckling under the weight of the sagging upper towers.

The gold on the minarets was melting, rivers of molten metal coursing over the stones. It would run down the streets. There was enough gold to encase the whole city and soon it would flow down until it reached the outer walls.

There were no other noises beyond the fire. No one screamed or spoke, no one cried or whispered. There was no one left to do those things. They were all dead.

The gates had shattered, then the walls had been breached, and once inside, the Horde had killed anyone who survived the siege. There hadn't been so many of them left. Not at the end. Half the city had gone to the White Snake—the child of an assassinated emperor, son of a revered empress—a ruling prince and merciless tyrant. He'd offered favorable terms: come willingly, be under his rule, and live.

Living was all that mattered.

The rest had been slaughtered.

Sorcha hurried down the center of Ruby Road. There were no shadows to hide in, no place to find cover. The only way to avoid the flames was to walk down the middle of the main road that spiraled from the Citadel gates to the high castle. The other roads were narrow, villas only a few feet apart in places, with footbridges built to connect buildings, potted plants and grapevines trained over wooden arches to bring much needed green to the city. People lived as much in the streets of the Golden Citadel as in their homes here.

Had. She corrected herself. *Had lived.*

The stink of singed hair clung to her, the strands of golden thread and pearls hopelessly tangled in her messy dark braids. Her left shoulder throbbed painfully, relentlessly, as a result of a falling ornament in the temple. The gown clung to her, wet with the blood of the final ritual, the bodies of those she'd come across in the streets, and one bloody knee. She'd tripped and landed hard in the courtyard before the temple gates. Each breath pulled in fine drifting ash, leaving her eyes and lips gritty and the back of her throat coated.

Sorcha wanted a cool drink of water and shade, the comfort of a plush sofa with downy feather cushions and fresh silk against her skin. Already, her last meal haunted her—the uneaten rubbery chicken, a bruised pear with only a single bite taken from it, and a goblet of wine left half-full. There was nothing like that behind her anymore and nothing like it ahead.

Run, Rohan had said. *Make your way out of the city. Find the Androphagoi dedicated to the Saint. Always go south, keep the golden star burning on the horizon to your right—keep to it faithfully—it is a symbol, a sign that the Saint will return soon.*

Then everyone, even the White Snake, would know the true power of the god.

The star would lead her to safety. It meant hope. Beneath it, she would find someone to guide her. Sorcha was going to need their help to find all the scattered relics, to do what she'd been born to do, and resurrect the Saint.

But it would take time.

Time was an enemy as great as the Horde.

Both waited for Sorcha beyond the city gates.

———

A soldier found her before she reached the fourth switchback on Ruby Road.

The street had been empty, and the growl of the fire rumbled around her, beams crashing in a shower of sparks and splinters, roofs collapsing in waves. A street away, a temple to a minor god shivered and came crashing down, stones exploding outward, toppling into the surrounding buildings and sending out a dark cloud that reached her.

A distraction, only a second of distraction, and in that moment, a man appeared in front of her. She froze, hand going to her mouth in surprise, smothering the exclamation of fear. She cursed herself for hesitating, cursed the fear coursing through her veins while her legs refused to move.

He smiled, his pale eyes glittering with hunger. He had rough features, with hair shaved close to his skull and a fresh scar running from temple to ear. When he spoke, the words were harsh, coming from deep in his chest, but she couldn't understand the language.

Shaking her head, she took a step back, mouth dry and unable to speak. She took another step, and for a brief moment, she wondered if she might be able to outrun him.

But he moved swiftly, darting forward and blocking her path, closing the distance between them in a blink. He leaned in, his face inches from her own. Foul breath washed over her face, metallic and sharp, and with a shudder, she realized his mouth was dark with a mix of blood and ash.

"Don't touch me," she whispered, clearing her throat and repeating the words with more strength.

The man laughed, throwing back his head, eyes squinting.

Sorcha leaned away, looking around wildly for someone, anyone. *There is no one left. They're all dead.* She stepped closer, kicking his shin, her soft slipper coming up against thick, studded leather.

His laugh deepened, the bite of his fingers becoming unbearable.

"Help!" she screamed, frustrated with herself for wasting precious energy. There would be no help for her now.

"Help!" The man mimicked—mocking her—the word strange in his mouth. He spoke again, accent distorting his language, but she caught it clearly enough. *There is no one to save you.*

And of course, he was right. She knew it.

But a flicker of movement over his shoulder stopped her heart.

A tall, ashen man walked calmly up behind her captor, eyes an unusual pale yellow, flat and dead. His face was expressionless in the flicker of firelight. Without speaking, he thrust a dagger into her captor's back, holding Sorcha's horrified gaze, twisting the blade with a jerk of the wrist.

Sorcha stumbled back, the dying man going with her, his weight taking her to the ground. They landed together in a heap, pain shooting through her as she was caught between the weight of the man and the cobblestones.

Her captor tried to roll, eyes wide, mouth open, his grip on her finally easing.

The stranger followed him down, plunging the blade into his back again and again, the motion frenzied even as his face remained serene.

Sorcha sat frozen, unable to move, a scream echoing through her mind even as her voice failed her.

Get up! Run!

As if the man had heard her internal voice, he turned to her. Blood speckled his cheeks and splattered his black armor, and it dripped from the hand still gripping the blade. The attacker wiped the blade on the dead man's cloak, his eyes leaving her face for a second.

She surged to her feet and bolted, clutching the fabric of her crimson dress, desperate to avoid tripping over it. But the man was up and moving more quickly than she'd anticipated, following with an ominous creak of leather and rattle of chainmail.

Sorcha glanced around, mind racing. The buildings to either side were burning. There was nowhere to run. The flames or the man? She made the decision in an instant, cutting to the left, focused on an open doorway where fire burned beyond.

The man grabbed her, jerking her backward, away from the flames she'd been so eager to embrace.

"Don't be a fool," he hissed, blackened teeth flashing. "There is someone who wants to meet you."

His accent was strange, but he spoke her language more smoothly than the last man had. Even if she hadn't understood, his message was clear. *Don't die before I get a chance to kill you.* She didn't bother to answer, fighting his grip, twisting to dislodge his strong fingers.

He watched her, a hunter studying a rabbit caught in a snare—dispassionate and calculating.

Her skin crawled, the hair on the back of her neck rising. This man was more dangerous than the other one had been.

Without another word, he began walking, dragging her behind him with one hand tight on her wrist. He didn't pause when she stumbled, keeping her upright through force and determination.

She gasped as her bones creaked and squeezed together, and wondered if he'd break her wrist before they reached whatever destination he had in mind.

Sorcha's head buzzed with *what-ifs*, fuzzy and disconnected from the world around her as she stumbled down Ruby Road beside this stranger. Her mind spun back, returning to the temple of the Saint and her final moments there. She tried to see what was around her, ground herself to this moment, but it was just as horrible as what had already happened. The memory, the horror of it, came to her like the visions that had been a constant since her childhood.

Blood. There had been so much blood. Spreading out, reflecting the fires, reminding her she had promises to keep. The faces of her friends and family, the temple elders and fresh initiates, the people she loved.

Gone.

Tears threatened, a stone in her throat, lungs on the verge of giving way to heaving sobs.

No. She wouldn't expose those parts of herself, her terror and sorrow, the weight that had settled so completely in her bones. *Don't think about it.* She would escape this man and find her way out of the city. There was a chance, she was still alive, and there was always hope.

Turning her attention to the part of the city they were now moving through, she was surprised to see how far they'd come. They were close to the outer wall here. It towered above her, throwing deep shadows across thatched and tiled rooftops, the shade beginning to scatter and flee as the fire spread out from the city center.

The man steered her down a smaller street as yet untouched by the fire, toward one of the larger plazas near the main gate. They passed shopfronts with shattered windows, glass gleaming on the ground—reflecting firelight—splashes of blood on the walls and cobblestones. But no bodies that she could see.

In a way, that was worse. To know people had died, to see the evidence, but not the bodies. Where had they been taken? Or had they risen from death to walk the streets like the old legends described?

A shiver rippled through Sorcha, cold lingering as they rounded another corner and came out into a plaza with a fountain bubbling at the center.

The area was full of armor-clad figures with their hands on their weapons.

All eyes focused on her.

Sorcha lifted her chin. Countless times, she'd moved through the court of King Roi, talking with advisors or generals, courtesans, or minor nobility. She knew who she was in every room she entered. There had been men as bloodthirsty as any in the Empire of the White Snake. She'd passed among them all—oracle and extension of the Saint— without ever questioning her safety. But this was different. These were the men who had brought the Golden Citadel to its knees.

"Keep walking."

Her captor jerked Sorcha forward when she hesitated. If the man who gripped her arm so tightly wasn't in charge, who would be?

Then she saw him. Sorcha stopped, brows pulling together, curious despite herself.

The man radiated power, an intensity that commanded attention and forced everyone else into the background. He had unusual features, with hair and eyes as black as onyx, which made her think of silence at midnight. No stars, no moon, only a watchful void. The black armor and leather gloves he wore were just as dark, the war horse beneath him a similar shade. A white wolf skull was tied to the saddle. The stories she'd heard said he wore it into battle, that his sword was always wet, that the blood on his hands would never dry.

The Wolf.

Chapter Two

Adrian had been instructed to find the Saint's vessel—a young woman, twenty-two years old, with dark hair and blue-green eyes. The description had come from a high-ranking temple priestess who had come to the prince. The woman had said the vessel would have tattoos—a history and map of the dead Saint on her skin. She might try to hide her identity, but those markings, she wouldn't be able to hide.

Her skin told the Saint's story, her flesh would point the way.

So far, they hadn't located the woman. But it was only a matter of time.

Any hope that the Golden Citadel had held for a reprieve from the death sentence that was the empire's ever-conquering Horde had died as the gates fell inward and the fires took hold. If there was anyone else left alive in the city, they would know her, and they might give her up when the pain became unbearable and release was offered. If there was no one left, he would search every building, even as they burned and fell around him.

He refused to accept that she might have perished in the fire.

Prince Eine had offered riches beyond measure in exchange for the woman: promotion to the Black Tomeis, enough gold to last several lifetimes, and a personal favor from the prince himself. The favor, the ear of the prince, was the most prized. It would be something to hold tight in the face of the long months ahead and coming battles.

Anyone would welcome these rewards. Each man listening had been hungry, ready for the pale light of morning as the siege came to an end, so they would have the chance to enter the city and find the woman.

"What do we do when we find her?" a man asked, a stranger unknown to Adrian. The others in the crowd had turned to him, focusing hard eyes on Adrian, searching for any hint of deception.

"Bring her to me."

The men had nodded, more than a hundred of them fanning out into the city as the gates came down. His own men, the Black Tomeis led by Revenant, were already gone, moving on Adrian's private orders.

Find the woman as quickly and quietly as possible.

Make sure no one else did.

———

Adrian saw the woman before she saw him. Revenant marched her toward the group of waiting men, his face blank but eyes blazing, as the woman fought him. She pried at his fingers, working to loosen his grip, but she grimaced when he squeezed. She was singed and dirty, the hem of her crimson dress dark with blood and the long, loose sleeves torn. Her hair was a wild black halo around her pale face, bits of gold and jewels tangled in the mess.

This was the woman the prince wanted?

Adrian considered her, cataloging details, collecting what he might be able to use to his advantage later. She didn't look like a woman of wealth and power. Or whatever it was she was supposed to be. She was bejeweled and wearing fine things, however damaged, but without an air of command. He would have passed over her in a crowd without a second glance, a forgettable woman in a sea of faces and nothing like what he'd pictured.

An oracle, priestess, and vessel of the Saint.

Her gaze landed on him finally—the only man on a horse in the square—and the shock of her anger sizzled between them. Her eyes narrowed and her mouth opened as if she planned to yell—yell for help or yell at him, he couldn't be sure. But the directness of her expression and the fury in it changed everything. It transformed her face. The woman's eyes were a vibrant, striking green. His breath caught as an arrow of desire pierced him, lodging in his chest—a dangerous surprise.

But the anger in her gaze shifted, eyes widening, skin going pale as she realized who she was being taken to. Understanding settled in her features, her knuckles white with pressure as she squeezed her hands into fists.

Monster.

She didn't need to speak the word for him to hear it. It filled the air around them all. He saw it on her face, the moment of realization. A tall man on a black horse, wearing black armor, black gloves, with the bone-white skull of a monstrous wolf.

The Wolf.

The monster who wanted her.

Revenant jerked her to a halt several feet away, out of reach from his horse's sharp bite. Nox shifted beneath him, turning to look at the pair who'd dared to come so close.

Adrian didn't speak—waiting, watching the woman. She hadn't looked at him again, her eyes elsewhere, searching for a way out. But there wasn't one. Everywhere she looked, there was fire and death.

"The vessel." Revenant tugged at her sleeve, pulling it back to reveal a tattoo. Black ink crawled up her arm and disappeared beneath the fabric at her shoulder.

She tried to pull free, twisting in Revenant's grasp, but the man tightened his grip until she cried out and her knees buckled.

"Enough," Adrian said.

His voice was soft, but every single man in the square turned their attention to the three standing together. He could feel their curiosity, even their bitterness at not being the ones to find the woman. But Adrian knew Revenant didn't want or need favors from Prince Eine. Those gifts were wasted on such a creature.

Revenant's brows lifted slightly at Adrian's command. It was more emotion than the man generally showed, but he quickly smoothed his expression, easing his grip on the woman's wrist.

"Are you the vessel?" Adrian asked, studying her.

She shook her head, glancing at him and away, searching for an escape. She was tense, poised to run, stubbornness plain in her features and the way she held herself. A flicker of humor shot through him. She was afraid, that was clear, but that she held on to her anger.

"Do you know who I am?"

She nodded once.

Adrian raised an eyebrow, waiting to see if she would say more. When she didn't, he looked to Revenant. "Was anyone else with her?"

"Lane had her. I killed him."

Adrian swore internally. Lane had crossed Revenant a month ago, leaving the man in a difficult position during a battle. Revenant had promised to repay him for that favor, and he'd finally had the opportunity. But that was something Adrian would address when there was no one else to overhear.

"Give her to me," he said.

Revenant shoved the woman toward the horse. Nox snorted and stamped in warning at the sudden movement.

She caught her balance and flashed Revenant a glare. Her gaze came back to Adrian before shifting away, still searching for a way out.

Adrian held out a gloved hand, palm tingling, wondering if she'd bolt or stand her ground. He waited for her to accept his offer, but she silently refused. Nox sidestepped beneath him, uneasy with his rider's sudden tension.

"You ride with me or them," Adrian said.

The woman glanced at the men who'd been staring and then over her shoulder to where Revenant stood with that dead-flat expression he'd perfected. He bared his blackened teeth in a snarl, and the woman paled.

"You're an animal to them. They will not hesitate to kill you."

It was a lie. Anyone who touched this woman would die. But she didn't need to know that.

"And you won't?" she asked, meeting his gaze with a challenge.

Revenant stepped forward and shoved her once more, sending her stumbling into Adrian's grasp. Before she could twist away or cry out, he had a hold of her, pulling her up into the saddle. He shifted, his arms a cage around her, as she settled on his lap. The scent of smoke and singed hair came with her, and below that, the copper stink of blood and fear. She sat ridged in an effort not to touch him, breathing heavily.

"Make sure there are no survivors," Adrian said with a nod to Revenant and the others.

They brought their right fist to their hearts in acknowledgment and a salute as he turned Nox toward the main gate. The woman shifted, leaning forward as much as possible, slipping as the horse walked.

"Do you want to fall and be trampled?"

When she didn't respond, he looped an arm around her waist, pulling her into his body. Even with clothes and armor between them, he felt her soft warmth, and it sent a shiver racing over him. Her hair brushed his face, the top of her head bumping his chin, as he urged Nox across the square. Adrian worked to ignore the feel of her against him, the way she trembled, her hands balled into fists.

He tilted his head to get a better look at her, catching a curve of her cheek and the sweep of thick dark lashes.

"I won't hurt you," he said.

She half turned to him—green eyes wary—her distaste a physical force. "I'm not stupid enough to trust a monster."

There, she'd said it aloud. Her tone was as sharp as his had been soft —words cutting like broken glass flung at him with full force. It could not have sat so long between them without being given solid form.

He smiled grimly, a part of him pleased that he'd pulled a reaction from her—pleased with her anger.

An angry woman was easier to deal with than a sad one. He had no time for tears. But anger he understood. Anger he could handle. Sorrow, tears, the wailing of deep wounds was something he had wanted to avoid at all costs.

The woman in his arms would never give him her tears; he'd known it the moment their eyes met. Adrian could feel her making promises to herself, the frantic whirling of her mind and emotions. She would give him as little of herself as possible.

But he would take everything from her.

Just as he'd taken this city. Already, the fires had eaten so much of it. The death cries of the survivors had been silenced hours ago. There was no more clashing metal, no more shouts or pleas. There was no one left.

Those who had accepted Prince Eine's terms had departed weeks ago, already moved on to live beneath the eaves of the Traveling City or at the farthest edges of the Empire of the White Snake. Those who had held out, remaining in the city because they thought the prince's soft-spoken voice made him weak, were all dead.

Prince Eine might be soft-spoken, but the edge of his blade was sharp and his mind cruel. There would have been torture and mutilation before death, incredible pain and despair. Repayment for the insult their refusal had caused. But soothing his own emotions wasn't the prince's only goal. The stories of what happened spread and were another weapon against those who challenged his dreams of expanding the empire.

The woman jerked in his arms and gasped. There were bodies in the streets near the main gate. Blood pooled between cobblestones and on the flat pavers. The stink of gore fought to overpower the smoke, a foul scent that would cling to his clothes for the next several days.

"You did this." Her voice was a harsh whisper, emotion choking her. "You killed them all."

He remained silent, unable to and uninterested in denying it.

"You truly are a monster," she hissed, twisting abruptly in his arms, wriggling until his hold slipped and she dropped to the cobblestones.

The horse lunged for her, teeth snapping, and Adrian snapped the reins in a warning. Nox quieted, but his ears were laid back in warning.

The woman scrambled away, panting and pushing awkwardly to her feet. She turned in a circle, taking in her surroundings and freezing as she looked out over the main road leading away from the Golden Citadel.

CHAPTER THREE

The gates stood open, splintered and hanging from giant hinges. The iron portcullis was twisted and stuck in the up position. They had withstood the attack at first, the invading Horde chipping away at their defenses, but it had only taken a few days for the gates to be breached.

Had it only been a few days? It seemed like months. Years. Sleep evaded her, the sounds of death creeping closer, with the blood of her sisters all around her.

Now she stood beyond the temple with new blood soaking the hem of her dress, the scent of copper filling her head and coating the back of her throat. Closing her eyes, she swallowed back bile, breathing out through her nose. The urge to scream was building beneath her breastbone, a throb that pulsed in time with her racing heart.

A harness jingled, and Sorcha glanced back at the Wolf. The man held out one black-gloved hand, patient and silent. The giant horse stomped and pawed at the ground. One eye rolled to her as he tossed his mane, impatient and ready to leave. The man watched her, waiting.

Right now, she might be going with him, but she didn't want to touch him. She shook her head.

"Walk then," he said, voice expressionless.

Soldiers and civilians were crumpled together—armor and spun cotton, heavy boots and simple leather slippers. But no one seemed to belong to the empire. These were all citizens of the Golden Citadel.

Tears filled her eyes, blurring the world. So much death, so much pain and suffering. The weight of it pressed on her, leaving her gasping as her thoughts raced.

There was nowhere to go but across the bridge or back into the city. One was certain death, the other an unknown.

This man, this monster, wanted her and, for the moment, had promised not to harm her. But how long would that last? Her value to him was tied to her skin and the tattooed map hidden by her clothing.

Someone had shared her secret, though it had never truly been one. Anyone who came to the temple could see her, their oracle vessel, the woman capable of resurrecting their dead god if the need arose.

Sorcha had believed it.

Believed it right up until those around her had slit their own throats.

Stop it.

Their deaths—their belief and faith in her—were as crushing as the death and pain surrounding her right now. She wasn't going to think about that.

Turning to the bridge, Sorcha let out a breath.

She had crossed this bridge thousands of times—laughing with friends, and once when a friendship had soured and she'd cried all the way to the temple. She'd crossed it holding the hand of a lover, under blue skies and in the rain, running for the shelter of the wall.

Now bloody and broken bodies covered it. The heat of the burning city was at her back, the Wolf beside her, and death lay before her as far as she could see.

A sob ripped from her aching chest. Her sisters were behind her. They would burn soon. And all these men, even the women and children she saw. They would be bone and ash soon as well.

She took a step and then another. The horse moved behind her, the saddle creaking as the Wolf followed.

Then she recognized a face. A man that lived nearby, a craftsman of some kind, nice enough but never friendly. A face she had seen almost every day as she went from the temple to the market or the palace to sit silently beside Kira in court. She couldn't even remember his name.

Tears blinded her, and she stopped, knees buckling. She landed hard in the filth covering the cobblestones, hands cupped in her lap, and let the tears come.

"I can't," she whispered, closing her eyes.

It was too much. The terrible numbness that had overtaken her before threatened to recede, and that scared her as much as the death around her did. She wanted to hold on to the emptiness, needed it to remain. Otherwise, she would go insane with grief.

The Wolf was beside her, moving so quietly she wasn't aware he was there until he'd scooped her up. He carried her in an iron grip—one arm under her knees and the other around her shoulders—cradled against his chest as he carried her to his horse. Sorcha glanced up, catching a glimpse of his hard jaw covered in dark stubble, a muscle jumping in his cheek. Then he was putting her on the horse, shoving her into the saddle in a quick, efficient motion. Where he'd touched her, the strangeness of his hands tenderly holding her, lingered with a prickling heat.

Sorcha looked down at him, and his dark eyes met hers. A shiver passed over her, the hair on the back of her neck standing up. When he turned away, she was relieved, not wanting to examine the feeling he'd given her too closely. She waited, wondering if he would ride behind her like before. But he left her there alone, taking the reins and leading the horse across the bridge.

Sorcha clutched the pommel of the saddle as the Wolf led the horse along the road raised slightly above the surrounding landscape. She kept her gaze fixed on the horse's ears, looking only ahead and refusing to see the destruction to either side. It filled the periphery of her vision, a terrible temptation she struggled to ignore.

The Wolf didn't speak as they walked, and soon her eyes drifted to him. His black hair was long and tied at the base of his neck, slightly mussed from being beneath his helmet. Taller than most men with broad shoulders, he moved as if the world held nothing to fear. The leather armor he wore was unmarred and well cared for. The rumors said he was untouchable on the battlefield. The bleached wolf skull bumped against her knee as she rode, a reminder of who the man in front of her truly was. Tentatively, as if it might bite, she reached out and touched it. The bone was smooth and cool beneath her fingers, the teeth sharp as knives.

What kind of a man wore such a thing into battle? *Not a man,* she reminded herself, *a monster.*

A tall monster with broad shoulders and hard muscle beneath the black and red armor he wore. She could see the strength in his arms; he must have wielded the sword at his side with skill. He was handsome, and it surprised her, going against what she'd expected. But hard beauty could hide a monster easily.

Though she had never expected to be in his presence.

The stories she'd heard talked about how deadly he was with a blade, his mercilessness and relentlessness. A man everyone feared. A man who had not hesitated to kill the prince's brother. He'd destroyed cities and kingdoms, brought down famous warriors, and did all these things as if it were as easy as breathing.

But if she'd seen him walk into the temple or through the streets of the Golden Citadel, he would have caught her attention. He would have kept it. That thought was unsettling and stung like betrayal.

Sorcha looked down at her hands and realized dried blood was caked beneath her nails. A streak of blood was flaking off her arm. She scrubbed at it, wishing for soap and water. The sudden desire to wash it away—remove it permanently—was overpowering.

Maybe if she was able to do that, the water would take the memory with it.

Ines had died so quickly. Sorcha had tried to stop the bleeding, hands to Ines's throat, the blood pumping through her fingers. Her eyes had gone glassy and distant, then she'd been gone. The end, her death, so quick and final. One of so many over the last few days, in those last few hours, as the gate fell and the Citadel was overrun.

With a shudder, Sorcha closed her eyes, breathing in through her nose and out through her mouth. A knot of tension throbbed in her chest, filling her up and making it difficult to breathe.

But behind her closed eyelids, those images waited—inescapable.

She opened her eyes, preferring the horror of the world around her to those inside her head.

Ahead on the road, a division of soldiers marched away from the Citadel. Their black and red armor splattered with mud and gore. She watched them for several minutes, counting their number and wondering how many more there had been. There must have been a camp somewhere nearby, a place the Wolf was taking her.

Sorcha searched the landscape around her, the plains she'd once been so familiar with, the trees planted at the edges of fields to break the wind and shield the crops. A stream cut through the landscape, one she'd waded through to collect watercress. It was now polluted and over-run, the banks churning into mud.

The plains beyond were as full of the dead as the city had been. Bodies were piled into burning heaps, the earth churned into a muddy, bloody soup, with any and all crops and vegetation trampled.

The siege engines that had breached the Citadel walls burned, black smoke flowing down. It moved in a strange way, thick and creeping along the ground, spreading out to blanket the earth.

The mutilated dead were everywhere.

Her stomach seized, clenching as saliva filled her mouth. Sour bile burned as it climbed up her throat. Sorcha threw her leg over the saddle and slid from the horse, folding over as she gave in and purged her stomach.

Chapter Four

The woman vomited in the road, hands on her knees, bent over and shuddering.

He watched without commenting, waiting for her to finish. It had been a long time since sights like those around them had bothered him. He'd stopped seeing carnage a long time ago—even embraced it as the Wolf.

Adrian stepped forward, not sure what he intended to do, a coil of something soft unraveling inside him. The urge surprised him as much as the death around him didn't.

"Don't touch me!" she hissed, jerking away and narrowly missing her vomit.

He turned to the small saddlebag and pulled a leather waterskin from it. Water sloshed inside—barely enough for a swallow—but he opened it and held it out to her.

She watched him as if he were a snake poised to attack.

"It's not poisoned," he said, keeping his voice neutral. "The prince wants you alive."

She hesitated only a moment before snatching it from his hands and sniffing the contents. Keeping her eyes on him, she took a small sip, swishing it around before spitting it out. Then she swallowed what remained.

All that was left. The last of the water, and he hadn't even considered it for himself. He'd handed it to her without a thought—an instinct. Somewhere beneath his armor and blood, past muscle and into bone, had been a ripple of pleasure when she'd taken it from his hand—an offering, a sacrifice to the beautiful defiance all over her face.

Handing it back, she kept her eyes locked on his face, wiping her mouth with the back of her hand. Soot and sweat smudged her face and body, the terror of the day stamped across her features.

He knew it would stay with her. And maybe she would learn to live with it. Or maybe she wouldn't.

He nodded, putting the waterskin back in his pack, mind racing. His reaction to her surprised him—disturbing and unexpected.

She was nothing. Could be nothing. He couldn't forget that.

"We have several miles to go," he said, turning to her, watching her as she watched him.

She looked ready to run, ready to sprint across the fields until it was all well behind her and nothing but memory.

"Run and I'll hunt you down."

Her face paled, expression falling. It had been all over her, obvious for anyone to see.

"You'll ride," he said, gesturing to his horse. "Come here."

"Your horse will bite me," she said, keeping back.

Nox twisted his head to look at the woman, the whites of his eyes showing, his ears laid back. Nox might bite her. He tried to bite everyone, including the horsemen, and other horses. Adrian was the only exception.

"Get on," Adrian said. "Or I'll put you on."

When she didn't move, he grabbed her arm and pulled her toward him. He was done playing nice. The prince had insisted she was to be treated well—as a guest and not a prisoner. But Adrian wasn't going to waste time with her in the middle of the road.

The woman lurched in his grasp, twisting away from Nox as he swung his head around and nipped at her.

Adrian moved between them and swung her up into the saddle in a smooth motion, keeping the horse from achieving his desire. She was small and delicate, weighing almost nothing, and gripped the saddle so tightly her knuckles turned white. The horse dwarfed her, and she made a noise as the animal sidestepped, muscles quivering.

He made a shushing sound, smoothing a hand along Nox's neck, and the animal settled. Then he took the reins and began to walk, considering the best route to take.

The Traveling City wasn't far now; it had covered hundreds of miles as the siege slowly wore down the Golden Citadel. It had taken longer than anyone had anticipated, and the prince would be displeased for months. But the blame fell on the generals and commanders. Adrian would watch each one die impassively and refused to acknowledge the spark of relief that flared in his heart.

"Where are you taking me?" she asked.

"To a waypoint," he replied after a moment.

"And then?"

Was that a tremor in her voice? "The main camp."

"And the prince is there?"

"No." Adrian shook his head. "We'll go to the Traveling City."

The woman didn't speak again.

He glanced back once, curiosity getting the better of him, to find her staring off into the distance. She appeared calm outwardly, but a muscle jumped in her jaw, her inner thoughts clearly in turmoil.

Her eyes flicked down, meeting his flat gaze, and then she looked away again, searching the horizon.

There was an air of a cornered animal about her, the sense that at any moment, she would dart away.

She would learn soon enough that there would be no escape.

———

Sorcha turned in the saddle at the sound of approaching horses.

The man who took her from the Citadel was at the head of a small group. She recognized his strange yellow eyes even from a distance. They seemed to glow in the fading light. Others rode behind him, all armor similar to the Wolf's.

Behind them, the Citadel smoked in the distance. She'd avoided looking back, even as a low rumble of collapse filled the air. She hadn't wanted to see it fall, to witness the final death throes.

They weren't as far as she'd expected to be. But they'd been moving slowly with her in the saddle and the man leading the horse. It wasn't long before the group traveling behind them caught up.

They paused as the group joined them.

"The city is empty," the man with the yellow eyes said, his gaze moving from the Wolf to Sorcha. "I expected to find you in camp."

"Go ahead and make sure there's food. Rest your horses. It will be a long day tomorrow to the main camp."

The man nodded, gesturing to the others to follow him.

Sorcha kept her eyes down as they flowed past her. But she could feel their interest.

Soon they were small figures on the road ahead of them, and then gone as the sun sank in the sky.

It wasn't long before they reached the small camp he'd spoken of. It was nothing more than a hastily dug fire pit and a circle of saddles and horses. There was room around the fire for people to sit, and someone had dragged a small log near the fire. Two men sat on it holding cards, a small pile of coins between them.

No one looked up when the Wolf entered camp leading the horse. There were maybe thirty men sitting or standing around the area they'd marked as their own. Some talked in small groups, and several were bundled in blankets with their heads resting on their saddles, sleeping on the muddy ground.

No eyes were on her. But Sorcha could feel them *not* looking. They were more than aware of her among them. Some of it was pure curiosity, but there was hostility in the air as well.

Sorcha slid from the saddle before the Wolf could offer any kind of help. She dodged the horse as he turned his head and tried to catch her with his teeth. Moving several steps away, she wrapped her arms around herself.

The Wolf glanced at her, looking from head to toe in a heartbeat, before turning to the group around the fire and gesturing to a man with blond hair. He came forward but didn't look at Sorcha, one hand on the dagger at his hip and the other gripping a medallion on a thin leather cord around his neck.

"Hugh, find a blanket for the woman."

The man nodded and turned away, hands dropping from his dagger and charm.

Another man stepped forward and took the Wolf's mount to the line of other horses. This one did throw a glance her way, but his expression was unreadable.

Sorcha's skin crawled with unease, standing hesitantly back as the Wolf went to speak with the pair playing cards.

A copse of trees rose to the right, the grouping spindly and short. Even if she made it that far, there were barely enough trees to conceal her. The rest of the land around them was farmland, trampled fields, with nowhere to hide but the shallow ditches.

Sorcha took a step backward, still facing the group of men. Then another. No one seemed to notice or care that she was slowly easing back toward the road.

Hugh returned from the group of horses carrying a gray blanket. Even from a distance, Sorcha could see it was stained and filthy.

Between noticing Hugh had returned and taking another step back, the Wolf was there beside her, moving so silently she hadn't even heard his chainmail rattle. He gripped her arm with one black-gloved hand, dragging her toward the fire. She stumbled, but he kept her upright. He indicated a flat stone, barely large enough to perch on, and let her go.

"Sit," he said, then turned to Hugh. "Find a clean blanket."

"The witch doesn't deserve one."

The Wolf stared at Hugh, radiating cold, not speaking.

Hugh paled, turning away to search for another blanket.

In a smooth motion, he removed his sword and sat beside her with a creak of metal and leather.

She glanced at him, his profile so near to her own, the long dark lashes and smudged soot on his cheek.

Sorcha was painfully aware of him. His cruelty frightened her, the obvious strength and fear he commanded from those around him. He was a palpable force beside the fire, a man made of anger and darkness.

But he drew her eye as he took out a cloth and a polishing stone and began to clean his weapon.

It took only a moment before Hugh returned with a cleaner blanket. He offered it to Sorcha without looking at her, his attention on the Wolf.

She took it, grateful despite herself, because the cold seeping up from the ground was already sinking into her bones.

"How do you know this is the vessel?" Hugh asked, mouth set in a hard line. "What if this is some other witch hoping to escape the sword?"

The Wolf didn't look up from cleaning his weapons, and when he spoke, his voice was deceptively soft. "Why are you asking questions?"

The camp fell silent as the men paused, watching the three by the fire, tension building.

Sorcha looked from one to the other.

In a lightning-fast movement, the Wolf removed the dagger from Hugh's hip and pressed it to his throat. A trickle of blood appeared, sliding down into the high neck of his undershirt.

Hugh's eyes went wide, the whites visible all around the iris. When he swallowed, the blade cut into him a little, and more blood trickled down his neck.

No one said a word.

Sorcha forgot to breathe. Would he kill the man right here? Like the yellow-eyed man had killed his compatriot. Was there no honor among killers, then?

"I'm not asking questions, sir," Hugh said, voice rough as he swallowed, and the blood continued to flow.

The Wolf released him, turning away.

Sorcha looked away from them, not wanting to see if either one threw a glance in her direction. She didn't want to be any more involved than she already was.

The other men returned to their conversations, and Sorcha watched the fire.

The Wolf did not take his seat beside her again. He went to speak with another man, one she had not heard a name for yet, and she was grateful for the small solitude it gave her.

As the sky darkened, a man put a collapsible cooking pot over the fire and poured water into it before adding hunks of some unrecognizable dried food. When it had boiled, the men gathered around the pot, holding cups close to their bodies and talking quietly. The Wolf was last, making sure all his men had eaten before receiving his share.

Sorcha's stomach growled, but she didn't think she'd be able to eat. There had been so much blood, the last few hours a blur of panic and pain. Yet her body betrayed her, the scent of the food overpowering.

Adrian crouched beside her, extending the cup he held.

The scent of cooked vegetables reached her, and it smelled better than anything she could remember. But she hesitated, watching him, too aware of the tension between them.

"Take it," he said, voice flat and expressionless.

Sorcha shook her head. Even as hungry as she was, she didn't want to eat what this monster offered. She would rather starve. But it smelled so good, and the ground beneath her was so cold.

He shrugged, setting it beside her and moving to sit a few feet away.

The sun set and the moon rose, the men going silent one by one as the card game stopped and they packed up their camp. Hugh brought more wood for the fire, building it up and taking a place among the others. Adrian remained beside her, the cold cup of soup between them.

Exhaustion took its toll, sleep coming on hard, offering a reprieve from the horror of the day, and she welcomed it.

———

Adrian watched the woman sleep. Her brow creased as she mumbled through dreams, twitching, her hand fluttering up and falling back. She didn't wake, and he didn't move to wake her. She cried out once, a sharp sound in the night, drawing the attention of the men around the fire. He waved them off, and they dismissed her easily, turning back to the campfire.

The horror of the city hadn't touched him. But he wondered what had happened to her there to disturb her dreams. The blood on her dress had dried, and there had been a lot of it. He hadn't ridden into the city, leaving that for the others, but there must have been many other people with her. Other priests and priestesses, people whose place it was to protect the vessel.

He was curious about that—her destructive faith and worship of the dead. What did it take for someone to believe in such things? He had faith in his sword and nothing else.

Exhaustion hung heavy on his shoulders, lodging in his back and making his neck ache. But he couldn't sleep. Despite the prince's explicit orders that the woman wasn't to be touched and must be treated with the utmost respect, Adrian's men were superstitious. They'd already proven themselves to be more wary of what they didn't understand than beholden to the prince's word.

It would be a mistake to leave her unguarded until they'd come to terms with the fact that her life was more valuable than theirs right now.

CHAPTER FIVE

Dawn arrived, and frost collected on the trampled earth around them. The tips of her fingers were cold despite the blanket pulled tight around her shoulders. Half the men had been gone when she'd woken up. The other half were preparing to leave now. Sorcha was surprised the Wolf had let her sleep so long when there was still so much ground to cover to get her to his prince.

He sauntered over and picked up a waterskin from beside the fire, then extended it to Sorcha. She didn't take it, and he crouched down, holding it out once more. He waited, and someone chuckled nastily behind him.

Sorcha glanced at the man. Hugh. More than anything, she wanted to shut him up.

Sorcha snatched the heavy waterskin and took a sip, the water cool and tasting of earth. When she thrust it back at him, the blanket slipped away, and the sleeve of her dress rucked up to expose a section of her elaborate tattoo. Hurriedly, she smoothed the fabric down, but the Wolf stopped her with a rough hand. She flinched with a gasp, pulling back against his hold but stuck tight.

He stilled, the two of them breathing together, locked in the moment.

Gently, he pushed the sleeve back with one gloved hand, revealing more of the tattoo—detailed and complex, starting just above her wrist and disappearing into the sleeve.

She watched, transfixed, as he traced a line across her skin. A road yet to be traveled, a destination yet to be reached. Each location was carefully detailed, nothing hidden, her skin a map and promise of what could be found at the end of the journey.

"Did your prince tell you about me?" she asked, intensely aware of his grip on her arm.

Who had been the last person to touch her with such gentleness? Ines before the fall of the Citadel gates? And now, this monster with black leather between them.

His dark eyes flashed up to her face. "Yes."

"How much?" She raised an eyebrow, wanting to remove his hand even as her heart raced with the connection. "Everything?"

"No." He shook his head. "I don't think he knows it all."

"About me or the Saint?" she asked.

"You are one and the same to him," he said.

"And to you?"

Her words hung between them. He didn't respond, watching her without emotion.

"It doesn't matter." She shook her head, pulling her sleeve down to hide the small part of the larger tattoo. "He won't get what he wants."

The Wolf rocked back on his heels. "He will. I will make sure he does."

"Do you even know what that means? What the Saint means?"

He shook his head. "I don't know the stories here. I grew up thousands of miles away. I only know what the court whispers."

"And what do they say?"

"He'll bring back the dead."

"He will bring *death*." Her eyes glittered, hardness and slow simmering anger building. "He *is* death. Walking, consuming, physical death." The words came out softly, belying the fury inside. "Does the prince think the Saint will do his bidding? That he can bend a god to his will?"

"I don't know."

"I thought you were his monster. Shouldn't a dog know what his master is thinking?"

The Wolf's hand clenched, his face betraying nothing—eyes black pits of nothing. The leather across his knuckles creaked, pulled taut.

Sorcha watched his fist until his fingers relaxed, the angry response quelled. Or maybe saved for a better moment, when others weren't watching.

"His mother is dying," he said, voice flat and hard.

Sorcha sucked in a breath, surprised. She hadn't expected something like this, so ordinary and very human.

"People die," she said.

He nodded.

"No one comes back from the dead," she whispered.

All the blood in the temple, her sisters and brothers—the only family she had ever known—all dead around her, all trusting her to do what she had been born for. The only thing she was good for.

Resurrect the Saint.

"Don't they? Isn't that what your religion teaches?"

She bit her lip, looking down at her pale hands and the dried blood beneath her bitten-down nails. "Are you religious?"

He shook his head, waiting until she looked up to speak. "You're a death cult."

You will be the instrument of our resurrection. He will walk the earth again because of you.

They'd killed themselves so easily. It had shocked her how quickly they brought blade to flesh, poison to lips. The gates breached, houses burning, the air stinking of death. The earth beneath her trembling, quaking, as if it might split at any moment.

She closed her eyes, squeezing it all out, forcing it down and away.

He grasped her chin, turning her face to his, forcing her to look at him. His grip was strong, unyielding, and her heart began to pound, her skin tingling with his touch.

"You don't believe it," he said.

Not a question, a statement, seeing it all on her face.

"I don't have to believe it for it to be true."

He grabbed her arm, pushing the sleeve back again to reveal the tattoo. "And these?"

The words spilled out of her, flowing without thought. "I was chosen, born beneath the right stars at the right time. Divine. I grew up in the temple. There is always a vessel. Always a girl at the right time and place."

She pushed his hand away, reaching up to tug at the high neckline of the dress. The tattoo on her chest began beneath her collarbones, wrapping her breasts and torso, following the line of her hips and down her thighs. Ankles to wrists to neck. Her whole body covered in the history of the Saint.

She pulled the neckline down enough to show the edge of the tattoo beneath her collarbone, a swirl of gold and blue. "In my seventeenth year, I took the final step and began the map ceremony."

He touched her collarbone with one gloved finger, following the line of bone beneath skin. The contact made heat writhe within her, a horrible mix of desire and disgust. He touched her with his gloves on, a layer between them, and more than anything, she wanted to take those gloves off. She wanted him to touch her with his bare hands.

His hand dropped away. "How long did it take?"

"It takes years to finish the map." She bit her lip, mind racing.

The map on her skin was incomplete. She'd not yet completed the rituals. Now, she never would.

"And you believe the pieces of the Saint can be found in these places?"

"Your prince believes it. Don't you trust your prince?"

"Always." He stood, staring down at her. "But I am not blinded by the impending death of someone I love. I won't be fooled by your death cult. I won't be taken in by your innocence."

She snorted, angry with his coldness, with herself for sharing so much without a second thought. "And what will you do if you find out it's nothing but a myth after all?"

"I'll kill you myself," he said. "We leave in a few minutes."

He turned away, his broad back to her, and walked through camp toward his waiting men, leaving her cold by a dying fire.

Chapter Six

The Wolf rode behind her on the way back to the army. Sorcha kept her spine straight, wanting to avoid any contact with him, but it was impossible. Awareness coursed through her, the contact inevitable, as his arm brushed her or when he leaned forward. His thighs were on either side of her, and even as she leaned forward, it was impossible to escape the contact.

Briefly, she wondered if he was leaning into her on purpose, keeping the contact even as she tried to wriggle away as far as possible.

"Can you not sit so close?" she asked finally, wriggling forward in the saddle for the hundredth time.

Behind her, the Wolf snorted, switching the reins from one hand to the other, brushing her leg as he did.

Sorcha shivered at the delicate contact, stomach twisting. She didn't like the way it made her feel, the way his warmth at her back was somehow comforting.

Sorcha wanted comfort, needed to be held and told that everything was going to be okay. It felt as if nothing would ever be the same, and she knew it wouldn't. For a little while, she wanted to pretend, to forget. But the blood beneath her nails and dried on the hem of her dress was a constant reminder. And the hole in the middle of her chest would never be filled, the grief never relieved.

Bring us back.

But how? How was she going to find all the relics on her own with an army searching as well? How would she find them if the Wolf was on her heels? She needed to escape. Rohan had promised there would be help in the other temples, that she would never be alone.

There would be an opportunity to escape, and she would take it.

———

The Wolf's men were waiting for him as they reached the outskirts of the main encampment of the army of the White Snake. The man she'd heard called Revenant had ridden ahead to ensure hot water would be waiting and to dispatch a messenger to the Traveling City.

As they approached, a group came forward, men she recognized from the small camp from the night before. Then, their teeth had been blackened, tongues dark, but now their mouths were pink and clean. Sorcha wondered if it were a ritual of sorts, a superstition.

Revenant stood at the head of the group, and she felt his yellow-eyed stare boring into her. She shivered, not liking the sensation, feeling his dislike as if it were a physical force.

When Nox reached them, Sorcha slid off the horse before the Wolf could dismount and help her down. As she'd come to expect, the horse turned to nip at her, and she darted out of the way, his teeth barely missing the sleeve of her dress.

"You're a mean horse," Sorcha whispered, glancing up to catch the barest curve of the Wolf's lips as he dismounted.

"The general is here and wants to speak with you," Revenant said.

The Wolf nodded. "Take her to my tent. Don't let her leave."

Revenant stepped forward, reaching for Sorcha, an unpleasant gleam in his eyes.

She shook her head, leaning out of his reach, not wanting his hands on her again.

"Don't touch me," she said.

The hatred in Revenant's gaze intensified as he kept coming, the intention on his face clear. He would do what the Wolf said, but he would make it as painful an experience for her as possible.

The Wolf held up a hand, stopping Revenant in his tracks.

The man nodded, accepting the silent rebuke, and turned back to Sorcha. "Follow me."

Sorcha looked from one to the other, the Wolf's face promising force if she refused. She fell into step behind Revenant. Walking through the camp was like walking in a dream where you've forgotten your clothes and you're on display for everyone to see. Faces turned to track her progress, curiosity and distaste on their features.

She'd never been in a war camp, surrounded by thousands of men, smoke from fires curling into the sky. Campfires and blood, ash and death. In the distance, she could hear horses and people calling to each other, and farther away, the sounds of steel grinding against stones, being sharpened and honed for the next fight.

The camp around her was as big as a city, but without the stone walls, slate tiles, and thatched roofs. Here, the round tents were heavy shades of gray and black, colorful banners limp on long poles stuck into the ground beside entrances. Some of the tent flaps were open, revealing low-lit interiors, shadows moving, a woman laughing.

She turned at the sound, wondering who it could be. What woman would want to be here? A shiver touched her. She wouldn't be here if she had a choice.

The noises died down a little as they entered an area with smaller tents, a circle with a large fire in the middle, and one large tent. Benches circled the fire, and cooking pots and other clutter—a spit for roasting—gathered round.

She looked around, the quiet unnatural compared to the way she'd come. All the banners here were black, solid, and as if each had been cut from the darkest of skies. No moon or stars, no light. Only the blackness of a dead heart.

"In here," Revenant said, his accent running the words together.

He held the tent flap back, revealing a dim interior, a brazier burning at the center.

She glanced at him, but he was looking away, back the way they'd come. His expression was carefully kept in check—smooth and unbothered. Whatever he might think of her, he kept it to himself. Still, he radiated animosity.

She stepped inside, and the tent flap fell behind her with a heavy thump, cutting her off from the noise of the camp. Hesitating, wrapping her arms around herself, she remained at the entrance, looking around the tent.

Dim light filled the space, flowing from a round opening at the center of the tent. A brazier flickered below it, smoke rising and disappearing through the hole. There were minimal furnishings in the large space. Two folding chairs made out of tan canvas and sleek polished wood and a lightweight desk covered in maps, letters, and sheaves of parchment. It all looked easy to pack up and travel with.

On the far side of the tent sat a cot covered in furs and blankets. A stand with an oval mirror and water basin was beside it. Steam curled up from the basin, calling to her—cajoling and tempting. More than anything, she wanted to be clean. There was a low bench beside it with bandages and soap, a collection of what looked like medicine bottles, and a rack to hold the Wolf's armor. Two chests completed the room's contents, one open and full of clothing, the other closed with a book resting on top of it.

Sorcha removed her filthy slippers, leaving them beside the tent door, stepping on the woven grasses that made the smooth floor. It felt like a house, more permanent than she'd expected it to be.

Slowly, she moved around the space, looking over the papers on his desk but not touching them. There was a map of the Citadel, the familiar lines jarring in this place, the roads and landmarks named, and the temple of the Saint circled in red ink.

They'd come for her. They'd known she would be there.

But who had told them? The Wolf had said a priest, but what priest? From where?

The other maps on the desk were of the continent—the Black Stone Mountains to the north with a pass marked, the ruins to the south and the volcanoes that rumbled constantly there. There were maps of cities and forests, maps of small cities and even smaller villages. Some were well-worn, the edges frayed, the ink faded. Others were newer, the colors brighter, with flourishes and other details.

Places the Wolf had been, places he had yet to see.

Places to which he would bring death.

Sorcha's stomach twisted at the thought, and she fought to clear her mind—Ines's face going pale, the feel of her life leaving her body, the warmth of blood on her hands.

Turning to the steaming water, she began to wash the blood from her hands.

————

The tent flap lifted, the scent of cooking food drifting in, roasting meat and the earthy richness of root vegetables. Men chattered around the fire, and someone laughed. The last vestiges of light from the setting sun touched her face, shocking her with warmth. She held a hand up to shade her eyes, pulling in a startled breath.

The Wolf stood there, taking in the interior at a glance—Sorcha curled by the brazier in two of the folding chairs, a book on the history of the Empire of the White Snake in her hand. He moved to the wash-stand and peeled his cloak away. After hanging it on the stand, he sat on the oak bench beside it to work his heavy boots free.

Sorcha sat up, stiff in his presence. The energy he brought to the space crackled through the air, settling to buzz beneath her breastbone.

She watched him, her hands clenched around the book. He didn't look at her as he stood and began to strip. Layer after layer came off, the red leather armor shed like a second skin. She couldn't look away as he removed the tunic, pulling the thin cotton shirt over his head to reveal his muscled torso covered in fading scars. When he reached for the waist of the pants, she sucked in a breath and turned away, cheeks heating.

"What's your name?" he asked as clothing rustled.

"Don't you know it?" Her question came out breathless, and she fought to keep her gaze on the book.

Water splashed, and he let out a breath, not a sigh exactly, but close.

"If I knew your name, I wouldn't have asked."

"Then how did you find me?" she asked, turning to look at him.

The Wolf wore nothing but a thin pair short pants, his back to her, hands braced against the basin stand. Their gazes met in the mirror, and he arched an eyebrow at her. Dark eyes. Black in the light of the fire and in the shadows of the tent. Eyes so deep she could fall into them and lose herself. The muscles in his back rippled as he shifted, picking up the cloth from the basin and wringing it out. Sorcha swallowed.

"The vessel. A young woman with unusual tattoos. Dark hair, green eyes. On the run, looking for a way out of the city. Possibly guarded by a member of the Crimson Cult." He spoke so easily, so matter of fact—her life reduced to a few words.

He looked away, going back to the water, and smoothed a wet cloth over his face and neck.

"Who gave you all that information?"

"A priest from the Summer Palace."

"What happened to him?"

"He died."

She shivered. His tone was ice—so calm—as if death meant nothing. The temple had taught her that it was a brief moment, something to pass through to the other side, where the Saint waited. But this man? What did death mean to him when he meted it out so easily to others who didn't have faith?

"Why am I here?" she whispered.

"The prince wants you here."

"But why? I'm not important!" It was a lie, and she knew he saw through her protest.

"You aren't the vessel for the Saint?" he asked in a low voice.

She froze, terror racing through each vein, the hair on the back of her neck standing. Warning bells jarred in her mind. There was nothing to hide. There was no playing dumb. This man was a killer, a monster, and he'd killed members of the Aureum Sanctus. He'd killed entire kingdoms, slaying city after city. Right now, she feared him more than the prince. More than death. More than what might be waiting on the other side of death for her.

"Aren't you?" he asked again, setting the cloth down and crossing to her. He grasped her chin, tilting her face toward the firelight, studying her. "You're the woman with the tattoos. Your eyes are green. Your hair is dark. You're the woman I've heard so much about."

Sorcha held her breath, keeping her eyes on his face, refusing to look away. His face was impassive, showing nothing, no hint or sign of his thoughts.

Slowly, she reached up, placing her hand on his. The contact was electric, somehow more intimate than his hand alone on her face. Something flashed in his eyes, like a ripple passing across a still body of water and made by something far beneath the surface.

What is this? Her thoughts raced, tension coiling in her stomach—a snake poised to strike.

She pushed the Wolf's hand away, breaking his grip as easily as she would have a child's. He let her go.

The Wolf nodded, stepping back, the air around them cooling.

His touch, the heat of his hand on her face, lingered. Sorcha wanted to wipe it away, erase the lingering sensation of a strong, callused hand on her face. But she remained motionless, not wanting to give him the satisfaction of a reaction beyond what she'd already shown him.

"Have you eaten?" the Wolf asked, moving to a chest and rummaging through it. A black shirt and a pair of pants appeared. He pulled them on without any sign of self-consciousness.

Sorcha shook her head.

"Yes or no," he said.

"No," she said, an edge of irritation slipping into her tone.

The Wolf stepped to the tent flap, pushing it back and calling to someone unseen beyond the opening.

"Food and more hot water." He glanced back at her, going over her grubby clothes and torn slippers. "And a change of clothes for the woman."

The person beyond the tent murmured something she couldn't understand. A different language she hadn't heard spoken among his men yet.

Then the tent flap fell back into the place and the Wolf moved past her to the desk.

"Food and water aren't going to change my mind about you."

He glanced at her, something like amusement flashing in his gaze. "I would never expect it to."

"I refuse to eat," she said, anger boiling, overriding the small amount of self-preservation she'd displayed so far. "Your prince won't get the satisfaction."

The Wolf was in front of her before she finished speaking, pulling her up and forcing her chin up until their eyes locked. When he spoke, it was in a whisper, the tone so at odds with the strength in his grip.

"You will eat." His eyes roved over her face, dark gaze searching, and a line formed between his brows. "I will accept nothing else from you."

"Compliance," she said, gritting her teeth.

"Surrender."

Sorcha opened her mouth, struggling to find words, caught in his eyes. A corner of his mouth twitched, as if he was enjoying her discomfort. She clamped her lips shut, biting the inside of her cheek. He released her, letting her stumble back into the folding chair. She sat down hard and remained there, more aware of where he'd touched her than her surroundings. She watched the fire as he added more oil and went back to his maps.

Soon, the water and food arrived—another jug placed on the stand by an old woman who shot Sorcha a curious look out of pale gray eyes. The food—flat bread and roasted meat—was placed on the desk by one of the men she'd seen around the camp the previous night. But he didn't look at Sorcha. He didn't need to for her to feel his hatred.

Without speaking to her, the Wolf took the rough wooden plate and held it out to her.

Surrender. But what kind?

She stood and reached out without taking another step toward him.

The Wolf moved the plate out of reach. "What's your name?"

"I won't—"

"If you prefer to be only an object, I won't refuse you that right. *Vessel.*"

She opened her mouth, ready to tell him that was fine. But her tongue betrayed her. "Sorcha."

He extended the plate and waited as she took a piece of bread from it.

"Don't you want to know my name?" he asked, black eyes on her face, watching as she put a piece of bread in her mouth.

"I don't need to know anything more about you," she said, half turning away, tearing the warm bread into chunks as she sat. "I know enough."

"Do you?"

She left his question there, unanswered and ignored.

CHAPTER SEVEN

"There's a problem."

Sorcha recognized the voice. Revenant, the Wolf's second-in-command. It hadn't taken her long to figure it out. The strange man had come and gone several times, once carrying a carefully sealed letter and another time to speak softly in a language she couldn't understand.

Now the fire in the brazier was out, and the overcast night sky glimpsed through the opening in the tent. It was late, the noise of the camp had died down, and a strange sense of calm had overtaken the place.

The Wolf was out of the cot and following the other man in a moment.

She was alone, wrapped in the furs at the farthest point from where he'd been sleeping. Except, she didn't think he had been. His breathing had never evened out, never relaxed. He'd been as awake as she had been.

Now or never.

Moving as quietly as possible, Sorcha stood and slipped on the boots that had arrived while she'd been eating. They were perfect, as if they'd known her size and fit. Another woman's boots? And the fresh clothes she'd refused? Would they have fit her this well? Now, she'd never know.

One of the Wolf's black daggers was on the desk—sheathed in red leather—holding the corner of a curling map down. Sorcha took it and wrapped one of the furs he'd tossed at her around her shoulders. The metal of the dagger was cool in her hand, warming with her touch.

The scent of smoke and blood lingered around her. She'd refused the full bath he'd offered after she ate, refused the clothes. A bath would have been a luxury beyond imagining, but she didn't want to concede to that as well. There had been too many of concessions already.

It was almost too easy to slip through the outskirts of the encampment. She saw a few fires lit and men in the distance, but no one around or in front of her. No one kept watch at the edge when she reached the final line of tents.

The forest lay only yards away, thick and black. Mist curled along the ground, pouring between the trunks, bringing the clammy cold of a fresh fall morning. But they lived in a world of early winter—unnatural and a sign of things to come. Only yesterday, it had snowed. But strange warmth filled the air here.

In a few breathless moments, Sorcha was across the open space and into the trees. She stumbled through underbrush—cursing silently—terrified someone would hear her clumsy passage through the trees. But she didn't stop. Putting as much distance between herself and the Wolf was the most important thing. Maybe with enough of a head start, she would find a place to hide and wait until it was safe to move again. Then she would figure out in which direction the closest unconquered temple lay.

A sound or movement tugged at her senses, and she paused, heart racing.

Nothing. Not another sound.

A figment. Stress. But there was someone there.

She pulled the dagger free of the sheath, gripping it tightly and moving slowly. The sense that someone followed intensified, not in the things she heard but in the things she couldn't. The trees around her were dark, holding tight to the night, refusing to let it go and become day. She squinted into each shadow, searching for a familiar shape, a sign.

A soft rustle behind her froze her blood. She turned, and he was coming toward her out of the night—birthed and made of shadows.

She stood her ground, breathing hard, and lifted the blade up.

He didn't stop, didn't pause; his power and anger rushing toward her. She took one step forward, just one, ready to meet him with her own frustration and hurt and fear.

With a ring of metal, he drew his sword, bringing it up and down, striking the dagger. The hard contact vibrated up to her shoulder, the clash of metal filling the woods.

But she held on to the blade, bringing it up again as he circled her.

"Do you know how to fight?" His voice was calm, as if he weren't wielding a sword, attacking a woman in the early morning hours. "Did they teach you in that temple?"

They hadn't. Not really. A few basic techniques, enough to defend herself from an over-amorous visitor, but nothing that would keep her alive under a blade like his.

He brought the sword up again before coming down. The dagger faltered, her hand falling, and he pressed his advantage, shoving her with the flat of his blade. Spinning, Sorcha hit a tree, scrambling to keep her feet. As he went by, she reached out with the blade and caught his arm. Fabric ripped, revealing a shallow slash, blood welling up. Shock skittered across his face when he realized she'd wounded him.

The Wolf grabbed her arm as he turned. Tugging her sleeve, he twisted his fingers into the fabric. Sorcha kicked out with a foot, wincing as she connected with his knee. Grim satisfaction filled her as he swore, but it vanished the next instant as he fell backward, still gripping her sleeve.

Sorcha followed him down, landing awkwardly across his body with a grunt. He swore again—taking her weight—as she pushed herself up and raised the dagger above her head. The Wolf held her other hand against his chest, each breath fogging the air between them. Rage filled her, overflowing and blurring the edges of her vision. Fighting to catch her breath, to quiet the racing thoughts, she stared at the Wolf.

He lay on his back beneath her, dark eyes locked on her, mouth set in a firm line, body hard and unmoving. Everywhere their bodies touched burned—legs tangled, his hand encircling her wrist, her palm against his chest, with thighs and hips pressed close.

She opened her mouth to scream or cry, to tell him what would happen when the Saint came for him. Anything. Something. But she remained frozen.

"Do it," the Wolf said, voice low and emotionless as he watched her and waited.

Her arms shook. The rage began to recede, leaving space for the chill to creep in. The dagger dropped a fraction, her desire to plunge it into his chest drawing back.

In a rush, he rolled her over, pinning her beneath him and pressing her into the dirt with his full weight. The dagger slipped from her grip, her hand empty and grasping. Twigs and small stones bit into her back as she struggled, leaves rustling, the scents of damp earth and snow filling her senses.

The Wolf moved his hands to her neck, digging his fingers into soft flesh. Sorcha clutched at his forearms, pulling at his wrists in an effort to dislodge him, but his grip tightened. Black hair fell around her as he leaned down, their faces so close she could smell the soap he'd used to shave earlier. His eyes glittered with some suppressed emotion.

Sorcha twisted, seeing the dagger was only inches away. If she could loosen his grip, she might be able to reach it.

"Don't," he warned.

The single word was hard and final. If she went for it, she might not survive. He needed her, she knew that, but his stony expression promised nothing. The prince might be angry his monster had killed the woman he needed, but by then, it would be too late.

"Get it over with if you're going to kill me," Sorcha challenged, lifting her chin slightly.

He leaned into her, coming so close she could smell apples and a trace of mint beneath that spiced armor polish and sharp copper. In a sudden, graceful move, he rolled away from her and stood, gaze averted. Sorcha lay there panting, hand easing toward the blade. But he picked it up and tucked it into his belt without a word.

Sorcha began to stand, but he scooped her up before she could. He threw her over his shoulder, and her breath pushed from her lungs with a grunt.

"Do that again, and I'll kill you," he said, adjusting his hold on the backs of her thighs. "Do anything but follow my commands, and you die. Understand?"

Sorcha braced herself against his muscled back, cheeks hot and mind whirling. His large hand was warm, his hard shoulder digging into her abdomen. The contact was too much. She wriggled, wanting him to release her, to not feel how small she was in his arms—how breakable.

They reached the tree line before she spoke, pushing hair out of her face with one hand, too aware of where her other hand was.

"Put me down," she said. "I can walk."

"I don't trust you." His voice was flat, giving nothing away.

"I won't run," she promised.

The Wolf snorted, continuing without pause as they crossed the meadow and entered camp. Revenant stood at the entrance to the Wolf's tent, yellow eyes piercing in the gloom. As they neared, he opened the flap, letting it fall behind them once they were inside.

Without ceremony, the Wolf dumped her on the pile of furs that had been her bed before.

"In the morning, you'll bathe," he said, returning to his cot. "You stink. I'm not taking you into the Traveling City smelling like Nox's ass."

Chapter Eight

They traveled for two days before Sorcha saw the Traveling City.

The Wolf kept her close, sharing the saddle with her, leaving Nox irritated at carrying the extra weight. The horse tried to bite her every chance he got. When she wasn't sharing the horse with the Wolf, he was sleeping beside her when they camped, and when she needed some privacy to take care of things, he stood with his back a few feet away.

By the time they reached the prince's city, she was almost glad. But as they neared, her heart dropped, filling her stomach with acid and stress, sinking until it could sink no further.

The Traveling City rose from the plains—a dark wooden mass—floating above the dead grass and trampled snow. White banners with an emblem of a black snake flapped from the highest towers, easily several stories tall, though it was hard to know the exact height.

Sorcha would have called it a village if it hadn't been so extravagant. A traveling city, a moving palace, slowly overtaking a stationary world. It moved forward constantly on a grinding journey without end.

No, that wasn't right. It would end with the Saint. It would end in blood.

As they neared, the carvings on the wooden walls and towers became clear. Spring trees, flowing branches laden with blossoms covered the outer walls. Animals peeked around the trunks, gathered in small groups beneath the flowering boughs. Even the towers were covered in carvings of the sky—constellations and fluffy clouds, a lightning storm striking. It was strange and beautiful, and unlike any place she'd ever seen or heard of.

Curiosity got the better of her.

"How does it move?" she asked, searching the gloom beneath the city.

It was a forest of piers and giant wheels of wood banded in iron.

"Oxen." The Wolf nodded at the herds that had come into view behind the city.

Long lines of animals were tethered together with mounds of hay before them. There were thousands. Hundreds of thousands. She'd never seen animals quite like them, huge and broad with dark hides and long curved horns that weighed heavy on their heads.

The Wolf pointed to a village of gray canvas tents beyond the animals where cooking fires were lit and torches burned. "And men."

Sorcha nodded, wondering how it had all come to be. Who could have dreamed of such a place? A city plodding across the landscape, crossing rivers and mountains piece by piece. It was something from a dream.

As they reached the city, a wide set of stairs lowered from a hidden location beneath the large main doors. Metal gears grated and wood creaked as the stairs dropped the last few feet in a rush, thudding onto the ground and sending chunks of dirt flying.

The Wolf's hands slid around her waist, his chest warm against her back for only a few seconds before he lifted her up and dropped her from the horse without warning. Nox snorted, swinging his head in her direction, a glint of malicious intent in his eye.

"Stop." Sorcha held up a finger, and the horse's ears pricked forward, listening intently to her hard tone. "No more. No biting. No stomping at me. You're done."

One ear twitched backward and then forward again, and she took that as an acknowledgement.

"Are you a horse witch now?"

Sorcha turned, meeting Revenant's gaze—her irritation flaring. *Witch.* As if it were an insult. The man watched her with more malice than she would have thought possible for a stranger. More hatred than she'd ever encountered. But he averted his gaze, eyes shifting down and away, when the Wolf dismounted behind her.

"Inside," the Wolf said, drawing her attention and gesturing toward the stairs. "Now."

He began to climb the stairs, expecting her to follow without more prompting. They knew who'd won in the woods that night after all. She didn't have the backbone to kill him, but if she ran from him now, she wouldn't get far, and he might kill her despite the prince's orders.

———

"Does she speak?" The man looked her up and down, his gaze lingering on her torn sleeve and knotted hair—likely finding her unexceptional. His lip curled in a sneer, the heavy gold loops in his ears trembling and catching the light thrown by the torches. "Will you need to translate?"

"She understands," Adrian replied.

"Good. Speak when you are spoken to. Keep your answers short. Use 'Your Highness' when addressing the prince. Keep your eyes on the ground." The steward stepped forward, grasping her arm and squeezed until her knees bent. "Kneel, temple girl. Honor the prince who keeps you alive."

"Remove your hand."

Sorcha and Adrian spoke at the same time, his voice overshadowing hers. She glanced at him with a quick, furtive look, and he could see the surprise in her face.

"You forget yourself, steward," Adrian said.

The man released her at once, eyes glittering with malice. "I'm an extension of His Highness."

"As am I."

A gong sounded in the next room, deep and ominous, calling the courtiers to the throne room. The prince was ready for them. The steward gave her a tight smile, malice becoming pleasure.

Adrian kept his face impassive, a mask of nothing. It would be a mistake to let the steward, let alone the prince, see anything of his emotions. Even the anger could hurt him.

"This way," the steward said, gesturing to the doors.

They were tall and skinny—from polished floor to high painted ceiling—overlaid with gold and set with precious stones. Incense burned nearby, a sweet, heavy scent that reminded him of childhood. Despite the torches and the lit braziers that flickered beyond the opening doors, shadows clung to the corners of the room, hiding in the carved rafters of the ceiling.

Adrian took her elbow, guiding her through the door, ready to feed her to the wolves.

The court glittered in the dim light—exquisite fabric rustling, gold chains clinking. The people moved, restless as a flock of birds pinned to the floor. The opulence was beyond anything Sorcha could have imagined.

The Golden Citadel had been wealthy, full of rich and powerful people, and the temple she'd grown up in had been one of the richest in the city. But here, each person wore velvet, silk, and lace, each covered in gold and faceted gems. The women wore elaborate headdresses. Some had veils covering their faces and lustrous pearls woven into their hair, while diamonds glinted on fingers, and others wore dark eye makeup accented with tiny, delicate beauty marks in the shape of a snake. Faces turned toward her, sharp and hungry. The room was full of staring eyes.

Sorcha hesitated in the doorway, not wanting to move forward, unsure about being presented here. The Wolf grabbed her upper arm and pulled her inside, marching her across the polished wooden floor. They were as smooth and reflective as marble, deep green in color with flecks of gold gleaming down the aisle. The Wolf's boots clicked against the surface, her own soft shuffle following, as the court began to whisper.

Jeweled hands covered mouths; painted fans snapped open to hide the lower half of faces. Several different languages were being spoken, some she recognized, others completely foreign. She kept her eyes on the floor, refusing to acknowledge the whispered insults. At the end of the long room, the dark prince waited on a dais. There were two chairs, and he occupied the smaller of the two off to the side.

She wondered who was missing, who would have been in the place of honor.

The Wolf stopped her a few feet from the prince and kneeled, his leather creaking, head bowed. When she did not bend her knee, he pulled her sharply down beside him. She hit the floor with a thud, and sharp pain shot up her thighs.

"My prince—"

From behind them, the steward spoke, but the prince held up a hand and the man went silent. His eyes—ravenous and rabid—were fixed on Sorcha, but he spoke to the Wolf.

"Adrian, thank you for bringing me the woman."

Adrian. Sorcha wondered how such a monster could have a name at all.

"Your wish is my command, Prince." The Wolf kept his eyes on the floor.

Silence followed his words—expectant and heavy.

Sorcha gritted her teeth against the impending questions, jaw clenching against the answers she might have to give. The rustling, whispering, and quiet seething of the room faded.

When the prince spoke again, there was no mistaking that he was speaking to her. "Tell me about the Saint."

Sorcha closed her eyes and swallowed. She didn't respond and wasn't sure how to. She wanted to deny him a response but was afraid. The court whispered, voices low and distant. She opened her eyes slowly, keeping her gaze on the floor, biting the inside of her cheek.

"Your Highness," the steward began.

The prince made a gesture, and the steward took several steps back. The door opened slowly, and his footsteps disappeared from the room.

She could feel the heat of the prince's gaze burning though her clothes and into her skin.

Her mind raced. What could she tell him? What did he already know?

From behind her came a low groan, the sound of something heavy being dragged. Then two guards deposited a priest in front of her. The man sagged without their support, on his knees and leaning forward. She studied his face, what wasn't bruised and bloody. He was familiar but still a stranger. His clothes however, were unmistakable.

A priest of the Saint.

He wasn't from her temple; she'd known each person by name. He must be from another city, some other temple, another stronghold like her own. Half his face was horribly swollen, and a bandage covered one eye, blood seeping beneath it and crusting around his nose and ears. Dried blood coated his hair and clothes, cuts visible on his neck and what she could see of his skin beneath the ripped robes. She was afraid to look any closer. His one good eye was closed, and he was humming softly to himself, not even a song, just a gentle self-soothing hum.

"This priest has been helpful."

The prince's voice came from a distance, the man groaning with his words.

"He has given me information I sought." There was a pause. "But I require more from you."

The priest's one good eyelid began to flutter.

"I will make sure your life is unchanged. You will be able to worship and live as you always have. And when the time comes, I will ensure the temple you preside over is as beautiful and grand as any that can be built across the continent."

The priest opened his eye, the pupil constricted, rolling as he eased into consciousness.

"But if you don't help me," the prince continued, "your fate will be his. I have no time or mercy for those who don't serve me."

Sorcha watched the priest, heart pounding, as the man finally focused and saw her. A horrible hope filled his face, recognition dawning, and he began to babble excitedly. His words ran together as he reached for her with one broken hand.

"You'll do it. You'll bring him back. It doesn't matter. You'll save us all. Bring back the Saint, and you will change everything. This body doesn't matter. This broken flesh is dying. But he will resurrect us all."

She leaned away from his grasping fingers, tears rolling down her cheeks as he continued, voice rising and filling the silent court, shrill and bouncing off the walls. He was louder than her heartbeat, louder than her thoughts, louder than anything she'd ever thought to hear or hear again.

"You will save us all. You will bring him back. We will live again."

Horror filled her, devastation and sorrow, fear snarling behind it all, driving it all. She couldn't look away as the prince walked up behind the man and, without a word, slipped a dagger between his ribs. She met the prince's gaze, unable to stop herself, swallowed by horrible consuming darkness.

The priest continued to ramble, voice softening and trailing off as blood soaked his robe, face going pale. He slumped to the side, single eye wide and fixed, lying on the floor before her until his voice finally stopped and silence rushed in to fill the void.

The prince reached for her. She flinched away but was unable to escape his grasp. Hard fingers dug into her upper arm as he pulled her to her feet, turning her away from the cooling body on the floor to face what had been brought in while the priest died.

Two pieces of the Saint lay on a burgundy velvet blanket.

The last time she'd seen the gold and jewel-encrusted hand had been the day of the fires, when the gates had finally opened beneath the onslaught of the prince's army, the day her family died.

Anger bubbled up, furious sorrow, and she glanced behind her to the man on the floor.

"No," the prince whispered, leaning into her. "Don't look back."

The jewel-encrusted and gilded bones drew her gaze—the call of the Saint, the way they weighted the room and seemed to suck in all the light. She'd never seen this bone before. She'd only ever seen the hand that her temple had housed. Once upon a time, there had been talk of a tour to visit all the relics, a pilgrimage to cement her faith. But that was something else the head priestess had promised there would be time for.

Her fingers itched to touch the new bone, what must be an arm bone but was ten times larger than any human bone. It was proportional to the hand, the bones of a giant, a myth.

"You want to touch them," the prince said, keeping his voice low, the courtiers around them leaning forward. "I can see it on your face. Go on."

He let go of her arm, and she took a step forward, the crowd around her fading into the background as the bones called to her. She knelt and placed her hands on the forearm bone. It was warm, as if it had been held recently, as if it were still a part of the Saint and had never cooled in death.

Somewhere, deep inside, something shifted in her soul.

Behind her, the prince was speaking again, loud enough for the whole room to hear, loud enough so that there would be no doubt of his intent.

"I know more than you might expect. I know about you. I know about the map. I've shown you what waits if you refuse." He paused, studying the bones and the way she touched them, how her hands caressed them lovingly. "But how could you refuse? Your one and only purpose is to bring him back. It's the only reason you exist."

Sorcha paused, pulling back. He was right. There was no denying that. And she wanted to find the Saint, she needed to resurrect her people. They depended on her. But inside, another voice began to whisper, pulsing, growing stronger. *What if what she brought back was worse than anything they'd yet seen? What if the Saint refused to perform the resurrections? What if all the people she loved remained dead?*

Doubt. Fear. These things sat beside her desire to fulfill her purpose.

"What if I choose not to help you?" she asked softly.

"Tell me, priestess." The prince crouched down in front of her, studying her face, the dagger held loosely in one hand while blood dripped onto the polished floor. "What choice do you think you have?"

The threat of death colored his words, unsaid but present. She was afraid to die. And that was a betrayal of all she'd been taught—all she believed. Death was nothing. The Saint would be there—he would welcome her with open arms, his devoted follower, his most beloved oracle. But faced with death, she'd chosen life, time and again. Following first the Wolf's—Adrian's—commands and now the prince's.

But maybe if she survived long enough and pretended to give the conqueror what he wanted, she could find another way through. A way to keep her promises and keep her life.

Her gaze drifted back to the golden bones and then to the prince and his triumphant expression.

"I'll take your silence as acceptance."

Chapter Nine

"Take her to the Mapmaker." The prince turned to Adrian, indicating Sorcha with a wave of his hand. "Find the other relics."

Adrian nodded, moving to the edge of the velvet blanket, giving the woman a moment to collect herself and rise on her own. But she remained there, hands on the bone, focused on some inner thought.

"Come," Adrian said, waiting for her to look up, to stand and come with him. When she didn't respond, a strange glaze over her eyes, he said, "Sorcha."

The court ladies tittered, and the men chuckled. He kept the disgust off his face, shoving down the desire to turn to them all and tell them exactly how worthless and pointless their lives were. How he could cut them down and the prince wouldn't stop him. Not the Wolf. He hated that he'd said her name so they could have it, stood here with her name in his mouth, when he could have just grabbed her and avoided the whole scene.

She looked up, her eyes full of tears, her face pale. But she stood on her own, seemingly unaware of the gossip being whispered and the malicious curiosity on display. Her hands were shaking. Adrian led her from the throne room, the voices growing louder and the sweet incense doing nothing to mask the scent of fresh blood.

"Clothes have been arranged by His Highness." The steward met them at the doors, everything from his expression to his tone sour. "There is a meal and bath waiting in the Cerulean Wing. You have an hour before the Mapmaker will be ready."

Adrian nodded.

"There is a meal there for you as well." The steward smiled nastily. "And clothes."

"He's not—" Sorcha began, anger and disgust in her voice.

The steward's smile widened, venom surfacing in his gaze.

Adrian took a step forward, and the steward's smile vanished as he stepped back. Without a word, Adrian led Sorcha from the receiving antechamber and through the maze that was the Traveling City.

It had been built over time, hundreds of years, room after room being added—banquet halls and private suites, towers and kitchens and armories. It wasn't only the men and oxen that helped it move. Hundreds of years ago, the Empire of the White Snake had been full of magic, and there'd been a sorcerer capable of making even cities walk.

Once, he'd had a set of rooms here. Close to the bottom levels, where you could hear the wheels rumbling as it moved, oxen bleating, and the men shouting. The prince had offered others, but it was pointless when he knew he'd never stay. He'd never loved this city. He'd been here because the prince had ordered him to be. Being sent to war was better than being surrounded by memories of the past.

The Cerulean Wing was higher up, away from the noise of the lower levels. It was reserved for courtiers who were in favor with the prince at the moment. Which meant that the rooms' occupants were in constant rotation. Whoever had been there before Sorcha arrived had either been moved or executed.

Adrian wasn't surprised the prince was treating Sorcha as an honored guest. The man had learned long ago that a show of kindness with a sheathed sword worked better than a naked blade. The prince only killed these days to make a point. For all other things, Adrian was his weapon of choice.

There were no guards or waiting maids when they reached the

rooms. Adrian stepped inside, glancing around. They appeared unchanged, identical to the last time he'd seen them.

Floor-to-ceiling windows looked out over the plain, brass fittings polished to a shine. Thick carpets covered the floors, and there were a handful of simple wooden chairs and a low carved table between them. The walls were painted the intense blue of a late summer sky—before fall arrives and while insects sing in the tall grass.

"There are rooms through the doors to your right and a bathing chamber to your left." Adrian indicated either door, inset into the walls and painted the same color. At first, they were invisible, but after he pointed them out, they were impossible to miss.

"Bathing chamber?" Sorcha asked, stepping forward and wrapping her arms around herself.

She stared beyond the glass windows, a view so high up above the plains that it was possible to see over the thick forest in the distance to the west.

"Rainwater is collected and heated. You'll figure it out." He took a step back, leaving the woman in the overly bright and airy room, tired and dirty from the road and so out of place. "I'll return in an hour."

————

Adrian stood outside the door to her rooms, a guard and deterrent to anyone who might arrive full of curiosity and determined to see the oracle of a famous death cult. He wanted to plan for what would come next, needed to know what it was he would be conquering. But it was impossible to plan for a future with zero knowledge.

He would take the woman to the Mapmaker, and from her skin, they would learn where the relics were hidden. From what he'd learned, her skin only carried locations for less than half. How those would be enough to perform the resurrection, he had no idea. But that wasn't a question he needed to answer. He only needed to collect them and get the woman to the Red Tower.

Only the prince knew each detail, how they fit together and how it would all end.

When a series of bells chimed throughout the city—announcing the time and keeping the complicated motions it took to keep the city moving on time—he turned and knocked on the door.

"Sorcha."

It opened before he could knock again, though she didn't say a word. She stood in a crimson dress, layers of sheer fabric from her throat to her feet, with long sleeves kept close to her skin. Gold flashed in her ears and at her wrists, and a ring with a faceted ruby adorned one hand, all gifts from the prince. Adrian could see an open trunk behind her with more clothes scattered around the room—all the same crimson she wore.

The color of her crimson cult.

She'd worked the tangles out of her hair and brushed it smooth, her skin now completely clean with no hint of dirt or horsehair. Even though she'd cleaned up before they'd arrived, it had been with the very basics. Not the hot water from the taps and soap scented with lemon.

Adrian breathed in—breathed Sorcha in—the scent of sugared lemons filling his lungs.

The woman before him was completely different from the one who'd been found wandering in the Golden Citadel or the one in the woods who had held a knife and thought it might protect her. Not even the woman who had finally bathed in the tent and come out of the water looking more like a person.

Now Sorcha looked like the woman Prince Eine had originally described. A powerful figure in her community, an oracle of supposed great talents, and a vessel for a dead god. He believed in none of those things. But he knew his lack of personal faith didn't mean they weren't a reality. He'd seen more of the strange and unusual to know it couldn't be denied.

"What do you want?" she asked, pulling her sleeves down to hide more of her wrists.

"It's time to see the Mapmaker," he said, watching her pale hands against the sheer crimson, the way her tattoos were still visible beneath the thin fabric. "Are you ready?"

"Do I have a choice?"

————

The Wolf led her through a maze of rooms and corridors, some wide enough for four or more people to walk shoulder-to-shoulder, others so narrow they reminded her of the alleys in the lower levels of the Golden Citadel. Lanterns were spaced at intervals, with mesh screens to prevent the fire from spreading if they dropped. But even with those, there were long intervals of deep shadows. The walls were carved here as well, polished to a high shine, but not painted. Not the way her rooms had been.

And always, he led her up.

Soon skylights began to appear overhead, sunlight pouring through stained glass, falling on the polished, carved wooden walls and bringing color to it all. Sorcha watched the Wolf walk ahead of her, the patches of blue and green light touching his black hair and the armor he still wore.

Why hadn't he changed when she had? He'd had the same hour, yet he looked the same as he had when they'd walked up the stairs of the Traveling City. She refused to think about the throne room and what had happened there. Even now her mind shied away from it, blurring it all out. Even what had happened in the Citadel seemed to have happened months ago.

Had it only been days? It was too easy to lose track of time. To forget if she wanted to.

The Wolf stopped beside an arched set of double doors.

Adrian, she reminded herself. Hearing his name in the throne room, saying it to herself now, felt strange and unnatural. This was the man who had toppled her city, had been the driving force behind her friends and family—

Stop it. We're not thinking about that right now.

"In here," he said, gesturing to the closed door.

"What's in there?"

"The Mapmaker."

Sorcha buried her fingers in the dress, taking up big fistfuls of the luxurious skirts—soft, warm, and delicate all at once. How much would she have to remove? How much would she have to reveal? How much would Adrian see?

"How many people are in there?"

Nudity had never bothered her. Life in the temple had been open, with shared time in the hot springs, getting ready for feasts together, and sharing clothes. But she'd never been nude in front of strangers, never in front of someone whom she would have preferred to have been clothed in their presence.

"The Mapmaker."

"And?" she pressed, knowing there was more.

"Me," he replied.

"Why are you coming?"

"I'm not leaving you alone."

"Don't tell me you actually care about my safety?" Sorcha shook her head.

He sounded so matter-of-fact. A muscle jumped in the Wolf's jaw, his gaze focused farther down the hall.

He spoke softly, reaching around her to open the door they'd stopped in front of. "The prince cares, so I care."

"I don't want you in there," Sorcha said, crossing her arms.

"Would you rather be left alone with the vampire?"

Before she could respond, he pushed the door open. More light filled the corridor, and Sorcha had to shade her eyes. The room beyond was huge, lined with shelves, the center lit but the perimeter shadowed.

She hesitated on the threshold, the room seemingly empty, and Adrian gestured for her to go forward.

"Are you the map?"

The speaker was unseen, the voice dry, the question posed without inflection.

"Yes," Sorcha whispered.

"I am the Mapmaker."

A man stepped out of the shadows with a rattle. Sorcha's eyes were immediately drawn to the delicate silver chain attached to his ankle with a manacle. He wore a simple set of clothes, a deep green—the color of spruce in winter—and his feet were bare and so pale they were almost white. His hands were the same pale shade, his fingers long, and his hair bright and lustrous as a pearl. His beauty was monochrome, parched for color.

Sorcha opened her mouth and then closed it, not wanting to be rude—if he might feel that it was being rude—and ask.

"Yes," the man said, acknowledging her unspoken question.

Vampire.

She'd never met one and wasn't sure they even existed anymore. There had been stories, there were always stories, but no one like that had ever come to visit the Golden Citadel and King Roi.

"Come," the vampire said, gesturing to a small platform in the center of the room. "Let us begin."

———

Sorcha stood in the middle of the cold room, crimson dress clasped to her chest, skin prickling under the Mapmaker's gaze. But he didn't look at her with desire, simply the flat calm of someone paying meticulous attention to the task before them. He hadn't even touched her. She had the distinct impression that she was merely an object to be studied for a brief time before being cast aside.

She glanced at Adrian. He stood with his back to her, moving slowly along the line of shelves, pulling down books at random and flipping through the pages. She found herself wondering what his gaze would hold if he turned it on her now. What would it tell her?

When the Mapmaker had instructed her to undress, Sorcha had refused. To her surprise, the Wolf—*Adrian*—had insisted her wishes be honored as much as they could be. Prince Eine wanted her to be treated with dignity. The Mapmaker had agreed to let her keep the dress partially on, revealing sections of her body—and the map—a little at a time.

"Turn."

The Mapmaker gestured with his brush, indicating the direction he wanted her to move. She turned, exposing more of her shoulder and part of her back. The tattoo told the story of her youth and adulthood, the Saint's story interconnected with her own, the Saint and Sorcha in one being. The Mapmaker's brush created a perfect copy on the paper, connecting the lines on her skin in smooth, patient strokes. He took his time as Sorcha watched, memorized by his progress.

She had never seen the tattoos as a whole. This would be the first time, in this place. She shivered, pressing the dress tight to her body, wishing she could be done. Ignoring the men, she looked round the room, taking it all in.

Overhead, a skylight exposed a perfect square of the wintry world. It was a lightwell, the low stool she stood on directly in the center. Around her, the room was deep, the sunlight penetrating only so far, leaving the walls and the men in shadow. The shelves contained leather-bound books and scrolls, jars of inks, parchment, and loose pages. A workbench was in the far corner, covered with the detritus of bookbinding.

The Mapmaker sat in the only chair, knees hidden by a lap desk, a pot of black ink strapped to his right hand, a brush in his left. His glasses hid his eyes as he sat perfectly motionless, never looking down as his brush moved across the paper.

What would happen if she stepped down and walked past him, went through the door, found a way out of the city, and then across the plain? How far would she get? The smooth sound of the brush on paper filled the room as her life was translated onto paper, her past and future, all of it written down and decided. According to the map, she wouldn't walk out of this room. Her destiny lay in another direction.

"Do you have tattoos anywhere else?" the Mapmaker asked.

Sorcha twitched the dress to reveal part of her left hip and thigh, a swirl of clawed hands and femur bone, bare trees, and decorative scrollwork. He copied it in a few swift brushstrokes, accomplishing what had taken the temple artist careful weeks with ink and needle, hours on the table with the book of Saint open beside her, each line careful and methodical. Rohan had made sure each line was as it should be.

But she'd never seen them all together, on one piece of paper or even one book. She hadn't seen how they connected, what tied them together, because the map wasn't done. That would have come later. There were still more tattoos to get. There would have been a ceremony. Privately, the head priestess would have held up a mirror and explained each one, how they all connected. But that wouldn't happen now. That part of her life was over.

Now her skin was mapped for someone else's eyes.

"Anywhere else?" the Mapmaker asked.

Would it be worth keeping one small piece to herself? Would hiding it be worth it? Even knowing the map wasn't complete, that there would be no other way for the prince to discover the other pieces, would it be worth risking?

The prince knew how many locations there were. Adrian had told her a priest in the temple near the Summer Palace—the prince's mother's private city—had given him that much information. She didn't blame him. She would have done the same. No one could be expected to withstand torture. And she hoped that once the priest had told the prince everything, his death had been swift.

She would keep one piece hidden. A small piece.

"Anywhere else?" the Mapmaker asked again.

Sorcha shook her head, meeting the Mapmaker's flat gaze. They stared at each other, the rustle of pages in the corner of the room pausing, and Adrian turned for the first time since entering the room. Her gaze flicked to him, and her breath caught as their eyes met. Heat and fear clashed, stomach dropping as she made her choice.

"No," she said, her voice firm in the quiet of the room.

As soon as the map was complete, the Mapmaker lost interest in Sorcha, reflective eyes fixed on the parchment before him. The landscape was incomplete. But the promise that certain relics could be found in those locations had been taught to her as the needles had penetrated her skin over and over. She'd read sacred texts. The Red Priestess had tested her again and again, prodding for the weak spots in Sorcha's understanding.

Sorcha's knowledge, though incomplete, was solid. But would these pieces, barely more than a handful, be enough to resurrect the Saint and give the prince what he wanted? She had never come across any passages that laid out how complete the skeleton needed to be. But she hadn't finished her training. Her knowledge only extended to those on her body.

Adrian moved to look over the Mapmaker's shoulder.

"Here is the closest relic," the Mapmaker said, pointing to a spot on the parchment. They'd both forgotten the half-naked woman standing in the center of the room. "There is a temple. Or was. It might be ruins now."

"How far is it?" Adrian asked.

"Distance means nothing on this map," the vampire responded, tone flat and without inflection. "It is incomplete, but I've done what I can, knowing the landscape as it is. There is no way to know if the tattoos and locations have been updated to these modern times. These locations could be two hundred years old by now."

Adrian's eyes flicked up, his gaze lingering on her face despite her still clutching the dress to her chest, the rest of her still exposed. "Do you know?" he asked.

Shaking her head, she stepped down from the platform and moved to a darker corner away from the two men. Adrian's eyes were on her, burning a hole into her back as she fumbled with the dress, adjusting the sleeves and then the neckline.

"I must make a copy," the Mapmaker said, the silver chain clinking as he stood and moved toward his desk. "One for the prince and one for yourself. As soon as I finish, I'm sure you will want to leave."

"Yes," Adrian said.

"I will complete it as quickly as possible," the vampire said.

It was then Sorcha felt the vampire's gaze on her—cool, fleeting curiosity.

"The woman?" the Mapmaker asked.

"She goes with me," Adrian said.

"Then take her and leave," the vampire said, curiosity gone, the monotone returned. "The copy will be done soon."

Sorcha kept her back to the two as she finished adjusting her gown, grateful there were no buttons or ties to fight with. Her fingers trembled, fear hovering at the edges of her mind. *The woman?* The vampire's question had held the hint of hunger.

Vampire. Her mind swirled with the word.

"Come," the Wolf said, gesturing at the door when she turned. "You will need to choose what you bring with you."

"I have a choice?" She didn't bother to hide her surprise.

The clothes and jewelry the prince had given her were beautiful. Red velvet and silk, swaths of sheer chiffon. Everything that deep familiar color. The color of the temple, the red and gold that marked the devout. The color of blood and wealth.

"You will need to pack light," the Wolf said. "Your horse can only carry so much, and we will be moving fast. Bring only what you can't live without."

All of it. None of it. Some of it.

Sorcha had no idea how to pack for a journey she had never been prepared to take. But she knew, whatever she brought with her, she'd need to be able to run in. No matter what happened, she'd escape the Wolf somehow.

CHAPTER TEN

The empress's eyes fluttered as she came out of a deep sleep, cheeks washed of all color, hands withered and clawed. They reminded him of bird's feet—of twisted tree roots—the way spiders curled in on themselves when they died. His mother was doing the same thing. Slowly pulling in, tightening, curling.

Soon she would be dead.

The healers had warned him. But he didn't need their assertions to know that the light in his mother's eyes—once a shade of blue so piercing that men had come from all over the empire to see them, her beauty renowned, talked about in every court, every kingdom—was gone. Now they were milky, and her vision was gone. Rags and tatters of her beauty remained—a sharp cheekbone, the way her lip curled into a faint smile even now. But what had made her a true beauty had been the kindness she'd extended to everyone who climbed the stairs of the Traveling City.

In the end, it was her generosity that would kill her. She'd invited a snake into her sanctuary, into her home, into her life. Soon he would know who it had been. And he would kill that person—man, woman, or child.

But a more pressing matter was the Saint.

The mystics claimed there was no other way to resurrect someone. No magic. No other guarantee to return, to preserve her life, and with her death fast approaching, there was no other way to bring her back.

Eine was determined. It didn't matter how long it took, how far they would have to go, to reach each piece. He would have them all, and when his mother died, he would bring her back.

Before the city had burned, Kira, the famous Kahina of the Golden Citadel, had come to him. She'd slipped past her own city guards, through the Horde gathered around the thick walls, past the guards around the Traveling City, and into his court.

He'd refused to hear the witch speak at first. Waving his hand, the unspoken command to kill her given and understood, before she could even set foot before him. But she'd broken free of the guards in the outer chamber and fallen to her knees before him, hands smacking the hard-wood as she prostrated herself, pressing her forehead to the floor and whispering.

I can help you.

Of course, he'd let her live. He would take any help he could get. But he didn't trust her. A red witch, the leader of a death cult, untrust-worthy in every way. But he needed her.

He reached down and took his mother's hand—dry and soft, brittle as dying hope—and gently squeezed it. But he could not bring himself to speak. Her eyes closed again, hiding the milky, unseeing gaze, her breathing ragged. Part of him was relieved and wanted the unseeing gaze gone forever, wanted his clever-eyed mother to look back at him and smile.

But she couldn't.

He would rather she sleep if she could not be who she had always been.

The physician—a middle-aged bald man—in the corner feared the moment the empress would die. His life would end the moment hers did. The prince had promised him that months ago. *If she dies, you die.* And though he knew the man continued to do everything he could, he would not hesitate to keep his word.

He turned away abruptly and left them all behind, the serving women and physician at the edges of the room, and his gasping mother.

He moved through her quarters, past the guards stationed at the inner doors, through a connecting hall, and into his own rooms.

No servants lingered here, no averted gazes, no one to ask if he needed anything. He embraced the silence as he passed through a small receiving area, through a bedroom, a study, and finally to a staircase leading up.

His shoulders brushed the walls as he climbed, the way narrow and cramped. The risers were half lengths, wide enough for his toes and nothing more. He climbed up the turret, spiraling ever upward, the way lit by thin glazed windows. Wind blew down from the top, the trap door open, and he knew she would be there.

Kira stood on the platform, gripping the iron railing. She faced the window, her hair and dress blowing out in a stream of black and red. She turned dark eyes on him, this woman made of secrets and lies.

"The empress is worse," he said, coming to stand beside her and looking out over the plain.

The woman didn't respond, her gaze going to the small figures leaving the shadow of the Traveling City. The group was small, the rider leading the party wrapped in a black cloak, his black horse larger than the others around him. In the middle of the party, a woman rode a stocky buttermilk mare, the horse's flanks dappled with gray.

"Your temple girl has gone to search for relics," Prince Eine said, closing his eyes and welcoming the breeze that brought a hint of snow and ash. "How long will it take her to find them all?"

"Who can say," the woman replied softly.

"You can," Prince Eine said, a warning, a promise, in his tone. "Your life continues or ends with her ability to accomplish this task."

"She won't fail." There was nothing but confidence in Kira's voice. "I've trained her well. The empress isn't the only person she needs to resurrect."

"The empress is the only one who matters."

"Of course, Your Highness."

He turned away, leaving Kira standing on the turret to watch the small party of travelers until they were out of sight.

Chapter Eleven

There were several days of hard travel—nights spent half-frozen, rolled into a tight ball of fur-lined cloak and blankets. Each day, Sorcha woke exhausted despite the all-consuming sleep, the way it pulled her under, deep beneath the waking world.

One night, the Wolf shook her awake, night heavy around them, his touch on her shoulder lingering. She sat up and pulled the furs to her chest, blinking and trying to see the Wolf's face clearly. He was nothing but an outline, a black shadow within the dim tent—a monster in the dark.

When he spoke, his voice was flat. "You were screaming."

Sorcha sucked in a breath and let it out shakily. Sweat glossed her face, the back of her throat raspy and dry. Without speaking, he handed her a waterskin, waiting as she drank. She was grateful for the coolness of the water and the way it soothed her throat. The Wolf didn't ask what she'd been dreaming about. He merely took the waterskin back when she held it out and returned to his bedroll.

From then on, he would nudge her awake in the early hours without speaking, sending her heart racing into a fuzzy awareness. They didn't speak in those moments, alone together without witnesses, when the world could have been a different place.

What place? What world? Sorcha wondered. *Why would a monster take pity on her?*

Finally, the blackness she found herself in each night began to take shape. Beneath the bloody memories of Ines and Rohan in the Golden Citadel—sinking into the glittering swirl of prophecies—were half-clear visions of the Saint. Armies met on a barren plain. A woman in red walked across a black marble floor. A man with a wolf skull mask held out a hand for her to accept.

The dreams were impossible to decipher without Kahina Kira. The priestess's knowledge and understanding of the Saint was complete, her word final. She was the center of their religious knowledge—the ultimate voice and word—and the only person Sorcha had been completely honest with when it came to her visions.

Sorcha and the Wolf found a rhythm with their nights, falling asleep within a few feet of each other, his proximity something she was unable to ignore. He never asked about her dreams, and said nothing when he shook her awake, forcing the vision to release her.

In the mornings, she dressed in the beautiful items Prince Eine had sent with them. Boots lined with black fur, the outer leather soft and supple, the color as deep and rich as the crimson dress she wore. There were several cloaks with deep hoods, and thick leggings to wear beneath the simple split dresses made for riding—all crimson. The riders around her all wore the same black as the Wolf in various shades of wear. The Wolf's was the darkest, the others washed-out shadows of the leader they followed.

As they'd ridden closer to the Black Stone Mountains, the cold had turned biting, snow filling the air and collecting on the shoulders of the men and backs of the horses. But the Wolf led them through a narrow pass, a path Sorcha would have overlooked had she come this way alone.

It wound through the mountains; the way so narrow they had to ride single file. But the pass was removed from the bitter cold and sheltered from forces of nature. Always, she rode behind the Wolf. He kept her close to him at all times, sleeping or waking.

In the evenings, she listened to the soldiers' conversations, picking out the words she knew and working to understand the rest. Not all the men spoke the same languages though they communicated easily enough with one another. Several spoke more than one and translated for the others and everyone understood the tongue of the Empire of the White Snake. As the empire grew, conquering new lands and kingdoms, Prince Eine let the people keep their mother tongue as long as they understood his order to bend at the knee.

She'd watched and listened until she understood enough, picking up on most of their names and replacing the silly titles she'd given them in her mind. Holder of maps was Thompson. Yellow-eyes was Revenant. The Wolf's magician was Domenico. The bad cook was Wes. The good cook was Juri. The one who always complained was Lev. The one who never spoke was Till. Then there was calm Magnus, the too tall Soren, round Lev, bald Cas, broken nose Rui, scared hands Imre, and scowling Bran.

It wasn't long before she felt she knew them well enough, though she never tried to make herself understood.

Not that she needed to be. They had the map—the illustrated copies of her decorated skin—and wanted nothing to do with the *witch*. Whatever abilities they feared, she wished she truly possessed—to fly, to kill with a few words, to foretell the remainders of their lives and when they'd end. But her only ability was experiencing the murky dreams that came each night—a jumble of images and emotions—with nothing solid to hold on to.

If Ines had been with her—*alive*—she would have helped Sorcha to understand. They would have gone to Kira and deciphered the complications. But even in dreams, they were gone, shades waiting to be recalled when the Saint walked the earth once again.

———

Sorcha had never traveled this far before. It felt as if they'd crisscrossed the country, doubling back on the progress they'd made. The farther south they'd come from the Black Stone Mountains, the warmer it grew, though winter still crackled in the air.

The trees were different here, the landscape foreign, a place of imposing gray mountains and evergreen rolling hills. She'd grown up with the vast flat plains with thin thickets of trees, the remains of carefully cultivated fields and orchards—now fallow and barren in the early winter. This was a strange and beautiful landscape compared to home, but it was empty.

They moved through an abandoned world. Everywhere they went, cottages and little villages were silent. Everyone had fled the approaching Horde. Or some advance forces of the prince had come and gone, leaving a terrible silence in their wake.

Adrian rode at the head of their small band, Sorcha close behind, a soldier named Thompson behind her with the map. Revenant stayed at the rear, his eyes on her every time she turned in the saddle to glance behind them.

No one took the time to scout ahead or behind. They stuck together, easy and unbothered, confident they were the most frightening thing roaming the landscape.

They stopped to camp several times, which had Sorcha clutching her cloak around her and missing the warmth and privacy of Adrian's large tent. Here, she had a bedroll under the sky, a shared fire, and she was exposed to the men's curiosity and resentment.

The only member of the party who had warmed to her was Nox. She'd finally won him over after she began sharing the scavenged apples she took for Epona as a treat after their long days of riding.

Once, they'd slept in an abandoned cottage. She had lain in someone else's bed, listening to the night, expecting at any moment for the house's owner to come through the door and ask why a stranger was in their home. She'd been grateful for the bedroll and open sky after that. She'd hated the feeling of being in a space and not knowing if that person were alive or dead, a stranger in a private place—unwelcome and unwanted.

Sorcha had overheard the men talking among themselves about the Traveling City and the Horde. The city was trailing behind them, though she had no idea how it would make it through the mountains. There was no way it could pass through the narrow valley they'd traveled through.

While the Traveling City moved south, the Horde of the empire was moving north. There was a kingdom unconquered and a promise to be kept. Marius the Mad, a king of Cautes. From the info she'd been able to piece together, it seemed as if the man had crossed the prince. The price was death, and the Wolf was being sent to ensure it was carried out.

But between the Traveling City and Cautes sat the Silvas Wood. Her skin had promised there would be a fragment of the Saint there. They'd locate that piece first, and then she would watch the death of another city, this time from outside the walls. She would be the witness to Cautes's demise.

———

"There is a door," Domenico said softly, his gaze traveling over the deep shadows of the ancient forest. "That's the only way in."

Epona shifted beneath Sorcha, snorting and fidgeting. The trees radiated a sense of otherness—secrets and the promise of the unknown. Sorcha knew from the texts that a temple sat somewhere within, but it had never been made clear exactly where it might be. The Mapmaker had said distance meant nothing, and now they were all discovering the truth of that fact.

The men were on edge, irritated to be traveling with no clear goal in mind, and resentful of the woman in their midst. The Wolf remained unbothered by it all, cold and virtually silent as they traveled, keeping Sorcha near him at all times. Sometimes she could feel his gaze, hot and prickly, but when she turned, expecting to find his eyes on her, he was looking elsewhere.

They were at the border of an evergreen primordial forest—an ancient place full of palpable magic. Inside, waiting to be discovered, was a relic of the Saint. A piece she had never seen before, never touched. Her fingertips tingled with the thought.

"What does the door look like?" the Wolf asked.

Sorcha looked around when no one responded and then realized he'd spoken to her.

"I don't know."

"Your cult didn't teach you?" he asked, derision coloring his words.

Sorcha bit the inside of her cheek to keep from responding, refusing to give him anything he might use against her later. As quiet as she'd been, she knew the little bit of emotion she'd let escape was being stored in that black mind of his. Whatever weakness she might display, he would take advantage of.

"Domenico, can you find it?" the Wolf asked, gesturing to the man who'd spoken earlier.

Sorcha studied the man, someone who had yet to talk much and kept mostly to himself. Domenico was short and thick, with his pale hair trimmed close to his skull and a fresh scar running across the top of his left hand. His eyes were a strange, flat gray, as if they had been cut from a thunderstorm sky.

The man walked up to the tree line, standing with his hands on his hips for several long minutes. One of the men behind her said something, a single word in a language she didn't understand, and the others chuckled.

Domenico ignored them, licking his pointer finger on his right hand and holding it up as if to test the wind. The laughter died down, and the noise around them faded, birdsong vanished, the rustle of evergreens going still. Then he turned, waving them toward the right, and began to walk that way himself.

The trees they stopped in front of looked like all the others—dark trunks, spruce needles, with gently waving branches. But Domenico jerked a thumb behind him, mumbling something to Adrian as he passed to reclaim his horse.

"Thompson," the Wolf said, and the other man urged his horse forward, stopping beside him. "What does the map say?"

Thompson pulled the parchment from a spot beside his knee and unrolled it carefully, studying it in silence. They all knew what the map looked like at this point. The Wolf involved his men in planning their routes and places to stop.

Thompson sighed. "There are no doors marked on this map, but the temple should be in there." He gestured at the forest. "Near a path that crosses the length of the forest. It's the only way in and out. The temple is a few yards off the path."

"And we enter here?" the Wolf pointed directly ahead, glancing at Domenico.

"Yes," Domenico said, accent thick. "Through those two trees. It is a door."

A door.

Sorcha peered at the two trees. A door. How could that be? The forest was thick, trees growing so close together that it appeared impossible to weave through them on foot, let alone on horseback. The forest swallowed the light, sucking it in, pushing it down. It seemed as if nothing but the night survived beneath those branches.

"The witch should go first," someone whispered.

A flush crept up Sorcha's cheeks, heat spreading beneath her skin, burning her ears. She couldn't be sure which man spoke and she refused to twist around in the saddle to check. If the Wolf heard, he ignored it, motioning Domenico forward. Though it pained her to be grateful to that monster for anything, she was grateful she wouldn't be leading them into the trees.

Domenico mounted his horse and urged it toward the spot he'd indicated. One moment there he was moving forward, and the next he'd vanished between two tree trunks as if he'd never been. Nox went next, urged on by a silent command from his rider, and Sorcha's docile Epona followed. The rest of the men followed after them, their whispers dying down, each one quiet and listening for whatever would come next.

———

It was warmer beneath the trees and not at all what she'd been expecting. It was summer here, not late fall or early winter. It was as if crossing the border had transported them through time as well as space.

They rode single file down the narrow track. Overhead, trees stretched toward each other, limbs tangling in the canopy, the under-layer and ground cover thick in the shadows. Everything appeared peaceful and quiet, but she felt watched from all directions.

There was something in the woods. They'd all felt it as soon as they had crossed the border. The men behind had exchanged a few words before going silent again. She could feel the intention of whatever was out there building as the sun slipped lower and the shadows lengthened.

The night was waiting, the moon ready to rise, and a sense of impending doom filled her. The others must have felt it too. They were quiet and watchful observers. Around the last campfire, the men had talked about this forest, but she hadn't caught more than a handful of words at the time. Now, she wished she'd paid more attention.

To them, this was simply a stopping point along the way, just a temple—one of many. They would recover a relic of the Saint here and then move on to the next one. Epona balked, snorting and thrashing her head. Sorcha patted her neck and made a low, soothing sound. But the animal sensed something, aware of more than Sorcha's human eyes could discern.

Maybe Epona was aware of the temple. Sorcha could only guess how they might find it in all this tangled growth. The forest on either side of the track was a solid wall of greenery. Every now and then, a low-hanging branch caught at her hair or sleeve, a sharp tug catching her attention, and she would have to free herself before they could move on.

Ahead, Nox took bites of leaves or latched on to branches, holding on as long as possible until they snapped back, stripped of all their greenery. But the Wolf didn't seem bothered by it. He kept the grip on his reins loose, letting the horse take the lead. The man appeared relaxed in the saddle, and if he felt any tension, it didn't show.

A large branch snapped off the path to the left, invisible but only paces away. Sorcha jerked in that direction, scanning the trees and searching for movement. Behind her, Thompson rustled the map, the sound of the scroll unfurling as familiar to her as her own breathing—the places they'd gone and the places they had yet to be. It was all laid out, bit by bit, and her skin tingled with the thought.

"It should be up ahead," Thompson said.

"How far?" asked the Wolf.

Thompson snorted, speculation and uncertainty clear. "I'm guessing this isn't the most accurate of maps. There's no scale for distance."

"Take a guess."

"A hundred yards, maybe?" Thompson rattled the map again. "It's hard to tell where we started, the markers could have changed. I have no idea how far we've come."

The Wolf glanced back, his gaze sweeping over Sorcha before moving on.

Thompson held up the map and pointed to a spot. "I believe we came in here, but the markers on the map don't correspond to anything we've passed. I think 'map' is stretching the word when it comes to actual locations. It's more about ideas than places."

Ahead, a huge tree stretched over the path. It was larger than those around it, with nothing beneath it but bare dirt and the collected leaves from years past. The wide trunk twisted upward, the pale bark peeling to reveal crimson beneath. The leaves were narrow and a vibrant red. It reminded Sorcha of the trees in the inner courtyards of the temple. In the Golden Citadel. Where she'd lived. Where Ines had last breathed.

Don't think about it!

"That tree!" Thompson waved the map. "It's on the map."

The Wolf turned in his saddle until he caught Sorcha's eye. "Did you learn about this place?"

She shook her head.

"It's on your skin," he said.

She stared back at him, face carefully blank.

As they came around the tree, the ruins of a temple came into view. Overgrown pillars and arches, pale rock and shallow steps. The forest was pressed close like a lover, trees intertwined with stone, becoming something wholly new and otherworldly. It was a ruin of a place that had once been immaculate and imposing. Fallen branches littered the steps, and vines crisscrossed the arches. Leaves had drifted, concealing sections of the stairs and what might have been fallen statues.

The men rode their horses up the first shallow flight of steps into an open courtyard. More steps led up to dark arches, the stairs too steep here for the horses to climb. They dismounted and began to spread out, swords in hands—wary and watchful. Sorcha kept her seat, Epona shifting beneath her and ears flicking back and forth.

Revenant and Domenico went up the steps together and passed under the arch into the darkness of the inner temple. Thompson rustled between the relic map and another she hadn't seen before—the parchment dark with age, the lines on it faded. Adrian dismounted and crossed to Sorcha's horse, reaching up to take the reins with one hand and offering the other to help her dismount.

"I don't need your help," she said.

Sorcha shifted in the saddle, ready to drop down on the other side away from the Wolf. She was tempted to kick him or nudge Epona forward and force him to drop the reins, but he reached up, wrapped his large hands around her waist, and lifted her down from the saddle in a smooth motion. She gripped his forearms, steadying herself, their gazes locked.

The Wolf's eyes were so brown they were almost black—framed by long lashes—and with his full mouth pressed into a thin line, Sorcha found him hard to read. Was he in a hurry? Or was there another reason he'd pulled her from the horse? Sorcha exhaled, brows coming together, a question half formed on her tongue. His gaze shifted to her mouth, and for a moment, his grip tightened.

"Adrian," Revenant called from the top of the stairs. "You need to see this."

The sound of dripping water drew Sorcha, tempting, promising. More than anything, she wanted the chance to rest and drink something that hadn't been in a waterskin for several days. But as she rounded the corner and saw the entrance to another large room, it wasn't the fresh, clean smell she'd been expecting. A heaviness filled the air, cloying and thick, metallic tinged with heat.

Behind her, Thompson held a torch high, the light catching on the details of the room. Carnivore. Predator. Everything in this room spoke of the hunt, the chase, the conquest. The head of a giant wolf had been carved from a single piece of black stone. It dominated the wall and was ornamented with ruby eyes and clenched, golden teeth.

Sorcha hesitated in the entryway, watching as blood seeped from between its clenched jaws and collected on the bottom jaw, falling into a wide pool below it.

The blood dissipated in the water, a spring fed from an unseen source, the surface moving—shifting—the blood dissipating as the water circulated. A shallow step led into the water. The bottom was visible but distorted, a mix of white animal bones and waving green plants.

"Where is the water going?" Wes asked.

Sorcha shook her head, though he hadn't been asking her.

"It must flow beneath the stone," Thompson said. "Or there's a tunnel or something."

"Is it drinkable?" Lev asked. "Our waterskins are almost dry."

"Would you want to drink that?" Magnus asked, pointing to the clenched jaws of the wolf as a trickle of blood fell.

"Do not drink from this place," Domenico said from the back. "Take nothing from this place."

"That's what we came here to do, Dom," Juri said. "And now you're telling us not to?"

"Do what you want," Domenico said, shaking his head. "But I wouldn't drink from that pool."

Sorcha could hear the shrug in Domenico's voice. She had to agree. Even if she'd had nothing to drink for days, she wouldn't dare drink from this spring. It wasn't only because of the blood-stained wolf head. The bones visible at the bottom were unsettling. Who had put them there? Why?

But even as she wondered those things, the water called to her.

"What is this place?" Lev asked. "Was it on the map?"

Thompson shook his head.

"Is it on her skin?"

Lev took a step toward Sorcha, but the Wolf was there in an instant—a silent, solid figure between them. She couldn't see the Wolf's face, but she saw Lev's expression shift from determination to startlement to acquiescence. Adrian would never let any of them touch her, even if they'd been tempted to offer some small kindness, which they never did.

Sorcha walked forward—the men keeping their distance—as she moved beyond the immediate circle of light thrown by the torch. The room was cool, and her skin prickled with magic, an electric sensation, as if lightning crackled through the stones waiting to be released.

Slowly, hesitating as if the carving might come to life and snap, she reached out.

She heard shuffling behind her, as if several of the men were leaving the room or possibly they were stepping forward. She ignored the distraction and focused on the imposing carving of the wolf. It was as tall as her torso, finely carved though not detailed—it was the impression and idea of a wolf, without each hair defined.

Blood continued to well from the clenched golden teeth, as if the jaws held back a flood, and the ruby eyes threw back the light of the torches behind Sorcha. Or did they hold their own glow?

Tentatively, she touched the snout, shocked at the warmth of it. Her brows drew together as she smoothed her palm over the jaw, avoiding the dripping blood.

Behind her, the men whispered, but she ignored them, keeping her gaze on the ruby eyes. A part of her believed—understanding in her bones—that it was alive.

"Witch."

The wolf jaws snapped open, lips pulled back in a snarl, the sound of stone grating on stone filling the chamber. Blood flowed out of its gaping maw, no longer a trickle, but now a steady stream splashing into the pool, mixing with the water, swirling and clouding it until the bones at the bottom were hidden. Someone swore, and there was more scuffling.

A heavy hand dropped on her shoulder, turning her away from the carving. The Wolf stood over her, studying her.

"What did you do?" he asked, voice soft—no accusation, only curiosity.

"Nothing." Sorcha shook her head. "I only touched it."

The scent of blood, flowing so freely from the creature's mouth, was overpowering. Impossible to ignore, impossible to escape. Stepping back hurriedly, she retreated to the safety of the torchlight. The ominous feeling of being watched heated her skin, leaving her mouth sour with the sensation. But nothing else changed. The wolf jaws remained open, the blood flowing freely now, steadily.

———

The relic they were searching for was gone.

The room obviously had held it at some point—the ornate alcove in the far wall with an altar would have been the perfect location. Ancient gilding still clung to delicately carved stone, along with painted flowers, vines, and skulls. The gold was flaking now but still caught and reflected the light of the torches. The ground around the alter glimmered here and there with pieces that had fallen away.

Sorcha held the torch up to the walls, fascinated by the remains of the murals. The walls carried a painted history, glimmering stones inset here and there—fiery rubies and clear deep green emeralds. A beautiful decay, untouched by thieves or passersby. The only thing that had touched this temple was time.

The Saint walked through the stories on the stone. The Saint as the past had known him. The Saint that had been hinted at in her teachings —conqueror and death dealer—but she'd never read or heard the full story. Kahina Kira had said there would be hard things ahead—hard truths. But the Saint had always been fair with his punishments. Only the unbelievers and unfaithful had ever paid a price.

What price?

Death.

It was here on these walls, as illustrated on stone as the ink on her skin. A golden skeleton, striding through a landscape, holding a body, blood running down the open chasm of his mouth. People were prostrated before him, people dead behind him. But never one of the red-robed figures, they came behind in single file, hoods pulled up to conceal faces, anonymous believers doing nothing to stop the destruction that preceded them.

Sorcha had only seen one book with illustrations like these. Kira had been angry with her for taking it from the area reserved for the most senior priests and priestesses. It had been so heavy, weighted with history—the story of blood and rubies. She'd been caught before she'd been able to finish it, only a few pages in, stomach tightening with a terrible sense of foreboding.

Was this what she believed? Was this what she was a part of?

Don't think about it!

Don't question. Don't think. Accept the role and embrace the ordered life.

It was the only thing she'd ever known.

But the walls in this ancient temple told another story—a darker Saint stalked these walls. This was the Saint the world had known, one of blood, death, and destruction. Was this the future the empire was racing them toward?

A different mural caught her attention, this one not as well preserved on the opposite side of the room. Sorcha crossed to it, tracing the deep gouges in the stone that looked like claw marks. A temple surrounded by woods, high above the treetops, painted gold with inlaid tiles. It was beautiful, and even now, Sorcha recognized the shape. *This temple. These woods.*

Red-robed priests writhed on the ground all around it. So there *had* been members of the Aureum Sanctus who had paid a terrible price. She traced the outline of one figure, a man in the midst of becoming a wolf. A shifter. Farther down the wall, there were more shifters, all kneeling before the Saint with their hands raised, exaggerated tears falling from their eyes.

"They were cursed," Domenico said. "See here? A punishment."

Sorcha jumped, surprised she hadn't heard him approach. But he wasn't speaking to her. His attention was on the wall, and he raised his lantern, following the story. Who had added the murals if the priests had been cursed? Why had the Saint cursed them? And how? She had no one to ask. Only Kahina Kira would have known.

She wouldn't have told you though.

"Why?" Thompson asked, coming to stand beside him.

"Who can guess at the mind of a god?" Domenico shrugged.

Sorcha turned away, scanning the room and the men in it. Her gaze fell on the Wolf, tall and dark, handsome features set in a scowl. He paced the room's perimeter, one hand on the sword at his hip. For a moment, his eyes rested on her, and she blushed, wondering if he read the thought hovering at the top of her mind. *Handsome. Monster.*

"Where is the relic?" he asked.

"I don't know." Sorcha shook her head, folding her arms across her chest.

Revenant walked past her, out of the small inner room into the open air of the temple beyond. Domenico and Juri followed. She could hear the others in the room beyond, talking in hushed tones, words lost, only the intention clear.

Anger. Frustration. Distrust.

"What aren't you telling me?" the Wolf asked, grabbing her arm and turning her to face him.

He stared down at her with hard black eyes, the flickering light of the torch beside the door so far away, so distant, leaving her alone with this dark stranger. The voices in the other room faded as the men went back the way they'd come.

Sorcha opened her mouth, mind racing.

"Don't lie to me," he said, voice so soft it barely registered.

"Why would I lie?" she asked with a swallow, the heat of his hand on her arm sinking into her, spreading out. "My goal is to resurrect my Saint. A goal I share with the prince."

The Wolf narrowed his eyes as he took a step into her, crowding her backward. Sorcha took a step back, and he followed, his hand still locked around her arm. She stopped when she felt the smooth stone of the wall at her back. Out of the corner of her eye, she could see the details of the Saint. *My Saint*. But was he? Even if her faith wavered?

"Vessel. Priestess. Oracle. Whatever you are, I don't trust that your goal is the same as the empire's."

His eyes roved over her face, a line appearing between his brows. Sorcha breathed heavily, trapped between this man and the wall, held in place by his iron grip. Heat gathered between them, an uneasy sensation coiling in her belly.

"You're seeking death," she whispered, unable to stop herself.

The Wolf dropped her arm and stepped away from her, then strode across the empty space.

Sorcha pulled in a breath, smelling the dirt of the temple and the green of the trees crowded around it. A strange cold filled the space he'd occupied in front of her only seconds ago.

"No, priestess," he said. "I am seeking life."

In a rush, he was at the door with the torch in one hand. The fire danced, light shifting over his face, reflected in his black eyes. He indicated the door.

She hesitated, rubbing her arm.

"Come," he said tersely. "There are other places to search."

———

If the relic had been anywhere, it would have been in the sanctuary.

But it wasn't.

They searched the remaining ruins, beating through the underbrush, moving fallen branches, even pulling up loose pavers. But no, it wasn't anywhere to be found, no matter how hard they searched.

Sorcha felt a perverse kind of joy. The Wolf had failed to acquire one of the relics—the first relic he'd been sent to collect with her in tow. It would displease the prince, Sorcha knew it would, and maybe if the prince was unhappy, someone else would take over the Wolf's position here.

The man who had killed the Golden Citadel and set fire to the rubble corpse.

Sorcha wanted to escape him as badly as she wanted things to be as they had been, as badly as she wanted to turn back all the hours and days, take back the fall of her city and home. She'd washed her hands hundreds of times, yet still she saw the blood on them, felt the sticky heat of something that could never be washed away.

Go back, go back to the way things once were.

What if the prince didn't recall the Wolf? Or what if the replacement was worse? She didn't want to find out, not really. The evil she knew might be better than the one she didn't. But maybe the Wolf didn't need to be recalled or replaced. Maybe she could walk away. Walk until she fell exhausted to the earth and wait until leaves covered her, hiding her from the curious eyes of the world.

With no relic here and no promise of finding any if they continued on, maybe she really could walk away from this. Sorcha touched her shoulder, the tattoo beneath the fabric showing this place—the Silvas. The arm bone, depicted surrounded by ferns and branches, had been stolen or destroyed. Could the Saint return if pieces were missing? She wasn't sure, couldn't be. Nothing she'd read had specifically addressed missing relics.

Sorcha considered all of this as she returned to the area they'd claimed as their camp. The horses were tethered in the entrance within the first arches they'd passed through, but they'd refused to go up the stairs. The men had been uneasy about leaving them in the woods. There had been too many strange sounds with no visible cause.

They were all uneasy with the watchfulness of the Silvas.

Where they were now had once been a large chapel, a place for worshippers to come and make their petitions. It would have been crowded at one point, full of the faithful, each person searching for an answer to their prayer.

The temple she'd grown up in had been like that, with pilgrims coming from all over to see the hand of the Saint—a hand capable of miracles. A hand to bless them or hurt them. Sorcha had witnessed it once in her childhood—before the tattoos had begun, before the teaching had started in earnest.

There had been a man with graying hair, hard eyes, his jaw clenched around his pain and anger. He'd touched the relic with his eyes closed, lips moving with his silent plea. But when he'd opened his eyes, they were no longer clear. Blood leaked from his tear ducts, and his skin aged rapidly, wrinkling and drying out in a matter of seconds. She'd brought her hand up, covering her mouth to contain the cry of horror. A priest had led him away, out of the temple and onto the street where the man had been left to find his way home.

Not a true believer. Not a faithful worshipper.

Until then, the powers of the relic had only been hypothetical. She'd never witnessed the response of a true believer's prayer and only read about what might happen if you asked for something but didn't believe it.

For months, she'd been afraid to touch the relic, searching her heart and wondering if, deep inside, she had something in common with the pilgrim.

Kahina Kira had chuckled and squeezed her shoulder, offering comfort and compassion. *Sorcha, you have been chosen. You could never fail him.*

Guilt touched her then. She should have wanted the relic to be here. She should want to bring the Saint back into the world. Instead, she found herself thankful, relieved to find it missing.

Gone.

Gone like the priests who had taken care of this place. Gone like the pilgrims who had filled this temple. Gone and forgotten here in the heart of the Silvas.

A howl filled the night, spiraling out, expanding as it rose above the tree tops. The call caressed the moon as it climbed above the trees and into view.

Sorcha stopped breathing, frozen as another howl joined the first. Then another. She turned, searching the faces of the men around her. The Wolf was not among them.

The men were looking at each other, questions on their faces.

"Wolves?" Thompson asked.

"Possibly," Domenico replied.

Wolves. Were they here to pay their respects to the Wolf? Or were they here to drag each person out of the temple and into the woods? Fresh meat—dinner and dessert all in one. The watchfulness of before, the feeling that something lurked beyond the screen of trees to either side of the path, must have been those wolves.

The Wolf appeared through an arch that led deeper into the temple, a direction they'd already searched. He gripped his sword in one hand and a long dagger in the other. Briefly, he surveyed his men, gaze skating over Sorcha and finally landing on Revenant. They exchanged a nod.

Long, mournful cries filled the air. They came from beyond the walls in every direction. The calls echoed through the trees, lingering like a lover's words, threats and promises of what would come.

"What is that?" Juri asked.

The Wolf moved to the arch, standing motionless and looking down the steps and out into the Silvas—listening. The men watched him, waiting for their leader's response.

With a slow shake of his head, he replied, "I don't know."

Sorcha wrapped her arms around herself, listening to the cries and trying to pick out one that might be closer than the rest. Anything that might indicate something was creeping up on them. But it was impossible to be sure. Everything, even the scuff of boots on stone, her own breathing, seemed to be amplified by the space.

When the Wolf turned back to them, his face was stone, eyes as dark as the temple around them. Sorcha could feel how the men changed around her, how they were tuned to him, shoulders straightening, hands going to their sword hilts.

"Light a fire. Stay in groups of three if you leave this room. I don't want anyone going out alone for any reason. We're all on watch."

Several men nodded, others looking around the space for anything that might burn. Sorcha followed their gaze, wondering how far they would have to go to find wood for a fire. Wondering if something else would find them first.

"Someone had a fire here recently," Domenico said. He kicked at a few scattered ashes, the remains of a half-burnt branch. He picked it up, gesturing to the small alcove. "It wasn't a large fire though. Looks like they burned anything worth burning in this room already. Maybe they gathered more from the woods."

"Maybe," Adrian agreed.

"Who's going?" Thompson's gaze swept the group.

But the ruthless faces staring back at him were washed out and drawn in the flickering light of their few torches.

"I'll go," Juri said. "Who's coming with me?"

Till lifted a hand without speaking. Magnus said he would go. The three left the ruins quietly, swords drawn, leaving the torchlight behind.

"No longer than ten minutes and remain within sight of the ruins," the Wolf said, nodding to another group of three preparing to go in the opposite direction. "Be quick. Be quiet."

"And her?" Revenant asked, drawing his sword and moving to keep watch over the arch as the men passed through it.

"Not your responsibility," the Wolf replied, weapons remaining in his hands.

The Wolf turned, and warmth spiked through Sorcha as their eyes met. He looked away first, a strange sensation tickling across her skin. Sorcha forced herself to watch the remaining men as they adjusted their weapons and dropped their cloaks, testing the buckles on their leather armor. Beyond the arches, the horses whickered and stamped, restless as the howls filled the air.

The group left behind sat or stood together, listening to the night, hearts racing with a shared dread and unease.

———

"Are you afraid?" she asked the Wolf.

The question surprised her, and she bit her tongue, keeping whatever else she might say inside. But she searched his profile, wondering if she might catch a glimpse of the truth. He stood just beyond her reach, a barrier in the night against the unknown, guarding her because his prince demanded it.

"No," he responded flatly, turning his dark gaze to her.

I am, she thought, wanting to offer him comfort so she might receive some in return—wanting something else to be happening in this moment other than what was. *But why? Why do I want comfort from a killer?* It was the fear. It was the howling filling her head, the wolves beyond the temple walls, the sense that they were creeping closer and would soon be on them.

But besides wanting comfort, now, even as she hoped to escape, even as she hoped the prince would be displeased and separate the Wolf's head from his body, she also wanted a shred of warmth.

Sorcha was disgusted with herself, shifting her gaze away, turning inward. It was better not to meet his dark eyes, better not to look too long into the handsome face of this monster.

"I won't let anything in these woods touch you," Adrian said, his face expressionless, voice pitched low.

Sorcha nodded, accepting the comfort, the small amount of warmth he offered.

A scrabbling sound reached them, like massive claws on stone. A horse screamed, and Sorcha jumped to her feet, pressing her back against the wall. A figure appeared in the torchlight, filling the entrance, hulking and covered in fur—it stood on its hind legs, as tall as the lintel. Orange eyes swept over them, and bloody saliva dripped from the creature's muzzle.

———

A werewolf.

Adrian's childhood nurse had scared him with folk stories about them. She'd warned that if he misbehaved, they would come for him in the night under a full moon—a moon like the one above his head. She promised he would be turned into one of them, cursed to see the world through the eyes of a wolf and he would never again play or eat sweets or walk under a clear sky. He would be forever tainted.

A wolf. It twisted in him, the thought that he'd become what she'd warned him against being. He'd ended up on that road anyway—he *had* become a wolf. He'd believed her wholeheartedly as a child. As an adult, he'd roamed the continent, had seen things from myths and legends. There had been creatures, people who were not people, and he now understood the truth in her stories.

He simply drew his sword and hoped it would be enough.

"What is it?" Thompson hissed.

"Werewolf," Adrian replied without taking his eyes off the beast.

It stood seven feet tall, a huge, broad-chested wolf-human hybrid with a sharp pointed face and orange eyes. Sharp claws tipped its fingers and feet, furious anger rolling off it in waves as it lifted its head and let loose a piercing howl.

Others answered.

There would be no way out of this place without facing them. Adrian heard other swords being drawn around him and Domenico murmuring a prayer to one of his gods. Adrian didn't take his eyes off the creature. What did it take to defeat werewolves? In the stories, it seemed impervious to whatever weapons might be brought against them. But nothing could survive if you separated the head from the body.

"What do we do?" Thompson asked.

"Cut its head off," Adrian said.

Armor clinked, and low whispers were exchanged. He couldn't make out the words clearly, but their collective fear was a siege arrow directed at his gut. Tensing, he waited for the creature to step into the room. But it didn't cross the threshold. It stood in the arch, staring at them, chest heaving, saliva dripping from its open maw.

"What's it waiting for?" Thompson asked.

With his question, the creature began to growl—promising violence, promising dismemberment and pain.

But that was it. It was just a promise.

The creature vibrated on the threshold, held there, unmoving.

Revenant picked up a pebble and tossed it at the creature, striking it in the leg. The werewolf roared, the sound deafening, but it remained where it was.

Relief and understanding flashed through Adrian. It couldn't enter the temple. The howls beyond the crumbling walls continued, mournful and persistent, circling and closing in. They were surrounded, and if they left, they would all die. The others were probably already dead: Juri, Till, Magnus, Soren, Wes, and Lev. Six of his trusted unit. Six men he'd fought and bled beside.

"I don't think it can enter," Revenant said.

"You're right," Adrian agreed, relaxing his stance slightly.

"What happens next?" Domenico asked.

"We wait for dawn," Adrian said.

"Do you think they'll leave then?" Thompson rolled his shoulders, looking from Adrian to the werewolf growling in the doorway. "Moonlight is their thing, right? Isn't that what the myths say?"

"I wouldn't trust myths if I were you," Revenant replied.

"Werewolves are myths, though, aren't they?" Thompson whispered.

"This one seems pretty damn real to me, Thompson."

"Enough," Adrian said. "Once the sun rises, we'll leave. For now, everyone is on guard. No one leaves this room. Understand?"

The werewolf growled, snapping its teeth, but remained where it was.

"Where's the witch?" Revenant asked.

"What?" Adrian turned, scanning the space. Sorcha was gone. "Thompson, did you see her? Domenico? Where did she go?"

The men shook their heads, and Revenant's yellow eyes gleamed with malicious pleasure.

Somewhere beyond the walls, wolves snarled and howled—sounding as if a small army of creatures waited for them in the night. A piercing scream filled the air, climbing in pitch until it abruptly cut off, leaving tense silence behind.

They exchanged glances, wondering who it might have been. The werewolf standing in the door lifted its muzzle, sniffing the air, and then darted away.

"Was that the witch screaming?"

Adrian's stomach dropped.

———

Sorcha ran out into the darkness of the inner temple beyond the room they'd been crowded in, panting and fighting the panic in her chest. Soon the torchlight was gone—the murmurs of the men faded—and overhead, the full moon was huge and bright. Sorcha felt as if it were hovering directly over her, leaning closer to get a better look.

Moss and tiny delicate ferns covered the stones of the passageway. The cool scent of water filled the air, and for an instant, she wanted to stop and find the spring, swallow mouthful after mouthful in an effort to cleanse the panic from her body, and ease the ache at the back of her throat.

Under different circumstances, she might have enjoyed this place. She would have walked through the ruins, stopping to touch the stone or admire a trembling frond, but in the dark, her heart pounded, and the cries of the wolves reverberated against the stone. As she wove deeper into the ruins, each desperate breath filled her head until nothing remained.

Sorcha hadn't planned to run, there was truly no escape, but it had been instinct. The Wolf would follow. Or worse, Revenant. She shuddered at the thought of the two men on her heels. But one scared her more than the other. The Wolf might be a monster, but he was alive. There was nothing living in Revenant's gaze.

There was something in the Wolf, a twisting knowledge that was slowly unfurling in her mind. When he looked at her, there was something beneath the vicious cold he exuded. A shred of humanity. Maybe she was fooling herself, maybe there was nothing left, or there had never been anything there in the first place. But the voice inside telling her otherwise was growing stronger.

A stone rolled beneath her foot, and she fell, landing heavily on her hands and knees, crying out as she caught herself. Sharp pain shot through her wrists. The howling stopped, and she gasped in the sudden quiet. Every hair on her body stood on end as she eased back onto her heels and wiped her dirty hands on her skirt. She stood slowly, looking around, wondering how close the wolves were now.

The space around her was open, not the narrow way of the passage, but an area where several halls met and divided. Dark openings waited, five paths to choose from, and she wondered which way she should go. Where would she be safe? Would she be able to find a place to hide that the prince's men wouldn't be able to find?

Maybe.

It was a chance she was willing to take.

Sorcha took a tentative step forward, choosing a path at random and continuing her run into the night.

———

Sorcha was being followed. Something had been behind her since she'd left the last of the ruined temple behind. She was out in the wildness of the Silvas now, the howling fading behind her.

It was working. The Wolf, if he'd noticed her absence, was back there. She would lose herself in the woods and move south. Away from the winter blowing down from the north—a winter that would soon be here. It would be hard to navigate on her own, but she could make it.

The temples would be dangerous. The prince would be collecting their relics, searching for her. But the priests and priestesses would hide her, provide sanctuary. They would want her to be safe.

Another voice, this one cynical and bleak, whispered of other outcomes.

She would be discovered in an inner sanctum surrounded by the dead. Just as it had been before. From there, she would be forced to carry on this journey, marching ever onward to resurrect the Saint. And it might not even be the prince. At this point, with so many believers gone, other believers would want her to continue as well.

Only the Saint could bring them back now. And only Sorcha could bring back the Saint. There was no hiding who she was, what her life was meant for. Nowhere was safe, but there was no going back. No matter how far she ran, no matter where she hid, it would be impossible to outrun the voices filling her head, the feel of Ines dying in her hands.

The prince would put someone else in charge of her. She thought she'd wanted that, wanted it so badly she'd fled the temple as soon as the Wolf's back was turned. But if she stopped now, he would find her and she'd continue forward with a *different* kind of protection—from the worst and by the worst—by a monster.

Her fate was the same. It didn't matter which direction she ran. It didn't matter if she ran now or even if she made it out of the woods on her own. Her fate was tied to the Saint. He was at the end of all roads for her.

They were connected by unbreakable chains.

She would always find the relics. She would always resurrect the Saint.

There was no reality where it could ever be any different.

But she didn't stop, she didn't turn back. Sorcha crashed through a bush, branches catching at her hair and skirts, scraping her legs and arms as she fell heavily. She groaned, swearing as she stood, continuing forward even as she fought to keep her balance.

She was tired of falling. Tired of scraping her hands. Tired of landing on her knees. They were already bruised, her palms scratched. The skin burned and stung, threatening infection, and her head ached with the urge to cry.

Slow anger simmered in her gut, frustration and exhaustion vying for space. She would use it to propel herself forward. She would keep the anger close and use it to stay alive, whether she made it out of the Silvas on her own or not. She wouldn't give up trying. Maybe it was better to steer her own fate, to leave the monster behind.

But even as she ran, she shivered. He would never let her go. He was relentless.

A creature crashed through the trees beside her. An overwhelming animal stink filled the air—blood and fur, hot breath and musk. A large paw tipped with claws swiped at her, catching her dress, and she toppled to the ground. It rushed forward, pinning her in place.

A growl filled her ears as she lay panting in the leaves. The scents of damp earth and moss vied with the animal smell—wild and melding together to be one thing instead of many. A scratch burned on her face, and something sharp was digging into her shoulders.

A werewolf crouched over her, radiating heat, lips pulled back from sharp teeth.

She waited for the snap of iron jaws tearing into tender flesh, for razor claws to sink into her. It panted, its orange eyes intent as it stared down at her.

Nothing happened.

She scrabbled in the dirt, hair catching on twigs and leaves as she moved to sit up. Her heart pounded and bile rose in the back of her throat as seconds raced by and death failed to arrive.

In the moonlight, the creature was huge—a hulking beast with a pointed muzzle and eyes lit with an eerie orange glow. The gaze was intelligent, cautious and curious and angry all at once.

It snarled and she froze.

Soon, so soon, she would feel hot blood soaking into her clothes. Her own blood. There would be terrible pain as it tore out her throat, ravaged her face. But it didn't come.

She inched backward again, tentative, watching the creature for any hint of movement.

It didn't stop her as she wormed away, putting a little distance between them. Its stance changed, the attack pulled back, eyes intent as she scooted backward. She panted, nostrils full of that animal scent— predator, meat eater, hunter.

Heartbeats passed, seconds, moments, minutes, as they sat staring at each other. She had no way to measure the time except by the beating of her own heart.

They remained locked together, staring each other down, until her breath came more easily and the fear began to recede. The creature's posture shifted, tense and poised, but more relaxed than it had been. Tensed in a new way.

Would it bite her? Stop her from moving? Let her go?

"Why are you here?" she asked, voice rough, emotion welling up. Slowly, oh so slowly, she reached out with one hand. "Do you know me? Or about me?"

The werewolf breathed out against her fingers, its hot breath rolling over her. A noise came up from its chest, a sound she felt in her own chest—a vibrating echo. An acknowledgment.

Excitement crashed through her, a moment of crazy, blinding hope.

The werewolf knew her.

But would it be able to help? It had snarled and snapped but not lunged to kill. And maybe it was tied to the Saint as well. Just as she was. Maybe this creature was tied to her.

A noise startled them both. A cry from a familiar throat. The werewolf turned its head.

She gasped and then screamed as a blade severed the werewolf's head from its shoulders.

———

Steel bit into flesh, severing through taut tendon and bone, skin and muscle parting beneath the blade. Blood gushed over Sorcha. The scent of copper filled his nose—metallic and bitter. The beast's head dropped into her lap as the body slumped to the side, paws twitching. She was screaming, a mixed wail of surprise and anguish.

"What have you done?" Sorcha gasped.

She looked up at him, face spattered with blood—dark in the light of the full moon—anger flashing in her eyes. Struggling to free herself of the dead thing, she stood and stumbled away from him, an arm outstretched to keep him at bay.

"It wasn't going to hurt me!"

"You don't know that," Adrian said, tone flat, gathering a calm and disinterested demeanor to him like a cloak. "It would have killed you."

He hadn't expected thanks, but he had expected relief at being rescued. Instead, she was angry and distressed at the creature's death.

Adrian had forgotten his anger with Sorcha's escape the moment he'd seen the werewolf hunched over her. The prince would kill them all if something happened to the woman. Adrian wanted to keep his men alive—himself alive. Saving her was nothing more than saving his own skin.

That's a lie.

Sorcha's voice had gone hoarse, tears threatening to spill out of her wide green eyes.

Adrian looked down at the creature. It shifted subtly, the canine features fading, the body shrinking. Second by second, the beastly features receded until it became a bearded man with matted hair all over his body and long, yellowed fingernails.

It would have killed her. It had already killed several of his men. Juri and Lev, both excellent swordsmen and unmatched on a battlefield but caught off guard by something so strange and new.

More werewolves were out there, hunting in the night and lurking beneath the silver moon. Their animal gaze bored into him from the shadows, heating his skin, heavy as fists, menacing and feral. He needed to take Sorcha back to the safety of the temple. The creatures had not come into the ruins. And there they could keep the walls at their backs and defend the position until morning. They were too vulnerable here.

Sorcha took a step back, moving away from him and putting distance between herself and the dead thing.

She held up a trembling hand and whispered, "Stay back."

Adrian remained motionless, aware of the silence around them, listening to the way her voice fell into it like stones into water. *Stay. Back.* Her voice rippled out, lapping up against the trees and the things hiding in them—watching them.

"You're a monster," she whispered, eyes darting back to the werewolf, mouth twisting in sorrow.

It would have killed you.

But he'd already said that, spoken the truth, and she'd denied it. Denied him. He'd protected her because the prince would skin him alive and leave him to rot in the sun on the outer wall of the Traveling City. That was all.

"I am not the monster here," he said, voice flat, pointing at the corpse with his sword. "There is your monster."

"You think just because you don't look like one, you aren't? You wear a human face. You pretend to be a person. You are the worst kind of monster."

Something shifted inside him, slithering free of his soul, curling around the sudden pang of hurt and hiding it away. No, he wouldn't let her words dig in, cling to him with claws of steel and iron. He would let anger replace it. He would let anger and disdain override this situation.

He stepped over the creature, stalking toward her, and she gasped.

The sound thrilled him. He wanted her to be afraid, to obey him. He wanted her to be quiet and still, and maybe, just maybe, then she would disappear from his thoughts. Maybe then he would learn to slide a cool gaze past her without lingering, without stopping as his heart caught, stuttering.

He reached for her.

"Don't touch me," she hissed.

"If you don't wish to be touched, follow me, listen to my commands, and I won't lay a finger on you."

"Why should I?"

"Because you're spoiled. You've lived your whole life protected in a temple. Worshipped as a living god. Do you really think you would survive out here? With those?" He pointed to the werewolf with his sword again, dark blood dripping from the blade.

"Better them than you!"

"Do you think so?" He stopped, considering her fierce expression, the hard set of her mouth and glint in her eyes. She was covered in blood —hair, face, body. The metallic scent would linger on her for days.

"Yes."

A wolf howled, the sound climbing, spiraling higher until it cut off abruptly.

Sorcha spun in a circle, searching for the direction the call had come from. She glanced back at Adrian, an expression he couldn't read flashing across her features, and then she bolted into the underbrush.

He didn't hesitate, plunging after her and swearing under his breath.

Sorcha stopped abruptly at the edge of a clearing, her figure haloed the moonlight, a shadow haloed and held motionless.

An arrow of desire pierced him. To capture or claim her?

He didn't think about it as he crashed into her, arms coming around her, clamping her to him in a fierce embrace. With her back pressed tight to his chest, her hands came up, squeezing his forearms with more strength than he'd expected—fingers digging into muscle. His heart pounded against his ribs, anger roiling in his gut.

She could have gotten away. She could have been attacked.

He closed his eyes, willing away the anger and fear, pulling in a deep breath to calm his mind and heart. Sorcha was small and warm against him, the top of her head resting below his jaw, her hair tickling his chin. Soft. Warm.

Even sticky with blood and sweaty, there was some underlying sweetness, whatever she'd washed her hair with last—a faint floral scent.

The urge to remove his gloves and stroke her hair was overwhelming. He wanted to touch her with his bare hands, run his fingers through her hair, cup her face. He inhaled sharply, surprised with the sudden rushing desire, the vividness of it all playing out in his head as he clutched her against him.

Sorcha's hands fluttered against his hold, patting his arms, pulling at his gloved fingers. He thought she was trying to pry him free, wriggle from his grasp, but she wasn't trying to pull away. She was trying to get his attention. He opened his eyes, seeing their surroundings for the first time, understanding what they'd almost stepped into.

In the bright moonlight, the clearing head was visible—the horror happening at its center plain. Two werewolves were eating what remained of a man. There was no way to know who it might have been. Nothing that would have hinted at an identity remained. The armor had been stripped, the hands gone, with most of a leg eaten. There was no face. No identify marks.

As they stood transfixed, one werewolf snapped at the other. The creatures snarled at each other, one tugging at the body, the other refusing to let go. The snarling grew louder. A yipping came from across the clearing, and then another howl. One of the creatures dropped the dead man long enough to howl. Then the two were fighting over their dinner, roaring, the sound deafening.

"Adrian," Sorcha said, voice shaking, body trembling. "Adrian, please, let's go."

Adrian. A name. His name. But in her mouth, it sounded unrecognizable. She'd spoken to him grudgingly and never addressed him directly over the last few weeks. She'd never said his name. In surprise, his hold loosened.

Sorcha turned in his arms and buried her face in his chest, smearing blood across his leathers. He held her, so focused on the woman in his arms that he barely registered the snarling from the clearing. She curled into him, breathless in the dark.

"We need to move," he whispered in her ear, the words barely there. "We need to go while they're distracted."

Sorcha nodded, following as he turned, his arm around her as he led them away from the clearing. Behind them, the snarling continued, the pair of werewolves still bickering over their dinner. The wet sounds followed, clinging to the inner shells of their ears, holding on to the backs of their minds.

The howls stopped as soon as they reached the temple. His men were waiting within the walls, the horses untouched. Sorcha was sticky with blood, and she'd put a little distance between them as they'd trudged back through the trees. The men had studied her briefly as Adrian shared what they'd seen in the forest, and then he'd told her to get cleaned up in the spring.

Adrian sat beside the spring as Sorcha washed the blood away. The water was teeth-achingly cold, but she sank into it as if it were a warm bath. He kept his eyes averted though he could see her pale skin glowing out of the corner of his eye.

Sorcha didn't speak to him again, didn't meet his eyes. But she accepted the blanket he handed her with one hand and a dress he'd pulled from her pack with the other.

"There's a fire," he began, motioning to where they'd been gathered before the werewolves had appeared.

The spring was red, and at first, he thought she'd been hurt. The water couldn't have been that red from what she'd washed from her skin.

He bent and scooped up a handful, letting the liquid fall through his fingers. It was no longer water. Now, the spring was made of blood.

"Do you turn water into blood?" he asked, not sure if it was a genuine question.

If her Saint could resurrect the dead, maybe this woman could turn water into blood.

She looked from him to the spring and then shook her head.

He led her back to the fire, a hand on her elbow, grip tight. He knew she wouldn't run from him again. But he needed to make sure his men were aware of it as well. The rest of the night, Sorcha's teeth chattered. She sat close to the fire, with two blankets wrapped around her shoulders with a glassy-eyed gaze.

They had found nothing but death here. No relic to carry out. No answer to any of the questions the men had. And now several had died. The prince had given him one more task to complete before they could leave the Horde and the Traveling City behind.

Cautes and King Marius lay between them and the next location on the map. Several battalions had broken away from the main body of the Horde and had begun marching in that direction. The prince had tasked the Black Tomeis with meeting them there.

Adrian had a king to kill.

Chapter Twelve

A hazy tower rose above a steaming, rocky landscape. Everything was various shades of red, as if Sorcha watched it all through stained glass. Hot air filled her lungs with each breath, rasping over her tongue and burning her throat. The hiss of steam and a distant voice echoed in her ears: words spoken but not understood.

A golden figure stood beside her, one hand reaching out. The Saint. Magnificent and fierce, he towered above her and she tilted her head back, moving to meet him. She wanted him—to be held, cradled by a being of eternity. The security he offered. Protection.

But from what?

He wavered, his gold skull shifting, jaws opening.

"Sorcha."

Her name cut across the vision. Sensations faded, the burning becoming memory. She turned to Adrian, caught off guard by the easy tone of his voice. He looked at her strangely, as if he might have been worried. For her? Surely not. Sorcha shook off the fleeting thought, pulling at the rope around her wrist. It was connected to another rope stretched from Epona's saddle to Nox's. Revenant had insisted. The whole group had been furious with Sorcha's escape in the Silvas. No one wanted it to happen again.

"You were somewhere else, weren't you?" Adrian asked.

She nodded, reaching for her waterskin to wash out the lingering taste of dust and heat from her mouth. It had been so intense, a few heartbeats in another place, the vision clearer than so many others had been. The Saint had been so close and yet so very far away.

"The murals in the temple," Adrian jerked his head to where it lay several days' ride behind them. "Is that the full history of the Saint?"

"Of course not," Sorcha's face scrunched. "That's only what came later."

"What came before?"

She sighed. "Are you truly curious?"

"A smart man understands his enemy," he responded, chin lifting slightly.

Would it matter if he knew? Sorcha decided it didn't.

"Once in Ostos, there were two brothers who received the dead and judged them. Haran oversaw the living, Hakan oversaw the dead. If you lived a life worthy of them, you remained. But if you displeased them, you would be sent to Bram."

"Bram?" Adrian asked.

"A devil," Sorcha shuddered. Souls sent to Bram spent eternity in his darkness. There was no escape. Not unless the Saint came for you. "He's not spoken of in our texts much."

"Are you afraid of the devil, then?"

"Aren't you?"

Adrian shrugged. "What happened to the brothers?"

"After eons together, they succumbed to the greed for power. They fought, one wanting more power than the other and Hakan—who became our Saint—was banished to our world. For a time, he appeared as a man; unchanging and living for centuries. He performed countless miracles. Trees fruiting in the dead of winter. Cities built overnight." She paused, lowering her voice. "He resurrected the long dead."

"And your people embraced him." It wasn't a question, and he did nothing to mask his contempt.

Sorcha chose to ignore it, carrying on. "The Aureum Sanctus grew around him. He promised to ensure our place in Ostos and be our sole judge. When he was killed, he became the golden Saint you saw on the temple walls back there.”

“How do you kill a god?” Adrian asked.

“Temple historians say he was killed by a sword gifted to the heretics by Bram.”

“And you believe all of this?” Adrian shot her a disbelieving look.

Sorcha shot him a hard glance, mouth pinched. “Do you want to know? Or are you just trying to keep me talking so I don’t decide to slip out of these ropes and run?”

“If you think you could get far on foot, you’re mistaken.” He tugged gently on the rope between them, and Epona adjusted her stride to get closer to Nox. He raised an eyebrow, waiting for her to respond. When she didn’t, he asked, “How did oracles become important?”

“The oracles came to speak for him, an extension of himself.”

“How important are your visions, priestess?” Adrian glanced at her, dark eyes meeting her quick glance. She blushed, belly tightening.

“Important,” she said. But how important? While Kahina Kira and Rohan had always carefully cataloged her visions and dreams to add to the extensive library, others had rarely questioned her second sight. Even Ines had only asked a handful of times. The only thing that seemed to matter was that she was the vessel.

“Tell me about the Saint.” Adrian spoke softly, keeping his gaze forward as they rode. His dark hair was pulled into a knot at the back of his neck, his grip loose and easy on the reins. Behind him the mountains loomed, snowcapped peaks sharp against the blue sky, framing him and presenting a sharp contrast. “Our world is full of gods and goddesses. Even in your Golden Citadel there were temples to numerous deities. How does the Saint compare?”

Sorcha straightened, curious about the religions he’d grown up with. While the existence of other deities was taken as fact, the Aureum Sanctus embraced the belief that the Saint was the only one who truly cared for his believers. None of the other gods and goddess promised to return to their people, remaining removed—occupants of other realms who might or might not bestow their favors.

The Amor Aeternus, the sacred text that contained the secrets of the Aureum Sanctus, was rumored to have been fashioned from the Saint’s heart. Few had even seen it, let alone touched it. Eventually, Sorcha would have become one of the chosen. But to her knowledge, only Kahina Kira had studied it. It held the story of the Saint's birth and death but also promised that one day he would be reborn. Those secret pages shared how it might be possible.

"The Saint will return," Sorcha replied, voice flat. *My blood, my body, will ensure it* she thought, but kept that fact to herself. Instead she said, "He keeps his promises. What gods do you follow do the same?"

"I follow no god."

"Do you believe in an afterlife?" Sorcha turned, studying his profile, waiting for his dark eyes to find her. Epona snorted, as if the horse might be aware of the uneasy desire Sorcha felt beneath her breastbone each time Adrian's eyes found her, the intensity in them crushing her into a new shape.

"If there is something after this," Adrian waved a hand, taking in the whole of the world—mountainous terrain, the Black Tomeis, White Snake, and the weight of his crushing past. "Do you think I'm anxious to meet it?"

Hundreds of thousands of people had died as the White Snake slithered across the continent. There would be more deaths in the coming years as the destroyed farmland failed to produce. The population that had supported and maintained the cities and kingdoms was scattered. Prince Eine had done what he could to ensure the survival of basic infrastructure, but this was war. In the end, the empire only cared about control and expansion. Each death along the way might not have happened at the tip of Adrian's sword, but the blood was still on his hands.

If there was an afterlife—if the Saint plucked his soul from the stream of time and dropped it into eternal torment, would Adrian be met with a sea of angry dead? Sorcha couldn't imagine living a life so full of death and knowing there would be no release, only an unending existence of horror.

Sorcha might embrace the idea of nothingness. Already, it flickered at the edges of her mind. For years she'd repeated the prayers and knelt in the temple before a relic, absorbed the rituals and practices of the Saint into herself, making it an integral part of her. She'd believed in the

Saint, and continued to, but her faith had never been tested. Weakness was creeping in, fear and doubt splitting her in two.

She wore the Saint on her skin, kept him in her mind, knew his power in her bones. But her heart quickened with terror when Ines and Rohan surfaced in her memories. Those last moments in the temple haunted her. Would she truly see them again? Would the Saint pluck them from the stream and return them to this world? Living, breathing, and whole in mind? It had all been so simple, so easy to believe before Prince Eine had ripped her world apart.

"No," he said, breaking through the whirl of questions in her head. "I do not believe there is anything after this. We're here now, doing what we can to survive."

"The man who kills everything he comes across talks about *survival*?" Sorcha snorted. The word struck her as an odd choice. Adrian, Wolf, and monster of Eine, didn't seem to be the kind of man who had to fight for his survival.

"You've been sheltered in your golden temple with people who waited on you hand and foot," Adrian responded without emotion, his words all the more unsettling in its lack of feeling. "You have no concept of world beyond yourself. Even now, with the changes you've experienced, you have no clue."

Sorcha opened her mouth, a sharp denial poised on her tongue, but Adrian stopped her.

"You don't understand survival yet. But you will."

For the first time in a week, Sorcha wasn't tied to her saddle or Adrian. At the clearing in the woods, she'd stopped thinking of him as the Wolf when—*Stop! Don't think about it!*

They'd come out of the Silvas and made their way through a region of low mountains and hills dotted with farmland. It wasn't winter here, sheltered by the surrounding mountains—autumn lasted longer in this part of the world with hints of summer lingering beneath. She'd enjoyed the ride through the landscape, though it was abandoned here as well, just as it had been before the Silvas.

She tried not to think about that too much either.

Smoke from the encampment fires caught her attention first. They crested a ridge to find a city of tents spread out before them—waiting and expectant, ready for the Wolf to arrive. A rider came out and met them, passing over a sealed scroll and sharing news.

The men around her had been relieved. They didn't say it, didn't express it in any outward fashion, but she could feel it. They'd lost too many in the woods; several had been killed by the werewolves. The others had been wounded and would remain with the Horde as the others carried on the search for the relics.

Adrian and Revenant had spoken softly as they entered camp, faces serious, but she'd been able to catch enough information to piece together what was happening now.

This was a small part of the Horde. There was a city to take. A king to kill.

Now, Sorcha watched the city in the distance.

The city was mostly dark—eerily quiet—and much smaller than the Citadel. She wouldn't have considered it a city at all, more a castle surrounded by a small town and fortifications. But it was the largest collection of buildings they'd come across so far.

Cautes would fall in two days. It appeared to be almost abandoned now. The only lights remained around the castle, groupings of bright torches—what might be men moving along battlements or on top of towers.

Was this how the Golden Citadel had appeared before the battle truly began? There had been the siege, the slow buildup to blows being exchanged, the hurriedly constructed siege engines approaching with a terrible certainty.

Had the Wolf and his men watched from the darkness, contemplating all those lives being lived? All those people praying to their gods that the morning would be like any other, that what they had known would go on, that the sun would break over the horizon and the Horde would have vanished?

But Cautes wasn't the Golden Citadel. The buildings surrounding the castle were dark. Even the little villages and homesteads leading to the encampment were empty. The whole world appeared to be inhabited by ghosts.

Sorcha shivered and wrapped her arms around herself, feeling cold despite the warmer air. Loneliness touched her—a familiar friend—and she turned away from the city, back toward the tent she'd been shown to when they arrived. Adrian's tent.

Somewhere, one of his soldiers shadowed her—Ivo or Imre. Neither one she knew well despite having traveled so far with them already. But as soon as she'd paused to contemplate the city on the hill waiting for death, the man had melted away.

A spiced floral scent filled her senses—a *familiar* scent. Sorcha turned in a circle, searching for the source. The Kahina Kira had worn a similar scent. Kira with her red-painted hands and rubies at her wrists and throat. The scent had clung to her—closer than a second skin. Sorcha half expected to see the woman step out from between two tents.

None of the faces around her were those of her family—the priests and priestesses who had been closer than any blood relative could be. The scent of cooking meat replaced the spicy floral. Had she merely imagined it? Recalling it out of desperation for the comfort it might bring?

Slowly, avoiding the curious stares as she went, she wove her way back through camp. In each grouping of tents, a large fire sat at the center, usually being tended by a woman, though, sometimes a young boy rotated the spitted meats. It was hard to understand how anyone could eat knowing what would come in the next day. Blood. So much blood. So much death that the stink of it all would spread for miles around, cling to them all—a trailing wake of decay.

But the camp ate and watched the living city. She wondered how it appeared to them, if they saw shades of their homes and families. Adrian had said the men in the square hadn't seen her as a person, so how could they relate to the unwitting victims.

"Priestess!"

Sorcha turned, pausing as she swept her gaze over the maze of tents nearby, searching for the speaker. An older woman with sharp eyes and thin mouth was walking toward her with long strides and an air of intention. Her head was wrapped tightly in a dark blue scarf, and she wore simple black blouse and trousers with sleek knee-high boots the same shade as the scarf.

"Yes?" Sorcha asked, taking a step back as the woman walked right up to her.

"I'm Toren." The woman put her hands on her hips and looked Sorcha up and down, eyes full of speculation. Her accent was strange to Sorcha, not one she'd heard before. But that wasn't new. So many of the accents she'd heard in the prince's court had come from faraway places. "The prince sent me to meet you. To make camp life a little easier."

Sorcha nodded, swallowing.

"The prince values you," Toren said, lips curving into a bitter smile. "For now."

"Oh," Sorcha said, not sure what other response she could give.

It wasn't as if she hadn't had that realization herself already and was more than aware the prince's sentiment wouldn't last forever.

"Come," Toren said, gesturing toward Adrian's tent—her tent. "I spent the last ten minutes wandering around camp. I have some things for you."

Sorcha fell into step beside the woman, shooting curious glances her way. Toren had a short dagger belted at her hip, but that was the only weapon Sorcha could see. Her clothes were clean and well taken care of, not at all what Sorcha would expect from a woman who had been traveling with the Horde for an extended period of time.

"They say you've bewitched him," Toren said, raising an eyebrow. "Have you?"

Sorcha laughed and crossed her arms, trying to keep herself from breaking apart. "How could I bewitch the prince? I've spoken to him once."

"No." Toren furrowed her brows, confusion crossing her face. "Not the prince. The Wolf."

Sorcha opened her mouth and then shut it. Adrian's banner came into view, rippling in the lazy breeze that shifted the smoke from the fires. They wove through the remaining tents, large circular constructions, similar to the ones she'd seen at the main encampment when he'd taken her from the Golden Citadel.

The fire in the circle of tents was unattended, though it burned as if fresh logs had been added moments before. Sorcha glanced around and saw two men, possibly one of whom had been sent to follow her, coming from two tents behind them.

Toren reached Adrian's tent and went in ahead of Sorcha, holding the flap back.

"Have you enchanted the Wolf?" Toren asked again.

"No?"

A question, not a statement as Sorcha had intended it to be. And beneath the doubt was a growing suspicion—that Adrian moved through the camp always searching for her face. Not because he'd been charged with her safekeeping but because something had changed between them in the Silvas.

Sorcha lifted her chin, meeting Toren's curiosity. But the woman shrugged, moving past her toward the center of the tent where a crimson trunk sat in the light—new and an obvious gift from the prince. Toren glanced at the low cot piled with furs where Sorcha slept, then to the opposite spot where Adrian slept at night.

"He's told the camp to leave you alone, instructed his men to guard you. Not only on the prince's command but his own." Toren's eyebrows went up, and she tilted her head to the side. "These men have been with him from the start. They'll be there at the end as well. But you won't be. I wouldn't trust them to keep you safe. They'll protect him from anything and everything, including you."

"I'm not dangerous," Sorcha said, watching as the woman lifted the trunk lid and removed crimson clothes—riding trousers and gowns meant for travel. These were rougher and sturdier than the ones he'd gifted her in the Traveling City.

"Aren't you? But you've already said no." Toren came toward her carrying a high-necked dress of heavy cotton lined with a shade of red so dark it was almost black. She held it up in front of Sorcha, gauging the size. "What men find dangerous about women is everything. Even if you were not an oracle or child of the Saint, they would find you dangerous."

"Why?" Sorcha whispered, unable to stop the question, her mind racing.

"Because you've caught the attention of a man who has lusted for nothing but blood all his life." Toren studied Sorcha, looking from the dress to her face. "This is a good color for you. I assume you don't require help dressing?"

"No," Sorcha said.

"I will have a bath prepared, and you'll be able to change into something clean. You won't be here with us very long, but as long as you are, I'll make sure you're comfortable."

"You have bathing tubs here?" Sorcha couldn't disguise the surprise and excitement in her voice.

"It's a glorified bucket," Toren said with a laugh. "But yes, I'll have it sent over soon. Are you hungry?"

"Very." Sorcha's stomach rumbled and she pressed her hands to her abdomen.

"I'll have food sent over as well."

"Thank you," Sorcha said, emotion collecting in her throat and behind her eyes.

"You're welcome," Toren said, gesturing to her right in a vague way. "If you need anything, I'm a few rows away. The banner at our tent is green and blue."

"You have a banner too?" Sorcha had only seen a few in this camp. From what she'd been able to discern, it meant a soldier of some kind of rank, more than a foot soldier.

"Yes." Toren nodded. "My husband will fight in the morning with the others. He's honorable and stands beside his men in battle. Sometimes, I go with him. But not this time."

"What's different about this time?" Sorcha asked, curious.

"You."

***

Sorcha heard Adrian's voice before the tent flap parted, cold air sneaking in to curl around her shoulders. She was sitting in the warm water, arms around her knees, steam billowing up to dissipate above her head. She didn't move, startled but not scrambling to cover her nakedness. He'd seen enough of her in the Mapmaker's rooms—half naked under the unforgiving light of day, her tattoos telling a story only a few could understand.

For a moment—less than a second—Adrian's face was open to her, surprise crossing his features. But it passed, and he was once again closed to her. The flap fell back behind him, cutting off the cool air and muffling the sound of men talking around a fire nearby.

Adrian didn't speak as he crossed to his desk, moving a scroll to study the map beneath it. Parchment rustled and his leather armor creaked as he shifted from one foot to the other. He didn't speak. He ignored her completely.

Sorcha dipped her cupped hands into the water, lifting them slowly, letting the water slip between her fingers. The sound filled the tent, echoing alongside the rustling pages—making strange music.

"Have you eaten?"

"What?" Sorcha asked, realizing a second after she spoke what he'd asked. "No. There was a woman. She said she'd have something sent over but it hasn't come yet."

"Toren?" he asked.

"Yes."

"Good."

Sorcha nodded to herself. *Good.* A scroll was unfurled behind her, something heavy set on the table. She waited, wondering when he'd leave. Would he leave? How long could she wait? How long would the water stay hot? Already, it was barely warm. She'd put off getting out several times, hesitant to leave the warm water soothing her saddle-sore muscles and relishing the quietness of the tent. She'd been enjoying the space to not think.

"Do you plan to stay in that bucket all day?" Adrian asked, something close to humor touching his words.

She turned to find him watching her, leaning one hand on his desk.

"And if I am?" she asked, raising an eyebrow.

Adrian sauntered toward her without breaking eye contact and knelt beside the tub. She stopped breathing, eyes wide as he dipped a cupped hand into the water near her thigh, letting it fall from his fingers —mirroring her gesture from before.

"It's getting cold."

Her heart thudded in her chest—hard against her ribs, climbing up her throat. Adrian held her gaze, eyes black with challenge.

Have you bewitched him? No. When she'd denied it earlier, she'd been so confident in the truth. But now? He looked as if one word from her mouth could change their situation in a heartbeat.

There had been men in the past, a handful of friends who had become lovers. But no one she could name in this moment. Each face, each name, vanished the moment *this* man dipped his hand into her bath. Adrian. The Wolf.

Monster!

Sorcha couldn't let herself forget it.

"Don't you have someplace to be? Checking in with your men? Sharpening your sword?" she asked, putting derision and ice in her voice, willing him to stand and walk away.

Adrian continued to hold her gaze, and tension grew between them.

A buzzing sound grew in Sorcha's ears, rising in pitch as she clenched her jaw around whatever else she might have said. *Walk away,* she thought, *because if you stay, I think I could change my mind about you.*

"I do," he said, standing with a creak of leather, turning away from her.

Sorcha watched him retreat from the tent, pushing the flap aside and escaping into the open air. She ran a hand up her arm, smoothing out the goose bumps, telling herself it was the cooling water that left her cold and not his departure.

———

Dinner arrived in the form of an invitation. Well after she was out of her cold bucket of water and dressed, Adrian opened the tent flap and asked if she would like to eat by the fire. Sorcha agreed, wanting more warmth and light, the sky over her head and the feel of the breeze on her face.

The fire at the heart of this circle of tents was unattended, Adrian's men off doing other things within the camp or in their private tents. She'd watched how they were treated by the rest of the Horde, and it was with the utmost respect. In most areas, she'd seen several men sharing a tent, but not the ones she'd traveled with.

The Wolf and his men—his pack—weren't subject to the rules and hierarchies of the Horde.

Sorcha moved a stool as close as possible to the fire, making sure she wouldn't singe her skirts, as Adrian passed her a fine porcelain bowl filled with meat in brown gravy and a piece of bread.

"Where did you find such lovely dishes?" she asked, unable to stop herself.

"Do you think we're all barbarians?"

What was in that question? Humor? Derision? Sorcha looked up, catching a muscle twitch at the corner of his mouth. Amusement then.

"I didn't expect an army to travel with such delicate items," Sorcha said, stirring her bowl and searching for anything too suspicious to eat. "I didn't expect you to be so human."

Human? Sorcha bit down on her tongue, cursing herself for even opening her mouth.

Adrian didn't respond, and the fire popped—a log collapsing in a shower of sparks. He moved to add another to the stack, wiping his hands on his trousers before picking up his own bowl. He sat across from her, always at a distance, unless there was some kind of necessity.

Maybe she'd been mistaken about the moment in the Silvas. His arms had come around her at the edge of that clearing—when death had been so close she could smell it—but it hadn't held that edge of desire. Only fear. And the moment in the tent earlier when he'd dipped a hand into her bath was nothing more than Adrian testing the temperature. There was nothing else between them—captor and captive, killer and victim.

Knowing that, it didn't matter if she asked questions, did it?

———

"What was your childhood like?"

Adrian paused, surprised by her question. She seemed softer to him somehow beside the fire—less angry and defiant. He hadn't expected that from her.

"Will you tell me?" she asked softly, eyes focused on the bowl cradled in her hands.

He considered her question. It had been a long time since he'd thought about the years before he became the prince's favorite killer. Adrian had lived longer with the prince than without him. Life before the empire felt like a dream—even less solid than memory. His father had been a king, and there had been a queen, as well as brothers and sisters. Some had died, and the others had been married off, shuffled around the empire until everyone had forgotten where they'd come from and who they'd been. If his siblings were still out there, he had no idea where they might be found. Or even if they could be. He wouldn't know them by sight, or even name, at this point.

His father had been offered the same terms as countless kingdoms before him, as countless kingdoms after.

Accept my terms and you will live.

Adrian's father had looked at the waiting Horde and accepted the conditions. It made no sense to fight—a little kingdom with no army, small and insignificant—and sacrifice so much when it was all so inevitable. His father was practical and valued the lives of his people more than whatever honor might have been found in trying to withstand a relentless empire.

"Do you know what the prince does with the people who accept surrender terms?"

Sorcha shook her head.

"The families—kings, queens, princes, princesses, dukes, whatever they might be—are broken up. They're sent to the four corners of the empire, married off to one of their countless cousins, moved into minor positions of state beneath the prince's most trusted people. They're buried so deeply within his court, in his way of life, so there is never any hope or chance of escape. Until you forget what your life had been like before."

"Is that what happened to you?"

"Yes," he replied softly. "I was separated from the family I'd been born into and forged a new one within the Empire of the White Snake."

"Have they been good to you?" Sorcha's voice held curiosity and a hint of disbelief.

But he knew her life had been similar. He'd spoken to the priests from the other temples they'd come across. The Oracle, the Vessel of the Saint, was chosen as an infant—taken from her birth family, given to the temple.

"Were the priests and priestesses in your temple your family?"

"Yes," Sorcha said, brow wrinkling. "Of course."

"It's the same thing."

"And these men," she said, waving at the camp around them, "they're as close as brothers?"

"Some are."

"Some?"

"There was someone who was my closest friend."

"But isn't anymore?"

Adrian shook his head.

"How did you come to be the Wolf?" she asked, picking at her plate, keeping her eyes down. "I've heard stories."

"There are many stories," he replied.

"Tell me which ones are true."

"All the bad ones."

He hesitated, watching her. There was no judgment in her expression, only curiosity. A desire to understand.

Adrian began to speak, and he was surprised at how easily it all came, the words flowing out of him. His father had been an advisor in Prince Eine's court. He stood beside the throne, an aging man with a sharp eye and a carefully blank expression, but Eine wouldn't let Adrian stay. Adrian had been sent to live with the prince's older brother. Prince Thueban had been fighting in the east, expanding the empire, growing their riches and lands. Adrian had learned to fight there, grown up there, and he'd been given a new name and a fresh future. Soon, it was as if his life had always been this and nothing else.

But there was tension between the brothers. Empress Isolde favored Prince Thueban. She'd built the Traveling City to be near him, forsaking her seat in the Summer Palace—following her oldest son's progress across the continent. Prince Eine was envious, and it poisoned him. But with Thueban expanding the empire, Eine had grown comfortable ruling from the Summer Palace. When his brother had sent word that he planned to return to take his place on the throne, Eine made a choice.

Prince Eine devised a plan to kill his older brother and take the throne for himself. But Eine would not survive if Thueban attacked. And anyone who had supported him would die with him. If the brothers went to war, Adrian's father would die because Adrian's father was in Eine's court, a trusted advisor.

Adrian went to Prince Eine and offered his loyalty. He would kill the man who had raised him, who had become a second father, in the hopes that his birth father would live. Eine was elated. Even then, Adrian had a reputation on the battlefield. He was not yet the Wolf, the Monster of the White Snake empire, but his name was known.

Prince Eine sent Adrian back to the Traveling City with a contingent of men. His instructions were to take the city, execute Prince Thueban, and escort Empress Isolde back to the Summer Palace.

If you do not defeat my brother, I will know you have betrayed me, and your father will die. Then I will hunt you down and kill you. But if you are victorious, I will reward you beyond your wildest dreams.

Adrian would never forget the bleak expression on his father's face beside the throne. There was no escaping that twist of fate. Finian had gone with him. Finian. That was a name he hadn't thought about in several years. One he'd avoided until now.

"I returned at the head of a small army and killed the man who had raised me." He looked down at his hands, pale in the light of the fire, seemingly clean. "I proved my loyalty."

"And you did it alone?"

"No," Adrian said, hesitating. "Most of the men here have been with me from that first battle."

"Most," Sorcha asked. "Have you lost many of your friends in battle then?"

"Yes." Adrian leaned forward and stirred the fire, sparks rising. "But there was one who left."

"I didn't think anyone left the Horde alive. I've heard stories about deserters being hunted down. Is that true?"

"It is."

"How did this man leave then?"

"We made a deal," Adrian said.

"I didn't realize monsters made deals."

Monster.

Looking up, he found Sorcha's eyes on him—luminous green in the firelight, the crackling flames reflected back at him. It was impossible to read her face. He couldn't tell what she thought of his history in the empire. But he didn't want her pity, not even her understanding.

That's a lie.

"It seems like a sad life," Sorcha murmured.

Adrian stood and set his bowl down, swallowing a lump in his throat—wanting to ignore the offer of kindness in her voice. Distrusting it as much as he distrusted his reaction to the woman who could be nothing more than a way to accomplish a goal.

"Make sure you have one of the men with you if you decide to leave the tent."

He walked away, the heat of her gaze boring into his back.

———

Sorcha finished her dinner, listening to the sounds of the encampment. Going back inside the tent didn't hold any appeal. There were too many hours between now and when full dark would arrive. She would be forced to retreat to its confines then. Adrian would have to return then as well.

Their conversation haunted her. The parallels between their lives were surprising. Taken by the temple and the empire at a young age, raised within a confined world, believing there was no other option available. She'd been the oracle, the Saint's chosen. And Adrian was the empire's most powerful monster.

He'd told her how the empire viewed everyone outside their close-knit world as animals, cattle to be driven before the Horde, to be made to serve a purpose.

Unless Prince Eine invited you into his circle and you accepted his terms. Then there would be grudging acceptance. It had happened. In the temple, they'd heard the stories of the wealthy or aristocrats accepting the prince's offer to join his empire. He took the families into his court and split them up, divided and conquered even within his kingdom, and made sure they were always watched by his closest advisors.

To Sorcha, that didn't sound like acceptance.

She hadn't wanted it when it had been offered. Not when emissaries arrived with scrolls sealed with purple wax, and Kira read them aloud to the gathered temple. She hadn't wanted it when another offer had been extended to King Roi, and the man had addressed the residents of the Golden Citadel.

But there had been those who had accepted—disappearing in the night, gone without any warning. There had been empty villas and businesses. The court had thinned rapidly. Many had remained, refusing to believe such a tyrant would keep his word. And Kira? Sorcha hated the feeling of betrayal that rose when she thought about the older oracle. Her teacher. Her confidant. Her mother.

Mother. Mother in every way that counted aside from birth. There had been no other woman in Sorcha's life who was influential. Was she out there? Had she escaped the Horde, fled the prince? And if she was alive, why had she left Sorcha behind?

With a sigh, Sorcha left the circle of tents, wandering off into the encampment, wanting to think of anything other than Kira and the fall of the Citadel.

In the morning, there would be fire and death—screams and the stink of guts and blood.

No one in Cautes had accepted the prince's offer. *Join me or die.* He'd extended it as always. But Marius put too much faith in thick walls. The people who had not fled were now trapped.

Death had arrived, and the reek of fear coming from the city was overwhelming.

What would follow would be anything but cold and calm. The

prince demanded torture and fear. Terror was a weapon, one he wielded expertly. He needed the next city, and the next, to know the horrible things that happened when the Horde arrived. There was control in fear—the inability to resist. Adrian understood it and used it.

Expectations and eagerness buzzed throughout the camp. Some of the men were resigned and accepted what the day would bring without any joy for it. The men here had been through many cities. They were the survivors of countless battles. Most of them, if not all, would make it through the day and come back to their fires still smoldering in camp. They'd remove the armor and wash the blood away, then rest and wait for the next city they'd be ordered to kill.

Cautes was a small city compared to some. One that could have been easily handled by any general of the horde. But it was personal for the prince. A rumor had reached him: Marius was interested in collecting Saint relics in an effort to outmaneuver the empire. So, the prince sent Adrian personally to make sure Marius died.

He wondered if they might find the missing bone from the Silvas inside the Cautes. After the gates were destroyed and any resistance had been dealt with, he would bring Sorcha in to find it. He didn't want to touch the bones. A year ago—a lifetime—he would have said he carried no superstitions. He was a cold and logical man. And while the world contained many things he couldn't explain—magic and monsters—the Saint seemed different somehow.

The Saint could resurrect the dead and they returned as they'd been in life.

Growing up, he'd believed with certainty no one could come back from the dead. He'd sent many people off to meet their end—to fall into that place with no way to return, often in bloody and terrible ways. He'd never considered they might come back.

But the way the prince had talked about the Saint had gotten under his skin.

As they traveled to uncover more bones, and finally found the woman, he'd seen the insides of the temples and encountered the believers who followed this creature. For centuries, they'd worshipped his bones and believed he would return to change the world. But none of them, not one, had been able to tell him in any detail what that change might be. They'd babbled about people rising from the dead, about the world being made new, and disbelievers being taught the error of their ways.

Prince Eine believed them.

And deep within the Traveling City, the empress lay dying. *Poison. Death. Treason.* It had been whispered about behind closed doors, in hallways when people thought there might be no one to overhear. The prince knew something of what ailed the empress, but he spoke to no one. Once, Adrian thought the prince would confide in him about such things. Hadn't he earned his trust? And yet, the empress lay dying, and the prince remained silent.

The Saint had become an obsession for the prince. He was filled with ferocious determination. It was unlike anything else. Not his desire for the throne, his desire for power, to expand his empire, or to be the myth and leave the legacy he dreamed about. Nothing meant more than finding the Saint.

A woman's cry broke through his thoughts—a familiar edge to it tickling across his brain. To the left, he could see a small group of men standing in a circle. He heard one of them laugh, and in the middle, he saw a face he knew. Without a second thought, he moved in their direction, a hand on the hilt of his sword.

Sorcha stood in the middle of the group, hands at her sides, cheeks red with embarrassment or anger. A blond man wearing a maroon leather jerkin smirked at her, then leaned in and reached out a hand. He was one of General Zlatko's men—a face Adrian had seen in battle, but he couldn't remember the man's name. A tough soldier, skilled with a bow and arrow but better with a short blade.

"Come, priestess, bless me for tomorrow." The man leered, a glinting promise of pain in his eyes.

She leaned away, taking a step back, but the crowd around her didn't move as the blond man grabbed her upper arm. A smile split his face, something inhuman lurking beneath it—a killer for the joy of it, a torturer for the pleasure of it.

Adrian moved quickly as Sorcha pulled her free hand back and slapped the man across the face. The blow connected with a sharp sound, but he didn't even flinch—the smile remained firmly in place.

His knuckles whitened as he jerked her forward, raising his hand to return the slap.

But Adrian was there, slipping his blade strategically between the man's ribs, watching as his raised hand fell limp. But the hand holding onto Sorcha's arm remained. The group around them stepped back, eyes wide with recognition. With a jerk, Adrian pulled the blade free and kicked the man behind the knees so he went down, tugging Sorcha down into a painful bent position. Blood soaked the man's tunic and flowed into the trampled grass, the dry earth soaking it up greedily.

The men surrounding them were silent. Blood pounded in Adrian's ears, buzzing at the back of his brain, drowning out everything. Everything except Sorcha—face pale and eyes wide, mouth slightly open.

The man he'd stabbed still gripped her arm.

"Don't," she whispered, shaking her head.

The word failed to register with him until he'd brought his sword up and severed the man's hand at the wrist. Blood spattered Sorcha— streaking across her crimson dress. Anger suffused him, crawling along each vein, thundering in his head.

"You're alive right now because we have a castle to take in the morning," Adrian said in a low voice. The man on the ground let out a low animal sound of pain. "If you survive the battle, I'll kill you."

Sorcha lifted defiant eyes, meeting his cold gaze—likely seeing the anger he made no effort to hide. Tears trembled on her lashes, and blood flecked her cheeks. She sagged, but he was there, tugging her upright and slipping an arm around her knees, lifting her before she could pull away. She was stiff in his arms, holding herself rigid as he walked away from her attacker.

Could she feel his pounding heart? For a split second, the desire to keep walking filled him, to walk beyond the tents, beyond the camp, out into the world to see what it might hold beyond all this blood and death. But he crushed it, turning to where his men were camped, furious that his order to shadow her had been ignored.

"I had an eye on her." Revenant stepped from between two tents, face impassive. "I wouldn't have let it go any further."

"It had already gone too far," Adrian snapped, holding Revenant's gaze. "The prince would be displeased."

Displeased was mild. If something had happened to her, the whole camp would have died. Revenant knew that. And yet, the man had let her wander into a dangerous situation. Sorcha shifted in his arms, and he instinctively held her warm weight tighter against his chest. He glanced down at her. She didn't look at Revenant, keeping her gaze averted, her mouth pressed into a thin line.

"Put a guard on her," Adrian said, jerking his chin in the direction of his tent. "Magnus or Aldo. They'll stay with her tomorrow. We leave at dawn."

Revenant nodded and disappeared into the camp. Adrian clenched his jaw, teeth shut against whatever he might say to Sorcha, whatever comfort he might offer her. There was nothing, so he said nothing at all.

Reaching the tent, he pushed through the heavy flap and let it swing shut behind them. The spicy scent of his armor polish and the citrus soap she'd used in her bath permeated the air. The opening in the center of the roof let in enough light to see by, and later, there would be a fire. For now, the fading daylight streaming in was enough to be able to see the tears tracking down her cheeks. Anger washed over him. Anger at the men out there, at Sorcha for leaving the tent and the small circle of protection around it.

"Why did you do that?" she asked, glancing up at him. "You didn't have to maim him."

He didn't respond. There had been no consideration on his part—no thought before action. He'd seen the man's hands on her, the way her face had paled with pain, and he'd stepped forward with a naked blade.

Adrian dropped her onto the cot, the pile of furs and blankets cushioning her fall, and a sound of surprise escaped her. He turned away, pulling his gloves off as he went, and moved to the desk to consider the map that lay spread out across the surface. He waited for her to speak, to thank him or accuse him, to call him a monster or worse.

But she said nothing else.

After he killed Marius, they'd leave the Horde—stepping beyond their protection and reach—and head out into the unknown in search of the Saint's relics. He'd studied the various destinations on the map and discussed the locations with his men. There were temples to the

Saint everywhere, but not all housed a relic. Those were fewer, farther apart, and there were whispers about supernatural defenses.

He traced the coastline to the south, a cliff face with a curling filigree of gold and bone. A copy of the one on Sorcha's collarbone, which brought to mind the way it had flowed beneath his gloved finger in camp when he'd seen it for the first time. Then again in the Mapmaker's room. It was different on paper, not like the living, changeable thing it seemed to be in her skin. He turned to find her watching his hand, wondering if she'd been thinking about that moment by the fire too.

"We leave the horde the day after tomorrow and carry forward on our own."

"Because of me? This?"

She pulled up her sleeve to expose the red marks left by the soldier's grip. Anger flared instantly at the sight. He shook his head as he moved away from the desk and crouched down before her, studying the mark. It wouldn't bruise. In an hour, it would be gone. But he wouldn't forget how he'd reacted. That was something he needed to consider. His orders were clear, and emotion had no part in it.

"My name is enough to keep you safe."

"Then what was that outside?" she asked, laughing bitterly.

"A mistake on my part," he admitted.

"Mistake?"

"I should have been clear. Not everyone is privy to the prince's desires." Adrian stood, turning away from her, and moved to the medicine chest beside the washstand. There was a cream there for bruises. He found it and returned to her, holding the milky glass jar out to her. "Take this. It will help with the bruising."

"And Revenant?" She took the jar and opened it to sniff the contents. "I thought he knew."

"You saw him?" It was a stupid question, but he had no answer for her. He had no answer for himself. He went back to the maps—the country around them, with several detailing the layout of Cautes.

"I'm not deaf, Adrian."

He glanced over his shoulder, a thread of humor weaving through his words. "Am I no longer a *monster* to you, then?"

"Would you prefer it?" she asked sharply.

His name in her mouth, her voice in his ear, was like finding a tender spot, a newly discovered section of bare skin, unprotected. He wanted to hear her say his name again.

"You can call me whatever you want." He shrugged. "It makes no difference to me."

Chapter Thirteen

There had been no king to kill in Cautes after all. Marius the Mad was dead in his throne room by the time Adrian passed through the city gates. Not by his own hand, nor that of his guards, but by someone else.

Finian.

A ghost from Adrian's past had appeared in that courtyard. It was as if sharing the story of their youth with Sorcha had conjured him from memory. He hadn't thought about Finian in years, not since Finian had left the Horde behind. Even now, Adrian wished he could forget him and everything that had happened before the world had changed.

They'd all seen Finian. And they'd all seen Adrian fail to keep his promise. The news would reach Prince Eine, and his old anger would flare. Eine had released Finian from the Black Tomeis because of Adrian's request. No one else would have dared ask. The only way out of the Horde was death. But Adrian had made it possible for one person.

"What happened back there?" Revenant demanded.

The question rang in Adrian's ears. What *had* happened back there? He'd never hesitated before, never broken his word. He'd promised Finian he'd kill him if they ever saw each other again. He'd promised to kill his brother. Not a brother by blood, unless you count other people's blood, but a brother in the soul—in the heart.

The pair had grown up together in a strange court, prisoners who became sons, sons who became captains and generals, leaders of the Horde. Finian had wanted out and Adrian had let him go. But with a stipulation, a promise.

If I ever see you again, I will not hesitate to cut you down.

Adrian had failed to follow through. Revenant's confusion and anger clouded the air, a stinking heavy fog that roiled around them—poisonous and deadly. The man was horrified. Adrian, someone Revenant had known and followed from a very young age, had proved to have a weakness. Adrian could sense his second-in-command's churning emotions. Doubt. Distrust. Disgust.

He'd failed in an extraordinary way. The kind of failure that could change his past as well as his future. In the middle of that burning courtyard, he'd faced down an old friend, and Finian had been ready to die. Then, a woman had run to his side—small and pale, blood on her skirts, soot on her face, afraid but determined.

The sword had been heavy in Adrian's hand at the sight of them, and he'd felt a sharp pain in his chest, his hands tingling. He'd failed to raise his sword and cut them down. Even while his men waited hungrily for their leader to do what he had always done.

"He betrayed you," Revenant hissed. "He betrayed us all. He abandoned us. And you let him live. You swore to us—not just the prince."

Adrian didn't respond, mind whirling with questions of his own.

"He's a traitor," Revenant spat.

Adrian held up a hand, and Revenant fell silent, anger seething between them. Adrian let out a breath, warm air puffing out, steaming in the cold night. He could feel the chill in his fingers and toes, making his bones ache, even through his gloves and heavy boots. Clouds hung low, rolling in and concealing any stars that might be overhead—the face of the sky covered and unable to witness these two companions ripping themselves apart.

The fires of the encampment were distant specks in the darkness, flames small in the night. It wasn't enough to hold off the siege of the relentless darkness. But dawn was only a few hours away—a promise that could be taken back.

Adrian had proved that all promises could be broken.

He wanted to get on his horse and ride out into the night—travel away from this place, this confrontation. He wanted to see the next relic and know they were that much closer to things going back to the way they had always been. The way they should be. Before they'd taken the Golden Citadel. Before he'd seen the oracle. The vessel. The child of the Saint.

Get it over with and be done. He wanted to be out of Sorcha's presence. If they could finish the search quickly, it would be for the best. He resented each moment spent with her, each question he asked himself for the second or third time. It was all second-guessing, all past and present and future in danger of being rewritten because this woman had stumbled into his life.

From the moment he'd seen her in the Citadel, everything had changed. He didn't know how to describe it. He'd found himself wanting to alter how she saw him—how she *looked* at him. For the first time in years, he wanted to remove the mask he wore with everyone else and expose what lay beneath. He wanted her to see beyond the name and reputation.

But even he didn't know what might be found there.

It had been a long time since he'd wanted a woman. It was the first time he'd been unable to control the emotion. He'd never given in to desire before. He'd never broken or bent his own private rules. He'd kept himself apart from everyone—the whole seething Horde, the glittering spoiled court, even the White Snake Prince himself.

He'd kept them all at a distance.

Especially his men after Finian had gone. That's what it took to survive the prince's ravenous empire. But the walls he'd nurtured were trembling and threatening to fall when Sorcha stood before him. Somehow, she'd slipped through the cracks, stepped inside the inner circle, and touched his heart. His mind. His soul.

He would never be the same.

He turned to face Revenant, trying to make out his expression in the dark. How long had they been together? They'd fought side by side, following orders for years. But Revenant hadn't been a boy with Adrian and Finian, he'd arrived much later in their lives. He'd never been part of their inner circle of two. Adrian had kept him at a distance even then. There had been too much darkness in Revenant's heart.

Adrian killed as Prince Eine commanded. Revenant killed for the joy of it.

The title of City Killer and Monster belonged to Revenant as much as Adrian. Revenant had never spared a life, never hesitated when he raised his sword. He never had the desire to do so. But Adrian had never reined him in, never stopped him.

How long had he been detached from it all? He'd pulled so tight in on himself, looked no further than the second, minute, and hour of each day. Never looking toward the future. There hadn't *been* a future. Not until Sorcha.

Adrian met Revenant's gaze, just a glitter of the distant firelight reflected in his eyes, overlaid with an animal sheen. A predator. A killer.

"Do you remember our first meeting in the Traveling City?" Adrian asked.

"It was a long time ago." Revenant nodded. "Lifetimes. We've changed."

It was Adrian's turn to nod. They had changed. Back in those early days, Revenant had controlled his darkness. He hadn't been so quick to kill. Now, the darkness controlled him,

"Our past changes nothing," Revenant continued. "Finian is still a traitor. You are a leader. Your weakness is infectious. Why should we follow you when you can't keep your word?"

Adrian's fingers itched to draw his sword, the sensation so intense he almost gave into it. The blade could solve this problem. And it was a problem, one that would only grow as the days passed, as Sorcha moved among them like a ghost—a siege weapon, a trickster goddess intent on ruining them all. This growing venom poisoned the air. Their relationship was souring right before his eyes. But Finian was a symptom. They both understood the cause was Sorcha.

"If you wish to leave, do it," Adrian said.

"No." The word was harsh, a stone thrown at Adrian, meant to wound. "I will not abandon my position."

Implication and accusation colored the words—threat and promise all in one. The prince would know of all this. He would be told everything in a loud, clear voice, loud enough for the whole empire to hear and understand the truth if Adrian did not make a correction now.

"I would not disobey the prince." Adrian spoke softly.

Doing so was a death sentence. And Revenant loved death.

"It's hard for me to separate the past from the present at times," Adrian continued, disgusted with himself for showing any kind of weakness, for exposing his throat to Revenant. He continued slowly, careful with each word. "And seeing Finian was a reminder. One of when things weren't so hard. When life was easier."

Revenant said nothing, stepping back into the night, and Adrian let him go. There were no footsteps, no trace that the man had been there at all. But from the darkness came a whisper.

"The man I knew would have kept his promise."

———

The Red Priestess, Kira, studied him with a gaze that reminded him of a cat watching a mouse—predatory and calculating. Prince Eine needed her knowledge. He'd thought he could do it without her help before, with his own mystics and sorcerers, but now he knew better. When it was over—when the empress recovered—he would make sure she would never see with those suspicious eyes ever again.

"What is it you want?" Kira asked.

He leaned back in the chair, arms resting on the armrests, hands limp at the wrists, feet stretched out before him. He tipped his head back until the painted ceiling came into view—a summer sky with clouds, colorful birds, and, in the corners of the room, hints of flowering trees. His mother had it painted long ago. She'd made the Traveling City what it was—a grand creation, the talk of the empire, an unbelievable reality.

The empress had ensured its safe travel over the mountains, overseeing the careful dismantling of it—piece by painted piece—to move through narrow passes. How many men had died in that process? How many oxen had succumbed to the cold and crushing burdens of turrets and polished floors? But she'd seen to it all, observing with a cool, steady gaze. She'd taken the city over the mountains and into the plains so that as the empire expanded, the city could follow.

It moved from place to place, across kingdoms, swallowing the worthy from the cities they razed. She oversaw the conquering, collecting artists and philosophers, astronomers and seers, and anyone and everyone who could add beauty and culture to her city. They had filled the blank walls and turned a house full of shadows into one of light. If the oxen and men could have borne the weight of tile and stone, she would have covered it in every manner of precious thing, but it needed to remain movable, as light as possible, so she had it painted to reflect all the finest things the world held.

Every day, he moved within the world his mother had created, the thing she loved, a small part of her heart. It could not go on without her.

"My mother will be dead soon."

His voice was crisp, not wanting to leave the woman across from him any room to wriggle in under his skin, to pry his eyelids back and examine his thoughts. He could feel it, the way she spoke to him, the way her attention lingered. She was searching for a way to control him.

"Your mother is dying," she agreed. "But what would you like me to do about it?"

He sat up straight, hands clasped in front of him, staring at her now. Silence unfolded, heavy and absolute between them.

Her eyes flicked down, to the side and away from the heat of his gaze, moving across the ceiling to the sparse furnishings.

"I've already told you what I know, shown you how it will happen." An edge of uneasiness colored her words, confidence wavering. "And you've begun the journey. Already, pieces of the Saint are in your possession. You have history books and sacred texts. You know more than many in my own order."

The corner of his mouth twitched up. "And yet you came to my court and offered me your loyalty. You offered your help. So far, you haven't given me anything more than what I'd already discovered from the others. So many of your faithful dead, so much knowledge given freely. But you claim to have more, something they did not."

She opened her mouth to speak, but he held a hand up.

"You've said that when the time is right, you will reveal secrets. I'm choosing to accept this answer for the moment. But each day, death moves closer. It is reaching for her, and I'm still missing relics. What good are rotting bones if I don't know how to put them together?"

"The vessel—" Kira began.

"Will bring him back. So you keep saying. So did the others. I must believe you because I have no other choice. And your sacred texts say very little about the actual resurrection. Each member of your order that has died has been convinced they would return, that your vessel would recall him, and I would face judgment."

She remained silent, waiting for him to finish.

"So, if I killed you now, here, in this room beneath a false sky, would the Saint be able to resurrect you?"

She swallowed, muscles in her throat moving, a muscle in her jaw tensing.

"If I burned your body, cut you into a thousand pieces, if I ground you beneath the hooves of the oxen and the weight of my city came down on you, would there be anything left that the Saint could call back?"

"I don't know," she said, voice subdued.

"And my mother? You've been unable to tell me how he would resurrect her. I had hoped to understand how everything works before she died. I had hoped you would be more helpful than you have proven yourself to be. I am out of time. You are out of time. And death is here."

"The vessel," the Red Priestess began again.

"The vessel has gone to find the missing pieces. I've seen her tattoos. I understand it's a map, but not every piece is listed. It's all there, laid bare on her skin, but it is incomplete."

Kira remained frozen.

"Where are the others?"

She jerked back, denial written all over her face, poised to fall from her lips.

Lie, lie, lie.

The prince leaned forward, the chair creaking beneath him, the room held captive by this moment around them.

"Tell me about the other pieces," he said. "Tell me what happens when those are found."

Chapter Fourteen

Cairns—carefully stacked stone towers ranging in size from a blade of grass to as tall as man—began to appear as the distance between them and the next relic lessened. The narrow dirt road they followed seemed unused, an out-of-the-way path that few people followed. They wove through a sparse wood—huge trees reaching overhead with open glades and stretches of fields between them. This forest didn't have the same feel as the Silvas. There was no watchfulness here, only a quiet, peaceful calm that Sorcha relished.

But the cairns unsettled her as they became a forest of their own. There were small and large stacks, some as tall as a man and others reaching well above ten feet. Others were one or two, a handful of stones gathered together—the beginning of something or the end.

"Don't touch them," Domenico warned. "There's something about them—"

"Magic?" Thompson interrupted.

Adrian glanced from one to the other, his eyes sliding over Sorcha as he turned in the saddle—a dark gaze, flaring as it touched her. But he didn't speak, and Domenico only nodded in response.

Sorcha didn't need his warning. They were strange and gave off an air of otherworldliness, as if they might come together to stand and stride away from this place. Or reach out with rocky fists to pummel them from their horses. Not watchfulness like the Silvas, but something that could become awareness if it was disturbed.

Eventually, the dirt track brought them to the lake. On the map, it was small, but reality was much different. It stretched in either direction, the opposite shore a distant hazy line of old-growth trees. The shores were alternating stretches of rocky and sandy areas, the water a clear blue, the bottom magnified and visible. Beneath the surface, the stones were a myriad of colors—bright as gems—worn into smooth, irregular shapes.

The men set up camp near a crescent stretch of rocky beach near the tree line, with Adrian's tent set apart from the others. These shelters were much smaller than the ones they'd used while traveling with the Horde. Sorcha was grateful they weren't sleeping out in the open, subject to the elements. But since these tents were much smaller. Adrian and Sorcha were now sleeping beside each other—separated by furs and nothing else.

As they traveled, she had ridden beside him—Epona the only horse Nox let get close—while the rest of the men fanned in every direction. There had been more empty villages and towns—smoke curling up from burned homesteads, livestock roaming freely. Along the way, the men had hunted, returning with small game and once a goat. Sorcha tried not to think about who had taken care of the animals, who had lived in those ruins.

Each night, Sorcha turned her back to Adrian, and each night, she felt his hot gaze between her shoulder blades. She lay awake and listened to him breathe, wondering what she would find if she rolled in his direction. She hadn't turned, not yet, but soon she would—it was inevitable. The tension between them thrummed and shimmered, practically visible in the air. She'd wake in the mornings to find the tent empty, the flap buttoned tight to keep the cold out, and her gloves laid carefully on her boots. Adrian set them out for her each morning.

After the Silvas, there had been a hundred small things like this. A piece of fruit that had survived the war and cold seasons, extra attention paid to Epona at the end of a hard ride. Things that she never would have thought twice about with anyone else. But Adrian? What kind of man killed so easily and yet brought her fruit and set her gloves out for her each day?

She hadn't had the courage to ask yet.

The others had noticed. Well before she'd been fully aware of it herself. Revenant was the only one in the group she truly feared. Toren had warned her that these men would kill her the moment they had the chance. It wasn't that Sorcha had disbelieved her; she knew they would. But she hadn't expected any of them to go against the man they served with such devotion.

But each time she felt Revenant's gaze on her, she knew. If he had his chance, he'd put a blade in her gut without blinking. And the others? They would follow his lead. Adrian—the Wolf, the monster—was the only reason she was alive.

Magnus started a fire while Soren and Ivo went hunting. The other men tended to their horses and went about their personal business. Adrian was going over a set of maps with Revenant and Thompson. Domenico was with them, but he never spoke much. Even now, he stood with a finger to his lips, listening as the three compared maps and debated routes to the next relic.

But first, they would need to find this one.

What would the prince do when he discovered there had been no relic in the Silvas? That ruined temple still tended by the cursed, where blood flowed so freely? He would be angry. But who would he blame? Her or Adrian? But that was a stupid question.

Sorcha wrapped her fur-lined cloak around herself, tucking her hands into the pockets. The wind coming off the water was cold—bringing the scent of sap and a hint of smoke—though the surface remained calm. She'd never seen water so clear before, and part of her wanted to jump in—discover how far the bottom really was. But she'd never been a good swimmer, learning in the Aevum River by the Citadel as a child but never swimming much in her adulthood.

Instead, she picked her way down the rocky beach, pausing to pick up stones—deep red, slate blue, black with veins of transparent quartz. She tucked them in her pockets as she went, moving toward a familiar line of boulders that stretched out into the water—a stone arm reaching for the other shore. It was a landmark on the map, an indication that a relic waited in this seemingly anonymous location.

Reaching the edge of the water, she stopped and rubbed a hand over the tattoo on her arm—a skeletal hand cupping water, the surface rippling out, an eel twisted around an outcropping of stone. She'd seen no eels and doubted that the prince and his men had interpreted the map correctly. They'd already failed to collect one relic. But what did that matter? The prince already had so many, and it was only a matter of time before he obtained the rest.

And then? She would fulfill her destiny. A shiver passed through her as a cold breeze came across the water and rustled her hair, pressing the skirt of her dress against her legs and sneaking down the neckline.

She felt his gaze then, warm on her skin as if he'd reached out to touch her. An emotion rushed through her—excitement or fear, a thread of desire. *Don't think about it!* Fumbling with the stones in her pocket, she tossed one into the water. There was no splash, barely even a noise, as it hit the surface and sank. In the distance, thunder rumbled, though no clouds were on the horizon.

———

Adrian watched Sorcha pace along the shore, the hem of the red riding dress damp and half tangled around her ankles. He could see Ivo at a distance, watching her, honoring his duties as a guard. The others had moved off to find something to eat or take care of the horses.

Revenant and Thompson had gone over the maps again, and Domenico had given his very brief opinion. The relic must be here; it was on the map—on Sorcha's skin. They had only to find it. They'd chosen a spot near an outcropping of rock that looked similar to the one in her tattoo. But the lake had others. They could spend days here, searching along the shore, trying to find the exact spot.

Days wasted while death slunk toward the empress. But he couldn't think about that or the prince's anger when the inevitable arrived. Finding the relic here would take as long as it took. It must be beneath the water. If they'd had a boat, he would have sent her out to find it, but they would need to construct a raft, and that would take time. Until then, they could do nothing but wait.

Sorcha made her way back toward camp, head down—moving slowly along the rocky beach. The scent of water and citrus came with her, fresh and bright. How close would those scents be on her skin if he pressed his face into the place where her neck curved into her shoulder, if he tilted her head back to run his lips along her jawline as he wove his fingers into her hair?

Adrian closed his eyes, turning away from Sorcha. He could not forget she was the oracle and vessel. She could be nothing more than that. But the intoxicating vision of her pliant in his hands would not leave.

"Food is ready," Wes called out from the cooking fire.

The men drifted in, gathering around the central point and exchanging words in low voices. Wes and Bran portioned out roasted bird and bread—ignoring the complaints that the bread was slightly burnt in places.

They'd filled their waterskins at a sweet spring they'd come across, and Adrian was relieved they wouldn't be drinking lake water. The idea that they might consume something touched by the Saint gave him an uneasy feeling.

Sorcha came into the circle, accepting the meal from Wes with soft thanks. She sat on a canvas stool and began to eat slowly, watching the fire. The light glistened in her pale eyes, flushing across her cheeks, catching a strand of lighter hair in her dark curls.

"A raft will be done in the morning," Revenant said.

"Good," Adrian said, looking away from Sorcha and feeling his second-in-command's gaze. "We'll begin the search at dawn."

"And if it isn't at the bottom of the lake?"

"Then we move on to the next relic."

"And that one?"

"Are you having doubts?" Adrian asked, turning his full attention to Revenant, searching his expressionless face for a hint at what might be working in his mind.

"There are no guarantees. This could all be a diversion, a chase with no end or reward."

"Then we follow the map to the end and tell Prince Eine exactly what we didn't find."

"How do you know the witch isn't lying?"

"I've seen the map."

"We've all seen the map." Revenant pressed. "How do we know it's correct?"

"I've seen the tattoos."

Revenant was silent. In the quiet, Adrian could hear his heart pounding. He stood, turning away from his trusted companion, a man who had been beside him for so many bloody years.

What Revenant implied was death. They could kill the woman and be done with the whole thing. Revenant didn't believe in the Saint—none of them did—and each man here would rather be with the Horde, taking the next city.

Sorcha met his gaze, and he wondered how much of that she'd heard. She knew what these men thought of her. And he was sure she thought she knew what *he* thought of her. If she knew what he wanted from her, it would be the end of everything for him. It was dangerous—a show of weakness.

"I'm not going to wait for a raft," Sorcha said, standing abruptly. "Dusk is hours away. There's time to search now."

"How far do you think you'll get if you swim? You don't even know where the bone is," Adrian said, stomach clenching at the idea of her swimming out alone, slipping beneath the surface to never be seen again.

"Why do you care?" she snapped, standing and setting the remainder of her meal on the stool and turning away from the group,

Why do you care? The question came and went, and Adrian refused to acknowledge it.

It was too late to examine why her fate mattered to him. If he didn't admit it aloud—if he was able to keep these things hidden—then things would go back to the way they'd been before Sorcha had arrived. But he needed her alive, and drowning in a lake would irritate the prince.

That was the only reason he followed her to the shore.

———

Water lapped gently against the rocks, barely moving, the surface farther out completely still. Nothing but sky and lake for miles. The trees on the opposite shore were shrouded in a rising fog. The sounds of camp had faded—the murmuring of the men, the whickering of the horses, the cooking fire popping.

Sorcha scrambled out onto the rocks jutting into the lake, noticing the cairns stacked beneath the surface now—as many as there had been along the road. Who had built them here? Or had the water risen over time, drowning them?

"Sorcha!" Adrian called, the sound of his boots on the rocks following her.

But she didn't wait. Reaching the last boulder extending out into the water, she removed her cloak and sat to take off her boots and stockings. She dipped a foot into the water. It was warm, not the jolting cold she'd been expecting. She stepped down, holding onto the rocks, and slipped into the water, up to her shins, then her waist. Her dress floated around her, billowing up, drinking in the water.

"Sorcha," Adrian said, nearer now and getting closer.

There was no emotion in his voice; it was simply her name.

Looking back, she met Adrian's gaze. Unreadable—face impassive—hiding whatever emotion might be beneath the surface. If there were any. Even now she wasn't sure if he had a heart.

The others remained in camp; a few faces turned to them—out of earshot but within sight. If he gestured, they would come. If he wanted to stop her, he could. But she knew he wouldn't. They needed the relic.

Sorcha turned away, back to the water, skimming her hands through it. There was no way to know how deep it was—feet, inches, over her head, or just up to her chin. Reaching the last of the submerged boulders, where the cairns began, she stepped down, and the water immediately engulfed her.

A startled cry escaped her, mouth filling with water, the cry becoming bubbles and pure terror. For a moment, she thought there was a cry from the shore, answering her own. But with water in her ears —deafening her—there was no way to know. She kicked, weighted down by the dress. It had been stupid to jump in the water wearing everything, assuming she would be able to feel the relic and find it quickly in a shallow area.

Stupid! she thought. *You're an idiot! And now you're going to drown.* Deeper down, buried so far in her mind that she could almost ignore it, another thought uncoiled like a snake. *Wouldn't that be better?*

Something huge and rough wrapped around her ankle, jerking her down and dragging her farther beneath the surface. She fought against it, kicking out, but the grip tightened. Sorcha looked down and met a pair of strange eyes, wide and flat and dark, the face and body thin and rocky. A collection of stones brought to life—a cairn taken human form.

Its grip moved from her ankles to her knees, then her thighs, hips, and finally to her waist. It brought her closer, their faces almost touching. She struggled, inhaling water in a gasp, and terrible pressure built in her chest. Then the creature moved, propelling them deeper down, farther into the lake. Sorcha choked and inhaled more water, fighting the creature, desperate for air and the surface. But it held tight as the world went dark.

Chapter Fifteen

Cold stone floor. Smooth beneath her fingertips. Pain behind her eyes, lungs burning.

She coughed raggedly, expelling water as her stomach cramped.

"A waste of good water." The voice was gravelly—grating stones and shifting fault lines.

She rolled onto her side, trembling, fighting the urge to moan or yelp with fright.

The creature sat beside her, legs crossed, hands on its knees. It leaned closer, peering into her face, on the verge of touching her without bridging those last few inches.

"You're the Lacus," Sorcha whispered.

She'd heard the stories, as all children had, of a lake guardian made of the bones of the earth, a creature who could give or take away, fortune or misfortune held like a pebble in the palm of one four-fingered hand. A fitting caretaker for something as precious as the Saint.

"And you are either brave or stupid to trespass. Or possibly both. I have not decided."

Sorcha pushed up on one arm, her clothes clinging to her, her damp surroundings sinking in. It was a cave with a pool of water to her left and a light high on the ceiling. Not daylight. Something magical, something unreal—shimmering suggestion of the sun. There was nothing else in the space except the pool, the light, the creature, and herself.

"I've come to ask you for something," she said, knowing in her heart it was not that simple.

The creature's face moved, but she could not read the expression—living stone with flat eyes, body language impossible to understand.

"I have nothing for you," the creature said.

"But you have something for the Saint."

It hissed and stood abruptly, moving away from her—stones grinding. She moved slowly, carefully, worried that it would pounce on her if she surprised it.

"It's not yours to take."

Sorcha pushed back the sleeve on her dress, exposing tattooed skin. "You don't have a choice. I've come to collect him."

"And if I refuse, Oracle?"

She shrugged. "Nothing."

"Nothing?" The creature turned, pacing. "Nothing means nothing. Something would happen—would come. Nothing is a lie."

"It's not my lie. I don't know what would happen. I would be dead."

"And with your death, he would walk again."

Sorcha swallowed, mouth dry despite the water all around them. Kahina Kira had shared very little of what might be required of her. Only those higher up within the Aureum Sanctus knew everything. The others believed and trusted she would do the right thing by them. But it would mean her death. She'd refused to contemplate it until now, forced to see it and embrace it. Or run. Become a traitor to those she'd loved.

"That's what I've been taught."

"But not what you believe?"

"My belief is unimportant."

The creature stopped with its back to her, controlled anger almost visible between them, a volcano on the verge of exploding. Sorcha held her breath. There was no escape here. She had no idea where exactly she was or how she might be able to reach the lake shore again. Even then, she would come back empty-handed if she could not convince Lacus to help her.

Do you really want his help? The question threaded through her mind, weaving between her guilt and sense of obligation. *Yes! Of course I do*, she thought. But even in the privacy of her head, those words felt hollow.

"I walked the earth with him," Lacus began, his tone bittersweet—no longer avalanches and landslides. "We traveled thousands of miles, and I saw how it all fell before him—trees bending, water ceasing to flow. I saw the sun go dark and the moon fail to rise. The death of everything, even among those he claimed as his own. You would call him back? Give him a place in the world that is finally free of him?"

"I don't have a choice," Sorcha whispered.

"Another lie. You are ignoring your choice in favor of something else. There is always a choice."

"There's no choice for me."

The prince would kill her if she failed. He would kill her if she succeeded. If the ritual of the Saint's rebirth didn't kill her first.

Lacus turned, coming for her, moving more quickly than she would have thought possible. He reached for her, his stony fingers on her throat—gentle pressure but the promise of a viselike grip.

"Would you like to die here?" The creature's breath washed across her face—cold water and damp stone. "There is a man on my shore that speaks your name like a lover. He is calling for you. I can hear him even now. I could kill him too."

Sorcha shook her head. *Calling for me? Lover?* Adrian's expressionless face flashed in her mind—his bottomless gaze, the hint of a rarely seen smile. His hands on her body, arms going around her, the solidness of him at her back. The warmth of his stare when he thought she wasn't aware. The uneasiness she'd caused between himself and his men—his brothers-in-arms.

"If you want me gone, give me the relic and let me go." She swallowed, the hand around her throat twitching.

Lacus studied her, strange eyes crawling over her features, a grating rumbling growing from somewhere deep within his body. Then he released her, stepping back with a sound close to a sigh, and nodded.

"A test. A fight. I will give you nothing freely."

"I understand," she said.

"The bone is not here."

Cold overtook Sorcha, chattering through her teeth down to her fingers and toes. If it wasn't here, where else would they have to travel? Would they be able to find this new place on a map?

"Where is it?"

"I put it where no one would find it, Oracle." Lacus stared at her—his eyes unreadable, unfathomable—a gaze unlike anything else she'd ever experienced. "Not even those who would want to bring him back."

"Can you retrieve it?" she asked.

"If you want the relic," he said, "you have to retrieve it on your own."

She nodded.

He pointed to the hole in the floor. "Through there."

"And then what?" she asked.

"You find it."

"You won't tell me anything else?"

"Why would I?" he asked. "I don't share your desire to resurrect the Saint. I will not help you bring about the end of the world."

"How do you know it will be the end?" Sorcha studied the film of water between his fingers—the nothingness of it and what it promised.

"How do you know it won't be?" he responded with a shrug.

"I think," she said, words coming carefully, each one formed with thought and intention, "it will be the end for me."

Lacus shrugged with the sound of grinding stones, a rumble that echoed through the small cavern and shivered up her spine.

Lacus gestured for her to step forward. He made a ring with a bulky thumb and finger. A sheer, thin film of water shimmered there—caught like a sheen of soap in a wash bucket. "Open your mouth, Oracle," he rumbled.

Sorcha did as he instructed, fighting to stay in place and not flinch away as he leaned toward her and blew on the film in his fingers. A bubble formed, small and perfect, and heavy with clear water. A shimmer twirled gently in the center—a tiny whirlwind. It broke on her tongue, and cool water filled her mouth, tasting sweet and cold enough to freeze her throat as she swallowed.

"It will last only a little while," he said. "Your time is limited. Keep your mouth closed, keep this gift of water inside you. If you lose it—if you let new water in—you will drown."

Sorcha nodded as she bent down and pulled at her skirts, ripping until the underskirts plopped to the floor. The things she'd put on to keep her from freezing were now half-frozen with chilly water trapped between skin and fabric. She took it all off except for the final thin layer of cotton, transparent with water, plastered to her like a second skin. She almost removed that too but stopped. Nakedness didn't bother her, it never had, but a small twinge of modesty hit her at the base of her spine.

It didn't matter that Adrian might have seen more than enough in the Mapmaker's room or that she'd never thought much about walking around nude in her private chambers. She didn't want *Revenant's* eyes on her. Even if the only thing between her flesh and his gaze was a transparent film of cotton, it was better than nothing.

Sorcha nudged the bundle of wet clothes with her foot. She wouldn't be back for these and didn't need the creature's confirmation to know it was true. She would never see this room again. The creature would dispose of them, or maybe they'd stay right there on the floor until they rotted. But either way, she wouldn't be back for them.

But there were other clothes. There was a trunk full of them in a tent on the shore.

A gift.

A bribe.

Another way to bind her to the Empire of the White Snake and Prince Eine.

The cool taste of water still filled her mouth as she contemplated the opening in the cave floor. She would leap, drop into the depths, and swim until she found what she needed. Not wanted. She had no desire for it. She *needed* it to keep living, needed it like breath and blood.

Sorcha lifted a foot, hovering over the opening, heart pounding.

"How guilty will you feel when millions are dead?"

Lacus's voice stopped her, low this time, a soft shushing of falling pebbles. It didn't matter what she wanted or how she would feel when it was all said and done. Her desires had no part in any of this. The journey was not hers to choose. She could only hope that she survived it all once it was over.

Without answering, she dropped into the water. It was warm—as warm as bath water. Sorcha fell like a leaf from a tree, drifting in slow motion. Down and down into the sparkling depths. All around, the water was clear, but nothing was visible. Far overhead, the surface rippled and light shone down in beams. She sank through shimmering and dancing light, the thin cotton of her chemise rippling around her.

It was impossible to know how much distance she'd covered. It felt like an age had passed—an eternity spent contemplating the way water bent the light. Then the view beneath her began to change.

A rocky floor began to take shape, the texture similar to the rocky shore above, blurred with distance but coming into focus. It wasn't a flat bottom, not littered with rocks and plants, not the bottom she would have expected to find buried beneath a sea of water.

It was a city.

Elaborate spires and domes took shape below her—arched windows and graceful buildings. There were streets, narrow and wide, overgrown with water plants of blue and green, and splashes of purple flowers. The buildings were a similar color, a mottled blue and green, smooth as glass and reflective. If the water could be drained and the sun brought to this shadowy blue place, the city could have been inhabited in a few days, bustling before the water had fully run away.

Sorcha pressed her lips tight, terrified of letting any water in, knowing she would never be able to reach the surface before her breath ran out. She looked up at the towers rising around her, her view all spires and distant sunshine.

They were passing her now, all curved and beautiful lines, flowing flowers, and animals carved into the blue-green surfaces. But these flora and fauna belonged to another time and place. A few were familiar, but others were new and foreign; strange snarling faces and shapes. They were the creatures of myths and legends.

Down and down she went, shadows gathering as she dropped into the heart of the city. But even here, between the tall buildings, there was a little light. A faint glow emanated from the stones, as if they were lit from within, shielding an iridescent flame.

The road she stood on would have been wide enough for several carts and horses. It swayed and moved with water plants now, the vegetation coming up to her knees. Delicate purple flowers on pale stalks waved in the gentle current, variegated leaves brushing against her bare legs.

Sorcha pushed forward and the plants parted for her, swaying and dipping away. A flash of movement caught her attention, and she turned, searching slowly. A huge domed building topped with a reaching spire, half-hidden by the buildings and rooflines, was immediately to her right. That had to be where the relic was.

She never would have imagined that there would be so many sacred places left to decay, never intended to be found.

The Saint hidden with the hope there would be no resurrection.

Not right now, she thought. Sorcha needed to find the relic without letting herself get distracted by worry or doubt. Or too much curiosity about this place. But her mind overflowed with questions. Everything she'd ever thought she'd known. None of it was as it seemed.

Pressing her tongue against the roof of her mouth, she held on to the hint of sweetness from the water Lacus had given her. For a moment, her thoughts drifted to Adrian, the Wolf who had been calling to her like a lover. But as monstrous as he behaved, he showed gentleness with her. She didn't have time for that right now either.

Sorcha pushed off the ground, reaching and pulling herself forward, turning the corner of a building and coming out into a much wider boulevard. The temple was at the end, massive and imposing. The road rose up to meet it, with wide stairs leading to a set of open double doors. They were covered in plant life, and a faint glow came from within.

Pausing, Sorcha looked around, studying the way she'd come. The buildings were empty, slowly crumbling, but glass was still in the windows and shut doors. The houses and shops reached up and up, several stories tall. The slow decay made her wonder how long it had been here. How long had it been submerged?

In the shadows between two buildings, she caught movement again. Her heart dropped, skin tingling, and a cry of surprise lodged in her throat.

There was nothing. Only waving water weeds, light filtering down from above, the buzzing silence filling her ears. She shoved down the scream and swam toward the open doors of the temple, throwing glances behind her as she did.

Reaching the stairs, she kicked off them, half walking, half swimming as she passed over the threshold. With one last glance at the city behind her, she went inside, disappearing into the greenish glow.

The interior of the temple was imposing—grander than the one she'd grown up in and loved in the Golden Citadel. Overhead, the dome arched in perfect pale marble, pillars of the same stone all around, and more arched corridors led off the main room. There were no paintings or murals here, only the same pale stone making up the floors, walls, and ceiling.

At the peak of the dome, the cause of the glow was apparent. A mass of large glowing eels writhed together, swirling and twisting, their incandescent skin the palest green. There were maybe fifty, maybe a hundred. It was impossible to count as they moved, slithering and twining as if they were one organism.

The movement she'd caught outside could have been an eel, one of these large creatures, or it could have been something else. She'd assumed she was alone down here, but she'd been wrong. She didn't want to think about that right now though. She needed the relic, needed to bring it to the surface, and time was pressing down on her like an impending storm.

She searched the room, thinking the relic would be in a place of honor, like her own temple, but no. The stone creature had no respect for the Saint. He no longer revered or worshipped him. The relic would be somewhere else. Hidden.

Arches led off the main room, shooting off into darkness, leading to places she could only imagine. She glanced up at the eels. In the silence, water muffling everything, the eel's movement was eerie.

She chose an opening at random and swam down a long hall, the faint light of the eels following. Reaching a smaller chamber with three more arches—three new choices—she paused. Two were full of an inky darkness. The one in the middle appeared to be lighter. Would it be eels or something else? But going into the complete night of the other tunnels felt too much like walking into a tomb.

The current was stronger coming out of the tunnel she'd chosen. Sorcha kept one hand on the wall to her right, following the twists and turns. A light began to grow—a rippling golden glow—and when she turned the corner, gripping the edge of the stone, the relic came into view.

The chamber was small, a barely widened space at the end of the corridor, as bare as the rest of the temple had been. An ulna and radius attached to one giant hand lay in a long alcove. It shone with an inner light, rubies throwing off crimson sparks, the gilding polished to perfection. It was enormous, and Sorcha's stomach dropped. How would she navigate the tunnels and bring it to the surface?

If she could reach it. The current was stronger here, becoming a force she'd not expected. It was as if the water didn't want her to reach the relic.

Closing her eyes, Sorcha tried to calm her mind and silence the doubt. She would reach it and bring it to the surface. *And then?* The next one and the next, until the Saint was whole. Her chest tightened. The taste of the sweet water was fading. And the bone, the relic—*Saint* —called to her. It was a wordless seduction, the feeling that part of her very soul lay within the marrow and the Saint could make her whole again.

Sorcha fought to reach the bone, fighting the current, desperate to drag it to the surface. But the force of the water was too powerful, and the pressure—the *need*—to breathe was becoming overwhelming.

Time was swimming away from her, faster than the current but just as forceful. She'd die down here, trapped beneath the stones, lungs full of water. She wasn't ready to die. But if she went back up for air, would she be able to get back down? Would Lacus help her again or leave it to her to figure out another way down?

Fight for me.

Me who? Herself? The Saint? And beneath that, curled in on itself, writhing like the eels in the temple behind her, another thought: *fight for Adrian.*

Sorcha pushed off the wall, arms outstretched, pushing against the water. The relic was within reach, so close that her fingers brushed against the gilded bone. It was warm as the water around her, warm as if it lived.

Pressure was building in her chest, the need to breathe overshadowing all other thought. The current caught her, twisting her away and back the way she'd come, knocking her into a wall. Skull connected with stone and then an elbow, and pain spiked through her. A bubbling cry escaped her lungs—the air getting trapped along the ceiling—as the current carried her away from the Saint.

———

Twisting and trying to orient herself, Sorcha bumped into another wall, panic clouding all thought, the pressure in her head bursting. The golden glow vanished, leaving her in darkness and desperate to figure out which way was up and out. Another corridor, another wall, and then the fast-moving water began to slow.

How far was the chamber with the three entrances? She'd counted corners as she'd searched farther for the relic. But now she couldn't remember. Not that it mattered. She had no idea how far the current had pushed her before finally slowing.

Sorcha gripped the wall, continuing to follow it. A faint sweetness still lingered in the back of her throat. Relief flooded through her. Her breath had been knocked from her, but somehow, she'd managed not to let any lake water in. But despite that, there was no way she would be able to go back the way she'd come. The relic was impossible to reach.

Left and left again, she followed the wall, hoping she would reach the main area of the temple. A pale greenish light was growing ahead of her, and she moved faster. *Please let this be it.* She kicked forward, pulling with her arms, and rounded another corner.

An eel came into view, shooting through the water. Its eyes focused on her, mouth open and widening as it approached. Sorcha kicked off the wall, pushing herself back up the narrow passage, desperate not to feel those sharp, yellow teeth sinking into her flesh.

Sorcha was too afraid to turn her back to it as it barreled forward.

Afraid the moment she did, it would strike. She would rather face it—rather know when she would die—and not be struck down as she fled. Sorcha studied, terrified of what would happen next. It had terrible teeth jutting from its mouth like thorns and its skin glowing faintly. Its bite would puncture flesh, reach bone, and crush her here in this place where she would never be found. Her skin tingled with expectation.

The eel struck her, but not with its mouth, with the side of its head, shoving her out of the way and bouncing her off the wall. It slithered past her so quickly she didn't have time to process it. She was left swirling in its wake, bumping off the floor and scraping a knee. In her mouth, the sweetness was gone, vanished, and the warm water of the lake, tasting faintly of vegetation and stone, filled her.

The eel receded, taking its glow with it, leaving her in darkness.

———

Sorcha fumbled against the wall—rough stone beneath fingertips—pressure building and pounding through her head. It pushed her forward, drove her with racing heartbeats and the urge to breathe, shoving her into the darkness.

Something began to murmur in the back of her mind, a whisper she could almost understand. In the nonsense, a golden thread wove through it all, familiar and warm. A promise waiting to be fulfilled. She swam on, concentrating on her arms and legs, propelling herself through the water.

Without the sweet water, would she make it to the surface? Did she have enough strength in her legs? Enough oxygen in her screaming lungs? She wanted fresh air and sunshine, to leave the water behind and never return. She wanted the shore. She wanted Adrian.

The darkness seemed endless. Sorcha would never make it out—never leave. The sun would never rise again, the stars all winked out of the sky. It crushed her, compacting her bones and wearing her down until nothing but fear remained. A small inner voice began to whisper, drowning out the one below it, further down. This one was a shade of her own, controlling, tempting, offering.

This could be all over. You could stop here—in this place—now. You can make this choice for yourself, the only one you can. What would it matter? Die now or later? Die on your own terms or at another's choosing? That's what you believe is going to happen, don't you? That's what you've admitted to yourself up there in the sun.

Stop now.

Sorcha followed the wall, fighting against the voice, screaming to silence what was becoming a forest fire in her mind. She kept fighting forward, knowing that at any moment, she would no longer have the strength.

Spots appeared before her eyes, vision blurring. But through the blur, a glow appeared. Her eyes were playing tricks on her, the dark spots in her vision fading, the light expanding in the water to engulf her. With a shock, she realized an eel was ahead, the one that had swam past her earlier.

The creature moved languidly, not noticing or caring she was behind it, gliding through the water. And its tail was within grasping range. She didn't think twice. Refused to second-guess herself. Closing the distance between them, she grasped the eel by the tail with both hands, locking her grip and gritting her teeth.

The eel jerked and twisted in surprise. It flicked its tail, trying to dislodge the annoyance, but she held on tight. She could not let go now. She would never reach the surface if she did. The eel wriggled forward, building up speed, dragging her behind it. It bounced off the walls, Sorcha hitting one and then another, bruises building and beginning to ache.

There was no way to know which direction the eel was moving. She had no idea if it would take her farther into the maze or out. She hoped it would be out, out into the high-domed room, out beyond the doors where she could fight her way to the surface. But the walls all looked the same, the intersections unfamiliar.

She had not prayed to the Saint since her city had been razed to the ground. She had not prayed to him since she'd seen her family kill themselves—slit wrists and throats, blood pooling beneath their cooling bodies. She had watched them one by one, blood flowing over the altar, soaking into the hem of her dress. No prayers, no pleas, her heart silent even as she'd placed her hands on the relics in the Traveling City.

Now, she prayed. She begged that the Saint would carry her through this. She prayed the eel would take her in the direction she needed to go, through the darkness and into the light, into the room with the wriggling, writhing knot of eels, until she could go up and up and pull air into her lungs.

Please, she asked, repeating it. *Please.*

There was nothing else she could add—nothing more important. It was nothing like the formal chants, nothing like the words she'd memorized from the scriptures. Not organized or filled with piety and reverence. The word was raw, torn from the ache expanding at the center of her being, coming from the hollowness of her bones.

Please, please, please.

Closing her eyes, she concentrated on the way the single word flowed through her mind and body. One word would have to be enough. When she opened her eyes, the eel was dragging her into the huge domed room, swimming through the open double doors of the building and out onto the boulevard covered in waving water plants.

Pain throbbed in her throat and lungs, every muscle aching. The eel twisted, spun in a circle, thrashing until Sorcha released it. She hung for a moment in the water plants, suspended within the drowned city, aching and dying by the second.

Then she remembered to kick toward the surface.

Chapter Sixteen

The water around her was dim, and when she broke through the lake's surface, thunder crashed through the sky, vibrating in her eardrums and lodging in her teeth. Lightning raced after it, rain pelting down, hitting her face. It blurred her vision and drove her back down. She coughed and gasped, thrashing, drawing on whatever strength was left to turn and find the shore.

Sorcha tried to gauge where she'd surfaced, finally figuring out the lakeshore was behind her. It was a few hundred yards away, and there, waiting on the rocks, was Adrian. His posture changed when he spotted her, but she couldn't see his face clearly. Briefly, she wondered if there would be relief there. Lacus said Adrian had called for her like a lover. But what did monsters know of love?

As she swam, the wind picked up to whistle in her ears, howling and cold, pushing waves toward the shore. She struggled and fought to keep moving, the fatigue in her muscles intensifying. If she stopped, she'd never make it.

The storm churned overhead, dark clouds gathering and settling low over the water as more rain fell. Thunder rumbled, shivering through the water.

Reaching the shore was the only thing that mattered. The rest she could worry about after solid ground was beneath her feet. A shout caught her attention—her name or a word, she couldn't be sure—and Adrian waded out into the water to meet her. Something that might have been anxiousness colored his features, and her heart leaped, pushing her forward.

"Sorcha," Adrian spoke gently. "You're safe."

Adrian pulled her out of the water, arms so tight around her it hurt —his hands large and warm on her body. Sorcha clung to him, pressing her face into his neck and concentrating on how solid he was. *Safe.* He felt safe after everything that had happened beneath the surface of the lake. For a heart-stopping second, his mouth brushed her cheek as if he might press a kiss to her wet skin, but he didn't. Without saying anything else, he carried her through the shallows and up the rocky shore. The rain ceased as soon as they left the water, but the thunder continued to rumble, rocking across the sky.

Sorcha pulled out of Adrian's grasp as they reached the grass, landing on her hands and knees. She coughed up more water, trying to catch her breath and working to ignore the way every muscle in her body screamed with exhaustion, the way it pounded behind her eyes as a headache slammed into her.

The feeling of failure broke over her, a drowning force as powerful as the pull of the water. She'd been unable to reach the relic, and there was no way they could continue without it. She'd have to go back and convince Lacus to change his mind. But he'd already refused to help, so how would he react if she returned?

Wrapping her arms around herself, shivering with fatigue, Sorcha closed her eyes. Scents of late fall filled her lungs—pine trees and dead leaves—winter creeping farther south and closer every day. Her skin prickled with it, gooseflesh rising along her arms and legs, jaw clenched in an effort to keep her teeth from chattering. She'd almost drowned down there in the dark, lost in a sunken city with no way out, and then dragged to freedom by an eel. The terror of it sang through her body, a high, bright chord that thrummed in her muscles.

I could have died down there. I almost did.

She'd been so close, her desire to find the relic and resurrect the Saint at war with the building fear of what that meant. The Empire of the White Snake wanted him, the priests and priestesses were waiting somewhere in death to be recalled, and Sorcha had yet to truly accept what any of that meant.

More than anything, she wanted something to drive it all away—to silence the ringing and drive it from her mind. She wanted to be held. She sucked in a sharp breath, overtaken by the sudden desire to have someone pull her into their arms. She wanted someone to kiss away the sobs that threatened to rise from her chest in an unstoppable storm.

She wanted Adrian.

"Sorcha." When she turned, he held out his black cloak, light sliding across the surface of the silver wolf clasp. "Take this."

The clothes she wore, what little remained, were plastered to her skin—every line of her body visible. Adrian stepped forward when she didn't move, shaking out the cloak and sweeping it around her shoulders. The action stopped her shivering, the cold of her skin heating suddenly at his nearness. His black-gloved hand brushed her skin, and more warmth radiated outward from his light touch.

Holding her breath, Sorcha reached out and placed her hand flat on his chest. She kept her gaze on her fingers, her skin wrinkled after being submerged for so long. Beneath her palm, his chest rose and fell, and his heart was pounding. Slowly, she raised her eyes, caught on his perfect mouth and the muscle jumping in his clenched jaw.

Desire uncoiled in her stomach, spreading greedy tendrils through her body, warming her breasts and lower belly. Death and desire. She'd seen how people reacted to it. Remembered how she'd reacted in the past. The urge to feel alive when others were gone, when faced with mortality. Any second, she could die—she almost had—but right now, she was alive. And Adrian wanted her—she knew it in her heart—and with each breath he took, he was that much closer to giving in.

Did she want him, or did she just want to feel alive? She let out a breath and curled her fingers into his black tunic, remembering the clean lines of his body, the muscles and scars. Pulling in a shaky breath, she stepped closer, aware of where their bodies touched, a flush creeping up her cheeks.

"What are you doing?" he asked, the question low.

He didn't move, hands loose at his sides. But he breathed raggedly, and she imagined he leaned into her touch.

Sorcha met his gaze, seeing nothing but the careful expression he wore. Disinterest or disdain, she couldn't be sure which. No warmth. No answering desire. His jaw was clenched, lips thinning as she watched.

He didn't want her.

She removed her hand and stepped back on shaky legs. She'd been so sure before. Now she felt like a fool for crossing every boundary she had to touch a man she despised. She did despise him, didn't she? Emotions coursed through her. She hated him. Loathed him. Feared him. Wanted nothing at all to do with him. And yet, she'd been the one to reach out, to touch him. To *want* him.

"I don't know why I did that," she said, heart racing.

"You've called me a monster." Adrian's voice was soft, his eyes half-lidded now, jaw unclenched.

"You are." Her words were firm, but beneath them lay a shadow of another emotion—did he sense it? She felt as if it were written all over her face.

When you look at me, I see fire in your eyes.
And I want to burn.

Sorcha took another step back, slipping on the edge of the cloak before turning toward the distant camp. Adrian could see Domenico and Thompson sitting near the fire with their backs to them. Magnus and Ivo were with the horses. The others were out of sight in their tents or hunting. There was no sign of Revenant.

Adrian clenched his hands at his sides, the leather gloves stretching tight over his knuckles. Slowly, he released his grip, focused on the woman walking away from him. *Sorcha.*

If he said her name, would that tentative expression return? Had she known what she was asking? The silent question between them, had she realized what she'd offered? He couldn't want her. Couldn't even let himself think about it. About the warmth of her beneath him, her sighs in his mouth, the moment he could consume every inch of her skin.

If he didn't scare her, she would touch him again, and then he would never be able to say no. Without thinking, Adrian closed the distance between them. He came up behind her and slipped an arm around her waist, jerking her back into his body. She was delicate, shivering as he ran a gloved hand up her neck to tilt her head back against his chest. He lowered his mouth to her ear, brushing his lips against her soft skin, and breathed her in—damp and cold, a woman made of water and winter in his arms. He exhaled, enjoying the way she trembled, his body stirring with desire.

"Is this what you want, Sorcha? A monster in your bed?" She didn't move, rigid in his arms now. He stroked her throat, tilting her head to the side, exposing more tender flesh. He lowered his voice, tightness filling his groin, each breath coming more quickly. "Between your thighs?"

Sorcha's heart raced, pulse pounding against his fingers on her throat, the warmth of her seeping through the leather gloves.

Adrian slid the hand gripping her waist up, brushing the swell of one breast, and satisfaction coursed through him when a breathy sigh rushed out of her. It took everything he had not to rip the thin, damp cotton clinging to her breasts and thighs. He wanted to strip her down and kneel before her, wanted her hands to tangle in his hair as he drove her over a cliff and into white-hot release.

But that would be a mistake.

"Go back to camp," Adrian said, letting her go—turning her loose.

For a moment, she swayed on her feet, head turned a fraction of an inch in his direction.

Go, he thought, willing her to move. *Or I won't give you a choice.*

His gut twisted, anger spiking through him. He hated himself for touching what he could never have, for letting desire take control.

Finally, Sorcha stumbled away, slipping on the damp grass and clutching his cloak to her waist. He watched her, waiting until the firelight touched her—catching in her damp hair—her figure haloed in warmth.

Magnus watched her silently as she made her way to the tent they shared.

Adrian let out a breath, scrubbing his hands over his face. There would be questions. Sorcha hadn't brought the relic back, and they'd have to decide to try for it again or move on. He wasn't sure he could watch her disappear into the lake again. But he would never go against the commands of his prince.

———

The night had been long. Sorcha had slept with her back to him, her soft, even breathing filling his head. There had been almost no space between them. He could have touched her; he could have rolled her beneath him and forced her to open for him. To take something she'd almost offered. But that would be a mistake. She'd clouded his thoughts so much already. The desire to touch her, to feel her mouth on his, to touch every part of her, was a dangerous distraction.

Adrian had risen before the sun and began to break camp as soon as it was light enough to see. It wasn't long before the others were awake and taking care of their tents and horses, preparing for the long ride south.

Sorcha woke as the cooking fire was put out. A bowl of cooling porridge on a canvas stool outside the tent for her. She'd reached out for it—a long bare arm visible for a moment—and retreated to the interior to eat in peace.

He hadn't rushed her, letting her eat and prepare for the day at her own pace. The men were impatient, rechecking the bundles on their horses, stepping away to take care of personal needs one last time.

Finally, Sorcha emerged from the tent wearing head-to-toe crimson —a simple riding dress and her fur-lined cloak, the soft red leather gloves in one hand. He glanced at her, taking in her dark, loose hair around her shoulders, and vibrant green eyes. She tended to wear her hair in a loose knot at the base of her skull or wrapped in a scarf beneath the hood she kept up to shadow her face as they rode.

"We'll go south and west from here." Thompson waved two rolled maps—one in each hand—as he came to stand beside Adrian. "There are no caves marked on the map created over the last year by the prince's cartographers. But her skin promises it will be there."

Her skin.

Adrian hated the idea that this map was a part of her—a part everyone in the party consulted and referenced at all times. *Mine.* The thought shocked him. She wasn't his, far from it, and this was just another example of his private desires crossing over into the life he'd chosen as the prince's personal killer. There was no room for her in the decisions he needed to be making as the Wolf.

He turned, positive he felt her gaze—warm between his shoulder blades—but her eyes were somewhere else.

"Lacus!" Sorcha called, dropping her gloves and running for the lake's edge.

Adrian moved toward her, wanting to stop her from returning to the water. If she slipped beneath the surface again, he knew she wouldn't survive. But even as that fear expanded in his chest, it died.

A creature made of stone was rising above the surface, holding the golden bones of the Saint.

An arm attached to a hand, gold and covered in jewels. The rising sun caught it, piercing through the trees in shafts of warm light. A bird stopped singing; the wind died down.

The creature held it out for her to take, and he could see from here that she was crying. Tears slid down her cheeks, catching in the morning light. He was too far away to hear what they said to each other—their voices disguised by the lap of water on the shore. When she smiled, it sliced through him, leaving him gasping, a knot of anger and frustration in his chest that it wasn't him she was smiling for.

"Prince Eine will be pleased we didn't have to drown his witch to get the bone," Revenant said, adjusting his sword belt. Adrian made a noise of agreement without taking his gaze from Sorcha. Revenant pulled his gloves on and asked, "Are you?"

Adrian broke his gaze away from the strange pair at the water's edge, turning to his second-in-command with a question in his mouth. But he stopped, finding Revenant's eyes intent and fiercely cold.

"Is everyone ready? There will be several days of travel ahead before we reach the sea."

"Packed and ready." Revenant jerked his chin at the strange pair by the water. "As soon as the witch brings that cursed bone here."

"Unpack the velvet for the relic."

Revenant nodded and turned back to where the rest of the men were double-checking their gear before mounting up. Domenico was already unpacking the velvet and canvas sacks they'd brought with them to transport the relics. The others watched the stone creature with flat expressions—neither curious nor disbelieving. A few had hands on the hilts of their swords, but no one moved to draw their weapons.

They all watched as the creature disappeared into the lake, and Sorcha walked slowly up the rocky beach toward them. Magnus and Domenico met her with the velvets. She hesitated before passing the relic to them, hands lingering even as they stepped away from her. His heart beat more quickly when she began picking her way toward him, tears lingering on her cheeks, face flushed.

"How far until the next relic?" she asked, moving past him without stopping.

"A few days' ride," he said, falling into step behind her.

"Maybe this next one won't try to kill me."

Adrian didn't respond. Each location so far had been dangerous. Even the pieces they'd collected before finding the oracle had come with a price. Not for a moment did he believe it would get easier from here.

Abruptly, Sorcha stopped, her back straight, shoulders pulled back, resignation and determination in every line of her body. She let out a sigh before glancing at him over her shoulder.

"But you won't let anything hurt me." Her words were flat and matter of fact. "The prince doesn't want me dead yet."

It was a statement, not a question. Her tone was soft, and he would have missed it if she'd not turned toward him ever so slightly.

No, he wouldn't let anything hurt her. But not because the prince wished it to be so.

Chapter Seventeen

The relic was wrapped in layer after layer of black velvet and heavy wool blankets. It was then tied to a riderless horse that Domenico led. Sorcha could feel him—the Saint. He was there, traveling with them, awareness tickling behind her eyes and gathering in the hollow places in her body—between her ribs, in the chambers of her heart, in the emptiness of her stomach.

When they stopped to rest, she was drawn to him, unable to keep away—not wanting to keep away. At night, the relic was placed in its own shelter, a smaller tent erected in the center of their little camp. But as much as she was compelled to be near the Saint, she was thankful the relic was not in the tent she shared with Adrian.

If he'd offered—which he hadn't done—she still would have chosen to keep it elsewhere.

———

The clean, salty scent of the ocean reached them first. Sorcha had never seen the Prates Ocean. It was another of those things Kahina Kira had promised would happen. Before war had overrun the continent and the pilgrimage to visit each relic had been postponed.

Now she leaned forward into the salty wind, body thrumming with the relentless energy of the waves beating and wearing away the cliffs, calling to her, singing an endless song. She'd had the urge to leap forward into it, longing for cold water and pressure. Would she be dashed against the rocks? Or would the wind carry her away? A surprising thought, coming from the dark space in her mind where the suspicion of how this all would end lurked.

"Don't," Adrian said, grabbing her arm.

"What if I jumped?"

Sorcha hadn't heard him come to stand beside her—at the edge of it all. She didn't look at him at first, but when he didn't respond right away, she glanced at him. He was watching her, something without a name crossing his face, then he looked down at the churning water.

"I would have to follow you."

"Because you need the Saint," she said, a faint smile touching her lips—bittersweet and hinting at deeper emotion.

Adrian didn't respond, and she took a few steps away, walking along the cliff, searching the horizon for ships and the hint of Biser Islands the maps promised would be there. She couldn't see either, and the wind whipped her hair around her face, obscuring her vision and whistling in her ears.

Was it desire or desperation that brought his voice to her? The words punched a hole in her chest, leaving a space for the wind to sing through, leaving her breathless. Sorcha didn't turn, couldn't, but continued forward because she had no idea how she might react if she saw Adrian's expression.

Because I can't go on without you.

———

Sea caves dotted all along the shore. A handful were on the map Thompson held, but the map copied from her skin only showed one. Slowly, they matched landmark to landmark and followed the changing cliffs, hesitating if a section had fallen into the sea, trying to decipher how the change affected what they were searching for.

Finally, they found the location—after a heated debate between

Thompson and Domenico over the spot. In the end, Domenico's certainty that he could feel magic in the rocks won out. Ivo, Bran, and Cas had then disappeared into the scrubby, wind-whipped woods to cut down small trees and fashion a rough support system to lower her down.

Sorcha watched them from a camp stool with her hood pulled up around her face—buffeted by the wind, low gray clouds, and the thick fog rolling in from the sea. The horses were staked to a line much farther back, sheltered in a little copse of trees. Right now, Sorcha wished she was with them, wrapped in her sleeping furs and not about to be dropped down the side of an enormous cliff.

The men talked as they worked, and she caught a word here and there. *Witch. Monster. Saint. Wolf. Oracle. Crimson Cult. White Snake. Black Tomeis.* No one spoke to her directly. But they never did, and Sorcha didn't expect them to start now. She wondered, not for the first time, why they feared her so much. There was no magic in her heart or body, or rather, she'd never considered the visions to be magical. The Black Tomeis felt differently.

Adrian sat closer to the tree line with Magnus and Thompson, the three studying a map she hadn't seen before. Would it be the southern-most section of the continent? In her studies, she'd learned about the civilizations that had once thrived there—ancient and now diminished. There had been rich lands and powerful kings, tyrannical queens and legends about creatures that lived beneath the sands of the great deserts and in the water off the shores.

Now those places were mostly abandoned, a home to a few who wished to live their lives without a king or empress leading them. Sorcha wondered what they would find there. She had no doubt they'd continue south—her skin carried indications of mountains and deserts yet to be discovered.

Cas whistled, getting Adrian's attention and waving him over. The wooden frame that would lower her down was complete. They'd used every rope they carried to lash it together or create a makeshift harness to hold her. It didn't appear to be very sturdy. But Sorcha would need to trust them.

Trepidation built inside her, gaining momentum and threatening to overtake everything. Sorcha both feared and wanted to find this next relic. To bring more pieces of him together, to see the Saint as the illuminated pages and mosaics had depicted him. What would she find in the cave? What piece of him would she uncover? And what would she have to face?

"Take this," Adrian said, holding out a sheathed dagger.

Sorcha took it, recognizing the blade. It was the one she'd taken from his tent and used to defend herself in the forest that night so many weeks ago. She hadn't seen it since. It was impossible to hide much when they traveled with so little—speed was more important than comfort. Holding the weapon now felt so right, as if it were tied to her with invisible threads.

"Thank you," she said, unsheathing it and turning the blade so it caught the light. "I'm surprised you're letting me have this."

"Should I be worried you'll try to stab me?"

No, I might try to kiss you instead. Heat fanned across her cheeks with the thought, and her breath caught as he motioned for her to come toward him. She went, thankful to be in the shelter of his body and blocked from the wind for a moment.

"Where will you keep the dagger?" he asked, running his gaze over the riding dress and thick tights she wore. Adrian twitched her skirt, the red fabric snapping out in the wind. "Do you want to remove this? It could get tangled."

"It's cold." Sorcha lifted her skirt and tucked the sheathed blade into the right calf-high boot she wore. After stamping her feet to make sure it wouldn't move, she let her skirt drop back into place. "See?"

"And if you lose it?"

"I won't."

"Are you so sure?" he asked, gesturing her to hold her arms up. "Come here, I'll tie this around your waist."

Adrian tied the rope around her waist, each movement quick and efficient, no trembling hands or furtive looks. He kept his eyes on the rope, checking the knot and nodding to Magnus and Ivo as they tested the wooden support arm that would ease her off the cliff edge. They promised it was sturdy, but even as Sorcha watched, it swayed in the wind, blurred by fog and mist that was quickly becoming rain.

"Lantern and flint. Do you know how to use these?" Adrian asked, holding them up.

"Yes."

"Will you be able to if your hands are cold and shaking?"

Sorcha lifted one shoulder. "I won't have a choice."

Adrian nodded, handing them to her. Sorcha fumbled with the length of rope, her cold hands clumsy. Without a word, he stepped forward and took the lantern, then secured it to her body. He pressed the flint into her hand, his touch gentle and his gloved index finger making a small circle on her palm. Her hands looked so small in his, pale against the black leather.

"Where are your gloves?" he asked, voice soft, the wind whipping it away.

"What?" Sorcha was confused by the tone and needed a moment to digest the flurry of emotions and sensations his touch brought to the surface.

Any time he touched her, he wore gloves. There had been times—like when he'd dipped his hand into her bath—that he hadn't been wearing them. But whenever there was a real chance of skin-to-skin contact, he touched her wearing gloves.

"For your hands. It will help with the rope."

"Oh," she said, handing the flint back to pat a lump in her pocket. She pulled the crimson leather gloves free, quickly slipping them on.

She glanced around, eyes briefly coming into contact with Revenant. Hate. Pure and burning, and evident in the fists clenched at his side. Sorcha shivered, bringing her gaze back to Adrian.

"Put this in your pocket," Adrian said, holding the flint out until she took it. "We're going to wrap another section around your thighs to take some of the pressure off your waist. It will be more like a harness that way. When you reach the cave, you can loosen it around your hips, but don't remove it completely unless you are absolutely positive you can tie these knots again."

"What if the rope isn't long enough?"

"It will be." Adrian adjusted the rope, accepting another length from Thompson, who glanced at her and away with an air of indifference.

Sorcha stood with her arms out as Adrian adjusted the harness.

"And it will be strong enough to pull both myself and the relic back up?"

"Yes."

"You sound so sure." Sorcha snorted. "What if you drop me?"

Adrian paused, eyes resting on her before moving back to the rope—continuing to test the knots. "I won't let you fall, Sorcha."

"I almost drowned in the lake," Sorcha whispered, not sure if she was reminding him or herself.

"But you won't here," Adrian said.

Sorcha scoffed. "Only because the fall would kill me first."

Even now, several days later, she wasn't sure how she felt about Lacus and the lake. What she truly wanted was for things to return to how they'd been before the Empire of the White Snake had moved west and south. She wanted Ines to gossip with and Kahina Kira to help interpret dreams and Rohan to answer questions about the tattoos he had planned for her. She wanted to read all the books and scrolls in the library, wanted to read the most secret of them, and come to truly understand her place in the temple. As the oracle. The vessel. If she went on, collecting the relics at the behest of Prince Eine, then it was possible her friends and family would return.

But at what cost?

Sorcha followed Adrian to the cliff edge, holding her breath.

"Ready?" Adrian asked, ready to let her go, to drop her. "Hold on."

Sorcha nodded, looking down and touching the rope around her waist and thighs with the lantern tied to it—checking and double-checking. She met his gaze and searched for the man who'd whispered shattering words into the wind, hoping they'd take them away, that they wouldn't linger between them. She was sure now he hadn't meant for her to hear him.

Heart pounding, stomach in her feet, she let them swing her out. Rain misted her hair and face, the wind blowing up her skirt as she hung over the rocks below. With a creak of wood and rope, the Black Tomeis began to lower her.

Adrian stood at the cliff edge and fed out one of the guiding ropes, eyes following her down. But his expression gave her nothing.

———

Sorcha bumped against the cliff face, scraping her shoulder, and small stones tumbled away into the waves below. It was a boiling pot she would never come out of if she was dropped into it. Wind whistled in her ears, drowning out everything else, even the churning water below. It cried and wailed against her, against this intrusion, warning her away.

But she had to go on. There was a cave, and within that cave lay a relic—the Saint. She would retrieve it, pull him out of his hiding place, and into the light of day.

Above, Adrian and his Black Tomeis waited, silent and suspicious, stony faces unreadable. They watched to see if she would succeed or fail, fall or rise triumphant from the sea. And what did Adrian watch for?

Adrian.

Sorcha felt the change between them in her gut. The path they were on was beginning to alter. It wasn't the straight-and-narrow way Prince Eine had laid out before them any longer. But she wasn't sure yet. All she knew was how she felt, the suspicion, an edge, a hint, a whisper. A soft murmur that, if she listened too closely, would vanish. Yet it was there, at the edge of her consciousness, this feeling that Adrian was tied to it all.

Sorcha bumped slowly down the cliff, jerking to a halt, the rope slipping. She cried out, the wind whipping her voice away. For a moment, she thought there was an answering cry from overhead. She lifted her face to the sky as the misting rain intensified. A bank of fog rolled over the cliff edge, gliding toward her in a wall of soft white. She gripped the rope with two red-gloved hands. It engulfed her, bringing a deafening silence and wrapping her in a cloud heavily scented with evergreen and a hint of dampened campfires.

One breath and then another passed while she twisted at the end of the rope, suspended in a world of white. It morphed and swirled around her, shapes forming and blurring, her mind turning the nothingness into faces.

The rope creaked, and she dropped several feet, her stomach free-falling. Then she saw the mouth of the cave below her—a narrow opening, barely large enough to squeeze into.

"Stop!" Sorcha called up, still falling. "Stop!"

The rope jerked to a halt, and she swung back and forth. The lantern was unlit. She would have to scramble in the darkness, light it, and hope it would stay lit. She had no idea what the cave might contain. There was a relic there, and that was all that mattered, but no hint of what might protect it. She hoped it was the remote location and nothing more; the ocean and the cliff and the waves and the incessant wail of the wind fighting to blow her away. This was dangerous enough.

And yet, in each place they'd gone, there had been something—man or creature, monster and myth. The Saint had never been left alone. Each piece cared for, cherished in these out-of-the-way places. And waiting for her.

Reaching the opening, she stretched out a foot, scrambling for it. The wind caught her, twirling her away, sending her in an arc that brought her out farther across the water and rocks beneath. The taut rope creaked with her weight.

She was grateful again for the gloves, for the protection and warmth they provided. For Adrian insisting she wear them.

That was another thing, another part of the unconscious whisper at the back of her mind. Adrian recalling her from bleak visions in the night and riding beside her in the day, the hint of emotion in his black eyes.

She pushed it away and reached for the cave opening again as she swung back, foot catching on the lip and landing one hand against the stone. She gripped the rope with the other, fingers aching, fumbling for a firm hold.

Panting with the effort, cold with fear, she managed to get inside and tugged the rope to let them know she'd made it. She took several steps into the darkness, bringing the rope with her—a lifeline to the top of the cliff, to Adrian, to the world beyond this secret place.

After opening the lantern hatch, she fumbled with the flint. Orange sparks fell before it caught; light jumped, pale yellow with a tinge of blue at the edges. The wind howled at the cave mouth, frustrated with her escape, leaving her ears aching. She was free for the moment, her body filled with her pounding heart and gasping lungs. She took a breath and then another, closing her eyes and picturing the silent temple, the quiet of sunbeams with dust motes, the muted city beyond the walls.

She waited until her heart calmed, until breathing was easier, until the fear receded from her mind, before beginning down the passage.

———

The lantern light shone across the painted walls—the stone beneath smoothed to perfection, the paint bright even after countless years. It had been a time of peace. Each new section that was illuminated depicted prosperity and happy people. But Sorcha knew the Saint's life had also been filled with death and retribution. He'd brought vengeance with him, dealt out death to nonbelievers, and terrorized nations. But that had all been forgotten, his followers dwindling down to hundreds instead of thousands, his reach fading into history.

There were still believers, the faithful praying in temples, protecting his remains.

And she was one of them, wasn't she?

Then the colors changed, darker now, the tones richer. This was a new chapter of the Saint's life—a golden skeleton on a throne and riding into battle. A final battle filled a wall from floor to ceiling, an androgynous figure holding a burning sword high. The Saint fell and was broken apart, red-robed figures carrying away the pieces, disappearing into locations far and wide. She recognized the Golden Citadel and the sunken city right away, but there were other locations not tattooed on her skin.

Following the story, Sorcha held her breath as a line of worshippers came together. They carried the relics, moving in a single line across a barren landscape to an imposing stone tower.

The next section was an interior room with the relics laid out on an altar and a woman on the floor, a bright crimson flood flowing upward, converging on the relics.

Sorcha stopped, breathing heavily, with a hand to her chest—pressed flat to keep her heart in place. *Stay, you don't know for certain this is your future.*

But, of course, it was. She'd known this. Seen it in the night, been woken from this moment again and again by Adrian. For the first time in her life, she understood the visions without Kahina Kira.

The knowledge—excruciating truth—hurt as she swallowed tears.

Whatever the future held, she must continue. There was no true choice. She was the vessel.

Behind her, the wind called, rushing across the mouth of the cave but unable to reach her. The air was motionless inside, stale, with nothing but dry stone and the oil from the lantern to change the texture. The floor was smooth, flat stone—no rocks, no dirt, nothing. It looked as if it had been swept every day for hundreds of years. Even the paintings seemed bright and refreshed.

She paused, holding her breath to listen. An intense, watchful silence greeted her.

All hope that it had been the natural barriers protecting the Saint vanished. There was something else here.

But she had to keep going. There would be no returning without this piece, unless she untied the rope and ran straight out into the sea, plummeting to whatever lay beyond this life. But if she did, could she be sure the Saint wouldn't be there waiting for her?

The tunnel began to widen, easing open, the roof rising, the narrow path expanding. The lantern light fought to penetrate the darkness, the velvety pitch black that hadn't seen a light in countless years.

———

The cavern around her was vast. Darkness lurked beyond her circle of light, a hunter barely kept at bay. It swallowed her steps, soaking up her noise. She took a step and then another into the room, eyes going everywhere at once; the floor could drop away, or something could fall from the ceiling. A glint of light caught her eye, a richness so at odds with the surroundings.

A single rib bone encased in gold and encrusted with rubies glittered on a plinth.

It called to her, pulled her forward. A invisible wire attached to her ribs, a tether, an unbreakable line—an inescapable bond. A part of her rejoiced at the sight, the reason for her existence, the way that she belonged to the Saint and the way he belonged to her.

But what if what Lacus promised was true? The Saint would bring destruction and death. How could her family come back if all he brought was bleak horror? But the call of the rib bone was strong—imploring and sweet—whispering to her. The halo of light moved with her, around her. Her hand trembled slightly as her heart raced. Each piece that came together reminded her how close she was—what the prince had collected and now what she'd found.

Soon she would meet him.

Sorcha took another step forward and reached out tentatively to stroke the bone, jewels cool and bumpy beneath her fingertips. The sensation was electric—skin to gold, skin to bone, heart tied to this relic. But she hesitated to pick it up.

How would she be able to get herself and the bone up the cliff face in that wind? What if the rain had worsened? Or the fog was too thick? What if the rope snapped?

Stop it, she thought. *Don't borrow trouble.*

It made the most sense to tie the relic to the rope and have them pull it up first. If the relic slipped from her grip and fell into the sea—to the churning, angry waters beating relentlessly against the cliff—it would be gone forever. But if the bone went up first, there was a smaller chance of it being lost. Then the rope could be sent back down for her. They'd have to; they still needed her to find the other relics. The Black Tomeis wouldn't be facing any of these trials for the relics. Not even for their prince.

Holding her breath, Sorcha lifted the relic from the plinth, ten times as large as a normal rib bone, as if it belonged to an ancient prehistoric creature. But it did, didn't it? The Saint was an ancient creature.

A rustling sound broke the silence, and Sorcha froze.

It had only been her breathing and the sounds of boots on stone, the thrum of blood in her ears. There had been no other sounds. Even the wind had faded, abandoning her to the inner world of the cavern— lurking and sulky beyond its mouth.

In the dark, something rubbed against stone, a chink of pebbles falling. Almost not there, almost nonexistent. So faint for a moment, she wondered if her brain was playing tricks on her. If it was just her imagination wanting to fill the silence that pressed on her like slabs of ice.

But again, it came, the pattering fall of small rocks, a shift of sand.

Removing her hand from the rib bone, she stood breathless. Was this the moment she would meet whoever guarded the Saint?

She held the lantern higher and waited, counting heartbeats and wanting to speak but afraid to find out what might be there. Stepping away from the plinth, she moved toward the far wall, holding the lantern above her head. She walked until the light fell across the stone rising up and up, curving to where it must meet the unseen ceiling. But the light didn't reach that far.

She'd expected painted walls, but these were bare. Dark and polished to a high shine. They looked as if they'd been polished for centuries, smoothed over and over until all imperfection was rubbed away. The stone was so black it absorbed her light, the lantern flame unable to penetrate, barely even reflecting on the surface. It seemed to suck it up—all-consuming—despite the mirrored finish.

But something about it was changing. She reached out tentatively, worried about what contact might mean but unable to stop as she pressed her hand flat against the surface. As soon as her fingers connected, the stone began to crack, a hairline fracture shooting up from her palm. Others joined it, cracks spreading, connecting and branching off from each other. The surface began to crumble.

Stepping back quickly, she watched in horror as it continued to break apart and revealed what lay beneath. Something jerked, twisting free of the rock. Shards of the wall broke away, tumbling down to shatter against the cavern floor. A skeletal hand emerged—pale and polished—catching the light as if it too were gilded. Bones carved from mother-of-pearl. More sections of the wall crumbled, and another hand appeared. Then another.

They reached outward, grasping at thin air, fighting to be free as if the stone were not solid but thick, clinging mud. It released them reluctantly. Around the cavern, she heard other places crumbling, other cracks widening. Sharp cracks filled her head, ringing through her body. They beat against her skin and poured cold, hard fear down her spine.

As she watched, a shoulder blade emerged and a skeletal foot stepped out, the leg following. Then, a six-foot skeleton was struggling to pull its other leg and arm free. It turned to her, sockets full of shadows, so dark her lantern could not penetrate the hollows. It grinned at her, snapping pointed, serrated teeth, lunging and fighting to break free.

———

Sorcha's scream filled his ears, a piercing cry that seized his muscles, froze his blood.

"Pull me up! Pull me up!"

There was panic in her voice, so much fear the howling wind was incapable of sweeping it all away.

"Get her up!" he ordered Revenant and Thompson, and the others rushed to help.

They worked together, but he knew the moment he tugged the rope, it was too light. She wasn't on it. Panic brushed him, a lingering touch, a whisper at the back of his mind.

Sorcha, he pleaded. But he couldn't sort through the rest of his thoughts, the images flashing across his mind, her face, her hand on his chest, the feel of her quickening pulse against his fingertips. *Sorcha*.

"She's not on the rope," Thompson said.

"Keep pulling," Adrian responded, motioning with his hand.

The end of the rope slipped over the edge, and a golden bone bumped across the stone, muted in the half-light, hinting at the richness. It was a huge rib bone, the curve pronounced.

Working quickly, he undid the knot, and Domenico came forward with a length of velvet.

"Adrian!" she screamed again, a hoarse edge in the tone—terror and desperation.

He dropped the rope back over the side, hoping she'd catch it. Several long seconds—years of tense anticipation—passed. Wind wailed in his ears, carrying a drawn-out snarling, cry.

The rope jerked, then went taut—her weight on the other end.

They pulled on the rope again, but Sorcha swinging back and forth made it difficult for them to keep their grip. He pulled quickly, grunting with the speed and effort, while the men at his back took up the slack.

Finally, she crested the lip of the cliff, scrabbling for a handhold, searching for purchase on the bare stone.

"Hold on," he said, and he didn't know if it was to her or his men.

Moving quickly, he dropped the rope and reached for Sorcha, grabbing her wrists—fighting to get a better grip.

Her face was pale, with shallow scratches stretching from temple to ear. Blood was in her hair and snaking down her neck.

She trembled, and he pulled her into his arms, whispering against her hair. "I've got you."

Her blood was on his hands, on his armor, and when she looked up at him, his heart twisted. Fear and pain colored her features, but when she looked at him, relief washed over her gaze. He ran his hands over her shoulders, down her arms, and she winced. Her sleeves were damp with blood.

"What happened?" he asked, lifting her arms and inspecting them carefully.

They looked like bite wounds, ragged half-moons, but no flesh was missing, only punctures and nothing else. Pale sections of her skin could be glimpsed through ripped fabric; places he wanted to cover. He could smell the saltwater in her hair, and her cheeks were red with the biting cold rolling in from the water. The urge to pull her against him, hide her from the world swept through him.

"We need to leave this place," she whispered. "I don't know if they can climb."

"Who?"

"The things that guarded the relic. Please." She touched his chest. "We need to leave."

The heat of her hand warmed his skin, sending a shudder down his spine. Her touch was like being branded by fire, each time, again and again. He wanted to make her feel safe. He wanted to find out what her touch felt like on his bare skin.

Adrian gestured to Revenant to pack up. Thompson and Ivo lingered, studying Sorcha's wounds from a distance. Revenant, Ivo,

Bran, and Domenico watched the edge of the cliff with their hands on their swords.

A mad chattering filled the air, rising above the crashing waves and punishing wind. Sorcha glanced behind her, wide eyed and poised to run.

"*Now*," she whispered, clutching his arm. "We leave now or we die in this place."

CHAPTER EIGHTEEN

They rode through the night—under a crescent moon, the golden star blazing on the horizon—before stopping to set up camp. Sorcha was surprised that the small tent she'd shared with Adrian so far expanded to create a much larger space. The walls were thinner, not doubled over to keep the cold at bay. And with fabric stretched as tight as it could go, the interior was large enough for them both to stand comfortably.

The bites throbbed and were painful and swollen, but they weren't as bad as the fear had been. Watching those creatures come out of the walls, as if they hadn't been solid stone only moments before, had been a waking nightmare. She could live with the pain of the bites—and the scarring—as long as she didn't see those creatures again.

Sorcha stayed with Epona long after Adrian had overseen the camp being set up—it looked as all the others had. A central campfire with tents gathered around it in two circles. Adrian's tent was in the inner circle, but with enough room all around to give Sorcha an illusion of privacy.

The Tomeis ignored her for the most part. Occasionally, she felt the pressure of observation, but no one would ever meet her gaze except for

Revenant. He watched her with that unnerving silent malice. Sorcha could never hold his gaze for long.

"Your tent is up." Ivo reached out to pat Epona's flank. "Adrian is looking for you."

Sorcha turned to him, surprised he was addressing her at all. But then, maybe Adrian had sent him to find her. Ivo had been a kind of personal guard in the moments when Adrian left her alone. But he'd never spoken to her. Epona's ears pricked in his direction, and she turned a curious eye toward him.

He was a short man with pale eyes and a weatherworn face. Burn scars marred his hands, the flesh deep red and gnarled. But she felt no warmth or comradery with him beside her. Would he protect her because Prince Eine demanded it? Or because Adrian expected it? Toren's warning surfaced: *These men would kill you if they could.*

"Why don't you address each other with titles?"

The question was out before she could stop herself. Epona snorted, bumping Sorcha with her nose as if even she knew it was stupid to ask such personal questions. To her surprise, Ivo remained, watching her thoughtfully. She raised her hand to apologize, to tell him he didn't have to share any kind of information when he spoke.

"Adrian has never demanded it. He knows who he is. We know who we are. To those outside our circle, he is the Wolf, and we are the Black Tomeis." Ivo shrugged as if this had all been settled long ago and her questions were ignorant.

"Thank you," she said with a nod, giving Epona one last affectionate pat before heading for her tent.

———

The pressure of the relics—their nearness, the expectation—was almost overwhelming. The tent housing them was set up near Domenico again. The man sat before them as if on guard. But from whom? Were they worried she'd try to ride off with them? Or that someone would appear to claim them?

Sorcha wanted to touch them again, to search for that connection she'd felt fleetingly at times. It had ebbed and flowed, a voice growing louder, a whisper becoming a shout—a command—demanding things she could not yet understand. But a large part of herself, the one growing stronger day by day, never wanted to speak the Saint's name again.

To her surprise, Adrian was waiting for her at their tent, holding the flap open so she could pass beneath it. She did so, brushing past him, so aware of him she couldn't breathe.

"You need to clean and dress those bites," Adrian said, pausing at the tent flap. "I'll be back with hot water."

Sorcha nodded and pulled at the high neck of her dress, ready to peel it off and get clean. She turned to her pack, where a change of clothes was beside her rolled furs. Adrian had placed them there, opposite his own things. As he always did. Thoughtfully, Sorcha removed her gloves and boots and placed them beside the items.

Slowly, she began to remove the layers of clothing, wincing with pain. The bites hurt, but they were only a part of the whole—each muscle and bone was sore from riding for weeks on end. The last time she'd seen a real bed was the Traveling City. And a true bath. Sorcha would have crossed hot coals if there were a real tub on the other side.

———

Adrian paused as he entered the tent. Sorcha stood with her back to him, showing an expanse of bare skin dotted with purple bruises. Her rich brown hair hung over her shoulder and swept across her bare shoulders, the rest of it clutched to her chest. He could see several bites, but none of them looked serious—puncture wounds that were no longer bleeding. Painful, yes, but not infected that he could see. She hadn't been clear about what had been in the cave. What kind of creature would leave a mark like that? He'd ask her again when she was clean and had eaten.

"There will be food soon," he said, setting the small pail of warm water near the brazier. "I don't know whose turn it is to cook."

Sorcha snorted.

Everyone disliked Bran's cooking, but it didn't matter. They would all eat it. The Black Tomeis lived their whole lives at the behest of Prince

Eine. That meant rarely staying in one place, with most meals thrown together while they conquered cities or beheaded kings. None of the group enjoyed cooking, so they all took turns.

"Thank you for the water," she said, glancing at him.

Adrian watched as Sorcha turned to him, drinking in the sight of her. Even worn out and tired with several frightening bite marks, she was the most beautiful woman he'd ever seen. He vividly remembered the empress when the empire claimed she was the most beautiful woman alive or dead. He'd been in the court when a princess from the Biser Islands to the east had been presented, the most famous beauty in her father's court. There had been others. Prince Eine's court was full of women revered for their looks—pretty faces and cunning eyes.

He'd felt nothing for anyone for so long.

Until Sorcha.

His hands felt white-hot at the idea of touching her, and he wanted to place his bare hands on her skin, wanted to feel her against him. He watched as she carefully moved the skirt of her riding dress to reveal a pale thigh.

The tattoo he'd seen before was gone.

"When did that happen?" he asked.

Sorcha hesitated and then shrugged. "As soon as I touched the relic."

"How do you know?"

"I don't," she admitted with a sigh. She cocked her head to the side, staring into the middle distance. "I thought—" But she stopped and shook her head.

"What?" Adrian prompted.

"Maybe there was a tingle? Or burn? But maybe I'm imagining it now that I know what the result is." Sorcha shrugged, seeming disappointed with her inability to answer definitively.

"And no one told you it would happen?"

"Maybe they didn't know. Maybe they didn't think it was relevant. Maybe I would have found out later." She dropped her skirt and smoothed it down, running her hands across the fabric.

He wanted to lift her skirt over her thighs, watch her face to see if she would refuse or encourage him. He wanted to bury his face in her soft flesh, feel her tremble and weave her fingers into his hair. He wanted to know what sounds she made when she came.

His mouth went dry.

"None of the books talked about this. None of the books I've seen, at least. I think that as we collect the pieces of the Saint, as it comes together, the tattoos will continue to vanish. There's no reason for them to stay, for me to have them, once he's alive."

———

The paintings in the cave flashed before Sorcha—blood and gold, rubies and sharp knives. An army of skeletal vampires was coming for her, mouths agape, bare bony fingers clutching. Sorcha shivered. The Saint would live, but she would not. That much had been clear. A blood sacrifice must be made—an exchange.

There was one tattoo on her hip—where the bones connected femur to hip—that she'd kept hidden from the Mapmaker. No one had seen it, and she didn't intend to share it. She was struggling to accept the only thing she'd been raised to do. But what if there were a different way? What if it just required blood and not her life? Could there be somebody else who could lie down beside the Saint and accept the blade? Could there be someone else who could give the Saint the humanity he desired?

She didn't know.

She wished there had been more lessons. She wished she'd been more determined and curious, had pushed to know more. There had been so many days spent frivolously going to the perfumer's market and spending time with her friends, nights running through the city, sipping wine, and laughing. There had been so much time for her to go to the library or sit in the inner temple, time to seek out Kahina Kira or Rohan and beg for the answers to the questions now lodged in her chest like arrows.

But she hadn't.

A few months ago, she would have said she knew everything necessary for her position in the Aureum Sanctus. Every piece of history attached to the vessel. Sorcha had made too many assumptions. Now she understood she was merely the sacrificial lamb.

Adrian studied her. They stood close together—she could have reached out and touched him. Sorcha was so aware of him, his nearness in the space, and how badly she wanted to bridge the gap between them. If her time was limited—if the whole world was going to end—would it really matter if she took something for herself? Something she desperately wanted?

Without hesitation, moving before she could second-guess herself, she threw her arms around Adrian's neck and pulled his face down to her.

His hands remained at his sides, his eyes locked on her face.

"Kiss me," she whispered, watching his mouth. Then louder. "Kiss me."

Adrian's face was blank, his dark eyes giving nothing away. He didn't lift a hand to touch her.

Each breath came quicker as she waited for him to make a choice. *Kiss me.* She willed him to move, to place his hands on her body, to engulf her senses.

But he remained motionless.

Sorcha laughed, releasing him—returning the borrowed moment of intimacy. Embarrassment burned in her cheeks but left her insides cold. Of course he wasn't going to kiss her. He'd turned her down once already at the edge of the lake—tried to scare her into never touching him again. Nothing had changed. She closed her eyes, shivering with the memory of his black-gloved hand on her throat.

Do you want a monster in your bed?

Yes.

She shook the thought away, but it was replaced with the flash of Adrian in the dark at the ruined temple when he'd held her so close and promised to protect her from all the other monsters in the world. Each dream, each nightmare, held his shadowy figure, his hand outstretched and waiting. But she couldn't force him to take something he didn't want. Because of duty. Loyalty.

Adrian's hand clamped on her shoulder, and he jerked her back against his chest. Sorcha yelped in surprise. He brought his hand over her mouth—bare palm to mouth—as his other hand slid around her waist. His lips brushed her ear, and she shivered, nipples tightening, stomach dropping away in a rush.

"Sorcha." Adrian's voice was rough—full of tension. "Be quiet."

A rush of blood filled her ears, leaving a buzz and throb as the hand over her mouth slid down. He took his time, pressed against her, following the curve of her throat. She gripped his arm and squeezed her eyes shut as he paused, praying to everything holy and unholy in the world that he wouldn't stop.

He spun her around, leaving her dizzy with movement, eyes still shut. The night sounds beyond the canvas disappeared. Nothing mattered more than his hands on her and the way she melted into him, ready and willing to accept damnation.

"Open your eyes."

Sorcha did, but couldn't bring herself to meet his gaze, afraid suddenly that she would see rejection there despite the desire radiating from him. She trembled, longing and anticipation warming her veins. Adrian slid a hand into her hair and jerked her head back, forcing her to meet his gaze.

She gasped, and the moment she opened her mouth, he kissed her.

The world narrowed down to his mouth on hers, with one hand on her backside and the other still in her hair. His tongue swept across her bottom lip and into her mouth, forcing her to open for him. A whimper escaped her throat, and he groaned, tightening his grip on her.

The world stopped as she clung to him. Everything in her body screamed *yes*. The last few weeks vanished from her mind. None of it mattered. The only thing that made any sense was his mouth claiming hers.

His hands wove deeper into her hair and tilted her head, deepening the kiss. She pressed her body against his, holding tight. She gripped his shoulders, gasping as he ground against her. Adrian kissed her as if the world were ending and death would take them at any moment. Sorcha tipped her head back as his lips moved along her jaw, mouth brushing her ear.

"We have to stop," he whispered.

"Why?"

Her heart beat frantically in her chest—rapid, running away from what was coming next. Gently she placed a hand against his cheek, rough with a few days of stubble, and closed her eyes.

Adrian didn't move, keeping his face pressed into her hair and one hand fisted in the fabric of her dress.

Sorcha froze, hands falling from his shoulders even as he held her tight. When she moved, he released her instantly, leaving her cold as she stepped away and kept her back to him. The little fire in the brazier flickered, low and deeply orange, on the verge of plunging them into the dim shadows of early night.

"Because you don't want me?" she asked softly.

"Because you are the vessel and I am the Wolf."

CHAPTER NINETEEN

Epona's ears twitched back and forth—aware of Sorcha's uneasy mood. Daylight had changed nothing at all. She was still the vessel, and he was still the Wolf, a creature of the empire. What had happened between them could mean nothing, though it had changed everything. The path they were on, set by a madman, was inescapable.

Sorcha had woken to find Adrian gone from the tent, and she'd lain awake in the nest of furs listening to the Black Tomeis as they broke down camp and prepared for a long day in the saddle. She'd heard his voice long before he entered the tent, and she'd known how he would handle the situation. He hadn't disappointed her, though a small part had hoped for something else. But what could there be? What could he offer her? There was nothing.

He'd handed her a bowl of gelatinous, cooling porridge, holding her gaze for a long moment before giving her a single nod. As if their fate had been decided already. She supposed it had been.

Now they were riding toward the next location on the map. Her hand strayed to her shoulder that had depicted where the last relic had been found, and she wondered how long it would take before they reached the next one. Sorcha couldn't remember a time when her skin had been her own. It had always belonged to the temple. Over the years, tattoos had bloomed across her skin like flowers and vines. She had no idea how it would feel not to be the vessel.

Still, they hadn't found the relic in the temple ruins where they'd faced the werewolves. That tattoo was still on her skin. Maybe it always would be. It wasn't the only one though. She'd hidden the tattoo on her hip from the Mapmaker as well. And there were many more relics—some in well-known temples and others hidden but never added to her flesh. They hadn't had time to continue the map once the Citadel had been besieged.

How would this impact the coming resurrection? Sorcha had no idea. Anger flared through her as the questions circled and built upon each other. There were so many and no way at all to get any answers.

Again, her thoughts returned to Kahina Kira. What had happened to her? One evening she'd been in the temple and the next morning gone. No one had seen her come or go. No one believed she would have gone to Prince Eine. Maybe Kira had found some secret place where she could make the final choice of her life in peace.

When—not if—Sorcha resurrected the Saint, she would see Kira again. Then Sorcha could ask about what had happened. And she could ask about the tattoos. She would ask every single question she'd ever lain awake at night considering. Soon she would meet the Saint. His voice in her head would finally have form and shape, ring crystal clear through the air. Maybe he would answer all her questions.

Sorcha glanced at Adrian, heat touching her cheeks, pooling in her lower belly. He didn't look at her, but she knew he felt it too—he was as aware of her as she was of him.

The men were riding far ahead or behind them today. Revenant led a group scouting the overgrown road they traveled, and Domenico and the others brought up the rear to make sure nothing surprised them.

Each day, they ventured farther south. Away from the Empire of the White Snake and the lands it was so greedily consuming. Away from the fallen city she loved. Now they were crossing into the fallen cities and civilizations of the south. The roads they traveled, once grand, were now covered in vegetation of all kinds—ancient trees, thorny brush, a late fall wildflowers now frostbitten from the cold nights.

She'd read enough history to know those cities and kingdoms had squabbled over land and water rights—greedy fingers stretching and grasping for what wasn't theirs. It had happened hundreds of years ago, and out of that chaos, the Saint had been born. He came from a time of political upheaval. A god in the form of a man, walking among the mortals with a promise of peace and plenty.

But the Saint had been betrayed. A trusted member of the order had cut him down, and the Saint's death shook the entire world. Then he'd been reborn. The golden skeleton of the Crimson Cult had walked the earth until he'd chosen to rest. There had been so much war, and as hard as he'd tried to unite the kingdoms, it had been impossible. He'd left them, promising to return if he was truly needed, and his remains had been broken up and hidden.

It was strange to realize she would be seeing all these places for herself. Locations that many of the members of Aureum Sanctus had never seen. Would anything recognizable remain? She'd read so many histories of the continent as a child. The great cities of Hadad, Cilo, and Takhmaspa had sounded rich and vibrant. Each one much larger than the Golden Citadel, which she'd never thought possible. The Citadel had seemed to be its own planet when she was small.

But soon, they would cross out of the places known so well by the living to those places left to the dead.

At night, he lay awake, listening to her breathe and thinking about his past and everything that had come before—everything that had yet to happen. He had never had a future before, never desired anything other than the path he walked. Battle and blood. Death and another city to take. He lived for this life. But now, he could live for her instead.

The Tomeis watched them closely, observing with mouths pressed thin, swift glances. Revenant always stared with his hooded eyes—attention sharp as knives. They felt the change. Feared it. If Adrian displeased Prince Eine, they would all pay the price.

Adrian couldn't abandon them to that. He couldn't choose a woman over the men he'd fought beside and sworn to protect. They'd walked through hell, expanding the Empire of the White Snake, and survived it all because of each other.

Kisses in the dark didn't change the way the world worked.

———

"I'm going with you this time," Adrian said.

A narrow, rocky track led down into a mile-wide sinkhole before them. All around the landscape was jagged groupings of boulders scattered throughout shoulder-high thin scrub in shades of olive and sage. Sharp grasses clung to the sandy soil, and small, orange-striped lizards and soft brown rodents scurried from hiding place to hiding place. When anyone touched the plants, they gave off an astringent, sharp scent that reminded Sorcha of medicine. Mountains rose in the distance —faintly blue and topped with snow—stoic and patient. Soon enough, they would be riding into them.

The sinkhole brimmed with bare winter trees—trunks and branches reaching for the sky—the canopy even with the surrounding landscape. The variety was so at odds with the surroundings, as if a giant had picked a hole in the earth and planted a forest from a lushly distant location.

Domenico and Thompson had been scouting ahead when they came across it—shouting with surprise and triumph. Now the horses were unsaddled and resting, and the men were gathering wood for a small campfire. Everyone was grateful for a moment to stop and cook a hot meal. Adrian stood with his back to Sorcha, working to untangle a knot on his saddlebag.

"You can't," Sorcha said.

He didn't respond. Sorcha glanced at the others, avoiding Revenant's ever-present hateful glare.

"What if they won't give it to me because you're there?" Sorcha kept her voice low, working to keep all emotion from it. But her frustration crept in, coloring each word, evident in the sharp angles of her body. She felt prickly and stretched all over at the thought of Adrian being beside her as she retrieved the relic.

"Then you can try again after we get back."

"What if this is the only chance we get?"

"There are other relics to find."

Sorcha gestured to herself—her flesh, the map.

"There are others," Adrian insisted.

She knew he was right. But, it made her uneasy to have him come with her. It would show the men how their relationship had changed. Not that they needed any more proof. To them, Adrian had changed the moment he'd laid eyes on her.

"That way," Thompson said, indicating the direction roughly to their left. "Down into the valley as near as I can tell."

"You can't give me any more than that?" Adrian asked, nodding at the map.

"Respectfully, sir." Thompson cleared his throat, his brows going up. "I've said it before, and I'll stand by it now. This map makes very little sense. I've compared it with a map created ten years ago and one created over a hundred years ago, so I can only make an educated guess."

Domenico cleared his throat. "It's not only about the topography. There are magical elements at play."

"I understand the limitations," Adrian said with a nod. "I'm still asking."

"Then my answer stands," Thompson said, gesturing at the sunken wood. "It appears to be that way."

Adrian nodded, waving at Sorcha to join him by Nox. "Leave Epona here. Nox will take us down into the valley."

"That's not necessary," Sorcha said. "I can ride my own horse."

"If something goes wrong, I don't want to lose two horses. Epona is not a war horse." Adrian nodded to Revenant—a silent command to keep watch. "Let's not waste any more time."

———

The air grew warmer as they followed the steep track down. It curved along the bare rock wall in a spiral, looping the perimeter several times. The sinkhole was deeper than it appeared at first, the bare trees larger. Sorcha strained to catch any sound that might mean they'd be coming face to face with someone—or something—protecting the relic. But there was nothing unusual. Only the rustle and movement of normal, living things.

Sorcha fought to keep herself from melting into Adrian as they rode. He was so warm and solid behind her, his strong arms wrapped around her as he kept a loose hold on the reins. Comforting despite everything. Every nerve in her body screamed for him. *Touch me. Kiss me. Take me.* But he'd made the choice for both of them.

"Stop here," Sorcha said when they reached the bottom. "We should walk."

"Should we?"

Adrian's voice was low, his mouth brushing her ear as he spoke. She turned slightly and closed her eyes, feeling the stubble on his cheek against her own. Sucking in a breath full of cool woods and warm man, she sighed and whispered, "*Adrian.*"

"Let me help you down," he said, pulling away.

In a smooth motion, he dismounted and turned to help her out of the saddle. She leaned down, placing her hands on his shoulders, their faces close as he reached for her waist. He didn't move, remaining in place as she slid down along the length of his body; hip and shoulder, hand and arm. She was careful not to look at him, but the pull was unbearable. He was a mixture of sweetness and pain itching across her skin, lodging in her throat. His large hands held her carefully, gently helping her down and making sure she had her balance before letting her go.

Sorcha looked back the way they'd come. It seemed so much farther up—as if Nox and the path had worked some kind of magic to get them here more quickly. The path continued into the trees, urging them to follow, to discover what might be found at the end.

Winter trees arched overhead, and Nox picked his way through drifts of brown and red leaves behind them. Adrian didn't speak, focused on their surroundings, one hand on his sword. She listened to her heartbeat, so aware of the man beside her. He was a distraction she couldn't afford to have. But she was grateful he was here.

"Cold?" he asked.

"What?"

"You shivered. Are you cold?"

Sorcha glanced at him, but his focus was elsewhere. "No. I was remembering something."

"The cave."

It wasn't a question. She nodded, wrapping her arms around herself. Poor comfort, but she'd take it.

"There," Adrian stopped, pointing ahead to a shadow between the trees. "See it?"

"Yes, that's where we're going."

———

A pair of monumental stone hands rose out of the leaves, the fingers coming together to create a pointed arch. They were as tall as the tallest tree and the color of old blood flecked with hints of clear, bright rubies. They glittered under the overcast sky as if lit from within. But the forest beyond the arch was vibrant—a summer place in a winter wood. A place outside their own.

"Are the hands alive?" Adrian asked.

"I don't know," Sorcha said, nudging dry leaves aside with her foot to see what lay beneath—moist dark earth flecked with tiny rubies. Kneeling, she picked one up and held it out. "It's faceted as if it's been worked by a jeweler. It's not a raw stone."

Adrian held out a hand, and Sorcha dropped the stone into his black-gloved palm.

He inspected it, rolling it around thoughtfully—a line between his brows, a slight frown tugging at his lips. "It reminds me of blood."

"Don't people usually say that about rubies?"

"I've never seen rubies like these." Adrian held it out for her to take. "Have you?"

Sorcha shook her head and took the stone back, rolling it between her hands. It warmed with her touch, the color richer and deeper than any other stone she'd ever seen. It was as if blood had crystalized into this impossibly beautiful stone. It wasn't like the rubies she'd worn in the temple or those gifted to her by Prince Eine. These were something else.

Closing her eyes, Sorcha waited. It didn't take long. From beyond the arched hands, a voice rustled—like the leaves, like the sudden wind through the trees, like a temple chant heard at the gates of the Citadel when she was late for services. The Saint. He was here. Or a piece of him was.

"We go through," she said. "The relic is ahead."

"And you know this how?"

"Because I can feel it," Sorcha said, turning to him. She placed a hand flat against his chest, feeling him breathe, his heart beat. He covered it with one of his, staring into her eyes. "Nox should stay here though."

They remained frozen, unwilling to break the connection. But the voice was growing. No words. No sense. Only the incessant murmur. Was it aware of the other relics above them? Could the Saint feel himself coming together?

"Are you afraid?" he asked, his fingers tightening a fraction.

"Does it matter if I am?" Sorcha smiled bitterly.

She stepped back and ran a soothing hand down Nox's neck. The horse turned to her, ears pricked forward. With a smile she held out a hand and he nuzzled her palm, snorting softly. They'd come along way from their first meeting. Maybe it had been her stern voice warning him not to bite her. Or the apples. That might have been the making of their friendship.

Sorcha turned to Adrian, her shoulders set. "I go forward no matter what comes next. Are you?"

Adrian shook his head, one hand casually laid on the hilt of his sword, the other still covering the spot her hand had rested. "I'm not afraid to follow you."

———

Heat engulfed Sorcha as they passed through the stone hands. It reminded her of the moment they'd crossed into the Silvas—crossing into an unknown, into a place with only tenuous connections to the world she inhabited. Vibrant green and blue surrounded them now, birdsong broke the silence. Behind them, bare trees and an overcast sky waited. Which was reality? The place she'd come from, or this one?

"Where do we go from here?" Adrian asked.

We. As if it were that simple. And from here? Sorcha couldn't tell him. She only knew that the relic was here, and if they kept going, they'd find it.

"I'm not sure," she said, searching the trees, waiting to feel that familiar pull. "This place is different from the others."

"Different enough that you won't bleed for it?" he asked dryly.

The comment surprised her, and she threw him a look. Adrian wore that face—careful and expressionless—and she was finally beginning to understand it. She didn't respond, waiting to see if he would offer more. To her surprise, he did.

"Don't they want him back?"

They. Monsters and villains from the stories. Myths and legends given flesh and bone—brought out of hiding with the promise the Saint would bring about a new age. He would return them to light, a place in the sun, as soon as he walked the earth again.

"I think some do."

"Do you?" Adrian asked.

Sorcha stopped, chest tightening. All the destruction and rebirth the Saint would bring—the world washed clean. And the price of it all would be her blood. Her life. Her hopes and dreams for a future she could no longer see clearly. She lifted one shoulder, refusing to commit to an answer out lout—not wanting to leave room for more questions.

Ahead, the trees opened to a meadow, waist-high lacy white flowers with splashes of delicate purple and sharp yellow scattered throughout. A bird sang as it spiraled higher, the sound piercing her heart. A breeze ruffled the grasses, flowerheads bobbing, and in the distance, a femur sat on a flat black stone flecked with sparkling rubies.

Adrian started forward, hand on the hilt of his sword.

"Wait," she said, grabbing his arm and coming to stand beside him.

With the contact came a rush of emotion. It flooded her, taking her by surprise, coursing through her like a storm surge—unstoppable, consuming.

I want you to touch me. I want your hands on me. I want you to hold onto me so tightly that I forget my name, I forget your past. Let's remake the world, change our story.

Her attraction to him was something dark, coming from a twisted place in her heart, a thing no one would understand, and they'd be sickened by it, disgusted.

Adrian the murderer. Adrian the monster.

I still want him.

"What do you see?"

"Nothing," she said, searching the meadow. "Yet."

Overhead, a clear blue sky observed their progress, the distance from the break in the trees to the relic farther than it appeared. Sweat prickled along her hairline and under her arms, the air thickening as they drew closer to the bone. There were more rubies in the earth here, larger in size and faceted as if worked by a talented jeweler. Sorcha could image wearing them—a glittering, coldly beautiful woman on a dais surrounded by opulence. She shook herself, willing it away.

Not a dream, a vision, of something that could be.

Breathing heavily, as if they'd run the distance to the relic, she paused before the femur. A sense of impending doom fell over her. It would be a long run to reach those stone hands, to reach Nox. And she had no doubt they would have to reach that portal as quickly as possible as soon as she touched the bone before them.

"Where did you go?" Adrian asked. "Just now."

"Nowhere," she said, not wanting to think of herself that way again.

The air crackled around the relic, electricity filling the air. Stepping forward, Sorcha sucked in a breath and reached for the Saint.

"Wait." He touched her shoulder, a slight pressure, but he didn't break contact. His hand remained—large and warm. "What do you want me to do?"

"Stay with me."

Adrian inclined his head, a promise in his dark eyes. Sorcha didn't want to go back to winter and the cold eyes of the Tomeis. She wanted to remain here and see if Adrian's eyes changed, if his mouth would soften with her name.

Sorcha placed her hand on the Saint—this small piece—knowing that even as she did, it brought them all closer to the things she wanted to deny. As soon as she touched the relic, the sky morphed, a storm exploding out of the beautiful day. Rain swirled around her, sleet grating across her skin, a million points of freezing contact.

Out of the storm, a shape was coming for her. It could only be seen where the sleet hit it—an invisible, hulking shape, vaguely human but oversized.

She screamed as it lumbered toward her, quicker than anything could possibly run.

It caught her, the invisible being in the rain, suspending her in time, pinned like an animal.

"Sorcha!"

Vessel.

Chapter Twenty

Sorcha stood on a hill. A gentle breeze blew through her hair, rustling the grass around her knees, and brought the scents of the sun-warmed plains. Overhead, a sun shone in a clear sky, high and around midday. In the distance stood a city.

The Golden Citadel.

It was familiar but different. Smaller. Not as many towers. There were no walls yet. No high defenses. But it was her city. The one she'd last seen burning. The one Adrian had killed.

Was it new? Was this the rebuilding—triumphant and rising from the ashes?

"No."

She turned in a circle, searching for the speaker. There was no one. She was completely alone on the hilltop.

"This is how it was," the voice continued. "Long ago, when the Saint was born."

As she watched, the city began to change. It happened quickly, between blinks and breaths—towers rising, walls appearing. It grew and grew, becoming what she'd always been familiar with.

"It became this because of the Saint. This beautiful place. Your home would not have been here without him. This place would never have been born."

A traitorous thought skipped through her mind. *He wouldn't be here without me.*

The voice chuckled. "Maybe," it agreed. "But there would be someone else. There is nothing special about you, temple girl. You are merely the vessel. Your blood will resurrect him, but anyone's blood could."

Anyone's. Sorcha's heart twisted, gut clenching. She wanted to deny him, this mocking voice, but something at the back of her mind stopped her. A question. A doubt. She'd been raised to believe her place in this world was fate—an ordained occurrence. She was chosen by the Saint himself, born at a certain time and place, under the right stars.

A reincarnation of the original savior. Kahina Kira had promised that Sorcha was special and raised her to believe it was true. The voice chuckled again, grating against her nerves.

"Special? Maybe," it said. "Unique? No. There have been others. There would have been others. It would not only come down to you. *You* are replaceable. Would it have been now? Probably not. In a few years? Twenty? A hundred? His resurrection makes no difference. It is inevitable."

Now her city was burning before her eyes, and she knew that somewhere within the walls, she ran for her life. Her friends were dead. Brothers. Sisters. Priests. Priestesses. Her family lay dead by their own hands.

By Adrian's hands.

The monster she'd somehow come to accept.

"There is no shame in loving a monster," the voice said. "We all love monsters."

A puff of delicate air caressed her cheek—tender and gentle.

"You will be loved," the voice promised, tone softening, growing kinder. "The Saint will cherish you. Yes, there could have been others. Yes, you are replaceable, but still appreciated."

There was a pause, her chest constricting with the promise.

"And who knows? Maybe your monster loves you in return. Maybe the Saint will have a place in his new world for this monster of yours. The Saint loves monsters too."

In the city, towers were falling, stones were tumbling free, and walls were crumbling. Thick smoke curled into the sky, billowing higher and higher, drifting across the sun and casting a shadow where she stood on the hillside.

Out of the dark smoke and flames, a figure uncurled like a fire god rising out of the ashes of destruction. A giant golden skeleton towered over the landscape. It stood as tall as any of the toppled towers, taller than the vanished city walls. It turned its hollow sockets to the sky, moving in a circle just as she'd done, taking the whole world in. Gold glimmered in the sunshine, faceted gems catching rays and reflecting them back in a myriad of intense colors. The creature sparkled—a jewel, a precious thing, a treasure. And so terrible.

Then the Saint saw her.

Fear seized Sorcha's heart, the terror of being seen and the urge to curl in on herself painfully strong. She wanted to pull back into her shell like a snail, make herself small in the knee-high grass. She wanted to close her eyes like she had as a child, when she'd thought it would make her invisible during a game of hide-and-seek.

But she wasn't a child any longer. She could not hide from the Saint.

He stepped out of the city, great strides eating up the landscape, coming toward her with a terrible purpose.

"He comes," the voice spoke softly. "He comes for you."

Then the Saint was towering above her, so massive that she had to tilt her head far back to see him. Sorcha shaded her eyes against the sun and glare, staring into the skeletal face. He was beautiful in the intricacies of jewels and gold—the clean lines of skull and bare bones. Something in the hollow eye sockets locked on her—seeing her, knowing her. The Saint crouched, joint by joint, until he was closer but still so far away.

Slowly, gently, he reached out, a finger extended and hovering in front of her chest. She was gasping, as if she was once again fighting for air in the sunken city—mouth open and waiting for the contact she could not prevent. She thought he would push her down, pin her to the earth, and keep pressing until she was dead and buried. She would be nothing but worm food here in this strange place—a woman decomposing and forgotten.

A bird began to sing. A meadowlark trilling, notes rising. A bee buzzed by, and a breeze ruffled her hair and sighed through the grass. Vessel and Saint remained frozen together—a silent tableau. The moment stretched so far she was sure she'd shatter with the tension.

The Saint closed the distance between them finally—as if reading her thoughts—and pressed his giant finger to her chest. She'd thought he would be cold, a dead thing, but he was warm and gentle. His head tilted to one side at the contact, an unspoken question she could not understand or answer.

Then the images began to come. One right after another, blurring together and speeding up. A succession of things that could be or had been. Things happening right now, just beyond her reach. The Saint moved through the world, controlling life and death, each held in one golden palm.

She'd seen some of the story—his story—on temple walls. Paintings and mosaics, careful brushstrokes and gilt, the horror made beautiful. Those were remnants of his history, the dry and removed remains pulled from pages and stone. Now, she saw them differently. A terrible foreboding crept into her body and grew, a physical force threatening to tear her apart. Briefly, Lacus's words crossed her mind. *It would be a mistake to bring him back.*

Then the vision changed. She was no longer watching the Saint cross a landscape, towering above it all and wreaking havoc, rebuilding the world in his image through blood and death. Now she was seeing it as he would have seen it. Towns and cities, small villages, lone homesteads, and little bits of civilization. People ran and kneeled. They raised their hands to the sky and praised him. People screamed, and fierce, joyful cheers echoed. There were oceans of tears and people throwing flowers.

Sorcha saw them all from a great height, removed from it—a silent witness. In the vision was this sense of rightness. The world had aligned and become the place it should have always been.

Years raced past, a quick succession of temples rising across the continent. Cities were built as others fell. Fashions changed, the Saint's worshippers changing as old ones died and new were born. How many years? They rolled by, but she had no sense of time. A hundred years? A thousand? She witnessed it all, an unending stream, a spool of thread sent rolling out, a ribbon unfurling.

Then it was gone. All of it. Everything.

The past. Present. Future.

The hill and the Saint vanished.

Sorcha was back in the meadow with Adrian.

The storm had vanished, the summer world gone. An illusion conjured by the creature or the Saint. A vision. The rain had stopped, but the cold remained, the sky no longer blue and the flowers sagging and browning with the biting frost. Winter had followed them through the arched stone fingers, and Adrian was shaking her. His hands framed her face, fear radiating outward in a palpable cloud. Fear for *her*.

"Are you okay?" he asked.

She nodded and pressed her hands to his, feeling how cold they both were.

"What happened?" he asked.

"I met the Saint," she rasped, her throat dry.

She wanted cool water and hot tea, furs and a fire, a swift dip in an icy stream. She wanted sweet wine and something warm to eat. Things to drive away what had happened, to soothe not only her raw throat but also the horrible feeling blooming in her chest like a poisonous flower.

"The Saint," Adrian echoed. Surprise and curiosity colored his words.

"Yes." Sorcha moved, stepping beyond his grasp.

She needed to move, restless with knowledge, wanting to ride away from this place, wanting to take the relic and go. It weighed on her, everything she'd seen—intense and heavy, unforgettable.

Sorcha wanted to forget it all.

But this was coming. It was rushing toward her and inescapable.

The relic called to her, beckoning—willing her to fulfill her promise.

"We need to take the relic and go," Sorcha said, striding toward the gilded bone and lifting the heavy weight of it with a grunt. "I don't want to stay in this place."

As soon as she touched it, a wind began to howl, flattening the grasses that still stood, whistling in her ears. Out of the trees beyond the altar, a creature appeared. It stood as tall as Adrian but twice as broad, covered in thick white fur. But it did not resemble the werewolves. This was something else—something far stranger. Throwing back its head, it let out a long, mournful call filled with the promise of pain. Fear crystallized in her blood.

Sorcha stumbled under the weight of the femur. The Saint needed her—these creatures wanted her—but it made no sense that he would not make it easy. Adrian pulled out his sword and faced the creature determinedly. Snow fell from the sky, a blizzard obscuring their vision. It was impossible to see, blinded by snow and stinging ice.

The creature howled, and then the howls became words, undulating and drawn out.

"*Mine*. He is mine."

Sorcha shivered, but it wasn't from the cold.

"Get back to Nox!" Adrian urged Sorcha toward the trees.

She stumbled, managing to keep upright and moving. Returning to the stone hands took less time—distance covered in seconds. The creature's howls followed, but it appeared to let them go. They stumbled through the arched fingers—snow following, wind screaming.

Sorcha dropped to her knees, clutching the bone to her chest.

I've got you, she promised.

No, the relic replied, filling her head. *I have you.*

She cried out, shocked, and thrust the relic toward Adrian. "Take it!" she pleaded, not wanting to hold it a moment longer and keep the connection open. There would be enough of that in the future, the certainty rushing toward her like an arrow aimed at her heart.

But Adrian didn't. Instead, he dropped to his knees beside her and reached out, cupping her face in his cold hands.

She trembled at his touch, cheeks reddening beneath his intense gaze. He leaned in, one hand smoothing across her shoulder, wrapping around her lower back to pull her close against him.

"Sorcha, I—"

A voice interrupted him, calling his name, searching and closing in. Adrian dropped his hands. Tilting away from her, he pushed to his feet.

"Here!" he shouted, steel in his tone—hard enough to break the world.

Where had the softness gone? Vanished. Shoved down. And what of it? He wouldn't have kissed her, wouldn't have caressed her.

Sorcha studied the earth she knelt in. Dead leaves dusted with snow, bare trees rising around them. A normal winter. A softer place than the one they'd escaped. She got to her feet, not waiting for him or expecting he would help her. But he caught her arm halfway up, coming close again.

This time she saw it in his face, a promise in his dark eyes. He would have kissed her, had wanted to there in the leaves and winking rubies, surrounded by dead trees.

Sorcha leaned toward him, wanting him to keep his promise, and reached out to place a hand on his chest.

"Do it," she whispered. "Kiss me."

It was her own promise, her own dare. He focused on her mouth—hungry and wanting. If he kissed her here, it would all change. Would it be a change she could handle? She wasn't sure. But she wanted it anyway.

Adrian covered her hand with his own, staring into her eyes.

And that was how Thompson found them, locked in a private moment, a scene that made them look like lovers. But the hard truth was that they were far from it—captive and captor, monster and temple girl. Despite her desire, despite the wish to change it.

Sorcha could feel Thompson's sharp surprise and heavy suspicion—anger glowed in his eyes. Adrian took Sorcha's hand and carefully, deliberately, removed it from his chest. She let it fall limp at her side.

"Coward," she whispered.

———

The creature's howls had reached the men waiting above the sinkhole. Revenant, Thompson, and Domenico had ridden down to search for Adrian. They'd found Nox waiting calmly at the bottom and then split up to search the woods.

Domenico had come forward to claim the relic and wrap it in velvet.

His eyes briefly met Sorcha's, an expression of understanding in them. It vanished as Revenant approached, flipping the velvet back to glance at the bone.

"A femur." He turned to Adrian. "How many more?"

"Two more," Thompson replied. "Then we meet Prince Eine in the Wastes."

Sorcha snapped her head around, searching the man's face for more information. This was the first time he'd said where they would end up. Where they might be taking the relics. The wastes? What wastes? Where?

"We should go," Domenico said, taking the bone to his horse and securing it to the saddle.

"Yes," Adrian agreed.

He motioned for Sorcha to follow him and accepted Nox's reins from Revenant. The two stared at each other for a long moment, some silent communication happening that Sorcha could not understand. Then Adrian grabbed her, shoving her into the saddle before she could protest, and mounted up behind her.

———

They rode well past dusk. The horses picking their way slowly through scraggly trees. In the distance, a wild dog yelped, and one nearby answered. Nox turned his head toward the sound and snorted. It was obvious the horses needed rest, but Adrian wanted to put as much distance between themselves and the sinkhole. He wasn't in a hurry to meet whatever lived at the bottom of it again.

Sorcha hunched over Epona, exhausted but without protesting the pace he set. She'd been more than willing to relinquish the relic to Domenico. She'd practically forced it into his arms. What had she seen that had frightened her so badly? He wanted to ask, and maybe he would.

The afternoon played through his mind. Sorcha in the meadow beyond the hands, wading through a field of flowers—red dress, white lacy flowers, blue sky. Then the moment in the winter wood, on their knees in the dirt, rubies glimmering around them. Her hand on his chest, heat in her gaze.

Kiss me.

Coward.

Adrian had almost kissed her. But there couldn't be a repeat of the other night. It had been a mistake. He couldn't allow emotion to cloud his judgment. His role in the empire was set. *For now.* That traitorous voice slipped through again. But he couldn't let himself consider what might come after this was over.

He tried not to watch her as they rode, aware that his men were paying attention. Thompson would have told them how he'd discovered Adrian and Sorcha by now. Adrian had no doubt how the Tomeis' would feel about the situation.

When they'd reached the top of the sinkhole, Sorcha had slid from Nox before Adrian could help her down. She'd crossed to Epona in quick, sure strides and threw herself into the saddle without a backward glance. Her anger and frustration had been palpable. But between then and now, she'd grown cold toward him. He should be grateful. Sorcha was a temptation he must resist.

Who was he? Adrian returned to this question again and again. Prince Eine would be furious to learn that his heartless monster had retained a shred of his heart. Sorcha was to serve one purpose for the Empire.

But . . . the thought began. *Stop.* He couldn't let himself think of it.

———

Adrian finally called a halt, and they set up camp, pitching the simplest form of their tents—narrow and low to the ground, quick to go up and come down. Magnus and Bran had built a fire and were cooking while Cas and Domenico had begun to dig for water.

There was none above ground here, but if they dug down far enough, the hole would begin to fill. They pulled bucket after bucket out, painstakingly straining and boiling it. The horses drank first after it had cooled—guzzling noisily—and then the men.

Adrian gave his water to Sorcha, and she accepted silently, lips pursed around whatever sharp word she wished to use. It didn't matter. She could have said whatever she wanted, and he wouldn't have cared.

He hoped there would be cleaner water to be found ahead—anything that didn't leave his mouth gritty even after being strained and boiled. Their dry provisions were running low, but so far, they'd been able to supplement them with hunting.

It was hard to know how much longer they would last. But hopefully, he wouldn't have to move them to strict rationing. As disciplined as the Tomeis were, and as many times as they'd been forced to travel and fight on quarter rations, it was something none of them enjoyed. He was positive Sorcha would enjoy it even less. She might even come to miss the gummy porridge if they were starving.

Thompson and Domenico were studying the maps near the fire—avoiding the flames and the rotating roasting rabbits. Firelight danced over the parchment, the ink seeming to move with the flicker of flames, as if it might leap from the page to return to the source.

"We're here," Thompson said, pointing to a nondescript location.

"And the next relic is there," Domenico said, pointing to what appeared to be a marsh or bog of some kind.

"It's very close," Thompson continued. "Less than a day if we ride hard. We'd be there tomorrow afternoon."

"From there?" Adrian asked.

"The mountains. There's a temple of some kind. It's clearly marked, well known. The Androphagoi." Thompson looked from Domenico to Adrian. "It has a reputation."

"The cannibal temple," Domenico nodded.

"I've heard about it," Adrian said. "Are the stories true?"

"Who can say?" Domenico shrugged. "I've never been. But from what I know of the woman's cult, I don't doubt it."

"I met a soldier who had been through there," Thompson said. "He told me they walled priests into cells so they could slowly starve and live their last days worshipping that god of theirs."

It would be a slow and painful death—starving and dying of thirst, knowing relief was just beyond an impassable wall. Did the sounds from the rest of the temple reach them there? What would it be like to have nothing but the sound of your own body slowly eating itself alive?

"Which piece is at the temple?" Adrian asked.

Thompson turned the map around so Adrian could see it clearly, tapping the temple's location. A skull. Adrian nodded once. How many other pieces had Prince Eine been able to collect? How complete did the skeleton need to be for resurrection? Or would Adrian and Sorcha be sent back into the world to find the others? But he doubted that would happen. The empress was dying—her time was running out even as they sat around the fire—and the prince would make a resurrection happen with or without each relic.

"Show me this one." Adrian tapped the other map, waiting as Thompson unfurled it and held it open.

He compared it to the cult's map, noting the distance between relics. The distance between the mountains and the wastelands. Volcanoes rose along a distant coast, smoke artfully drawn. The rumored Red Tower would be there, somewhere along a broken road.

"Don't those death worshippers know there are literally hundreds of other colors?" Thompson sneered. "Everything. Red. It's an obsession."

"It's part of the religion," Domenico said.

"They're fools," Thompsons said.

Domenico snorted. "Just because you have no faith doesn't mean they're fools. We've all seen enough to know that nothing is what it seems in this life."

"Faith and reality are two different things," Thompson scoffed. "If their god is real, I don't worship him. And I won't, even if the prince demands it. Do you think he will?" Thompson's eyes found Adrian's.

"I can't give you an answer for that," Adrian replied.

"He will make it our new religion," Domenico said softly, eyes on Sorcha's map. He reached forward, tapping the skull. "If this dead god heals the empress, wouldn't you make it your religion?"

"I'll believe it when I see it," Thompson said.

They were quiet for a moment, contemplating what lay ahead.

Thompson sighed, rolling up the maps. "When do we leave?"

"First light," Adrian said. "We'll collect these last two pieces and send a messenger to Prince Eine telling him to meet us in the Wastes."

"How far south is the Traveling City coming?" Domenico asked.

"As far as it can get. But with time running out, they might come by ship. It's quicker by sea, and the remains of a city and port are along the coast."

"Who will take the message to the prince once we have the skull?"

"Wes. He has the fastest horse. It will still take a while, but he's the best option. You two get some rest."

Adrian stood and turned away, his back aching, muscles sore. He wanted to sleep without dreams—without any doubt creeping into his mind, no second guesses lodging in his gut. He caught sight of Sorcha across the campfire, light playing across her delicate features, shadows gathering behind her. She stood wordlessly and moved to the tent they shared, avoiding the relic tent as if it were alive and hungry for her.

With one more glance to make sure everything was organized—Revenant was nowhere in sight, Cas and Magnus were keeping the first watch, and there was a line of water buckets waiting to be boiled in the morning—the only thing he could do now was sleep.

The tents they'd set up were small and compact versions of what they traveled with before. There was just enough room to crawl in and sleep. He paused outside his tent, wondering if Sorcha would feign sleep or if he'd find her facing him in the dark.

What did he want to find when he went inside?

With an internal sigh, he knelt and parted the tent flap, then crawled inside and removed his boots. He placed them beside Sorcha's, keeping his back to her for as long as possible. When he turned, he saw that she was a lump in the dark, facing away from him on her side.

But she wasn't asleep. He could tell by the way she breathed, the tenseness in the space around them, that she was waiting for him to say something. Quietly, he moved to his bedroll beside her and lay flat on his back, keeping his eyes closed. He fought the urge to speak, counting silently until he fell asleep.

———

Sorcha awoke abruptly, throat sore and ears ringing. The dream—the vision—had been vivid, clearer than the others. The Saint had been seated on a throne in a red room, surrounded by creatures. Lacus had been there. A werewolf. The white beast from the meadow. There had been others as well—horrible figures and beautiful demons. A high-pitched hum, not unpleasant but insistent, filled the space. And Sorcha had been covered in rubies standing beside the Saint.

The vision released her, fading even as she fought to remember the exact details. But what would she do with them? Who would she tell? A rustle caught her attention. Adrian was awake, sitting up across from her, but she couldn't make out his features in the dimness. He didn't speak. Neither did she. The tent was cold. The only warmth here came from them.

So many nights, he'd woken her without speaking—a gentle nudge on her shoulder or leg. So impersonal even as he touched her. Sorcha wanted the warmth of his hands, his skin to her skin—body to body. She wanted whatever comfort he might offer in the dark. If any. What did it mean for her soul, for her, that she'd made room for this man in her life? A killer. A monster. Yet she'd stopped thinking of him that way weeks ago now. Even as she watched him maim and kill. Even understanding that he served the empire and it would always come first.

But Adrian was different with her. She hadn't seen it at first. But he displayed a softness she never could have imagined. The Tomeis were careful to keep their expressions flat. But they saw it as well.

Sorcha went to him. It was like crossing the world and falling joyfully into hell. With a shaky breath, she reached for the hem of the dress she'd fallen asleep in and began to pull it upward.

Sorcha dropped her furs and began to remove her clothing. In the dim tent, the colors were muted, but in daylight, they would be a deep red. A color he would associate with her for the rest of his life. Not as a follower of the dead Saint. Only and forever, Sorcha.

He knew what was expected of him, understood what he should do. Accepting what she offered now would be a betrayal. It couldn't happen. If he touched her now, it would change everything. In the morning, in the revealing light of day, things would be clear, and they would both be thankful if he stopped this now.

The dress fell to the ground, and Sorcha paused, breathing rapidly, as she waited to see what he would do.

Adrian reached for her, fingers digging into her hips—the contact shuddering through him. He ran his hands up her waist, enjoying the way she closed her eyes and shivered, and jerked her into his lap. She straddled him, her hands coming to rest on his shoulders.

She was so beautiful, it made his heart ache. *Did he still have one?*

Slowly, he caressed her face, sliding his fingers down her throat and over her collarbones. Her eyes were wide, mouth parted with expectation—desire and trepidation. He wanted to touch her everywhere. Every inch of skin. He wanted everything she was, all she would be, in his bed and inside his soul.

The thought startled him, and he stopped before reaching her breasts, listening to the rush of blood in his ears.

A mistake. He'd already let so much of her in, bending his world to contain this woman. He was already damned. If this happened now, how much worse could it be?

"Adrian," she whispered, her voice thick with desire.

Sorcha reached for the hem of his tunic, helping him pull it over his head. She hummed in satisfaction as she ran her hands over his bare shoulders and chest, sliding down his muscled abdomen to the hard ridge of his cock. Palming him, rocking forward slowly, she moaned softly and rested her forehead against his shoulder.

Adrian buried his face in her neck, breathing her in—a mix of citrus soap and the sweetness of her skin. Pulling her closer, tight against his body, he wove his fingers into her hair and tugged, tilting her face to his.

She smiled—the curve of her perfect mouth stealing his breath.

"What do you want, Sorcha?" he asked, voice rough.

She gasped, back arching as she pressed down against his cock, rolling her hips forward.

He groaned, gripping her waist with his other hand, desperate to take everything from her. Every shudder and moan, each panting breath, the slickness at the center of her body, he wanted to thrust into her and swallow each scream. He wanted to ruin her for any other man.

But only if she asked.

"You." Her eyes were dilated and half-lidded when she looked at him, stroking up and down slowly with one hand. "I want you inside me."

Adrian adjusted his grip on her, one hand cupping her ass, the other moving to her pussy to trace the outer lips, parting her slowly. She was wet for him, slick and hot, trembling as he barely touched her. He wanted her riding his cock, sweating as he told her how beautiful she was. With a low noise of satisfaction, he brushed against her clit, watching her face and continuing to touch her.

"Here?" he asked, circling her clit with his thumb.

He dipped one finger in her wetness and stroked slowly.

Her expression changed as he added another finger, curling upward to touch a swollen, inner part of her. He groaned as she shuddered.

"Adrian," she pleaded, her hands going to her breasts, squeezing the soft flesh.

Leaning forward, he nuzzled one of her hands aside and took a nipple in his mouth, sucking hard on the hard bud as her inner muscles tightened around his fingers. She tasted better than anything he could have imagined. He was desperate to bury his face between her thighs and feel her on his tongue. But that could wait. Right now, he needed her to come with his fingers inside her. She whimpered, meeting his thrusts as he rubbed. He increased the pace, rocking beneath her now. Adrian wanted her, but he wanted this more.

"Kiss me," he demanded.

Sorcha placed her hands on both sides of his face and kissed him. She wasn't tender or shy. Her tongue boldly caressed his, and she nipped at his lower lip as she took what she wanted. Hips twitching, his fingers stroking and applying the perfect amount of pressure, she came—shattering apart in his arms. Adrian swallowed her scream, their mouths locked as his tongue and fingers worked, drawing out the shuddering contraction of her inner muscles.

He stood, and she wrapped her legs around his waist, head against his shoulder and almost boneless in his arms. She gripped his shoulders as he eased her onto the pile of furs, and she curled languidly into them, eyes dreamy. Kneeling between her legs, Adrian touched her small, perfect breasts, massaging their delicious weight, tweaking a nipple between thumb and forefinger.

She gasped and bit down on her lip, fighting to keep quiet.

Sorcha reached for his breeches, pulling at the laces, silent but insistent. He removed them, his heavy erection slipping free, and she took him in her hand, stroking his length. She moved confidently, adjusting her grip and rubbing her palm over the head of his cock.

He twitched, and she smiled, eyes flashing up to his.

"Lie down." He pushed her down, taking her hands and sliding them above her head, pinning her in place. "Don't take your eyes off me," he commanded, pulling her leg over his shoulder and kissing her inner thigh.

Taking his time, he committed each inch of her skin to memory, every quiver of her body. He paused at her center, breathing over her clit, smiling as her hips twitched.

"Are you watching, Priestess?"

"Yes," she whispered, eyes barely open but locked on him as she lifted her hips impatiently.

Adrian lapped at her center, teasing her clit and groaning against her when her body tensed. Slowly, he ran his tongue over her before sucking at her soft flesh and thrusting two fingers into her. She came again, body arching up, eyes squeezed shut.

He waited, drawing out the last few shudders before pulling back to settle his hips between her thighs, cock pressing against her pussy. He lifted her leg and grasped his cock to tease her, closing his eyes as skin met skin.

"Sorcha." Her name was a prayer, a request for redemption as he ran the head of his cock over her opening.

She trembled, fingers digging into his waist, as she wrapped one leg around him.

He opened his eyes, staring down at her, barely able to control his voice. "You're going to come on my cock, and you're going to be quiet. Understand?"

She nodded and reached down to touch herself, running her fingers through her slickness. He grabbed her hand and brought her wet fingers to his mouth, sucking hard. She gasped, and he thrust into her. She was stretched around him so tight his head dropped forward with a groan.

He saw stars, her body so soft beneath him as he pumped into her, gaze fixed on her mouth open in a silent scream.

He pulled back, leaving her warmth, before snapping his hips forward and filling her with a grunt. She shuddered, clenching around him, hands tangled in the furs beneath her. Closing her eyes, she threw her head back, exposing the long, pale line of her throat, back arching. He pounded into her, driving her toward a cliff edge, focused on her inner muscles tensing and her legs trembling.

She moaned his name, biting her lip and struggling to keep her voice down. Hot triumph swept through him. He wanted to pull that sound from her again and again—he wanted her to scream his name and swear no one else would ever touch her like this again.

———

"You're mine," he said, voice low and thick. "Say it."

"I'm yours," Sorcha whispered, pressing against him, desperate for everything he was giving her and wanting more. "All yours."

He ground against her, changing the angle—going deeper—hitting that inner part of her that throbbed, the friction on her clit intensifying.

She was blind with pleasure, not seeing the tent around them, unable to see him clearly through the haze of desire—only aware of his hands on her hips and his cock stretching her wide. She whispered his name, wanting all of him in her mouth and in her body. Wanting him everywhere.

The orgasm crashed through her again, white heat sweeping her body, leaving her weak and fighting to breathe.

Adrian didn't give her time to recover before he flipped her over and pulled her hips up, slamming into her from behind relentlessly.

She fumbled a hand between her legs, desperate for pressure and friction against her clit. Biting the furs and squeezing her eyes tight, she panted as she circled the spot. Painful pleasure built yet again, the delicious fullness of his cock stretching her, his hands demanding on her body. She moved faster, release so close she whimpered.

"Mine." Adrian's voice was hard, but his hands were gentle as reached around her and moved her fingers. She choked on a sob, her pussy aching. "Ask for what you want."

"Touch me," she pleaded, hands fisted in the bedding. Adrian stroked her clit, slowing to draw out each long thrust. She shook her head. "More. I need more."

Adrian pressed down with the fingers of his right hand, increasing the speed of his thrusts. The fingers of his left dug into her hip, holding her in place under the demanding pace.

Sorcha sucked in a breath, on the verge of crying out, and buried her face in the furs to stifle her moans. She couldn't take the spiraling tension in her body—the way he demanded more from her, relentlessly moving inside her. It was too much. So much.

Sorcha sucked in a harsh breath, body trembling uncontrollably. Tears filled her eyes as the orgasm ripped through her. Her body worked his cock, throbbing around him, and she heard the sharp intake of his breath. Harder, deeper than she could have thought possible, he thrust into her and then went rigid, a low groan tearing from him as his cock pulsed with release. She felt warm and so full, his orgasm sending another shiver through her as she bit her lip and pressed backward into him.

Adrian collapsed on her, easing his weight to the side so she wasn't crushed beneath him. She lay flat on her stomach as they breathed heavily, sweat glossing their skin, and Sorcha's heart thundered so loud she was sure he could hear it. Before she could move, he reached over her, picking up the discarded tunic beside the cot.

"Lift your hips," he said softly.

Without ceremony, he cleaned her—moving slowly, pressing kisses to the side of her face. Sorcha gasped as the smooth fabric touched her, the soft cotton harsh on her swollen flesh. Adrian pressed a kiss to her shoulder, squeezing her gently before releasing her and dropping the tunic back on the ground.

Adrian rolled, taking her with him, adjusting her beside him until she lay with her head on his shoulder and one leg over his waist. He tightened his embrace, kissing the top of her head. It was sweet, not at all what she'd expected after he'd wrecked her so thoroughly. One hand trailed up her bare back, tracing the curve of her spine, following the line of her shoulder. He took his time, gently touching each part of her that he could reach.

Something had broken apart in her soul. The shards of past and present flying free, leaving only her wish that things were different. Reality was creeping back too soon. She wanted to banish it, refuse it, demand that it leave.

"Do you—" Sorcha stopped, the word she'd wanted to say stuck in her throat.

What? Love me? Is that really what I was going to ask?

———

The unsaid word hung between them, chasing up his spine and clawing through his mind. Something had been growing there, taking tentative shape as weeks rolled by—as he watched her walk fearlessly into danger again and again. But he'd been dreaming of another kind of life, glimpsing it in her face. Sorcha had shown him acceptance in the way she spoke to him separately from his actions and history that colored every waking moment.

He wanted this woman. Her body, her soul, her heart, her mind. He wanted each piece of her that she'd ever given away and all the pieces she'd kept to herself. Sorcha was everything he'd never let himself dream about.

If she were no longer a map and the Saint was in one piece, the creature wouldn't need her anymore. And Prince Eine wouldn't need the Wolf if the Saint could accomplish everything Adrian could but better.

Eine had promised Adrian he could eventually withdraw from the army and endless battles. Rewards had been promised. When the Empire of the White Snake had been expanded and established, when the fighting stopped and the farthest reaches of the Empire couldn't be reached in a matter of days or weeks, but months or years, Adrian could walk away from it all. They were getting closer to that goal each day. Then he could fade into obscurity, claim the land that had been promised, and vanish.

His mind raced with possibility. There would be nothing for Sorcha to return to, and as they'd traveled, he'd seen her faith in the Saint waver. If not exactly in the god, but in serving him.

She could come with him.

Adrian knew if he extended his hand and whispered her name, she would take it, would accept him. And they could vanish into obscurity together—forgotten at the edges of the empire. Maybe Prince Eine would let them remain forgotten.

"What happens after the Saint has returned?" he asked. "Will you be needed?"

"I don't know." One shoulder lifted in a halfhearted shrug.

"What if you came with me?"

The question crystallized around them.

Sorcha's eyes flashed up, filled with an expression he couldn't read but longed to understand.

"What do you mean?" she asked quietly.

He spoke slowly, careful with each word. "Come with me."

Her eyes were glued to his face, pupils wide, taking everything in.

"I have land to the east, a gift from the prince for expanding his empire. It's beyond everything. We can leave for it as soon as things are finished."

We.

The word buzzed and vibrated in his head, shooting along each nerve. He'd never once felt the desire to say *we* to anyone. Not in this way, not with the idea of running away from it all and pretending the world didn't exist if it meant this woman would accept all his darkness.

"We," she repeated.

He didn't nod, didn't move, couldn't bring himself to show any kind of emotion as he gave her space to consider the offer. If she refused, they would go on as they had been—killer and priestess. A pair of fools collecting the relics of a mythical saint so a prince might be pleased with their service and spare their lives. And when it was all over, Adrian would continue to burn cities to the ground. Would do whatever it took to forget her.

Her silence was killing him. He wanted answers, he wanted a reaction, he wanted anything from her other than that flat look she was giving him. He wanted to make as deep an impression on her as she had him. He thought he had. Sometimes, when she looked at him, he caught something else in her gaze. But he couldn't be sure she would act on it even now. He couldn't be sure she would trade everything she knew for a monster.

He knew what he wanted her answer to be.

"Adrian," she began but stopped. His heart twisted. "I don't know what will happen when all the relics come together. The things I see . . ."

He waited for her to say more, but she remained silent. She didn't speak about her visions, and he hadn't pressed for information. Each night, she woke screaming, following memories of the past or visions of the future, shivering in the dark. When they arrived tomorrow night, would she come to him then? Would she slip into his bed as easily a second night? Or was this it?

Sorcha took his face in her hands, smoothing back his hair, and curled her arm around his neck. She kissed him gently, brushing her tongue against his. Sorrow tainted her kiss, bitter on his lips. But he held her close, as if holding her might be enough to keep her with him.

"Sleep," he urged.

She could make no promises, and he could ask for none.

She nodded, rolling over onto her side. Adrian tucked her against his body—her back to his chest, his arms around her—and listened as her breathing slowed. Dawn was only a few hours away. In the morning, they would find another relic. Soon, he would hand her over to Prince Eine, and whatever he hoped for would change.

Chapter Twenty-One

"We aren't blind, Adrian. Or deaf. Do you think the prince will be?" Ivo threw his hands in the air—an electric mix of frustration and fury. "He will kill us all because you've displeased him."

Someone tried to quiet him, several voices pitched low, soothing and making promises to discuss this later.

Magnus put a hand on Ivo's shoulder, his eyes locked on Adrian's sword hand.

"No! I've had enough of this." Ivo shook Magnus off and pointed at Adrian, his eyes wild. "You value the life of a witch more than that of your men? More than the empress?"

Adrian let out a deep breath. His chest felt tight, and pressure was building behind his eyes. Ivo had been with him since taking the city of Oro. He was much younger than the rest. When he'd been made a Black Tomeis, they'd drunk half the night away and woken up before dawn to kill a city. Ivo never faltered, never hesitated. He was one of Adrian's best men. He'd even trusted Ivo enough to be Sorcha's guard on occasion.

"Are you still loyal to Prince Eine?" Ivo asked, voice shaking.

"Idiot," Magnus muttered, stepping away from Ivo.

Are you still loyal? The question throbbed in the air—caught in

Adrian's ears. For all his life, he'd valued loyalty over everything. Did he still? Could he still claim it was important when he'd chosen Sorcha over his men in his heart?

Ivo watched him, expression guarded, shoulders tense while the rest of the Tomeis' kept their faces neutral. The accusation throbbed between them all, a shared open wound. It could not be ignored.

He drew his sword, pointing it at Ivo.

"Now," Adrian said, keeping his voice low while adjusting his grip on the weapon.

The black leather glove creaked, tight across his knuckles. He exhaled slowly, waiting for the man to decide. He would either die with a sword in his hand or without. It was Ivo's choice.

With a grunt of acceptance, Ivo drew the sword he wore slung across his back. It was shorter than Adrian's, and the edge was serrated like a carving knife—pain and suffering shining darkly along the blade.

With a cry, Ivo charged Adrian, sword raised, face red.

Adrian let him come, rushing across the space between them. For a split second, their gazes met—resentment, fear, anger, hurt, and love. *Love.*

There was no ringing steel, not even a fight. It ended before becoming anything more than a swift kill.

With a smooth motion, Adrian drove his sword through Ivo's heart. The man's momentum carried him as he slid down the blade until it stuck through his back—a slick, meaty sound and the scent of blood filled the air.

Ivo slumped forward, and Adrian let him fall, pulling his blade free and flicking the blood off it. He turned to each of the Black Tomeis, giving them the option here and now for a quick death.

Thompson exchanged looks with Domenico and Bran. A faint smile hovered around Revenant's mouth—pleasure in someone else's pain.

"Take him away!" Adrian roared. "Go!"

When one of their own died, there was no burial, no remembrance of any kind. Dead was gone. Gone was nothing. They'd lost men through the course of this war—to cities and sickness, to the blade of another's sword, even each other's at times.

And now, to Adrian.

Sorcha stood beside Epona, a hand on the horse's neck, watching him from a distance. Her face was shuttered—emotions locked tight.

———

The empress gasped, sucking in air, fighting death. She stared wide-eyed into nothing—concentrated on some inner image, witness to an inner beast. One hand curled into a fist as her lips pulled back to reveal clenched teeth and bloody gums. Pink-tinged saliva pooled in the corners of her mouth as a low animal sound filtered through.

No one in the room moved. The space was full of advisors and handmaidens, physicians and mystics. Servants stood motionless in the periphery, bearing trays of medicine, tinctures, oils, and basins of cool water. Incense clung to the ceiling—the heavy scent unable to cover the sharpness of crushed herbs and sickness.

Each person had been entrusted to care for the empress. And yet, she'd been poisoned.

Whoever had done this— imprisoned her in a rotting body consumed by pain, whether asleep or awake—would die. He would make sure of it. Her death was coming—almost here. They all knew it. She knew it. And he raced against it, searching for relics and believing Adrian would find them no matter what. The Saint would bring the empress back. He would rip her from the underworld to place her once again in the court that loved her.

The court that feared him.

Eine could feel their eyes as they dreaded the rage that would follow. He welcomed the anger, embraced it, because it would drive the hated fear away and his inability to change the situation. He turned away from his mother and strode from the room. Her labored breathing followed, and a low murmuring from the advisors broke out.

"Get Adrian," he said to the short man scurrying after him. "At once."

"He is traveling with the woman, my prince."

"Find him. I wish to personally impress upon the woman that time is running out."

"But my prince, if you recall him, it will waste time."

"*I* am not the one wasting time." Eine turned, eyes hard. "She needs to understand there is no other way forward but the one I've given her."

The advisor swallowed and nodded.

Behind them, a wail broke the air, shuddering down the halls, filling Eine's head. Another voice picked it up. A woman sobbed. A priest began to chant a prayer to a foreign god—the words echoed and built upon themselves, becoming a chant of many voices. A white-faced servant stumbled from the room, eyes wild with fear. He fell to his knees before the prince, arms outstretched, tears streaming down his face.

"Have them killed," Eine said, jerking his chin toward the room, ignoring the man at his feet. "All of them."

The messenger found them on the road to the next relic.

Magnus, bringing up the rear of the party, heard the hooves first—a rider approaching at a breakneck pace—and he signaled for the others to move off the roadside. Soon, a thin man on a large roan mare came into sight. He used no saddle and carried nothing but a skin of water slung around his chest and a leather cylinder. On his shirt, a silver snake glinted. The mark of the empire.

Adrian rode to meet him, and for a brief moment, Sorcha thought the messenger might join them. He kept looking beyond Adrian to her, pale eyes intent and curious. But he turned and rode away after a brief conversation, his horse breaking into a gallop within a few feet and carrying the messenger away.

Sorcha's stomach twisted—uneasy with the expression on the man's face. He'd been studying her, searching for anything on her face that he might present to the prince upon his return. Only the prince would have sent someone. Sorcha had learned long ago that no other man held sway over Adrian's life.

But the continent was vast. The Traveling City had fallen behind them weeks ago. If this man had reached them so easily, it meant the Traveling City was closer than expected. They'd made it over the mountains and might have even had a few days' hard ride. Maybe there was an easier path, and the city had come the long way around. Not that it mattered. The relics would be reunited sooner than she'd anticipated.

Revenant rode out to meet Adrian, the two stopping their horses to continue a conversation without the Tomeis listening to every word. It was impossible to read Revenant—his faintly glowing eyes landed on her face for a moment before moving on—but Adrian's anger was unmistakable.

Adrian listened without speaking for a time. Then he shook his head, a single movement, as his gaze found her. Relief hit her as the two men rode back. But it vanished when Adrian's face remained stony.

"Prince Eine has sent an urgent message." Adrian turned to Thompson. "How far are we from the next relic?"

The man pulled out the two maps he consulted at every turn. He shook his head, shrugging. "Not too far. We'd be there by early evening."

"Good." Adrian nodded, voice terse. "We'll keep going."

A bog stretched out in either direction around them—miles and miles of murky water and half-dead trees. Tall, thin grasses quaked in the lackluster wind moving through, bringing the occasionally hints of the coast. The ground was soft in places, and the horses picked their way carefully, working to find solid ground.

Soon, the party divided. Adrian, Revenant, and Thompson continued on with her. The others turned back to wait for their return. The farther they traveled, the more a sense of watchfulness touched them.

Sorcha could sense something out there. A creature of some kind, frightening as the werewolves and the vampire skeletons deep in the cave. What else? Something like the creature in the blizzard? No, it would be something new. Something as equally terrifying.

As they rode, Thompson murmured to himself. Sorcha caught bits and pieces of it. He was watching the map, looking up briefly from time to time, and taking mental notes. No matter what happened, he would know the way out of this maze. Continuing on, Sorcha kept an eye on the sky, but it was overcast, making it impossible to determine the time of day. Morning or afternoon. Possibly evening. Or an exceptionally bright moon could be fighting the cloud cover in the hopes of lighting their way. No matter what, the light remained unchanged.

"Stop." Thompson rustled a map. "That stone to the right. See the carving?"

Barely visible and worn down by time, the engraving could still be seen on the broken pillar. A skull. Crude and possibly cut in a short amount of time. There was a quality that felt rushed to Sorcha. It made her uneasy.

"It should be near here."

"Sorcha?"

She jumped, startled out of her thoughts. Adrian was watching her —his expression giving her nothing.

Was this the man who had pushed her body to its shaking limits? Or the man who killed those around him without a second thought? Or was this the man who had talked about leaving this all behind and running away together?

"Which direction do we go?" he asked.

"I don't know," Sorcha said, turning away from him.

She closed her eyes, breathing in, working to calm her mind. No questions. No distractions. Find the relic. Resurrect the Saint. Nothing else mattered. Adrian didn't matter. He couldn't. Not yet. Maybe not ever. Despite what her body might be screaming for out of blind lust and terrible longing.

They were here for one reason.

"Tribute? Sacrifice?"

The question came across the water—up from the earth or down from the sky, it was impossible to tell. It held that note of *other*.

Sorcha swallowed. *Another guardian*, Sorcha thought. And what price would she have to pay here?

"Why have you come?" the deep voice asked.

"We're looking for something," Adrian replied.

"I have nothing for you."

"But you do for me," Sorcha said and dismounted, smoothing out her riding skirt. "I've come for the relic."

A laugh erupted, and a shiver ran across her skin. Fog, hugging the ground but slowly rising, rolled toward them. There was no other choice than to go forward. Sorcha hesitated at the edge of the bog, studying the hillocks and narrow waterways—the murky pools of water. Half-dead trees grouped together here and there, deep green moss clinging to the trunks and hanging from the branches. What might have been a path wound through it, leading deeper in.

"I can smell you." A voice came out of the fog, chasing chills up her spine. "Come and walk my muddy waters. Come to me."

Sorcha took a step forward, the earth undulating beneath her—the air full of decaying vegetation. It was impossible to tell if it were night or day, the world shrouded in half-light and suggestion. The suggestion of shape and time of day, the suggestion of safety and danger. Nothing there was solid. Nothing could be trusted.

Adrian followed her, their arms brushing. He reached out and grazed her arm with the back of his hand. Such a subtle gesture, barely registered.

"No, temple girl. Your lover stays behind."

She met Adrian's gaze, giving him the barest hint of a nod. Revenant's anger was a physical force beating fists against her back. He would have something to say about the word *lover* as soon as she was out of earshot. And from the look on Adrian's face, he knew it too.

It struck her that this was the second creature to call Adrian her lover. Lacus had said it so casually, as did this one. Was it so obvious, then?

The voice laughed, the sound booming out, rolling over them and taking their breath.

"Yes. You are easy to read. Your emotions taste sweet. But I prefer the bitterness of the yellow-eyed one's anger. His thoughts are delicious, like fire and ash."

Sorcha couldn't help it, and she turned to see Revenant's face. He was furious. She could see it in the way he held himself, the expression in his eyes, even though his face remained flat and smooth.

"You are wasting time. My curiosity is fading."

"No." Sorcha swallowed. "I need to speak with you."

"I'll be here," Adrian promised. "When you come out, I'll be right here."

————

Adrian had to send her in alone. It happened over and over, and each time, it became harder to bear, to watch her walk into danger, to face the threat alone. Revenant and Thompson watched him—hot focus and growing anger. Sorcha had changed it all, corrupted their leader, the monster, the man they followed into battle, the man who let the blood flow. He knew what they thought of him now. But he would not go back. He would not change it.

This woman had turned his world upside down. He watched her constantly, unable to pull his eyes away, wondering if redemption was possible. Prince Eine had promised to let him go. And if he did keep his word? Could she love a monster? Could the monster love her?

Come back to me, he thought. *Come back to me and press your lips to mine. Come back to me and change my skin, change my bones. Melt into me and change my life.*

With each day that passed, he wanted it more.

"Should we follow?" Revenant asked. "Will she come back with the relic?"

"We don't need to follow," Adrian said.

"You've made a mistake trusting her."

Adrian tensed. "There's no reason not to. She's done what the prince asked."

"And seduced you." Revenant's tone was flat, but Adrian knew him well enough to feel the accusation in it. "Do you think the prince will be happy that you've tampered with his witch?"

Adrian didn't respond, waiting. He knew there was more. Ivo had been the tip of a blade. Now Revenant planned to twist it. Thompson looked down and then away, noisily rerolling the maps.

"What are you suggesting?"

"You want to regain control? Prove to the Tomeis and Prince Eine that you're still capable of completing this task, and kill the woman now.

We'll take the pieces we have back to the Traveling City. The prince would not be displeased."

"It would go against his wishes. He wants her alive."

"What punishment could there be if the end result is the same?"

Adrian turned to him then. "You speak of treason."

Revenant shook his head. "We follow you. Into battle, to the ends of the earth. If you serve the prince, then so do we. If you do not . . ." His voice trailed off, the rest of the sentence implied.

"I serve the prince," Adrian said flatly.

"As do we. Long may he live."

The men stared at each other for a long moment. Thompson remained silent, shuffling the maps and keeping his gaze averted. If Revenant was speaking now, he was speaking for the unit.

Kill them, a voice deep within him said. *Each and every one. If you don't do it now, you'll regret it later.*

Adrian shifted his hand to his sword, resting on the hilt casually. Revenant kept his attention on Adrian's face, reading his next move there.

Behind them, back the way they'd come, Domenico was shouting.

The tension in his shoulders eased as Revenant looked away.

"There's another messenger!"

Chapter Twenty-Two

Fog swirled around her, obscuring the surrounding bog and leaving her to wonder if this was the right path. Or had she wandered off it, stumbling in the wrong direction, headed for sucking mud and the endlessness of preserved death?

"Who are you?"

Sorcha froze, heart stuttering, threatening to stop entirely. The voice came from behind and above her, so close—almost in her ear.

"Sorcha," she said, pushing her voice above a whisper, keeping the tremble out of it.

"You smell of dying cities."

"I've come from a dying city."

"Have you come here to die? The mud would have you. The fog would eat you. I could help you die."

She was too afraid to turn around and see what stood behind her. A creature. Those words—the booming, slithering echo—did not come from a human chest.

"I've come for the relic."

Silence. Consideration.

"It's time," Sorcha whispered. "I'm the vessel."

"Show me."

Sorcha sucked in a breath, fingers going to her bodice, turning slightly. The only proof she had was the tattoo—an inked map and curse in one. Her salvation and death wrapped tightly around her.

"Stop," the creature hissed. "I do not want your flesh, temple girl. I want your mind."

"How?"

"Close your eyes. Hold out your hand."

She trembled, couldn't stop it or help it, grateful for the darkness behind her eyes as the creature loomed over her. The mud shuddered, threatening to turn into quicksand and swallow her whole.

When Sorcha did not lift her hand, the creature took it. She gasped. Bones. Naked and bare. Stripped down to nothing. And claws, long and curved, sharp and pricking her skin, taking her gently by the hand, hovering at her side.

"Show me."

"I don't know how."

A snort full of derision blew across her face. "They didn't show you? Have they lost the gifts he gave them? Idiots. Worse than fools. Concentrate, what have you been raised for? Born for. Show me your memory."

She knew the day that would mean something. A recent memory. The siege had just begun, raging beyond the walls, a constant background grinding. But the temple had been quiet, morning sunlight pooling on the marble floor, coming through high windows. The hand of the Saint on the altar, gilded and encrusted with jewels. They winked in the light, and for a moment, the hand appeared to move—a finger twitching in her direction, a shift in the thumb.

"Take it," the voice hissed in her ear. "Touch him."

In the past, she hadn't touched him that day. She'd come to see the Saint, urged by the others to pray, to beg for mercy, for a way out of the besieged city. But she'd stood there—mind blank—listening to the sounds of violence beyond the walls.

"Touch him," the voice demanded again.

Its breath caressed her neck, the scent of ages coming with it, preserved bones, bones that had long ago fossilized.

Sorcha reached out through her memory—what was now a vision—and brushed her fingers over the gold and jewels. They felt so cold.

A sudden fear overtook her, terror at the thought of the hand clenching her own, gripping so tight it hurt. Then the city was burning, the memory morphing into something else, blood and fire, the night in the woods when she'd cut Adrian with her blade. His face in the flickering firelight, his mouth in the dark.

The creature moved, arms coming around her, cradling her in a cage of bones. A skull rested against her own. She squeezed her eyes tighter.

"Temple girl. Vessel. You are more beautiful than you will ever understand. The bringer of life, mother of death. You lucky child, able to bring him back, to unleash him onto this world."

She trembled, and her teeth began to chatter as a clawed hand covered her face, snapping her jaws tight.

"I know you now. It's been so long I had lost hope. I began to think he would never come again. And I have waited for such a long time. Stay here. Don't move. If you step away from this spot, the mud will swallow you."

Then it was gone, releasing her, leaving her with weak knees and struggling to remain upright. She counted to ten, taking her time, letting the words stretch until they broke apart in her mind.

Temple girl. Vessel.

Sorcha opened her eyes. Huge, clawed footprints led deeper into the damp ground, mist shifting as something large came toward her.

Sorcha stumbled out of the mist, clutching the relic. A foot, oversized and heavy, bejeweled as the others had been. She'd expected Adrian to be there, waiting for her as he'd promised. But it was Revenant's eyes she met.

"A messenger came. Adrian's presence was requested in the Traveling City immediately. I'll escort you there now. Prince Eine is waiting."

Her heart sank, fear overtaking her. The Traveling City must be even closer than she'd thought. Sorcha opened her mouth, tempted to ask questions, but Revenant would not be the man to answer them.

When she closed her mouth, he must have seen her realization because his upper lip twitched with venomous derision. But he didn't speak. He had no more words for her.

She stumbled toward Epona, who stood patiently beside him, as she clutched the golden bone. Revenant made no move to help her, and it took several tries to get up into the saddle and not lose hold of the relic. When she was seated, he clicked his tongue at his own horse, leading the way out of the bog.

"I will see you again, temple girl," the voice called out of the fog—a promise and a threat. "Mother of death."

CHAPTER TWENTY-THREE

A thousand torches and lanterns lit the Traveling City—tiny fires burning, the dark painted wood almost vanishing beneath the moonless sky. It rose above the trees, growing larger as they neared it—obscured, hinted at, until they left the forest. The city sat in a huge clearing. Trees for miles had been cut down around it, the earth trodden into mud. Snow clung to roofs and turrets—evidence of the weather farther to the north—and beneath the city, the oxen were penned up, out of the cold winds. Fires burned there as well, small campfires, the smoke curling up and sticking to the underside of the city, escaping in thin whisps around the edges.

It looked as if it had just begun to burn and soon flames would engulf it.

Sorcha rode between Domenico and Revenant, the latter's eyes boring into her back. The pressure made her uncomfortable and dread began to fill her. Why was she being called back? She'd done as the prince asked. At one point, she'd considered drawing this out indefinitely—still aware of the tattoo she'd kept hidden from the Mapmaker. But it was inevitable that he would discover it. Was that why Revenant was escorting her here now? Had the prince discovered the hidden tattoo? But it wouldn't matter. The story would end the same way.

Coming out of the bog, she'd expected to see Adrian. He might not have opened his arms for her to walk into, but at least he didn't look at her the way the others did. But there had only been Revenant. And he had been watching her closely, waiting for her reaction at finding Adrian absent. He could see that Adrian's feelings had changed. And he would tell the prince.

Adrian always aligned himself with the prince's desires. But she'd changed him. He wanted her, she knew he did. Would it be enough for him to go against the prince? She wasn't sure. Not when it came down to a hard and fast choice. She hadn't asked, and she couldn't force his hand.

Whatever might happen, she shouldn't count on him once they were before the court.

Sorcha watched the Traveling City grow—otherworldly in the night. A single bell broke the silence, and another followed. The sentries had spotted them. The prince knew they were here.

Adrian flexed his hand, his leather glove creaking. The desire to wrap his fingers around the hilt of his sword was so powerful he could practically feel the weight of it. The bells had finally stopped ringing a few minutes before, announcing the vessel's arrival. He'd hoped they would arrive without any fanfare, without alerting the whole court of their presence. Instead, they were forced to wait in an antechamber as various lords and ladies shuffled past them.

The lords and ladies had rushed to be here. Many hadn't even bothered to put on full court dress. Some had hastily thrown on rumpled finery, others breezed by in simple nightgowns and robes. Their curiosity had been too much to resist the call of the bells.

The steward rubbed his face and then covered a yawn. Even he had failed to put on his usual full court dress. He was so tired he didn't even speak, and for that, Adrian was glad.

The candles in the room dipped and jumped each time the outer door opened, the curious passing through, the inner doors sending the candles streaming out again. They wandered by one and two at a time, not even bothering to hide their excitement at what might happen. Each one was here in the hopes that blood would be drawn and someone might die.

Maybe even the Wolf would meet his end tonight.

Adrian kept his eyes straight ahead, muscle jumping in his jaw. It took everything he had not to turn to Sorcha and offer some kind of comfort. But Revenant and Domenico stood in the corner watching them. Domenico held the last relic Sorcha had retrieved—a golden foot crusted with cut stones, just as the others had been. Adrian's palms itched, the urge to protect Sorcha stealing over him. Danger waited for them beyond the doors. But there was nothing he could do about it.

———

A gong rang out—tones shivering through the air—and the inner doors swung open. Incense wafted through, thick and cloying, and reminded Sorcha of the temple. It hit her—vision or memory—an image of the temple on a late fall day with fresh incense burning and someone singing in the distance.

"This way," the steward said, gesturing them forward. "Prince Eine will see you now."

Sorcha glanced at Adrian, searching for some kind of sign or hint at his emotions. She'd wanted to run to him when they'd entered the antechamber—Revenant and Domenico two steps behind. But his face had not been welcoming. He'd nodded to his men and refused to make eye contact with her.

Now he walked beside her, silent and stoic, into a room full of people who wanted to watch them all die. Even Revenant and Domenico. It was a palpable sensation—vicious curiosity and blood lust.

Prince Eine paced at the foot of the dais. In the empress's chair sat a single wooden bowl. Sorcha was surprised that such a humble item would be placed there. But then it struck her. The empress must be dead. She could think of no other reason their presence would have been demanded.

As one, the group knelt before the prince. She'd been bathed and dressed before appearing in the antechamber to wait. Once again, she'd been gifted beautiful things, and the dress this terrible man had chosen for her was as lovely as all the others. It billowed and pooled around her in a swirl of crimson. Adrian was to her left, Revenant to her right, with Domenico behind them.

"What have you brought me?" Prince Eine asked, gesturing to the bundle Domenico held.

"A relic, my Prince." Domenico placed the wrapped bundle on the hardwood floor. "A foot."

Prince Eine bent and flicked the velvet away. Gold caught the light, reflecting on the prince's face before he covered it again. With a nod, he looked between the four of them. Finally, his gaze settled on Adrian. The entire court held its collective breath.

"What else have you brought me?" Prince Eine demanded. "You were trusted to escort this priestess to collect all of the remaining relics. Is this the only one?"

"No, Prince Eine," Adrian responded, keeping his voice level. "There are others being transported as we speak. They should arrive tomorrow or the next day."

"And the rest?"

"There is more to collect."

"Why hasn't this been accomplished yet?" Prince Eine's words were calm, but his face was reddening. Then he shouted, and the whole court jumped. "She is wasting time!"

"We are making progress."

Adrian's voice was steady, though Sorcha trembled. Every inch of her felt exposed—mind laid bare, terrified the prince could see what she'd kept back. The deceit floated at the top of her thoughts, waiting to be picked from her mind and examined.

"Progress," Prince Eine repeated.

"We would have accomplished more if we'd not been forced to return," Adrian said.

A gasp passed through the gathered courtiers, and murmurings followed—surprise, shock, and delight.

The prince darted for the guard behind his throne, pulling the man's dagger free and lunging for Adrian. Steel flicked out, and a line of blood appeared on Adrian's cheek.

Sorcha made a noise of surprise—fear and horror for Adrian wrapped in it.

Prince Eine's eyes moved to her, something dark and terrible surfacing. The intensity of the look pinned her to the floor, making it impossible to move or speak.

"Stand," he commanded, a calm veneer covering the madness.

Sorcha hesitated, keeping her eyes cast downward as she gingerly stood. Adrian twitched, as if he might stand, but remained kneeling.

Prince Eine grabbed her arm, yanking her forward. The room was silent now, breathless as they watched. With one hand, he pulled at the neck of her dress as he brought the blade down with the other.

The thin fabric split and fell away in ribbons—floating to the floor as if made of nothing. The remaining tattoos were revealed, but most striking was the absence of them. The court could now witness what was left for themselves—dark flowing lines and even darker secrets. Sorcha kept her head up with her hands at her sides—nipples tightening in the cool room.

"Where are the rest?" Prince Eine asked, circling her, the blade inches from her skin. "I saw what the Mapmaker copied. Either his map was wrong, or your flesh is lying. Priestess?"

"They disappear as I discover the relics." she said, swallowing, too afraid to tell him anything but the truth. "No one told me it would happen."

"And this one?" He touched the dagger to her hip—against the tattoo she hadn't shared with the Mapmaker. "I don't remember seeing it before."

Out of the corner of her eye, Sorcha caught the barest hint of movement from Adrian. She opened her mouth to respond but could think of nothing to say. What had seemed like such a clever idea before now had become a huge mistake.

"It doesn't matter," Prince Eine said, waving the blade dismissively. "We only require one more piece."

Before Sorcha could reply, Prince Eine grabbed her by the hair, their faces so close she could see how tired he was—bloodshot eyes and a muscle ticking in his jaw. When he spoke, it was to Adrian, though Eine never took his eyes from Sorcha.

"You have a map." Prince Eine's voice rose, hitting the high ceiling and ringing in her ears. He brought the blade to her throat, pressing it into the soft flesh. "How hard is it? Does someone else need to make her do it?"

Adrian shot to his feet, eyes blazing, hand on the sword at his side.

"I see," Prince Eine said. "It wouldn't do me any good to keep her here, to bleed her dry. I need the thing only she can call forth." The blade slid down her collarbone, tracing the lines of the tattoo, pricking the skin, drawing the faintest line of blood.

Adrian's sword rang as he drew it, but his face was a blank mask, eyes raging.

"Stop."

A single word. Treason. Instant death. The guards around the room drew their weapons and rushed forward, waiting for the command from the prince. The court gasped in delight, anticipating more bloodshed.

The prince smiled. A promise of painful things. Hideous things.

"Revive the Saint, and you can have her," he said as he dropped the blade at Sorcha's feet and stepped back. "But if you take her, if you lower yourself to this, you will no longer be welcome in my city. In any of my cities. And who knows what would become of you then, without my protection. The most hated man in the Empire of the White Snake. The slaughterer of thousands. A monster."

Sorcha's skin prickled, fear growing in her chest.

"Wolf," Prince Eine continued, low voice menacing. "How long do you think I'd let you keep her?"

The threat hung in the air.

Adrian crossed to Sorcha and took her arm, turning to face the prince. "She will find the last relic and revive the Saint."

The words were flat and final. Twitters of delight ran through the ranks watching them, whispers behind hands, delighted eyes focused on the flesh of the woman before them. They watched her hungrily, devouring the details, saving them to share later with the poor unfortunates who missed out on the entertainment.

Adrian turned her away from Prince Eine and hustled her toward the huge doors at the end of the hall. Her dress lay on the floor behind them, her nakedness on display—body open to the curious and prying eyes of the men and women they passed. Behind them, Prince Eine began to laugh, the sound growing and echoing, chasing them out of the hall.

———

"You made a mistake in there," he hissed, hand tight on Sorcha's upper arm as he guided her down the hall, looking for a dark corner.

They passed a handful of servants, who watched them curiously. The naked woman covered in tattoos. The dark man in full armor who brought the scent of death with him.

The Wolf, known at a glance.

She stumbled, staring at him, watching the blood sliding down his neck from the thin slice on his face. Her own blood snaked down from her collarbone, slipping between her breasts, more than she would have expected from such a shallow wound. They bled together.

Dazed, head fuzzy, she tried to understand his words.

Adrian found an alcove and pushed her into it, shielding her nakedness with his body. With a snap, he pulled the cloak from his shoulders, the broach popping free and bouncing on the floor. He swirled it around her, wrapping it tightly around her.

He was angry, his face white with it, and she realized, with shock, that his fingers were trembling.

"What do you mean?" she asked.

"He's reminded us both of our places." he whispered as he pushed her against the wall, his leather armor creaking, his full weight pressing her into the carved wood at her back. His hands were on her throat, shaking, his voice low and strangely calm. He buried his face in her hair, breathing her in. "You shouldn't care what happens to me. You made a mistake showing it in that room."

Sorcha shook her head and reached up to touch him, to wrap her arms around him.

But he grabbed her wrists and pushed her arms out, pinning her to the wall. "He'll use it against you."

"And you won't?"

He let her go and stepped back, leaving her cold. It had gone, the softness in his tone, the warmth of his body against her. She wanted it back, wanted the man who had been in the dark tent with her, desperate for the comfort he'd offered her then. But he was cold again—distant. A wall brought into place so quickly she was left reeling, struggling to understand.

Years ago—a lifetime—he'd made a choice, and now he was struggling to stand by it. But it had been the wrong decision. She knew it was. He did too.

"We need to go." Adrian took her by the arm and walked her down corridor after corridor. "The horses are ready, and we'll recover the last relic as quickly as possible."

———

The prince stared down at his mother's face—the smoothness of her pale features. The pain was gone. Behind him, her ladies were wailing, tearing at their clothes, scratching their faces—leaving bloody trails. Beyond the room, horns blared, vibrating through the city, echoing down halls and into rooms, searching for the source of their meaning, searching until they found her.

It all seemed unrelated to the woman before him. Cold, furious anger filled him. He wasn't sad. He would see her again. The anger was all for the temple woman. He'd given her enough time, and she'd failed to bring together all the pieces of the Saint.

Only the Saint could bring back his mother.

He whirled away, leaving mourners behind, walking until the fresh air of her private courtyard blew the scent of death from him. He was aware of a single advisor who had followed—silent and ready, ever watchful. The man waited—face impassive—for orders he knew would come.

Eine looked up at the blue winter sky. It was so cold outside. The magicians of his court promised that snow would fall soon. The empress had wanted to see the snow one more time—feel it on her lashes, let it melt on her cheeks. He'd promised to give her that. But it hadn't snowed.

Now she was dead.

But winter was just beginning. Before it had passed them by, she would experience the joy of a fresh snowfall. She would again be among the living. He would make sure of it.

"My prince, what would you like me to do?" the advisor asked.

"Have they gone?" Eine didn't look away from the sky, contemplating the stretching hour of dusk.

"Yes, Prince Eine."

"I want the fastest messenger sent to the Wolf's second-in-command." Eine crossed his arms over his chest as the cold settled in his hands. "What's his name?"

"Revenant, my prince."

"Send a message for his eyes only, and make sure the messenger is discreet."

"What message would you like to impart?"

"If it comes down to it, he needs to make sure the task is completed at all costs."

Behind him was death. His mother. His father. His brother. But ahead, shining like the golden star on the horizon, was life. It beckoned to him, sang a siren song he could never ignore. Soon, the death that filled his life would be driven away. And his mother would sit beside him in court. Eine nodded to himself and turned to the advisor, raising a finger in warning.

"But he cannot harm the woman. She must make it to the Wastes alive."

Chapter Twenty-Four

Sorcha split the small apple in one slice, contemplating the two pieces. It was bruised on one side but edible—a luxury after all the miles between the Traveling City and the foot of the mountains where they'd find another relic. Slowly, she sectioned the slightly wrinkled apple with the paring knife, cutting it into bite-sized pieces. Concentrating on the feel of the blade slipping through it, Sorcha inhaled the hints of late summer apple released.

There was more than enough to share. She popped a piece in her mouth and pressed it flat against the roof of her mouth with her tongue, cheeks tingling. She slid the plate in Adrian's direction with a scrape of metal on wood.

The brazier crackling in the corner lit his face—shadows clinging to him like smoke. He was absorbed by the map spread out before him on the cot. There were several of varying sizes and details, but none were the one they'd used to find the missing relics. These were for some other place. Maybe the places he would be sent to next. Sorcha slid the plate a little closer into the edge of his vision, and his dark eyes flicked up to her face.

"It's for you." He spoke softly, a reminder and remonstration.

"I know." Sorcha nodded. "I've decided to share."

An eyebrow went up, a question crossing his face—there and gone. But Adrian ignored the plate, which disappointed her. She shrugged, not wanting it to show, and took the plate back. She popped another piece in her mouth, savoring the sweet and tangy flavor. It was on the verge of being overripe. Another hour or day and it would have been too far gone. But here at the edge, it was perfect. She considered that thought: *here at the edge.*

Here at the edge of the world, at the edge of her sanity, at the edge of her soul, at the very edges of her heart. She stood at the edge of this man, poised for a coming change, poised to fly or fall.

She ate her portion of the fruit, leaving the rest for him. Sweetness lingered on her tongue, collecting in her belly. It was the ghost of past meals, afternoons in the market, late-night feasts. She stood and stretched, stiff from sitting cross-legged for too long.

Turning away from him, Sorcha worked to smooth her expression, not wanting him to see the turmoil racing across her features. From the night in the tent to discovering the empress was dead to the audience with Prince Eine, it had all been so much.

She crossed to the brazier and held her hands out, warming them, facing the light—ignoring the shadows cast behind her. If she had turned, she would have seen how her shadow fell across the desk, fell across him.

Waiting.

Waiting for him. Waiting for the map to vanish from her skin. Waiting to see how he might act in the daylight, when the sun was high, and they would be forced to face this thing between them in the light.

The mark of the Saint was slowly disappearing. Her body was being returned piece by piece. But it was an exchange, not a release. With each relic collected, she could feel him growing in her mind.

Still. Even then. A piece of her wanted to believe she would have a life of her own after this. That Adrian would change his mind about returning to the empire. That the whole damn world would change for them. But he could make no promises, and she could never keep them. All choice had been taken from her. The only thing she wanted for herself was Adrian.

What had they been before the audience with Prince Eine? Nothing. And after? Even less than nothing. They'd continued to share a tent, and Adrian rode beside her. But the strange, fierce thing that had grown between them had been driven back. Sorcha had no illusions. Though the details of the future remained uncertain, she knew in her heart what the ultimate outcome would be.

The Saint visited in her nightmares. His voice was growing at the back of her mind. No words, only intention. *Vessel.*

She shivered and shook the images of rubies and a burning sword away.

Sorcha wanted to go outside and stand in the cold until her fingers and toes numbed. She wanted a distraction from the way being near Adrian made her feel. They were connected by a tenuous thread, their eyes locked, hands reaching but never touching.

Without looking back, she stepped out of the tent. Adrian didn't stop her. He knew she had nowhere else to go. That fact was still a wound. The home she'd been torn from, letting go of the temple and her previous life—her connection to it all—by force or personal will. She'd divested herself of that other Sorcha. A woman who had smiled easily and made friends quickly. Ines's death had killed that Sorcha. The deaths in the Golden Citadel had ensured that version of herself would never return.

Not even the Saint himself would have been able to resurrect her.

Overhead, lights flowed and shifted across the sky. A blue and green aurora danced across the sky tonight—blue like sapphires and green as new mint in spring. The golden star in stark contrast to the rippling colors. Low as ever on the horizon, a constant reminder.

Sorcha wove past the campfire and the men gathered there, not stopping to see who they might be or who lingered at the edges on guard. It didn't matter. They wouldn't stop her from roaming. She was positive that most, if not all, wanted her dead despite the prince's edict. If she wandered out of camp and got lost in the wilderness, it would only make it easier for them. The horses were tied on the other side of camp, but she heard them rustling together in the dark.

A cold wind blew down from the mountains here, searching for travelers, seeking out the thin places in their clothes and getting close. She crossed her arms, trying to keep her body heat in and wishing she'd put the fur-lined cloak on instead of this one. If she had, she would have been able to avoid going back to the tent sooner. She didn't want to be anywhere near Adrian. Not when he avoided her eyes and refused to acknowledge her in any meaningful way.

I will never leave you alone.

The Saint. His words or pure emotion. It was hard to be sure.

A scuff of boots made her turn. Adrian came out of the dark, carrying the fur-lined cloak she'd been wishing for. Without speaking, he draped it over her shoulders and stepped away, turning his face to the sky.

They stood together, but Sorcha felt more alone than before.

"Are you really going to pretend it didn't happen?" Sorcha turned on him suddenly, throwing her hands in the air. "Really?"

"I swore an oath," Adrian said, keeping his eyes on the sky.

"Why does that matter? Right now? I'm not asking for anything beyond this." Sorcha spread her hands, taking in the landscape and golden star. "If the end result is the same, who cares how we got there?"

"Some would care."

"The prince? Revenant?" When he didn't respond, Sorcha nodded, a sour expression crossing her features. "Tell me you haven't been thinking about me."

"Do you want me to drag you back and show you what I've been thinking about?"

Sorcha's heart pounded, and she struggled to breathe. *Yes.* She wanted everything he could give her—pain as well as pleasure, heartache, and bottomless black joy. But not if he was going to be the empire's Wolf. Not with her. He could be the villain in everyone else's story, but not hers.

Or have I become a villain too? For wanting what I can't keep? For wishing I could leave the Aureum Sanctus behind and leave the dead to rest? They're counting on me. The Saint wants me. Sorcha bit her lip, wanting to scream with the pressure of it all. *But I want Adrian.*

"Adrian," she whispered and reached for him, placing her hands against the hard contours of his chest.

There was nothing else she could say. His name was all that mattered. No other promises could be made.

He looked down, searching her face. For what, she didn't know—would never know—because this man would only ever offer small pieces of his heart. And she didn't have a right to claim even those. She stepped back, accepting that this was what they'd be until the resurrection. Endless nights spent sleeping beside each other, but only one of them mattered. It would have to be enough to carry her through whatever lay ahead—the last thing she'd ever chosen for herself.

"Goodnight," she said, giving him a sad smile. "Tomorrow we can pretend we didn't have this conversation either."

He swore softly—the word brutal in the quiet—and reached her in a few quick steps, crushing her in his embrace. Their mouths met and locked, tongues caressing. Sorcha wove her fingers into his loose hair, pulling him down to her.

Take me, she pleaded silently. *You can't damage me any more than I already am.*

———

"I've made the choice I have to." Adrian fumbled with her clothes—hands rough, voice hungry. The fire in the brazier was almost dead, but faint light from the aurora penetrated the canvas tent, bathing them in an unearthly glow. "You know how this ends."

But do you?

"Don't talk," Sorcha said as she helped him remove his tunic and ran her hands over his chest.

So many scars. She would never hear the stories behind each one, never hold him in the daylight when the world belonged to the living and nothing more important than a breakfast choice lay ahead. But she would take this.

Adrian leaned down and took one firm nipple into his mouth as he massaged her other breast. She leaned into him, head falling to his, as she smoothed his hair back. After a moment, he moved to the other nipple, his hand moving to her pussy and gently parting her, exploring her slick folds.

She moaned and tilted her hips toward him as he slipped a finger inside.

"You're so beautiful," he murmured. "So wet."

She made a noise of agreement, struggling to think of anything clearly. He circled her clit, sucking on one nipple and then the other, sliding two fingers into her and stroking that inner place. Her knees buckled, and he held her up, fingers sliding in and out as she leaned into him. He moved to kneel, gripping her ass with one hand, ready to lick between her thighs.

"Wait," she said, stopping him.

Sorcha knelt and tugged at the laces on his breeches, pushing them down and taking his underclothes with them. His cock was heavy in her hand as she stroked him. Leaning forward, she licked the head of his cock, swirling her tongue over him, a small noise of pleasure humming in her throat. Adrian's hands were at his sides, and she grabbed them, placing them on her. He groaned, cradling the back of her head with one hand, the other cupping the side of her face.

He let her take her time, hips twitching, his grip tightening slowly.

She cupped his balls and stroked him with one hand, caressing the head of his cock with her mouth and tongue. He was close. She could feel it in his body, the way he tensed and clutched at her.

———

"Stop," he murmured, hands in her hair, fighting the urge to fill her mouth. "Come here."

Sorcha pulled away and placed a gentle kiss on the head of his cock, running her hand down the length of him again. He groaned, pulling her up and onto his lap, leaning back so she straddled him. She hovered above him, holding him and teasing him, his cock slipping through her arousal.

"What do you want?" she asked. Her voice was husky voice, her pupils dilated.

"You," Adrian whispered. *You and only you, for as long as I can have you.* But he didn't say that.

Sorcha's lips twitched upward—an eyebrow raised. He dug his fingers into the soft flesh of her thighs, waiting for her response.

"Then take me."

Adrian moved her hand and thrust up, sliding inside her warmth and filling her. She gasped, hands on his chest, staring down into his face.

Don't look away, he thought. *I want you to see what you do to me.*

Sorcha rolled her hips, head back, hands on his thighs behind her. Adrian swallowed and gripped her hips, every muscle tense as he watched her—enraptured. He would have given her everything. Anything she asked. Burn the world. Kill the prince. Race across the continent until they reached the ocean and then keep going. *Don't stop.* Her body tightened around him as her movements became frantic. Cupping her breasts, Adrian thrust up and massaged her soft flesh, pinching one hard nipple and then the other when she moaned. He hissed when her fingers dug into his thighs, her mouth falling open, brows drawn together as her release hovered.

"Come for me, Sorcha," Adrian whispered. "I want you more than I've ever wanted anything in my life."

The orgasm ripped through her, and she bit the back of her hand, muffling her cries. Her other hand dug into his thigh as her rocking slowed and then stopped, her chest heaving as she tried to catch her breath. Her eyes were hazy, face relaxed, and body boneless. He loved to see her this way, without the weight of the future dragging them down, when he was inside her, and nothing mattered more than the way the world broke when she came.

Sorcha leaned forward into his arms with a sigh, her breasts pressed against his chest and body slick with sweat. He rolled her over, letting the furs fall aside. He cradled her head in the crook of his arm as he braced himself over her. He breathed her in, squeezing his eyes shut, committing to memory each sensation she pulled from him. He took his time, filling her slowly, but she tilted her hips up, urging him to move faster.

"We have all night," he whispered against her ear. "I'm taking my time."

She groaned, the sound soft and shivering across his skin, as her fingers dug into his waist. "I don't have all night."

Without hesitation, he rammed into her, covering her mouth with his and swallowing her cries. They moved together, her knees pressed against his sides. She tensed beneath him, head tipped back, and eyes closed. He wanted this to last, to feel her body tight around his, but he couldn't stop. He came as she whispered his name, her voice almost drowned out by his breathing.

Adrian. Adrian. Adrian.

————

He might breathe and eat and kill after this was all done. He might find another woman to warm his bed at night. But it wouldn't matter. He'd already be dead inside.

"When did your feelings change?" he asked, needing to know, wanting to hear her say the words.

For himself, he couldn't pinpoint the exact moment. But he could go back to the first time he'd seen her—surrounded by fire and falling buildings, angry and hating him the moment their eyes met. It had crept up on him. At first, he'd been able to mask it as duty. But now he had to be honest with himself—with her—that it had not only been following orders. The moment in the Silvas when they'd been chased by werewolves, pulling her over the cliff and into his arms, promising to never let go.

I've got you.

His stomach twisted, excitement and fear—her acceptance or rejection. When had she come to see him as something other than the monster he was? Her embrace had promised redemption, had shown him a path through the darkness of his own soul—through the hellscape he'd built his life in. Could he be worthy of her after all that? He'd embraced the darkness long ago, time and again, at each turn, taking it in instead of turning it away.

There had been so many situations where he could have chosen a different path. He could have broken away from the prince, the empire. He could have run like Finian. But he'd never considered anything other than what the prince offered. Even now, he knew there were things about himself that would never change—he would always be a monster.

Slowly, they'd built an uneasy understanding, desire lurking beneath the surface, delicate with each other—tentative. He was desperate to preserve it. Desperate not to see a look of disappointment or sadness in her eyes. The fear had vanished, and if it returned, he knew there would be no coming back from it. They would never be able to regain that ground between them. It would be like shutting a door and sealing it behind stone.

"When did my feelings change?" she mused, voice coming from a distance, somewhere deep inside where she examined each emotion one by one. "I'm not sure. I don't know if I could choose a single instance. You?"

"In the city, as it burned."

He swallowed, unable to say more, holding his breath and waiting for her to speak again. Sorcha pulled her knees to her chest and wrapped her arms around them, resting her chin on her arms. She considered the shifting lights of the aurora penetrating the canvas, absorbed, and he could not tear his eyes away from this woman who had stolen his heart. She'd run into the wild and carried it with her. He'd followed, unable to resist.

"We can make no promises," she whispered.

Sorcha hesitated. Her tone held something else, hinted at more. She was holding it back, keeping a secret. She sat up, the furs falling away to reveal pale skin as she studied his face, drinking him in.

"I'm not asking for any." He adjusted the bedding, the air cold against his skin. "You'll freeze."

She reached down and took his hand, placing it on her breast, and whispered, "So, keep me warm."

Adrian pulled her down to him, covering her mouth with his own, and refused to think of anything other than this moment with Sorcha.

CHAPTER TWENTY-FIVE

The Black Tomeis had not been the same since Ivo's death. No one had said anything, but the atmosphere was different. The camp-fire each night was quieter. The afternoon rides no longer full of conversation. Adrian kept Sorcha closer than ever, but if he was gone for any reason, it was Revenant who stood guard—full of silent judgment and anticipation.

Sorcha kept her mouth shut, pretending not to hear when they called her a *witch* or worse. If Adrian was within earshot, they kept it to themselves, but sooner or later, the words always came out.

The Androphagoi could be seen from the foothills—growing in size as they neared. Nestled among the snowcapped mountains, it was the home to some of the most dedicated believers in the Aureum Sanctus. *The Crimson Cult*. She'd never thought of it that way before, but it was the truth. A death cult, revering a dead god and praying to join him as soon as possible. For them, death had never held any fear.

But she feared it now.

Ines. Rohan. The others sipping poison as if it were water, welcoming the convulsions and frothing mouths. She didn't want that to be her fate—following blindly and giving her life away so carelessly. There had been minutes and hours when she hadn't thought of her loved ones. The guilt that followed that realization was haunting. Letting life in, the small joys—a beautiful sunrise, a flower, the breeze that brought the scent of snow and pine. How could she enjoy those things when they were gone?

Not gone, said a voice in the back of her head. *I am coming.*

Sorcha shivered. It had been growing stronger, this strange pull that began in the center of her body and stretched out into the world. She wasn't sure where it would lead her. But the moment she would meet the Saint—a living, real-world creature—was coming. And they would collect the final relic in the Androphagoi.

This was one temple she'd never wanted to visit. It housed a relic—the Saint's skull—but this place was shrouded in mystery. No one talked about it. She only knew the skull was there because of the map on her skin. No one had ever spoken it aloud. No one wanted to talk about what happened within those temple walls.

Some whispered, though, when they thought no one in a higher-ranking position could hear. And Sorcha had never passed up the chance to eavesdrop.

Priests volunteered to be bricked behind solid walls, left to starve while they prayed and dedicated their last days to the Saint. Some claimed there had been a harsh winter years ago, and the men living there had been snowed in for months. When someone had finally gotten through the narrow pass leading to the temple, several people had been eaten. *Right down to the bone.*

Unease trailed them—a persistent companion—as they traveled. Adrian, Revenant, Thompson, and herself were the only ones going all the way to the Androphagoi doors. The others would continue across the mountains to a location Thompson had made sure they could describe—a place where the old road forked near a stream. Then, as soon as this final relic was retrieved, they would reunite and continue south.

Prince Eine would be waiting for them somewhere in the Wastes.

———

The walls of the city around the Androphagoi were jagged teeth—rubble and tumbled stones, with turrets crumbling against a gray sky. Statues of men in robes and women wearing halos were on every corner, gathered in the squares they passed through as if moments before they'd been speaking privately but now paused to watch these interlopers pass through.

Sorcha studied the stone faces, each one larger than life and coldly beautiful. They stood seven or eight feet tall, looking down on those who passed beneath them. She wondered if a person would emerge if the stone cracked. If that happened, she might scream. Epona tensed beneath her, tuned into Sorcha's unease.

But the statues weren't nearly as unsettling as the crows that sat everywhere. The birds watched them—silent and aware. Sorcha felt more than watched. It was inspection, critical and relentless. One bird broke the silence, stretching out its neck, its caw filling the air.

"Do you want me to shoot it?" Revenant asked, pulling his bow and nocking an arrow.

"No," Adrian's voice was hard. "Leave it."

Sorcha let her eyes sweep over the two men who had come with them without resting for too long. Revenant was bloodthirsty and always so ready to kill. Thompson, though outwardly not as vicious, was the same.

One pale as death, the other dark as terror. They made a striking pair, following their monster general. Sorcha couldn't stand them, couldn't meet their dead eyes. If they could, they'd put an arrow in her heart, a knife in her throat. They saw the way Adrian looked at her when he thought no one was looking—when he thought she couldn't see him. A look she struggled to understand, one that angered his men, made them distrust her even more.

Witch. Temptress. Oracle. They said she was many things. A priestess to a god, a harbinger, a woman holding more power than they thought she should have. Too many times, she had been alone with them. Too many times, she had felt their desire to end her life. If the prince hadn't wanted her alive, she would be dead, no matter what Adrian said. It had been true since the beginning, but it was worse after this last audience.

She could feel them at her back now, waiting, wondering if maybe, in this place, they could get away with pushing her into a crumbling wall or down a broken flight of stairs. If Adrian knew, he didn't show it, refusing to expose the weakness to them, but they had all seen him pull his sword on the prince as well as pull her up from the cliff and into his arms.

Safe, he had murmured against her ear. Safe with the monster.

Another raven cawed farther into the ruins. A receiver of the message. Whoever or whatever was in there, they knew Sorcha was here.

The Saint knew she was here.

Adrian turned to her. "Where will the relic be?"

"A safe place, deep within the temple. I've heard stories of this place, but none of them were clear about where the relic was located."

With a nod, he led the way, Sorcha following, and the two men remained behind her. The flat stone paving beneath her feet was cracked —dead grass wilting through the breaks. The broken gate loomed—iron rusted, wood rotted.

What happened here? Sorcha wondered. *How long has it been since anyone from the Citadel visited this place?*

She'd never met anyone who had, but there was never any hint that it lay in ruins. Why leave the relic here when this place was decaying by the moment? Another lie. Another dark truth. More illusions of security and well-being. Kahina Kira talked about the temples in the world as if each were as powerful and important as the one Sorcha had grown up in.

Lies. So many woven together to create the illusion of safety and importance. Sorcha was no longer sure what was true. And in her heart, she no longer cared. There was no choice but to continue. Somewhere, the Saint waited. She could feel him, just as he must feel her.

They passed beneath the arched gate into a narrow street beyond. Buildings rose around them with hollow, empty windows and tumbled beams blocking doorways. Human bones, bleached white and weathered, were everywhere. They were in the gutters and on the street, slowly breaking down beneath the onslaught of the seasons. So many people had died here, and she wondered if they'd chosen poison over whatever might have broken through the gates.

Turning away with a shudder, she concentrated on Adrian's back, trusting him to discover a path. Too much trust, leaning into him in a way she couldn't understand. A man despised across the continent, feared in a way no other person had ever been, hated. Yet she had never felt so safe. Her heart had never raced the way it did when his dark eyes met hers. What did that make her? Betrayer, lover of monsters. A woman sick with darkness, infected with it, soul corrupt.

———

At the farthest point from the gates, nestled in an alcove of a sheer cliff, sat the Androphagoi. It had been carved hundreds of years ago into the dark gray stone—veins of white quartz ran through it, threads of gold twinkling within those pale lines. Pillars lay tumbled down the stairs, singed by fire and pockmarked with age. Huge, wide steps led up to arched doors, six of them across the front of the building. The metal embossed doors had been melted with some forgotten but intense flame.

The distorted story they told was familiar, and a pang of unexpected homesickness sank through Sorcha, from head to toe. A benevolent Saint, bestowing blessings, the sacrifice he made for his followers, the promise to return. And the ruins of the world without him.

The group dismounted, the men murmuring to each other as Sorcha patted first Epona and then Nox. The horse nuzzled her hand, searching for some small bit of food.

"Not so scary after all, are you?" Sorcha whispered, running a hand over his nose before turning to Epona to do the same.

The mare's ears pricked forward and then back, listening to Adrian and Revenant as their voices grew louder for a moment before returning to whispers.

Sorcha went to her saddlebag, digging down past a second cloak and her gloves. There were a handful of small, wizened apples at the bottom —the remains of the fresh rations they'd taken from the Traveling City when they'd departed. Sorcha gave one to Nox and one to Epona, waiting for the men to decide their route.

"It's time," Adrian said, getting Sorcha's attention and jerking his chin toward the temple.

He paused, twisting the sword in his hand. She came to stand beside him, part of her wanting to turn away, to run back through the deserted streets and out into a world where she was no one and nothing. Another part—the child raised and loved in the temple, with mothers and sisters who surrounded her and filled her with safety and security—wanted to go inside and see if anyone was there. And even now, knowing what would come, how it all would end, a small part of her wanted to meet the Saint.

Sorcha glanced at Adrian. He'd broken all his rules for her—bent his world around her. He had no idea how much blood there would be at the end. And it would all be hers.

"I'll go first," she said, moving past him and going up the stairs.

He let her go, falling into step behind her, becoming her shadow. The men behind followed at a distance. At the top of the steps, they paused, the weak light of the overcast day barely penetrating the gloom beyond. The space reminded her of home. It hit her, a swell of homesickness for something that could never be. And it had never truly been what she'd thought it was.

"There." Revenant pointed at a far corner. "See it?"

A faint, glimmering glow reflected on a corridor wall leading deeper into the temple.

Adrian nodded, motioning for Thompson to stay behind as the three crept forward. Revenant lit the small lantern they'd brought, leading the way inside.

No one spoke as the light led them through the ruins of the sanctuary and deep within the twisting corridor. There were no stairs or diverging paths, only the corridor with brick walls that curved in on itself, spiraling in, around some hidden destination. From behind the walls came sounds—tapping or faint scratching. A smell of death and decay permeated the air, coming from deeper within the building.

"What happened here? Has the Horde been here?" Sorcha asked, pausing to listen to a knocking coming from the other side of the brick wall to her right.

"If they'd been here, the relic would have been brought back,"

Adrian said, motioning for her to continue with them. Revenant nodded. Adrian continued, irritation beneath the words. "It could have been any number of smaller kingdoms or warlords. Bandits. Temples are wealthy. I haven't seen anything of any worth left in this city."

"Bandits? Warlords?" Sorcha's brow furrowed. "You make it sound like ancient times. We don't have those anymore. The only army who could have been capable of this is yours."

"Prince Eine's army," Revenant cut in.

"Why do you think the Horde marches south?" Adrian asked.

"Because you're power-hungry monsters." The words were out before Sorcha could stop them. *Not you, Adrian. You aren't a monster,* she thought, unable to say it aloud. But that was a lie. They both knew it.

A bark of laughter escaped from Revenant. "Or could it be that no one south of the Summer Palace is fit to rule and keep their people protected and prosperous?"

"The two aren't mutually exclusive," Sorcha snapped.

"The kingdoms south of your citadel have been fighting among themselves for centuries. What do you know of world history?" Adrian asked, gesturing that they should continue walking.

Sorcha lifted one shoulder, refusing to admit how little she knew. She'd paid no attention to the world beyond her small sphere. Never questioned the decisions royals made or the trade deals that were brokered. Of course, there were alliances and marriages and treaties and there had been other small wars. But none of it had impacted her life. Until now.

"Prince Eine will unite the entire continent," Revenant said.

"And then?" she asked softly.

As a new section of the corridor came into view, they stopped, staring at the destruction ahead. Sections of the walls had come down, revealing dark expanses of nothingness, and bricks littered the floor. Emaciated bodies lay on top of the rubble. The smell here was worse than it had been, and Sorcha covered her mouth and nose. It reminded her of the Citadel—the way it had stunk before the city began to burn, when everyone was hungry and sick.

A scrabbling came from up ahead, around the next curve, and

Adrian stepped to the front of the small group. Adjusting the grip on his sword, he waited. Revenant crossed to one of the bodies and knelt, moving a piece of fabric away from a shoulder.

"A relatively clean cut made after death," he murmured, moving to the next corpse. He picked up a finger. "It's been chewed."

"What?" Sorcha looked from one man to the other, then down at the bodies.

A voice rose in song, a hymn she'd heard a thousand times. One of Ines's favorites. The notes wobbled as the words ran together, fading off into loud humming.

"I know that song," Sorcha said, stepping around Revenant and the bodies he was examining. "That's her favorite song."

"Stay behind me," Adrian said, holding out a hand to keep her back.

"But—"

The humming grew louder, and the light in the corridor shifted. Incense blew toward them, the scent overpowering the decay. A thin, bald priest came hobbling into view. The man wore the crimson of someone important—an elder and leader of some kind. But his robes were torn and dirty, the hems stained a greasy black. In one hand, he carried a sharp hatchet, and in the other, a ceremonial bowl. The man stopped when he saw them, mouth open, bloodshot eyes dancing between them.

"Who are you?" Sorcha asked, taking a step forward.

"Sorcha." Adrian's voice was soft but firm. "Stay behind me."

"Sorcha?" The priest looked from Adrian to her, pale eyes wide. "From the Citadel?"

"Where is the relic?" Adrian asked, at the same time, sword half raised.

"You came," the emaciated man said, dropping the hatchet and bowl with a clang. He shuffled toward her with an outstretched hand. "You are the vessel."

"How do you know?" Adrian asked.

"Sorcha." The man studied her carefully and then nodded. "Only the vessel would come to us after everything that's happened. We knew you would come for him."

"But you know my name," she said, voice barely above a whisper. "How?"

"Everyone knows. Your name was given to us as soon as your map ceremony began. Sorcha of the Golden Citadel, Vessel and child of the Saint." A sheen of tears reflected in his eyes, and he pressed one hand to his chest. "I knew you would come, but I wasn't sure I would be here to see it."

"And the relic is with you?" she asked.

"Yes, I will show you. He's with me." The priest shuffled back the way he'd come, toward the light, motioning for them to follow.

"Stay behind us," Adrian said, nodding to Revenant.

They followed the priest around the curve, coming across more open spaces in the walls, more dislodged bricks. But there were no bodies here. The light grew stronger, the air around them warmer.

"What happened here?" Adrian asked, keeping his eyes focused on the man.

"It was a long siege," the priest said, picking up the pace.

"But the walls?" Sorcha waved at an opening as they passed it, pausing to peer inside. "It looks like a cell? Or room?"

"The altar is around this curve," the priest said, avoiding her question. "We're almost there."

"Your priests are cannibals," Revenant said, his words echoing along the corridor.

"Stay focused," Adrian said, shooting his second-in-command a sharp look.

The corridor ended with an arch leading into a larger space. Candlelight illuminated everything, flickering and dancing in an invisible draft. A faint haze of incense covered everything, bringing memories of the temple to mind. It had been one of her duties as a child to light the incense that burned around the relic. It was different from the others burned throughout the rest of the temple. A richer scent, heavy with perfume. The same scent filled the air here, but beneath lay dark decay.

"Wait." The man stopped, turning to face them. "Sorcha, please give me a moment to ensure that you are meeting him under the proper conditions." The priest passed beneath the arch, muttering to himself excitedly.

She heard him moving things out of the way, something heavy hitting a wall.

"Kill him," Revenant said.

"No." Adrian shook his head, eyes straight ahead.

But he would have before. Sorcha knew he would have. Only her presence kept him from being the monster. But she could see his calm facade cracking.

The priest returned, shuffling forward, a wrinkled golden sash wrapped around his waist.

"Sorcha," the priest said, clutching her arm, rank breath steaming out of his black mouth. "He's here."

"How long have you been down here?" She kept her voice low, focusing on the priest as she followed him, working to keep her disgust and horror from showing.

All around the room were bodies that had been mangled and chewed.

"Since the city was sacked. We hid and stayed underground for many weeks. We protected the Saint. Only afterward was I able to bring him back here."

The priest gestured to where a large object lay beneath a swath of crimson fabric on a black stone altar. It was surrounded by hundreds of candles. When Sorcha didn't step forward, the priest did. He grasped the edge of the fabric with a trembling hand and pulled it away.

Empty eye sockets seemed to fix on her, seeing her from another world, ready to join her in this one.

Vessel. It wasn't a word so much as a feeling. The Saint's voice, here in this place. She felt him in her bones, in the space between each rib. Her mind was awash with a tide of images—a battlefield, a golden man, a burning sword.

"He's ready to leave with you. It will be a glorious return." The man smiled, exposing rotten teeth and bleeding gums. He held up one finger and hurried to a dim corner where a low bench was piled high with unlit candles and books. "I have something for you."

"Wrap the relic in the cloth. It's time to go." Adrian gestured to Revenant.

But the second-in-command was already moving, collecting the relic and grunting as he took the weight on his shoulder.

Sorcha skimmed the room again—chewed bones, rotten gums, the priest who looked more dead than alive. She would have given anything to leave this place behind.

The priest came shuffling back, carrying a bundle.

"A beautiful thing," he murmured, unwrapping layer after layer of soft cloth. His eyes darted up, searching her face, and a faint smile touched his cracked lips. The priest held out a golden knife, intricate scrollwork covering the blade, the handle a dark polished stone. A ceremonial blade—one meant for ritual and sacrifice. "Beautiful, like you."

"I have to go," Sorcha whispered, stepping back.

Not here. Not now. Not after everything else that has happened.

"No." The man shook his head, desperation in every line of his body. "You can't leave. Not yet."

Adrian grabbed Sorcha's arm and dragged her back the way they'd come. She stumbled past the exposed cells, avoiding the desiccated bodies, trying to block out the priest's cries as he followed. The tapping in the walls grew louder, as insistent as the man following them.

Revenant went ahead, calling to Thompson as soon as they reached the main area. Cool air blew away the stink of decay and the cloying incense. Sorcha shuddered, pulling her cloak tight as Adrian urged her ahead of him. Hurrying on, trying to block out the priest's pleas, she rushed for the doors and began to make her way down the stairs.

"Sorcha! Vessel!"

I am not those things. I am not a killer. I am not the only physical tie to a god on this earth. I did not choose this. I will not let things end like this here.

Revenant was telling Thompson what they'd seen. Adrian was beside her. Ahead, she could see Epona, Nox, and the other horses. She wanted to ride out of this place and never come back.

Adrian offered no comfort, no understanding, in front of his men. Right now, she hated him for it.

With a jerk and cry of surprise, she was brought up short as she was grabbed by the clasp of her cloak.

The priest gripped the fabric with claw-like hands—pale as death in the muted light of the overcast sky, eyes sunken and lips cracked and bloody. He was already dead, moving through the temple without realizing it. It would be a mercy to kill him now, before he wasted into nothing, gnawing on the bones of his brothers and sisters.

"Please kill me, Sorcha." The priest pulled at her cloak, the fabric straining and then ripping. "Sorcha, you must."

Shaking her head, she stepped back as the tear in the fabric widened. "I can't."

"Sorcha, please."

She wanted to cover her ears. Never again did she want to hear her name spoken this way.

"Keep going," Adrian said.

The priest's voice was shrill as he continued, one bone-thin finger pointed at her heart—accusation and demand in the gesture. "You will fulfill your duties! You are the vessel. You are his face in this world. How will you face his judgment knowing you left me this way?"

She shivered, tugging the torn cloak around her, looking up at the winter sky. He wasn't one of the many who had lied to her—promising one thing while meaning another—but it didn't matter. He was one of them.

He held the ceremonial blade out to her, hope filling his face, hinting at the man he might have been before the siege, before the deaths.

She took it, feeling its warmth from being held so close to his body. It was a heavy weight in her hand, full of expectation and intention.

"I will tell him how well you fulfilled your duties, Sorcha."

"You don't have to tell him," she said. "He knows."

He smiled, exposing black teeth and gums, fumbling with the soiled tunic and pulling it apart until he exposed his bony chest. Bruises covered his skin, dark discoloration that hinted at internal decay. It was kindness and mercy, the only thing left she could offer.

Sorcha plunged the blade into his chest, scraping against bone, hitting soft organs. There was little resistance, almost none, and it brought with it the memory of the priest in the prince's court, the quiet determination of her family. A sob broke from her throat, and she gritted her teeth, fighting to keep it in as the priest sat heavily on the steps, the blade lodged in place.

Revenant and Thompson were whispering, the crows screaming. Sorcha closed her eyes, straining to hear the old man breathe, waiting for the moment it stopped. It didn't take long. He was gone so quickly, so ready to depart.

I will tell him how you fulfilled your duties, he'd promised. But she hoped he wouldn't, that she would never face the creature who had begun to dream with her, who'd crept into her waking hours.

She turned, leaving the man on the steps, walking past the group she'd come with, continuing without looking back and leaving them to follow.

The skull murmured to her, the words not yet distinguishable but getting clearer.

———

There were more and more birds. Black messengers called to witness a rebirth so they could carry it to the ends of the earth.

She looked up to watch a flock of starlings dip and rise, an amorphous shape moving across the sky, liquid in a solid form. In their movement, she thought she saw things—the future and past, the present and what might have been.

"Do you see something, witch?"

She brought her eyes back to earth, to the muddy, bloody place she stood in. Revenant was watching the flock, standing so near, though she had not heard him approach. He held his sword unsheathed in one hand, drawn and ready, sharp and deadly. Had he come for her?

She glanced around. No one else was close. The camp was far enough away that if she screamed, they wouldn't be able to reach her in time to stop a killing blow.

"He's not in camp," Revenant said as if he read her mind.

"I wasn't looking for him."

"Weren't you?" He turned to her, staring her full in the face. His own expression was full of an emotion she had no name for—disgust or fear, anger or pity. "In the village where I was born, we had a witch. She was ancient, crippled, and blind. But when she channeled the demons of the underworld, she would dance and sing, her clouded eyes cleared, her face smoothing out."

Sorcha swallowed, an edge of fear creeping toward her, sidling in. "What happened to her?"

"I killed her." His voice was flat, matter-of-fact.

"Why?"

"Do I need a reason to kill a witch?"

"I am not a witch."

"You keep saying that. I don't believe you. He's been different since you've arrived, lost the edge that made him worthy of the prince."

"It's your prince that wanted me here. I wasn't given the choice."

"And when you've served your purpose, I will kill you."

She wanted to tell him. Shock him. Silence his threat. It was meaningless. She would die without his assistance. The idea warmed her, kept the fear from taking over. And there was a fierce pleasure in knowing she would deny him what he wanted. What he felt was revenge and justice for altering the man he'd sworn his life to. So, she shrugged, not giving him the satisfaction he craved, the fear he'd hoped to instill in her.

"Do you know about the Saint?"

"It's a cult. A myth and lies."

"Your prince doesn't seem to think so."

He shook his head, not wanting to speak the treasonous words. "You're nothing more than a witch. A temple whore. I've heard the creatures speaking to you, temple girl and vessel. I know what you are."

"You've heard them, seen them, so how can you deny them and believe the Saint is nothing but a story?"

Emotions battled on his face, his own personal beliefs at war with how he thought the world was, what he believed it was. Flat, black and white.

"You don't have to believe in them for them to exist. He will come for you regardless of your beliefs."

His grip tightened on the sword, fierce light in his yellow eyes.

"The prince believes. Others do too. You have no idea what I am, what is coming for you." She took a step forward, lowering her voice. "He will devour believers and nonbelievers alike. No one will be spared."

"Not even you, witch?"

He'd come to it without her saying it aloud. She didn't respond, turning on her heel and walking toward the camp. *Don't run or he'll cut you down.* A hunting dog scenting blood, the nearness of a successful kill.

He laughed, hatred and triumph in it. "I'm looking forward to your death, temple girl."

———

They came down out of the mountains and met the remaining Tomeis in the foothills. Sorcha barely registered it. Her mind spun around the priest's death—relived the dagger sliding into his thin frame, releasing him from the world he desperately wanted to escape. She hadn't even known his name. But he'd known her. How many others out there carried her name in their heads, waiting for her to perform magic she didn't understand and give up a life she'd barely lived?

Adrian rode beside her, silent and stone-faced, one balled fist resting on his thigh. He'd retreated from her again, because they could only share themselves in the dark. It had been a mistake to think she could be happy with those stolen moments. Now that he'd touched her, she wanted nothing more than for him to do it again. But each time she spoke to him or lingered beside him too long, the Tomeis stopped to watch.

The landscape was vastly different from anything they'd seen so far. A world of sand and bare rock in shades of rust and faded red. The maps had shown volcanoes to the east and a collection of towering rock formations. Thompson kept checking the maps as they went, muttering to himself while the rest of the men remained quiet. By the time Prince Eine's caravan came into view, Sorcha was relieved. With so many other people around, maybe Revenant would stop watching her with such intense hatred.

"Stay with me," Adrian said as they approached the group of fifty or more.

Sorcha nodded, sticking close as the others fell back and took up places in the line of slow-moving horses and richly painted carts.

When the prince saw them, he called a halt, the long line of people and horses stopping to rest.

"You have the skull?" Eine asked without looking at her, his gaze focused on the barren horizon to the east.

"Yes," Adrian said.

"Put it in the cart with the other relics." Eine waved a dismissive hand.

———

Sorcha was aware of the other women traveling with the caravan. They rode on the litter with the empress, perfuming the decaying body and rewrapping the shroud as it was soiled. It was a constant process of replacing it and working to cover the horrific smell. Every few hours, they sprayed a cloying perfume at the swaying curtains surrounding them, then each other, and then the empress.

Despite this, no one wanted to be close to the litter. But it traveled in the front of the column, behind Prince Eine, and was unavoidable. Sorcha had been curious—watchful and waiting until an opportunity presented itself to approach them. She wanted information, wanted to know what had been happening in the world, and didn't trust Prince Eine or the others to be truthful. And she missed Ines. More than anything, she wanted someone who would remind her of her friend.

They'd stopped to rest beside a stream, the horses taken off their leads, the men fanning out to relieve themselves in private locations. Someone had built a small fire.

Sorcha had gone down to the stream, wanting to wash her face despite the chill, desperate to clean her hands. The priest's blood had been washed away, but every time she looked down at her hands, she saw it. Thick and red. The end of his life. A life she'd taken.

A woman had been alone on the bank, crouched at the edge to collect water. Sorcha had greeted her, hopeful for a connection—struck with homesickness. The woman had not responded, shrouded in her layered veils, features impossible to make out. She'd stood, the two facing each other without speaking, a heartbeat passing, then a breath, before the woman turned away in a swirl of red and walked back to the waiting horses.

Sorcha hadn't tried to speak to her again.

CHAPTER TWENTY-SIX

The Saint traveled on a covered cart, jewels caught in filigree twists, light lingering in sharp facets and precise cuts. Huge gray draft horses pulled it at a slow and steady pace the entire group was forced to keep.

So much opulence made Sorcha's eyes water, her gaze drawn to the swishing curtains revealing and then concealing the glittering bones of the Saint. The huge jewel-encrusted skull sat facing her in the back of the cart, pointed so that his resurrector was always within sight.

Adrian rode beside her, stoic with gloved hands loose on the reins, eyes pointed straight ahead. She longed for him to turn to her—to truly see her now—in this fiery, burning place. She wanted him to repeat everything that had come before, every sweet word that had made her feel as if the world could change. But he didn't turn. He didn't speak.

Revenant rode ahead of the empress's litter with Prince Eine. She wasn't sure when the change had happened, but one killer had been exchanged for another. Maybe it had started in the prince's court, on those polished wooden floors where she'd been stripped, and Adrian had drawn his sword. But Revenant had been suspicious before, his unreadable eyes focused on the man he'd once called his brother.

Sorcha wanted to ask Adrian about the change—curious about his emotions under the circumstances. But she couldn't bring herself to point it out. It was obvious. It wouldn't do any good to force a conversation about something that would be painful. She was the heart of it all, the breaking point, the center of a tear in time and space, an unmendable rend in his life. A part of her hurt for him, knowing she'd upended it all, changing his life.

She considered it all as they rode behind the litter, the Saint watching. He lurked within her, whispering at the edge of her hearing. A faint, cool touch on her arm as he waited on the other side of this world. Impatient to be recalled from death. Ready to take her hand and accept her gift.

There was nothing she could do that would change it.

———

The Red Wastes were everything the name had promised. No vegetation of any kind, only the rocky landscape filled with abandoned fortifications. The air was hazy with red dust, the earth bubbling with steam curling into the sky, mud pots bubbling and gulping.

A winding path led through the fields of hot springs and geysers. Deep within the earth, something shifted, moving water and stone, the surface vibrating. Sorcha had to stand perfectly still and hold her breath, concentrating on the dirt beneath her feet before realizing the motion was constant.

Tall towers rose above the landscape, dozens reaching for the sky, the tops as ragged as broken hands. The stones were black with age, but here and there, gold glittered between the cracks, vibrant crimson paint flaking away. The tower they were headed for was the largest, the bottom full of arched entryways. No doors or fortifications surrounded it. No protection of any kind. But there was nothing in this place worth taking or protecting. Without the Saint, this place was meaningless.

Dead.

Warm air blew over them, rustling fabric, shifting through hair. Sweat prickled along her back, strands of hair sticking to her forehead. She wanted to brush it away, wanted to pull in a deep breath that held more than heat and pungent death. She wanted the temple in the Silvas again. Or the lake. Even the bog or the sea cliff. She wanted any place other than this one.

Behind her, the advisors murmured constantly. It grated along her skin, her name in their mouths drawing anger to the surface, disrupting her attempt at calm. The way they looked at her made her want to lash out. But they were relatively harmless, their power in words and persuasion.

Revenant was different.

He sent fear curling through her, as hot and dangerous as this place could be if she stepped off the path. His distaste was palpable like the steam. The advisors were merely gossiping and insisting on her death. Revenant wanted to taste her demise.

Adrian still rode beside her, face blank. A hardness returned to his eyes that she'd seen soften as they'd traveled. It had slowly disappeared with their weeks together, tender moments softening the edges. But there was nothing there now. Nowhere to run or hide, no way to avoid what would happen in the tower.

The end of the world, the beginning of a new one.

Chapter Twenty-Seven

"There," Adrian said, pointing. "Do you see it?"

Sorcha nodded. Thompson had gone over the map with Adrian within hearing distance, and Sorcha had made sure to pay attention. The tallest tower in this shallow valley was the destination. She would have recognized it even without the map.

In the years after the death of the Saint, the leading figures within the Aureum Sanctus had built tower after tower, searching for the place where the earth lined up with the heavens. A sacred location for prayer and contemplation. In the early years, there had been sacrifices here, the devoted split and left to bleed out beneath the sky in an effort to lure the god back to this world.

But it had never worked. That was when the Aureum Sanctus began to search for the chosen one—a vessel—the only person capable of achieving this task. But as the years passed, there were fewer and fewer priests within the order who felt the need to recall the Saint. Their lives were good, easy, and despite being a small religion, overshadowed by the myriad of deities crowding the continent, they enjoyed a large amount of respect.

Why change when things were good? But when the Empire of the White Snake began to move, the faithful began to whisper of the Saint.

When the golden star had appeared on the horizon, those within the Aureum Sanctus began to whisper too.

There had always been a vessel—their names recorded through time, children who had been chosen and then marked, growing into women who lived their whole lives within the confines of the Aureum Sanctus. But Sorcha would be the first to attempt to recall the Saint. There had been no training. Only her visions of the future and her body mattered. Nothing else was required of her.

Sorcha nodded, acknowledging the tower Adrian indicated. It was the only one in the landscape that looked capable of holding any weight. Around them, the other towers fell apart even as they watched—enormous blocks crashing down to rattle the earth, the grating sound of masonry shifting.

"What do you know about it?" Adrian asked, keeping his voice low as those around them stored their waterskins and remounted their horses.

"It's where he will be reborn," Sorcha said, keeping her tone flat.

"What comes after?"

The question was a knife to her heart. What would happen afterward? She had no idea. She would die, and then? Who knew. Those around her had believed the Saint would bring the dead back, rewarding his faithful with life. But Sorcha had begun to doubt what she'd been taught, eyes wide open to the faults within her world that she'd ignored for so long. She would have never seen the cracks in her life, the tenuous threads holding her religion together, if Adrian hadn't appeared to drag her across the continent.

Did it matter what she believed now? No. Because what was coming would happen with or without her acceptance. It would all be easier if she didn't fight it. There would be no running. There would be no dreaming beyond the end of the day. There would be no tomorrow, and it was pointless to pretend otherwise.

"Sorcha." Adrian dropped his voice, his eyes wandering the landscape, both of them aware of being watched by the others. "What will happen in that tower?"

"I don't know for certain," she whispered, turning her face to the sky, enjoying the weak sunlight.

"Mount up," Revenant said from the head of the group. "We're moving out."

Sorcha patted Epona. The mare dropped her nose to Sorcha's hand and exhaled a warm breath in return. With another pat, she got in the saddle, wondering how long it would take to reach their destination. The tower was huge, and the landscape difficult to cross, even following the decaying road leading directly to it. They'd taken several detours already because of sinkholes and chasms that had opened over time. It could be one hour or five.

With a shudder, Sorcha urged Epona forward, and fell she into step beside Nox. It took everything she had to ignore the desire to reach for Adrian.

The line of horses and carts slowed as they approached the tower. The landscape was broken and steaming, the paved road rotting away. Cracks zig-zagged across it, the carts rattling and jumping as they crossed them. A fine sand blew back and forth, driven by the warm air currents. It collected on the bridles and in the folds of clothing, catching in Sorcha's eyelashes and coating her skin. She kept her waterskin close, taking small sips to dislodge the grit gathering between her teeth.

He comes for you.

The Saint. The dead god. The head of her religion.

The creature in the valley had sounded pleased, as if it had waited its whole life to say those words. Had it been alive when the Saint first walked the earth? Had it seen the golden skeleton marching across the landscape with its own eyes? Those traveling with her would witness the miracle for themselves.

Soon.

Sorcha turned to the cart, seeking out the Saint. It was his voice beneath hers, weaving through her thoughts. *Soon.* A promise or a threat. It didn't matter. He was right. It would be soon.

Prince Eine and Revenant reached the tower first, stepping into the deep shade thrown by the towering structure, the litter carrying the empress following. Sorcha hesitated before letting Epona carry her forward. There was something about the coolness the shadow offered that made her think of death.

"Someone needs to see to the horses and set up a temporary camp." One of the prince's advisors spoke, dusting his hands together to remove the red sand. "Put Prince Eine's tent up near the road."

Servants scurried back and forth, pulling rolls of canvas from a cart at the end of the line while others set up a tether for the horses. The women traveling with the empress climbed down from the litter, their crimson robes flapping in the breeze, veils taut against their faces. Sorcha was curious about them, but none returned her interest. They wore the colors of her order, so familiar and yet foreign somehow in this place, and she wished for any kind of connection.

"Bring the vessel to me," Prince Eine shouted, his voice rising above the chatter.

Sorcha paused with one hand on Epona's flank, absentmindedly patting her, as she opened the saddlebag and searched the contents. The prince could wait. She wanted something to eat and a rest, as the last few weeks full of stress hit her all at once. It was an ache in her bones, a tightness at the back of her throat. Adrian appeared beside her—dark eyes expressionless. She jumped, pulling back at his sudden appearance.

"Prince Eine would like to speak with you," he said, his tone giving nothing away.

"I heard," she said with a sigh, keeping her voice low. "What does he want now?"

Adrian didn't respond. But it hadn't been a question she'd expected a response to. Prince Eine wanted her to resurrect the Saint. That was the only reason they were in this place, and it was pointless to play dumb.

Together, they walked up the line to stand before the prince. Revenant was there, silent in the background but present in a way that made him impossible to ignore. Thompson and someone from the prince's court were going over his maps while advisors and magicians moved around the prince in a flurry of activity. Sorcha paused before him as Adrian knelt in the dirt, head bowed and still beholden to the man who had taken everything from him and turned him into a monster the whole world feared.

"Right now, in this place, I will not require you to bend a knee to me," Prince Eine said, glancing at Sorcha and away. "In this place, you're the second most valuable person. The Saint and the vessel, my mother and myself. When this is finished, there will be no need for you to subjugate yourself. Stand, Wolf, until this whole process has been completed and we are on our way back to the Traveling City, I won't demand you follow protocol."

The steward's face contorted with displeasure, and Sorcha let herself enjoy the small spark of joy. The man was a petty, nasty person. She ignored the look Adrian gave her as he stood, the prince's words lingering in the air. *When this is finished, there will be no need for you to subjugate yourself.* Adrian's *why* was as loud as any shout.

"Do you know what will be required of you inside?" Prince Eine gestured to the tower, indicating the open windows at the top.

Sorcha kept her gaze on his face. He was thinner than the last time she'd seen him in the Traveling City, his face a pale waxen color that resembled illness. Had he contracted whatever the empress had died from?

When she didn't respond, he continued.

"You must enter the tower first," Prince Eine directed. "Then we will follow with the relics."

"How do you know I need to be the first one inside?" Not that it mattered to Sorcha, but his conviction was a force of nature, overwhelming her with certainty.

"Bring the priestess." Prince Eine kept his cool gaze on Sorcha.

The steward beside him hurried toward the dead empress and her retinue. A woman detached herself from the small group and followed the steward.

The woman appeared to float across the rocky ground, skirts swirling around her feet, the veil she wore flowing out behind her like the tail of a comet. Tall and elegant, despite not being able to see her features, the woman exuded confidence and grace.

"Tell her," Prince Eine said, gesturing from the newcomer to Sorcha, an unpleasant edge threading through the words. "Do you recognize one of your own, little Vessel?"

Chapter Twenty-Eight

Sorcha didn't respond, her gaze glued to the woman beside him. A veil covered her from head to toe—concealing her features and shape, only hinting at the tall woman beneath the fabric. Sweat prickled along Sorcha's scalp, the hair on the back of her neck rising.

The woman pulled at the fabric—yards and yards of sheer crimson layered with delicate cotton. Bracelets tinkled on her wrists, gold and rubies flashing. Familiar bracelets. Ones that Sorcha had seen every day for years.

A chasm opened beneath her feet, and her stomach dropped into it. Fate struck her, the truth of the moment emerging, pinning Sorcha motionless to the earth.

The woman threw back the last bit of fabric. That face. The high priestess—mentor, mother, friend. Hair so blonde it was almost white, and blue eyes the color of turquoise. Sorcha had wanted to be this woman, confident and contained, whole and her own person within the Aureum Sanctus.

Since the fall of the Golden Citadel, Sorcha had believed that Kahina Kira had been dead. Burned to ash like the others.

Sorcha had been sent out into the world to retrieve the relics. A duty she'd never expected to perform, but if she had, this woman would have been beside her for the whole journey. For months, she'd believed she was alone.

Yet here was Kahina Kira, the high priestess.

"I thought you were dead," Sorcha whispered.

Part of Sorcha wanted to run to the woman, to throw her arms around her and cry. Cry for everyone, for everything that had changed. For the horror that had entered the world and altered everything about their lives. She wanted the easy comfort of before—understanding and acceptance. But another part, one born in the months since the fall of the Citadel—born out of bogs and sea cliffs, the woman who had risen from the ruins, capable of slipping a knife into the heart of a believer— knew that if she did, she'd be giving it all up. It would be like turning her back on the woman she'd become. Fragile in so many new ways, but growing stronger, more certain of what she was capable of accomplishing.

And all this time, each grueling mile into the Red Wastes—the plodding of the horses and the pace the empress set—Kahina Kira had been within reach. There had been an opportunity to close the distance between them, to reveal herself in private, for a joyful reunion to happen.

But Kira had waited until now, standing before the Red Tower with Prince Eine as her witness, to reveal herself.

Sorcha sucked in a breath, aware of the group surrounding them.

The prince's men were watching, curious or uninterested, half laughing or sneering, or even indifferent. Had Adrian known? Or were they all witnessing this revelation for the first time?

It was wrong. It wasn't how someone who loved you would act— they wouldn't wait to be reunited in a moment like this.

Sorcha remained where she was, even as Kira's lip trembled and tears gathered on her lashes. She wanted to scream.

Have you been with the prince this whole time? Did you know I went out there alone to collect relics? To face monsters? Why did you leave me? Why did you wait until now?

"Have you been helping him this whole time?" Sorcha finally asked.

"I wasn't helping him," Kira replied firmly. "I was helping you."

"If you were helping me, why weren't you with me? Why did you let me believe you were dead?"

"I had to," she responded, irritation flashing across her features. "You had to do it on your own. Even if I had been with you, I would not have been able to help."

"What about supporting me?" Sorcha shook her head, squeezing her hands into fists. So many gazes were on her, but she wanted to search out Adrian, discover if his eyes would tell her if he'd betrayed her as well. "You could have simply been there. Instead, you're here, at the end of it all, with the prince. You've been here this whole time."

A memory skipped across her mind, the stream where they'd stopped before to rest. The woman at the water's edge, standing and silent, refusing to acknowledge Sorcha's greeting. "It was you by the stream."

Kira remained silent.

"And what do you want from me now?" Sorcha asked. "What do you think you can achieve here? Because that's why you're here, isn't it? Because this is the end of some long game for you. This is the moment your desires are realized."

Sorcha turned her green gaze to the prince. His face was set, blank and smooth, except for glinting knowledge deep in his eyes.

Kahina Kira snorted, drawing Sorcha's attention back, sending rage coursing along each vein.

"Are you enough of a child to want a confession? Or do you need an apology to ease your soul?" Kira's voice was harsh now.

Sorcha's tongue felt thick—mouth full of saliva—as Kira became the harsh mistress she remembered from early childhood. Sorcha refused to cry, focusing on the anger building in her chest, the heat and burn of betrayal—the sorrow of abandonment.

"I want nothing from you." Sorcha looked at the prince again, meeting his eyes, and repeated it. "Nothing."

"You will need my help," Kira said, taking a step forward. "You will need me in the days to come. This is not the end." She extended her arms, offering the warmth she'd withheld. "There is more to do. So much you wouldn't have been able to understand until now. I can finally tell you the whole story."

A sneer touched Sorcha's face, distorting her features, muscles twisting. "You mean my death? Will you help me die? That's something you never taught me. You never explained that my death would be the last piece of this magic."

"We all die," Kira said, voice low but fierce. "But some of us return."

"But not me," Sorcha gritted out between clenched teeth. A noise caught her attention, and her gaze flicked behind Kira. Adrian watched them, hand on his sword, but it was impossible to read him—to understand what he might be thinking behind his black eyes. "Why haven't you tried before?"

Kira shook her head, reaching for Sorcha, flinching when the younger woman took a step back. "It's never been that easy. It had to be at the right time, beneath the right stars. We've waited hundreds of years for this moment."

The golden star on the horizon. Of course, it was important, but it was also just a star millions of miles away. What would a celestial body know of a dead god and his little religion determined to resurrect him? It all washed over Sorcha, leaving her hollow. And it was as the creature in the bog had said—she wasn't special, she was only in the right place at the right time.

Sorcha turned away, turned to the cart where the relics glittered, glinting in the sun as it moved toward the horizon. It would set in a few hours, another night spreading through the world, and the golden star would shine as brightly as a small sun. But she would not be here to see it.

He was there in that moment when her attention was drawn to the relics. The Saint's voice, touching her mind—reaching across the vast distance between life and death. The words were unintelligible, but she understood the tone and rhythm—promises and endearments. She'd carry his voice with her now forever, the murmuring nothings, taking them into her own personal darkness.

"Sorcha," Kira began but paused, clearing her throat. "This can't happen without you. Time is limited, the window is small, and we need to act now. You can change the past and bring back Ines and Rohan. You're being given a chance that anyone would take."

"The Saint will return," Sorcha said, staring unflinchingly at Kira. "And I'll be dead. You never taught me that part."

"I don't know what will happen with the Saint," Kira admitted. "But yes, you will die."

"The Saint will bring the empress back." Prince Eine's voice was steel, cutting across them, reminding Sorcha where and who she was with. "It's time to begin."

———

DEATH IS NOT THE END.

The words over the arch were huge, cut into the stone in hard, straight lines. They appeared to glow from within, as if beneath the solid surface of the tower, molten lava surged and flowed.

Sorcha shivered, a pit opening in her stomach, expanding to sink down to her toes. The people behind her were afraid. No one knew what would happen when the Saint breathed again. Not even Kira. And now they knew even his chosen vessel would not survive his rebirth. What would it mean for them? She could feel their uncertainty, a counterpoint to Prince Eine's single-minded determination and Kira's strange peace. She didn't envy them. Didn't pity them. Everyone had made a choice to be here.

In the distance, thunder rumbled, rolling out across the landscape and echoing in the tower. The horizon was black, the volcanoes on the horizon smoking. She could stand here and wait for it to arrive—delay the final moment—but there was no point. More than anything, she wanted to complete the one mission of her life. Even as another part of her screamed in defiance.

"Sorcha."

She closed her eyes as Adrian's voice washed over her, consuming her. In the dark, when there had been no one else around, he'd said her name like that. With longing. With intention. *Mine.* She hadn't expected to hear it here, with Eine and Kira between them, with Revenant poised to kill them all.

"No!" Kira commanded, voice rising sharply. "Do not stop her. She must go in alone."

A shaky breath escaped Sorcha, sweat pricking along her scalp and beneath her arms. Had he taken a step toward her? If she turned and ran to him, would he wrap her in his arms? Would he drag her to Nox and Epona so they could ride off into the Wastes as if this were some lover's story? Death would follow them. And she would be dragged back to stand in this exact spot once again.

Forward. It was the only way. With Adrian's gaze hot between her shoulder blades, Sorcha passed beneath the words—their promise and threat—and into the dim interior. The building trembled, stone grating against stone as thunder rolled closer. Her heart raced, thudding painfully in her chest, the scent of dry decay rolling over her. She hesitated on the threshold, glancing over her shoulder.

Adrian stood beside the prince with hands clasped, stoic and calm, seemingly detached from the situation despite having spoken her name. Revenant stood beside him, glaring at her. But it was Prince Eine's face that made her heart skip with fear. He wore an expression of ravenous intent—pure hunger and determination.

He'd worn a similar look each time she'd met him. But it had intensified. She'd felt like an object at every turn. Now she was even less than that. Her only worth lay in opening a door he wanted to walk through. Sorcha, a key and missing puzzle piece, was on the verge of achieving his desire, and she could be pushed aside.

Soldiers were removing the relics from the cart one by one—preparing to carry them to the top of the tower. Sorcha wasn't sure which idea frightened her more. The Saint coming together and standing up in a world hundreds of years after his death or the pieces failing to align and Prince Eine killing her. Would Adrian be ordered to cut her down? No, Revenant would do it gladly and ensure it was as painful as possible.

"He's waiting for you, Sorcha," Kira called. "Prepare to meet your god."

———

Sorcha pushed through the glistening curtain of spider webs, tiny droplets of moisture trembling as she broke through to the inner tower.

It rose high above her, the interior hollow with an oversized staircase climbing the outside, circling all the way up to a floor at the top. A ribbon of light slid through an opening above, flowing down the walls, catching in the spiderwebs and illuminating threads of gold in the black and red stone. At some point, the tower had crumbled, cracking apart, and a huge hand had repaired it with gold. Beneath her feet, the tile was dirty, but she could make out the mosaic story embedded there. Another legend of the Saint, another piece of his history. A piece of *her* history.

Movement to her left, beneath the stairs, caught her attention. A large black spider with red markings skittered across the floor, heading for the opposite wall and moving up it quickly. Sorcha gasped, taking a step back.

"What is it?" Prince Eine called.

"Spiders," Sorcha replied, raising her voice to be heard.

There were more of them than she'd realized, crawling over the walls, camouflaged against the black and red stone. Some were tiny, and others were as large as cats. Bodies glossy and spindly, skittering with an inhuman and predatory grace.

Sorcha studied the stairs, hoping they would hold her weight on the way up, counting the landings silently. It would be a long climb.

Straightening her shoulders, she headed for the base of the stairs. The tower trembled, the floor vibrating with movement as something deep within the earth shifted and rolled. Sorcha extended a hand to steady herself on the wall and yelped, jerking back quickly. The stone was hot to the touch, her palm stinging with the contact.

The stairs were wide enough that she could avoid touching the wall again, but there was no railing or lip to catch her if she fell. Working to keep her mind calm and shutting down any stray *what-if* or *but*, she climbed. Even the memories. Even the feel of Adrian. Even the sensation of his mouth pressed to hers and the curling delight that had filled her body like light.

Sorcha worked to keep it all away. *Forget the past. Do not acknowledge the future. Concentrate on putting one foot in front of the other.* Breathe and climb, climb and breathe, until she reached the top. Everything would be considered then. But it was hard to keep her mind still, so she began counting golden seams in the stone, following the spiral up. Reaching the top step, she paused and glanced down, regretting it immediately. The height from this perspective was dizzying—leaving her gasping.

"Are you here?" Sorcha asked, turning to the room at the top. She felt silly the moment the words left her mouth. The Saint was below her still, waiting to be brought up, but she'd expected to feel him in this place the way she had in the valley.

This place was empty but expectant. The wall's open arches overlooked the boiling red plains with a peaked roof overhead. Here, each golden crack in the stone flowed together, meeting at a center point. They formed a perfect circle, slightly dished, from which each golden thread radiated outward—weaving through the tower like roots, like veins in a blackened heart.

Mosaics covered the ceiling. Everywhere she'd gone, carefully laid out stories waited to be rediscovered—the sea cave, the remains of the ruined temple in the Silvas, the dead city. A legend of the Saint everywhere, little collections, fragments of his story, and as she'd put it all together, horror had built, quiet, insistent, knowing dread of how it all would end.

He was a loving, generous Saint. That was what she'd been taught. A creature who protected and championed his followers. But the stories she'd seen were the opposite. Again and again, she'd seen destruction and death, dismemberment and torture, and here, a golden skeleton sat on a dark throne, watching this forsaken room and waiting.

The hollow eye sockets seemed to follow her as she moved, circling the room. She treasured each final second of solitude. The prince would be getting impatient. He would want to know what was taking so long. He would want to know if she'd uncovered any traps or hidden dangers as she'd moved up the tower step by slow step.

Kira had insisted that Sorcha enter alone. Now Sorcha wondered if it was because the woman had wanted to gift her a few peaceful moments before the end, here in this empty shell waiting for the Saint.

A voice called up from the foot of the tower, but she couldn't make out the words. The stone muffled them, and the wind pushing through the arches stole them away. She went back to the opening and stepped back inside to peer down the hollow interior. Small figures were grouped at the bottom, Prince Eine and his men. Adrian.

"Is it safe?" Revenant called up.

Sorcha almost said no. But it wouldn't keep them away. Revenant would simply find out for himself. It was nothing more than a delaying tactic that would gain her nothing.

"Yes," she called down.

The word echoed in the space, growing quieter, the mournful sound twisting in her stomach.

Yes, it is safe. Yes, this is the end.

She turned away and wrapped her arms around herself, gaze drifting back to the steaming plains.

There were no barriers to keep her from walking off the edge of the tower. She would simply plummet to the earth. Prince Eine would never get what he wanted then. But her own curiosity would never be satisfied either. There would be no way to know if everything she'd been taught was true. Her whole purpose in life had been—*was*—the Saint. How could she turn her back on the only thing she'd been raised to do?

Fear coursed through her, a river, an ocean with rising tides. Sorcha had to know. Morbid curiosity filled her. And if there was a chance, however small, that Ines might live—that Rohan and the others would return—she had to take it. Promises had been made. She couldn't bear the idea of turning her back on them now after coming so far.

Closing her eyes, she listened to the thunder rumbling and leaned into the warm wind. It pushed at her skirts, pulling at her hair. It brought the scent of the hot and pungent springs. Pulling in a deep breath, she held out her arms, and for a moment, she was on the edge of a cliff, water beating at the rock, a cave full of living skeletons waiting for her. The memory of that place echoed through her, and with it, the remembered warmth of Adrian's embrace.

"Will you jump?"

Adrian stepped onto the platform, rising out of the stairwell like a demon summoned by memory and desire. His dark eyes were unreadable, features set in a flat expression.

She wanted to run to him, to throw her arms around him and lean in, knowing he would hold her up and keep her safe. His touch would tell her the things he could not say.

I loved you in the ruins of a city. I loved you beneath a burning sky filled with stars.

I love you now when the world is ending.

Sorcha opened her mouth to ask him if what filled her exploding heart matched his. But neither one of them spoke, their gazes locked in understanding. He came to stand beside her, the back of his hand brushing hers, as they stood together overlooking the Wastes. Tears filled her eyes as she pulled in a breath, lungs constricting. The sounds of boots on stone reached her—the group reaching the top of the stairs with their heavy burdens and terrible intentions.

"Finally," Prince Eine said, breathing heavily from the climb.

His greedy gaze swept the room, taking in the two of them standing together. A tight smile flitted across his features. He was enjoying the torture of it all. The way they looked at each other and away, the inescapable fate rushing toward them like an arrow. Soon. It ended here, a journey of months and thousands of miles, brought to a point where the world could only turn in one direction, and there was no other way out of this tower beyond death.

"You have no idea how long I've lived for this moment." Kira appeared next, one hand lifting her skirts as the other went to her throat, eyes dancing across the mural overhead. She radiated joy—glowing, intense, painful exultation. Her eyes dropped, finding Sorcha. The smile was directed at her now, and she came forward, holding her hands out— golden bracelets tinkling, rubies catching the light. "You are such a gift, Sorcha. Let me help you with this."

"I want nothing from you," Sorcha said, pulling back from the woman's grasping fingers. The anger in her tone flattened, voice dropping. "You died in the Citadel. To me, you've been dead for months. You abandoned us."

"That's not true," Kira said, glaring now, reaching up to adjust the veil still attached with a ribbon of gold woven through her hair. Beautiful even now, with her vicious heart exposed, a woman Sorcha had wanted to be more than anything. "I made a choice. And even though you might not be able to see it now, it was the right choice."

"The choice to let us all die?"

"You have no idea what I've been through, Sorcha. What it's taken to reach this point."

"You could have talked to me! Explained things!"

Kira's eyes narrowed. "You could never understand."

"You made the choice to keep me ignorant."

"Lifetimes. Whole entire lives strung out like beads on a necklace, wrapped around my throat, suffocating me." Kira's hands moved to her pale throat, elegant fingers digging into the flesh. Her eyes glittered madly, chin lifted. "Let me help you, here, at the end. Let me help you."

"No," Sorcha said.

The word bounced off the floor, hitting the walls and then the high-domed ceiling over their heads—catching in the bones of the Saint, thrown back by the glimmering gold. The tower shivered, stone vibrating against stone, and in the distance, thunder boomed across the Wastes.

Kira closed the distance between them and grabbed Sorcha's wrists, cold fingers biting into her skin and holding her in place. Her face reddened with anger, eyes hard with malice.

"You stupid girl," she hissed, spittle collecting in the corners of her mouth. "You need me."

"I don't." Sorcha fought to keep her voice calm and level. "I understand enough."

"You think so? Then what does the Amor Aeternus say about this moment?"

The Amor Aeternus. A book made from the Saint's heart—living rubies and gold. It was a myth. Whispered about between the priests and priestesses, briefly mentioned in the texts shelved in neat rows in the library. Once, when she had been a child, she'd asked Rohan about it. The man had laughed and told her it was only a legend—the Saint's blood crystalized and solid, imbuing life well beyond the allotted years. An object capable of showing the past and present, a way to look at the world through the eyes of a deity. But the man had said it would have been destroyed in the war that killed the Saint. If it had ever existed at all.

"It's a myth," Sorcha said. But her tongue was thick in her mouth, heart beating erratically as unease overtook her. "Rohan said it never existed."

"I have it," Kira whispered, reaching for Sorcha again. This time, Sorcha went, their faces almost touching as Kira continued. "I have it with me now. It's not a myth. Not a story. I made it. He gave me his heart. He will be reborn here, birthed out of your blood and sacrifice, but he will not be complete. He will not be whole. There are more relics to find. Another sacrifice to make."

Gave her his heart? How? When?

Sorcha shook her head. "Someone would have told me. I'm the vessel."

Her whole existence came down to it, her reason for being—an empty object in which to collect the life of a god. She studied the rituals. She'd practiced each task they'd given her. She'd focused on each lesson, not wanting to fail or disappoint them. All of them.

But especially this woman.

"Do you think you would learn everything so soon? There are libraries that you have never even seen. Only a few know the Amor Aeternus is even a reality. Even fewer have seen or touched it. Less have read it." Kira let out a shuddering breath. "I've kept his heart close."

Sorcha held her breath, skin tingling.

"Beyond this place, beyond this life, more will be required of you," Kira said. "Death is not the end."

Sorcha tried to pull away, a noise of distress escaping. She felt Adrian beside her, tense and listening, the air thick with questions. Her gaze bounced around the room, landing on Prince Eine's hunger, Revenant's fury, and fear on the advisors' faces. The empress's body had been brought up, but Sorcha had been so focused on Kira, she'd been unaware of the room becoming crowded with people.

"He will need to find himself. He will need the other pieces of his body." Kira's fingers dug into Sorcha's muscle, breaking the skin on her wrists. "He will be vulnerable until they are all brought together, until he is complete."

"Then how can he be brought back now?"

"Blood is powerful magic."

"Is that why you're here, then?" Sorcha pulled free, stumbling backward. "You've promised to be useful and bring the remaining relics together? That's why the prince let you live, isn't it? And now you will stand before the Saint and promise to make him whole."

Kira shook her head, brows coming together. "No, you don't—"

"Stop." Sorcha held up her hand and closed her eyes, ears ringing. "You let our family die and hid yourself for your own selfish reasons."

"Because I love the Saint!" Kira shouted, her words bouncing off the ceiling. "If there was more time, I would be able to explain."

"There is none left," Prince Eine said, coming to stand beside Kira. He placed a hand on her shoulder, squeezing until his knuckles went white. "It's time to keep your promise."

Sorcha was steady now, heavy calm blanketing her—soothing even as it suffocated. There was no escaping the fate that had brought them all to this place. She could meet it on her own terms, or she could be forced to accept it.

She would face it.

The prince's advisors and soldiers had readied the space, placing the uncovered relics in the center of the gold circle in the floor. The women traveling with the empress were carefully unwrapping the decomposing body to one side of the bones. The putrid scent of death was barely covered by the incense they were lighting. Revenant stood by the stairs, sword in hand, as he watched it all unfold.

Prince Eine looked from Kira to Sorcha. Had Kira given him everything? Or had she let something slip now that she'd never intended him to know?

"I have to prepare," Kira said, eyes flat now, distant.

Sorcha swiped at the tears collecting on her lashes, tilting her face up. The women moved around the room, lighting torches and placing them in the brackets along the arches. Kira knelt among the relics and adjusted them, caressing them. Eine hovered near his mother, watching the priestess's hands. Revenant paced behind the prince, wearing an expression of distrust and revulsion, disgusted with the red witches and their blood sacrifices.

One of the women brought a basket forward, pulling items from it and handing them to Kira one by one. A shallow gilded bowl. A knife. A vial. A raw shard of ruby. A large golden circlet. Each object was carefully arranged as Kira murmured to herself—weaving prayer and promise together. Thunder rumbled, beams of sunlight piercing through the clouds, falling across the landscape, and moving toward the tower. Sorcha watched the world shifting and changing below her as pressure built in her chest.

"The Saint is waiting," Kira said, cold and distant, motioning to the floor, to the ceremonial dagger and a vial of poison. "Choose your death."

"Which will it be, witch?" Revenant called, yellow eyes filled with hate as he adjusted the grip on his sword.

Sorcha turned to Adrian, closing the distance between them until only the space of a breath remained. His eyes pleaded with her silently, promising to burn the whole world down if she walked out of this tower with him now.

"There is a life beyond this," Adrian whispered. "Come with me."

When had he forgotten to hide his emotions? He'd been so good at it, unreadable, a solid black force moving through the world. But here was a man with a pale face and haunted eyes—fear and sorrow mingling, intertwined in his features.

Sorcha shook her head. Their paths had been leading here, to this moment, where he would ask, and she would refuse.

"I can't."

"You can!" He raised his voice, angry, frustrated, wanting her to let go of the last vestiges of her life. One she had never really wanted anyway.

"You're talking as if I have a choice." Her own voice rose, matching his. "Look around you. This is the final piece. Do you think your prince would let me leave now?"

Adrian shook his head, denial all over his body—face fierce. His eyes burned, reflecting the fire of the torches. She reached out and cupped his cheek, searching his face—determined to take his memory with her.

He leaned into her touch, throat working as he swallowed.

"It was always going to end here," Sorcha whispered.

"Enough." Prince Eine's voice cut across them. "Choose your death, Vessel."

Without speaking, Sorcha reached for the dagger at Adrian's hip.

The one she'd taken from the tent and cut him with in the forest, the one he'd given her on the sea cliff. It had been passed between them—gifted only to be returned. A shared object, a totem of their bond. He stopped her and shook his head once.

No.

But if death was here for her, this was how she wanted to meet it.

———

"You can't ask me to do this," he whispered; the anguish was a crushing weight, threatening to bury him in the earth. The life he'd begun to see, the shape of the world with her beside him, was slipping away.

"I can't do it without you," she said, unspoken words lingering between them. *Bring me death. Take it. You're the only one who can. You're the only one I want with me in this moment.*

And if he didn't? Revenant would step forward, and her last moments would be brutal—full of unnecessary pain. He couldn't face that, knew that afterward he would draw his sword and cut into their bodies, hack and hack until their blood mixed with hers. Now, after all this, after all that had come before, all that he had been, he wasn't sure he could face that either.

Sorcha pressed the dagger into his hand, the tremble in her fingers so slight it could have been his own. The moment in the woods when she'd faced him, determined to draw blood, twisted into this one, pulling horror and darkness from the air to cloud his vision.

He took the blade and stepped forward, sweeping her into his arms and gripping her tight. She buried her face in his neck, wet tears touching him, as his heart split open. This was the end. The end of everything.

"Now," she whispered, mouth brushing his skin, a soft kiss sealing in the word.

In a few quick steps, he carried her to the relics and knelt with her in the golden circle. The room faded around them, a tense hush falling, even the thunder growing quiet. Adrian searched her face, taking her in —pale features, haunted eyes. The same woman who had melted with his touch, shattered in his arms, only to be woven back together. The woman he loved with a heart he hadn't known he possessed. The woman who had walked out of a burning city to change his soul.

Sorcha took his hand, bringing the blade to her throat, tears in her eyes. *Here.* Her mouth formed the word, but no sound came out. *Here.*

The stone was cold beneath them, ice creeping into his bones—into the cavern left by his dying heart.

His chest heaved. There wasn't enough air in the space, not enough light. Panic clawed at the back of his throat, pressure building behind his eyes.

Adrian shook his head, and she tightened her grip—knuckles white with desperation, her body pleading for action. The blade against her throat shivered and reflected the room—dancing light, gold, jewels, the story of the Saint in the ceiling above them.

"Adrian." Sorcha placed a hand on his chest—gentle but firm—touching the spot where his heart was. Would be. If he had one. "Now."

Swallowing, he pulled in a shaky breath and pressed his forehead to hers, squeezing his eyes tight. Blood pounded in his ears, his life without her spinning out—meaningless and bleak. Someone said his name, Prince Eine or Revenant. The priestess was talking to one of the other women. But those sounds came from another world, outside their trembling bubble.

"Sorcha," he whispered. Her name was barely more than a whisper, only breath ghosting across her skin.

He kissed her, demanding this last offering, taking it when she opened her mouth and her tongue slid against his. She tangled her hands in his hair, pulling him closer, even as he held the knife at her throat.

He broke the kiss, tasting tears, and spoke his last words into her mouth. "I love you."

He drew the blade across her throat, parting flesh.

She gasped, the sound bubbling, rasping, as she fought to breathe.

He closed his eyes, holding her as warmth spread across his hands and chest. Holding on even as she struggled and shook, hands fluttering, horrible sounds coming from her. Then she slowed, movements growing weaker, until her hands stilled, and she went limp. He choked on a sob, terrible aching pain flooding him—blinding and relentless.

"Put her down." The voice came from far away, and Adrian looked up to meet Revenant's gaze. "Time to leave."

Kira tugged at Sorcha's body, bringing the shallow dish to her neck to collect blood.

He stayed on his knees, watching numbly as the woman ladled blood over the relics, as the blood flowed out of Sorcha to pool beneath the Saint.

Revenant pulled on Adrian's shoulder, dragging him to his feet and away from the center of the room.

Adrian couldn't look away from Sorcha—bloody and lifeless. Beautiful in the way a dried flower is—a dead thing, a mimic of the living. Her eyes stared into nothingness, mouth open, as blood continued to flow.

Kira worked quickly, arranging Sorcha on the floor, folding her arms, and then closing her eyes. Her blood was everywhere—all over him, all over the Saint, all over Kira where she knelt in it and smoothed it over the golden bones. Prince Eine bent down, running his fingers through it, and turned to smear it across his decaying mother.

Kill them. Kill them all. Kill them now.

Rage—the color of Sorcha's blood—stole over him. It built, crashing through the cold places in his mind, tearing through the barriers.

"Don't." Revenant's voice was hard—a command, not a request.

The ground trembled, a vibration coming up through the tower, as a high note rang out. A bell chimed, high and sweet, the sound climbing and moving into a range beyond hearing. A woman shrieked, and an advisor came forward to pull the prince back, babbling about falling stones, the shaking tower. People were leaving, soldiers hurrying down the stairs, even as Kira remained, covered in blood, mouth moving in a silent prayer.

The sky was black, nothing but darkness beyond the arches. The torches smoked and jumped, yellow-orange light caressing the relics, catching in polished gems.

Then the relics began to vibrate. The bones danced toward each other, coming together, piece by piece, fitting together and held by magic.

The Saint sat up, head turning this way and that, a giant unbeliev-able creature. Without warning, he lunged and grabbed an advisor, drag-ging the man to his mouth. Blood gushed as golden teeth broke flesh, the man shrieking in anguish. An arm was torn away in one bite. In the next, the screaming stopped as his head was separated from his body. The Saint dropped the remains, reaching for the dead empress.

"Please." Prince Eine was on his knees, hands up in supplication. "My mother. The priestess promised you would return her to me."

The Saint gave no response as he picked up the empress—a leg detached, wrappings fluttered free—and bit into her.

Eine screamed, the noise coming up from his gut and echoing in the room. Thunder crashed, rattling the tower, and lightning raced across the sky to illuminate the scene. Eine darted forward, grabbing his moth-er's arm, tugging until the hand separated at the wrist, and he fell back.

Bones crunched, cracking in the Saint's jaw as he ate, the body vanishing into some unknowable interior space.

The priestess was talking so quickly her words ran together, jumbling and becoming nonsense. She laughed, reaching out to place her hands on the Saint—flesh to golden bone—leaning forward to press a kiss into him.

He paused before one hand came out in a wide, slow arc, fingers closing around her as his jaw opened.

"You promised!" Kira screamed, face twisting as she fought his grasp. "In every lifetime!"

The Saint paused, the words connecting with some distant part of himself. He set her down, and she stumbled away. Tears coursed down her cheeks, and one hand covered her mouth in an effort to smother the wails ripping out of her.

Eine screamed to get her attention, cheeks white and spattered with blood, his rich clothes disheveled. Kira stood rooted to the floor, sobbing and unable to look away from the Saint. Still clutching the decaying hand of the empress, Eine grabbed Kira and pulled her away, dragging her down the stairs after him.

The huge skeleton looked around, head swinging back and forth, empty sockets staring. His attention fell on Sorcha. The huge head tilted, taking in her crumpled figure, her blue-tinged lips. So much blood. He prodded her gently, and her head rolled to the side, exposing the wound. The Saint scooped her up in both hands, moving slowly—reverently. Sorcha's limbs dangled grotesquely, dripping blood, as he raised her off the ground.

"No!" Adrian screamed, terrible dread filling him.

His sword was in his hand, though he had no memory of drawing it. Revenant was gone. Only the women, cowering and huddled together near the stairs, and himself remained. And Sorcha.

The Saint would consume her. Crush her between golden jaws. And she would truly be lost to him—ground into nothingness. But the Saint's golden teeth remained closed as he stroked her bloody hair, cupping her skull gently as he brought her close. Delicately, cradling her as if she were precious, beloved, the creature pressed his huge teeth to her face—to her lips—in the mimic of a kiss.

Bile rose in Adrian's throat, a scream trapped as he swallowed. She's dead. *Dead.* He wanted to scream it, rip the world apart with his anguish. The only thing he was good for—good *at*—couldn't help her now. The sword was an unpleasant weight in his hand. But he couldn't move. Even as he screamed at himself to unstick his feet from the stone, he remained.

The Saint lingered over the kiss and stroked the small body he held, smoothing a finger over her neck.

A woman sobbed.

Sorcha's fingers twitched, stopping Adrian's breath—his heart a block of burning ice in his chest. Her eyelids fluttered open, a hand coming up to touch the Saint's cheekbone as his face pulled away from hers, leaving her whole, uneaten. He moved slowly as he set her on her feet, steadying her with one golden, skeletal hand. She studied the Saint with a calm gaze, gripping his fingers like a child.

Sorcha *lived.*

The Living Saint
Blood and Rubies Book Two

The Saint lives and the Empire crumbles.

The resurrection of the Saint brought death and destruction to the now fractured Empire of the White Snake. As cities bow and break beneath his merciless rule, people are desperate for a champion capable of reversing the terror he's unleashed.

Sorcha, loyal priestess and now confidant of the Saint, has forgotten everything before his rebirth. In an instant, he wiped her memories and left her with nothing but inexplicable loneliness. But pressure is building and fragments of her life before the Saint have begun to surface. In her nightmares a man wearing a wolf skull holds out his hand, waiting for her to take it.

Adrian, once the notorious Wolf and killer of cities, is tormented by the final moments he spent with Sorcha. Now, he scours the continent for those who might help him undo the terrible mistakes of the past. But the brothers-in-arms he betrayed are close on his heels, determined to have their revenge and prove that love is no protection from death.

Sorcha and Adrian will have to find their way back to each other if there is to be any hope of defeating the immortal Saint. But her stability has been shaken and she distrusts everything, especially her memories and the man who claims to love her. Adrian must convince her that their hearts were once connected by the delicate thread of fate—and their lives depend on it.

The future of the Empire will be decided by monsters or men—the world will end in darkness or light.

The Saint is ready.

Preorder your copy of *The Living Saint* now!
https://books2read.com/u/bMzBMB

Steel and Starlight
A Blood and Rubies Novella

A princess...

When war threatens the borders of her father's kingdom Daphne's life and happiness are exchanged for weapons and soldiers. To seal the deal, she will have to travel to meet her new husband and pray that love and respect can grow out of a marriage contract signed in blood.

A highwayman...

Time is running out for Finian as the Empire of the White Snake approaches. His men know what it's like to live in the hell that is a battlefield, and they'll do whatever it takes to avoid returning to one. The only way to keep ahead of the looming army is enough money to finance escape. Ransom is the perfect solution.

How much is one princess worth?
How much is one man willing to change?
One kiss can change it all.

Preorder Steel and Starlight and meet Finian and Daphne:
https://books2read.com/u/4Ne9qz

Preorder Steel and Starlight and meet Finian and Daphne:
https://books2read.com/u/4Ne9qz

SACRAMENT AND SMOKE
A Blood and Rubies Short Story

The death of a Saint. The birth of a monster.

Visions of war have haunted the oracle Kira for weeks. Those around her have ignored each warning—even her beloved Saint Hakan—leaving Kira with an impending sense of doom.

An enigmatic and charismatic leader of a growing cult, Hakan is on the verge of achieving the impossible. Monsters and men have gathered to discuss uniting the fractured kingdoms surrounding the Golden Citadel. But there is a dangerous faction who believe Hakan has become too powerful.

In one night, Kira's world is transformed and the love she thought would last a lifetime is reshaped.

Discover the origins of the Saint in this prequel short story to the dark fantasy romance The Dead Saint - book one in the Blood and Rubies series.

Get your copy of Sacrament and Smoke:
https://books2read.com/u/mq9711

Acknowledgments

I've had these characters living in my head for the last several years now; sinking into underwater cities, kissing beneath fiery skies, and rising from the dead to devour people at all hours of the night and day. It's exciting and terrifying that they're now alive in your head too!

What began as one novel expanded into a duet, a novella, and several short stories. And possibly a third novel about some characters you'll meet in *The Living Saint*. I can't wait to share book two with you soon!

None of this could happen without the support of all the amazing people around me.

Thank you everyone on my advance reader and street team. Without you reading and loving and talking about my books no one else would ever see them. Thank you for sharing posts and commenting and being supportive. Thank you for taking a chance on my book! It means the world to me!

Thank you, Gwen, for reading all those stacks of printed pages. Thank you, Amy, for being excited about Finian and Daphne character art with me. Thank you, Raven, for Sunday lunches and for being my person at the other end of the line to talk me off a ledge when needed. Thank you, Marnie, for being my writing person—if we can make it through the difficult books, we can make it through everything that comes next! Thank you, Ann, for being the most amazing assistant and friend—your knowledge and talent changed things for me in a big way. Thank you, Jeanine, for your kindness and support and skill and talent. Thank you, Amber, for endless amazing book recommendations and amazing word skills and letting me know that The Mummy was making an anniversary appearance in movie theaters again!

I'm so grateful for the support of my family especially. It's not always easy to live with an author and I'm so grateful and humbled by your faith in me. I recently discovered that my dad has bought or preordered all of my books (I did tell them that these weren't parent-friendly) while we were sitting beneath a mulberry tree waiting for a tow truck. He pulled out his phone and showed me all the little covers in his reading app, pointing each one out. It was a lovely moment. I had no idea. I love you both more than the whole world Mom and Dad.

Thank you, Graham, for your thoughtfulness each day. You have the biggest, kindest, most gentle heart. Thank you, Sloan, for each laugh and big hug. You have so much joy, curiosity, and craftiness in your soul. I'm so honored to be your mom. I love you both grain elevators full, miles high, city blocks long! (please don't read these books)

Thank you, Darrell, for believing in me and for working to convince me every day not to doubt myself. I'm sorry I'm hardheaded about it. I love you. All of this is meaningless without you.

About the Author

Kathryn Trattner is an award-winning author who has loved fairy tales, folk stories, and mythology all her life. Her hands-down favorites have always been East of the Sun, West of the Moon and the myth of Persephone and Hades. When not writing or reading, she's traveling as much as possible and taking thousands of photos that probably won't get edited later. She lives in Oklahoma with her wonderful husband, two very busy children, one of the friendliest dogs ever, and three cats who think they're in charge.

If you enjoyed this book, please consider leaving a review and signing up for my newsletter. You'll get information on new releases and exclusive content!

https://www.kathryntrattner.com/newsletter

facebook.com/kathryntrattner

instagram.com/k.trattner.author

bookbub.com/authors/kathryn-trattner

tiktok.com/@kathryntrattnerauthor

goodreads.com/kathryntrattner

ALSO BY KATHRYN TRATTNER

Deep Water and Other Stories

Mistress of Death

The Scent of Leaves

Magic and Myth: Short Stories

Magnolia House

The Glass Palace

The Blood and Rubies Series

Sacrament and Smoke

The Dead Saint

The Living Saint

Steel and Starlight

Coming Soon

The Sparrow King and Other Stories